WITHDRAWN

SEA FICTION GUIDE

by
MYRON J. SMITH, JR.
and
ROBERT C. WELLER

With a Foreword by
Rear Adm. Ernest M. Eller, U.S.N. (Ret.)

and Craft Notes by

Edward L. Beach
Edwin M. Hall
Wilson Heflin

Hammond Innes
Alexander Kent
F. van Wyck Mason

John D. Seelye

The Scarecrow Press, Inc.
Metuchen, N.J.   1976

Library of Congress Cataloging in Publication Data

Smith, Myron J
  Sea fiction guide.

  Includes indexes.
  1. Sea stories--Bibliography. 2. English fiction--
Bibliography. 3. American fiction--Bibliography.
I. Weller, Robert C., joint author. II. Title.
Z5917.S4S64 [PR830.S4]   016.823'008'032   76-7590
ISBN 0-8108-0929-X

for
SUSAN and ROSE

FOREWORD

The ocean, vast and untracked, surges through man's affairs in an ever rising tide. It reaches into every facet of his life to affect his wellbeing and destiny. In great waters he has found adventure, romance, power, the mystery of far horizons, growth in matching mind and will against its might, some understanding from its majesty and grandeur of the infinite majesty and grandeur of the Divine.

The sea has captured men's hearts in each generation. Hence from earliest times a rich sea literature has flourished. Initially this crested in the superb epic poetry of Homer, and Thucydides' history that for me still has no peer. Not until the 18th century did the novel join, bringing a new form of expressing the call of the sea--and a very powerful one indeed.

Myron J. Smith, Jr., has published a number of useful bibliographies dealing with the influence of seapower upon history. Now he has joined forces with Professor Robert C. Weller of the Naval Academy, and the two of them have turned their skills to giving lovers of nautical literature a bibliography of novels by British and American authors.

Tastes change. Favorites of one generation may be pushed into backwater by the next. Yet a truly good novel-- such as Stevenson's Treasure Island or Melville's Moby Dick or Conrad's Typhoon--cannot perish. They are timeless. They reveal the human soul in conflict and the wonder of great waters that ever enthrall us.

A fine novel that is good history richly rewards a reader. As a boy I learned to love history through the works of Henty, Cooper, Stevenson. In maturity, periods in history have become alive and more vivid through writers like Kenneth Roberts, honest researcher and skilled writer.

Recent years have seen America deluged with writings

of the basest human thoughts and actions.   Why this is so I
cannot fathom, for man ranges to the stars.   One welcomes
a bibliography through which the sea winds sweep clean and
refreshing.

The sea, and great rivers or lakes which support it,
is an impartial friend or foe.   It showers its beauties and
its disasters on all, the ready and the unready, the brave or
foolish, the strong or weak.   Even at their most peaceful,
the great waters may still shipwreck the careless on their
reefs or shoals or snags.   In anger, these waters spare no
error or dishonesty.

This bibliography will be of value not only to those
who are stirred by the magic of the sea or the beauty of inland lakes and rivers, but also to the serious student, librarian, and teacher.   May it serve many readers young and old
and may its entries lead them to a clearer understanding of
the influence of the sea in the destiny of mankind.

Rear Adm. Ernest M. Eller, U.S.N. (Ret.)
Former Director of Naval History,
    U.S. Department of the Navy
Wardour, Annapolis, Md.
19 April 1975

TABLE OF CONTENTS

INTRODUCTION

For more years than many can dream, the way of the
sea has been vital to the commercial lifeblood and national
security of Great Britain, the United States, and a host of
other countries. It has not been for naught that literary disciples of "sea power" have reminded us that national character, to say nothing of national growth or profit, has often
been forged afloat on the nautical anvils of revolution and in-
genuity, challenge and survival, plus a myriad other re-
sources attendant to national heritage. From the days of the
ancient Phoenicians into the present, this nautical development has been the stuff of song and story. "The sea is
valor's charter," wrote Robert Treat Paine a century and a
half ago, "A nation's wealthiest mine."

For most of us, far removed from the ocean, our
only experience with the sea, or "blue water," has been
pleasurable and rather close to shore. Bathing, boating, or
fishing is the closest most of us in the seventh decade of the
twentieth century come to the world of the sailor. For others, the "Huck Finn" experiences of inland seas, lakes, rivers, or streams, collectively nicknamed "brown water," has
been an equally enjoyable substitute. Regardless of location,
many of us who have known the quiet happiness available
around water probably echo in some degree the sentiments
of John Masefield, in "Sea Fever." We too must "go down
to the seas again" and ask, too, for a "merry yarn from a
laughing fellow-rover."

One pleasurable way in which we can vicariously experience the tang of wild waves or the turbulent eddy is in the
reading of nautical fiction, an imaginative rather than factual
type of literature usually called the "sea story." The novel
is its usual format although the short story (herein represented by anthologies only) has been used. Seated in a com-
fortable chair with the television switched off, one can let
his mind grasp the author's water-bound entertainment (and/
or reform), share the plights of characters whether realistic

or wooden, visualize the tall or grey ships or stately river-
boats around which the plot usually unfolds, and with some of
the more realistic or psychological tales, absorb a little prac-
tical or historical information or moralistic value as well.
This salty literature, universally popular over many years,
will continue to be read even as man rockets deeper into out-
er space and explores the depths of the world's oceans, or
"inner space."

Blue and brown water tales have been around in one
form or another since before Homer. The verbal old sailor's
yarn transposed into the nautical novel, with which this work
is concerned, is a form of literature perhaps most highly developed in the English language. From the early 1700's when
British writers first began the development of the novel as a
literary genre the sea has often figured in it. While it is
not our intention here to present a history of the sea story,
a task far better done by authors noted later in this introduction, we do want to explore some of the reasons why this
literature came into vogue.

Great literature has to a large extent been founded
primarily upon character delineation rather than plot or setting. Nevertheless, authors of nautical fiction have tradi-
tionally been eager to engineer complex characters through
the spectrum of natural rigors offered by nautical life. From
the beginning, writers such as Smollett, Marryat, Cooper,
Melville, Conrad, C. S. Forester, and many others have
taken full advantage of the ideal pressurized microcosm presented by the ship at sea to scrutinize man.

This concept was especially valid during the 19th and
early 20th centuries, when authors, particularly in Britain
and America, were looking outward to the world's frontiers.
Their eyes saw escape and movement and all its potentials
for growth and freedom in a sort of "outward vision," the
vision of sea literature. Thus beyond the entertainment
value, which was then and is now quite high, students of the
nautical tale can find in it a basic cultural record of the
psyche of nations. It is interesting that so many novelists
have found the nautical genre a particularly suitable forum
for airing national concerns, anxieties, and hopes. What was
true 150 years ago is significant even today: the essential
unrest, the search for adventure in new frontiers (spiritually
or outer-spatially or even within the self) shows clearly in
sea fiction.

Furthermore, the tradition of the salty yarn--the basis
of nautical novels--has been readily adapted by the writer of
books, especially the English-speaking writer, and we might
add, he has become through the years pretty good at it!
Like the lonely explorer or frontiersman in his existential
quest for communication, the sailor-author spins his tale.
Old and new salts weave yarns of heroes and villains that reflect their dreams and nightmares, their aspirations, humor,
utopian quests, their myths. Anecdotes of peg-leggers, island hermits or castaways, pilots, rovers, sea hawks and
sea dogs reflect the individualism and indomitable spirit so
carefully and thoroughly woven into the fabric of our Anglo-
American folklore.

From antiquity on and into the 20th century, the "bluejacket," for love of God and country, and often fearless of
both, has freebooted straight and crooked ships on and below
the sea. Adventures of villainous bandits, sea gypsies buccaneers, raiders, plunderers, smugglers, riverboat men,
and illegal treasure hunters, many historically founded, are
matched by heroic pursuits of fleets of chivalric skippers,
keeping the seas open and free for pleasure and profit. The
nautical war story, an important segment of the literature,
reflects the centuries-old strategic struggles for "sea power."

Serious students of sea literature have begun to see
new perspectives in the genre. You will note, of course,
that much sea fiction was written in the late 1800's through
the turn of the century when the oceans and inland waterways
figured most largely in the public eye, an importance which
is still valid today, only much more poorly seen. For example, reevaluations of the "Ned Buntline" variety of dime
novels are yielding fascinating understanding of our mythology.
Courses in sea literature are available today on a number of
college campuses, usually modeled on the "Literature of the
Sea" seminars pioneered by Dr. Wilson Heflin at the Naval
Academy and Dr. John Seelye at Mystic Seaport.

Here, then, is the stuff of nations, the full comple-
ment of humanity on its ship of state, aweigh, adrift, aground.
Here are free men, young skippers, ocean-born waifs, foreign
and domestic sea pups, midshipmen, foundlings, and similar
apprentices at sea. Female enchantresses, mysterious
nymphs of the oceans and backwaters, maidens, sirens, mermaids, captains' daughters and even a maritime nun or two
seek their fortunes in sea fiction. Landlubbering escapists,
dwarfs and giants alike, have scribbled their journals and

logs and scattered their stray leaves in bottles down rivers and across seas and oceans. Here is a world of adventure open in real life only to a few in which most of us can live, though, through books--free from the historical or modern difficulties or discomforts of the reality.

When most of us think of nautical fiction, we seldom consider any of the aspects of the above discussion and for most of us, casual readers that we are, the cultural or nationalistic overtones of a work really mean very little. We seek escape, romance, and adventure, conjuring up heroes or heroines in the swashbuckling molds of Erroll Flynn or Maureen O'Hara, or in more reflective moments, the likes of a Captain Ahab or Lord Jim. Regardless of your tastes, you are cruising in good waters; this compilation is meant as much or more for the casual reader seeking an evening's pleasant occupation as the serious student intent upon the motives of mankind.

In order to aid you in choosing an entertaining or reflective yarn, the criteria of selection in this book are basically historical, and basically Western civilization. The novels cited herein were written from the 1700's to mid-1975. We have noted for the serious student the most representative and important works penned during those years. With certain exceptions, for example Melville, the casual reader or "sea story buff" will undoubtedly be interested in those written in this century and currently available. Once a fad, as the spy story was a fad, only a few nautical tales are now being published; these are yarns expected to reach the largest audiences.

While these novels were written during only a few hundred years, the time span for topics chosen covers modern history of the Western world since the days of Prince Henry the Navigator and Columbus in the late 1400's. Prior to that first great period of exploration, events at sea were, as seen in Viking raids, based on land experiences and have thus been discounted here. With some exceptions, notably Homer's Odyssey, the basic blue water adventure dates to the time of the Portuguese caravelle, when daring mariners freed future generations from a world of fear and superstition, opening European minds to the excitement of expansion.

A word about pseudonyms: many writers, even today, have chosen for reasons best known to themselves to publish their works under a pen name. Whenever we have run down

and boarded such a case, we have made certain that both the
author's real name and pseudonym are included within the
body of his/her citation.   Also, a Pseudonym/Joint Author
index has been included on p. 221.

During the 19th century, a goodly amount of nautical
literature was aimed at "boys." Writers used the sea story
as a medium for disseminating ideas on what was often ro-
mantically conceived of as a wholesome life style, an ideal
not necessarily true in fact.   The product of these pens,
some of which is noted herein, might profitably be studied as
an early type of "YA" or young adult literature.

Despite the fact that sea fiction is remarkably free of
the sexual themes often found in spy, mystery, or western
adventure, and that the parent or other individual seeking fore-
knowledge of books with sexual themes will find little basis
for caution in any of the titles listed here, we have nevertheless for selection purposes affixed the symbol "y" to those
works aimed, regardless of publication date, at junior-senior
high school readers.   This is not to say there is no violence:
the sea by its very nature is violent and man's activities upon
its surface have not always been peaceful.   Nevertheless it
should be understood that, in our belief, all sea stories can
be read by persons of any station with guidance necessary,
if then, only for the young child.   We recommend that anyone over the age of 12 who is interested in the genre be al-
lowed to shift back and forth with freedom between any reading level or style best suited to his interest or taste.

Many of the titles in this compilation have annotations,
either as to content or author.   A few of the more important
writers, especially those who have contributed greatly to the
genre's development, are favored with extensive notes.   Some
of the titles are self-explanatory, need no amplification, and
receive none.   All comments are designed simply to amplify
the value of the whole.

Certain of the novels and anthologies which we will be
calling to your attention are now out of print; others have
been republished, often in paperback, through the years.   The
dates of publication presented in the citations to follow are in
almost every case those of original appearance.   Casual readers desiring a particular title are advised to consult their
public or school libraries or a favorite local bookseller.   Your
library can often obtain out of print books for you on interlibrary loan, while some specialized book dealers in larger

cities have a large stock ready to sell you.   Country auctions should not be overlooked, but beware of the antique dealer. Serious students will need to contact strongholds of nautical research, especially for the little-available 19th-century books. A few recommended libraries where such might be examined and/or borrowed (directly or by interlibrary loan) include: the G. W. Blunt White Library at Mystic Seaport, Conn.; the library of the Mariners Museum in Newport News, Va.; the Library of Congress; the Nimitz Library of the U.S. Naval Academy, Annapolis, Md.; and the Navy Department Library at the Navy Yard in Washington, D.C.

In addition to checking any of the many survey works on British or American literature, readers interested in additional literary history concerning the blue and brown water novel might profitably employ these adult listings:

Dickinson, A. T. , Jr.   American Historical Fiction, 3d ed. Metuchen, N. J.: Scarecrow Press, 1971. An excellent annotated bibliography.

Lewis, Charles L.   Books of the Sea.   Annapolis: U. S. Naval Institute, 1943. A basic reference covering the nautical literature (fiction, short stories, poetry, drama, etc.) of many nations.   Reprinted.

McGarry, Daniel D. and Sarah H. White.   World Historical Fiction Guide: An Annotated, Chronological, Geographical & Topical List of Selected Historical Novels, 2d ed. Metuchen, N. J.: Scarecrow Press, 1973.

Parkinson, C. Northcote.   Portsmouth Point: The Navy in Fiction, 1793-1815.   London: Hodder & Stoughton, 1948. Provides basic insights into the genre's birth in Great Britain.

Philbrick, Thomas.   James F. Cooper and the Development of American Sea Fiction. Cambridge, Mass.: Harvard University Press, 1961. Provides basic insights into the genre's birth in the United States.

Robinson, Charles N.   The British Tar in Fact and Fiction. Detroit: Gale Research Corp. , 1968.

xv   Introduction

A reprinting of the 1909 original edition; as valuable as Lewis or Parkinson.

Smith, Myron J., Jr. American Naval Bibliography.
    5 vols.   Metuchen, N.J.:   Scarecrow Press, 1972-
    1976.
        A basic background source, 1775-1941, for ma-
    terial on the U.S. Navy and such American authors
    as Cooper, Melville, Beach, Ellsberg, etc.

Wright, Lyle H. American Fiction, 1774-1850.   San
    Marino, Calif.:   Huntington Library Publications,
    1939.

Those interested in sea stories for younger readers
(elementary and intermediate) might consult the following three
references, aimed more directly than this work towards the
juvenile group.

Hotchkiss, Jeanette. American Historical Fiction and
    Biography for Children and Young People.   Metuch-
    en, N.J.:   Scarecrow Press, 1973.

        . European Historical Fiction and Biography for
    Children and Young People.   2d ed.   Metuchen,
    N.J.:   Scarecrow Press, 1972.

        . African-Asian Reading Guide for Children and
    Young Adults.   Metuchen, N.J.:   Scarecrow Press,
    1976.

Readers should also remember the H. W. Wilson Co. publications of Book Review Digest, Fiction Catalog, Junior High
School Catalog and Senior High School Catalog, all of which
contain relevant index or text headings (e.g., "sea stories").

For the benefit of those interested in the professional
views of contemporary writers of sea fiction, we have included a special section of comments, "Craft Notes," by some
noted practitioners.   We hope their insight will prove of
value to anyone using this work and we thank them all for
their valuable contributions.

For their encouragement and aid in the preparation of
this bibliography, we offer our sincere appreciation to these
good friends and colleagues:

Mr. Fred J. Reynolds, Librarian, Public Library of Fort Wayne, Indiana.

The Reference staffs of the Indiana State Library, the Library of Congress, the Navy Department Library, the Nimitz Library of the U.S. Naval Academy, and the library of the National Maritime Museum, Greenwich, England.

Dr. Edward Hall of the U.S. Naval Academy, for his help with James Fenimore Cooper and disciples.

Dr. H. Ray Stevens, a Conrad scholar, Western Maryland College.

Mr. Donald Judge, Librarian, G. W. Blunt White Library, Mystic Seaport, Connecticut.

Dr. Wilson Hefflin, of the U.S. Naval Academy, whose dreams must necessarily be of white whales, for insisting on the urgent need of this publication.

Rear Adm. Ernest M. Eller, USN (ret.), formerly Director of Naval History, U.S. Navy Department

The staff and board of the Huntington Public Library, whose assistants have lately come to know more about nautical fiction than most may have wished.

Now dear reader, with the necessary introductory victualling out of the way, you are invited to peruse this listing. If you cannot recall the author of a favorite title, we have listed them in an index aft. If you desire a certain topic or era, a subject index has been stowed in the same area. Set your sails for a look at life now largely historic, and clear your decks for some of the most exciting writing available in the Queen's Goode English.

Myron J. Smith, Jr.
Huntington, Indiana

Robert C. Weller
Annapolis, Maryland

December 7, 1975

CRAFT NOTES

The literature of nautical fiction, as one may see in this bibliography, has had countless noteworthy authors. To provide some insight into the feelings that men who today write sea stories have towards their craft, the compilers invited a number of them to contribute brief statements for this section. What follows will hopefully be of value to both the lay reader and the serious student.

A ROMANTIC NATURAL

Edward L. Beach

It was inevitable that one of the wellsprings of fiction, in our society, should be the sea: it is mysterious, unfathomable, limitless in all directions. It has been feared since man first looked upon it. The land has always been familiar. The sea is fierce and foreign. The sea has many moods, the land only one. Both land and sea are of course subject to the vagaries of weather, but the land is passive whereas the sea can roil up in a splendorous rage far transcending the winds and tides which have aroused its awesome majesty.

The sea carries no tracks; one disappears into it and leaves no trace, returns from it without a mark to show whence one came. It is no wonder that seamen, since the beginning of time, have embroidered their adventures or concocted allegorical ones. Fearsome beasts, lovely mermaids, Flying Dutchmen, Quetzalcoatl landing in Mexico and Leif Erikson discovering Newfoundland, Jonah and his whale, Noah and his Ark, Jules Verne and Captain Nemo's "Nautilus," Horatio Hornblower--some of these have more and some less of fiction in their makeup, but all belong to the romantic literature of the sea. All have made their mark on the world.

Three quarters of the earth's surface in ceaseless motion, possessed of deceptive gentleness and implacable fury. A mystery beyond the horizon and a phantasmagoric jungle, still very lightly explored by man, barely a few feet beneath the surface. Who is it who has not wondered at the spectacle of a great ship, a pinnacle of man's accomplishment, being totally swallowed up by the sea and becoming, therefore, as nothing? Yet this great transformation in most cases has resulted from some small disaster--a relatively small hole-- which would hardly have been noticeable, much less a fatal injury, on land. Who has not speculated upon the thousands --and hundreds of thousands--of wrecks of ships, some lost aeons upon aeons of ages in the primordial ooze, forever entombed on the ocean floor? What treasures must be there! What heroism, what villainies, what tragedies lie there buried forever from the inquest of man!

Sea fiction? The romance of the sea? A willing arena for the creative intelligence? What else! The existence of the sea could well have been the proximate cause of that development of the creative imagination which has distinguished man from the lesser creatures of the earth.

The sea and the most far-reaching expressions of man's fantasy were made for each other.

JAMES FENIMORE COOPER AND LITERATURE OF THE SEA

Edwin M. Hall

James Fenimore Cooper invented the sea story. The Pilot (1824) is the first of its genre.

There are, of course, other claimants. There always are. We speak of George Washington as the Father of His Country, but we also speak of the Founding Fathers. Many people will react to my first paragraph by asking how I can overlook the Odyssey, the account of St. Paul's shipwreck in Acts, Smollett's Roderick Random, etc. Let me therefore state my working definition of the sea story: It is a fictional prose narrative of which at least half takes place on shipboard and in which the handling of the ship is important to the plot. With such a definition, out go the rival claimants. The Odyssey is a poem, and most of it occurs on land; the narrative in Acts is presented as historical fact; Falconer's

The Shipwreck is a poem.   Even though Cooper acknowledges
an indebtedness to Smollett in his final preface to The Red
Rover, out goes Roderick Random too, for less than a quarter of that novel takes place on shipboard, and ex-Surgeon's
Mate Smollett pays little or no attention to the handling of
the ship.   Admittedly, however, my definition excludes some
of Cooper's own non-fiction, most notably his excellent History of the Navy and his interesting, if discursive, Lives of
Distinguished American Naval Officers.

        Cooper became a novelist in answer to a challenge.
While reading a recent English novel to his wife, he sudden-
ly announced, "I could write you a better book than that my-
self!" His wife laughed at him; therefore he wrote Precau-
tion.   He became a writer of sea stories in the same way.
At a dinner-party in New York, Scott's The Pirate was being
praised.   Somebody said that the author must obviously be a
seaman; Cooper said that a seaman would have made more of
the nautical portions of the book (which, by the way, consti-
tute less than half of it).   He insisted that a reader could be
interested in a book which made much of ships and ship-
handling.   When nobody agreed, he decided to write such a
book, and The Pilot was the result.

        He imposed on sea fiction much of its modern form:
much of the action takes place on board ship; the handling of
the ship is important; therefore the ship may be said to be,
in a sense, a major character in the story; the ocean becomes more than a literal expanse of water; it is a tester of
man's character and thus, to some extent, a symbol of life
itself.   For one element of sea fiction Cooper did borrow
from Smollett's Peregrine Pickle: the sailor character who
confounds landsmen by using sea terms metaphorically in
talking about life ashore.

        Which are Cooper's best sea novels?   To me they
are The Pilot and The Red Rover.   But these choices demand some explanation.   Under the leadership of Robert E.
Spiller, Cooper-scholars have been insisting for some years
that Cooper is to be valued only as a critic of society.
Since the later books, when Cooper was turning back from
romance to realism, contain much more of his social formu-
lae--America needs an aristocracy of merit and a greater
acceptance of the Episcopal Church--they are the books which
must be taken most seriously, these men say.   I cannot
agree.   Cooper the social critic had fairly shallow ideas and
accomplished nothing.   Had he been a social critic only, we

should never have heard of him today. It was as a teller of
romantic yarns that he gained his public. In that respect,
The Spy, The Last of the Mohicans, The Prairie, and the
later Deerslayer are the best of his land tales; similarly, I
contend, The Pilot and The Red Rover are his best sea
stories. They are once high romance and good stories.

The Water-Witch pushes romance too far; the business
of the mysterious figurehead troubles modern readers. Homeward Bound, Afloat and Ashore, and its sequel, Miles Wallingford, are interesting works that hold a pretty good balance between romanticism and realism. The Two Admirals combines
some of Cooper's best sea-narrative with some of his worst
land scenes. Two novels based pretty firmly on historical
facts are interesting: the story of Columbus's voyage in
Mercedes of Castile is well done, and the Mediterranean setting of The Wing-and-Wing is acceptable, though the characters of Lord Nelson and Lady Hamilton, who play minor roles,
do not come fully alive. As several critics have pointed out,
Jack Tier is a curious book, since it is The Red Rover up-
dated to Cooper's own time and de-glamorized. The casts
of characters in the two books are similar, even to the older
woman who consistently misuses sea-terms. The last sea-
novel, The Sea Lions, is spoiled for most readers by the
missionary efforts of the old seaman Stephen Stimson, who is
longwindedly trying to bring young Captain Roswell Gardiner
back to Christian orthodoxy. Yet no less a novelist than Melville, who reviewed the book for Literary World the year before he published Moby-Dick, may have been influenced by
Cooper's use of the sea as a backdrop for the drama of man.

HERMAN MELVILLE: SEAMAN AND AUTHOR

Wilson Heflin

Herman Melville (1819-1891) brought to the writing of
his fiction the experiences of a merchant seaman, a whaleman, and an ordinary seaman in the United States Navy. As
a "boy" (a landsman without previous seagoing duty), he
sailed in the irregular trading ship St. Lawrence of New York
for Liverpool in June, 1839, spent his twentieth birthday
there, and returned to New York in October. On Christmas
Day, 1840, he signed on as a green hand for the new whaleship Acushnet of Fairhaven, Massachusetts.

Acushnet took Melville to Rio de Janeiro, round Cape
Horn, to recruiting ports in Peru, to the Off Shore whaling
grounds, twice to the Galápagos Islands and, after eighteen
months, to the green and rocky isle of Nukahiva in the Marquesas. The ship had stowed down 750 barrels of sperm oil
and had sent home an additional 200 barrels, but Melville
forfeited his eighteen months' share in the voyage by jumping
ship in July, 1842, at Nukahiva. After a month of living
with Polynesians, he joined an Australian whaler, the barque
Lucy Ann of Sydney, and served briefly aboard her, until the
captain became sick and had to be put ashore at Tahiti. Because Melville and a number of his shipmates refused to continue the voyage under command of the mate, they were imprisoned in the Calabooza Beretanee at Papeete.

Soon thereafter Melville made his way to the neighbor-
ing island of Eimeo (Moorea), where he joined the Charles
and Henry of Nantucket. In this whaler, which was truly a
luckless ship in the fishery, Melville seems to have found
the only experience afloat so far which he really enjoyed.
The Charles and Henry, after six months on the whaling
grounds, took Melville to the Sandwich (Hawaiian) Islands.
At Lahaina on the island of Maui, he was honorably discharged
in early May, 1843.

At Honolulu three and a half months later, he enlisted
aboard the frigate United States as an ordinary seaman in
the United States Navy and served in this flagship of the Pacific Squadron for fourteen months. The frigate ended its
tour of duty at Boston in October, 1844, and Melville was
among the many enlisted men who were discharged there.
This fairly extensive and varied maritime experience made
it possible for Melville to write with authority about the sea.

In Melville's early books the land is dominant. A
ship brings the narrator to a savage island or a civilized
port, and, after many adventures, his own or another ship
takes him away. But there is a clear progression in his
fiction toward landlessness, until the Pequod of Moby-Dick,
leaving Nantucket, sails on and on toward its destruction with
never a stop ashore.

In "The Lee Shore" chapter of Moby-Dick, Melville
wrote that "in landlessness alone resides the highest truth,
shoreless indefinite as God...." As Melville developed as
an author, the ship became increasingly a microcosm of the
world, and the events on board reflected the universal prob-

lems of mankind.   The ocean came symbolically to represent
speculation on man's fate:

> Glimpses do ye seem to see of that mortally intol-
> erable truth; that all deep, earnest thinking is but
> the intrepid effort of the soul to keep the open in-
> dependence of her sea; while the wildest winds of
> heaven and earth conspire to cast her on the treach
> erous, slavish shore.

Melville's greatest sea stories--Moby-Dick, Billy Budd
and perhaps White-Jacket and "Benito Cereno"--are engaging
and exciting on the simple level of narrative.   But in each of
them there is a "lower layer," a courageous symbolic effort
to comprehend the universe and the roles of mankind in it.

NAUTICAL FICTION: A BRIEF APPRAISAL

"Hammond Innes"

Marryat and then Conrad set a standard of accuracy
in modern nautical fiction that has been constantly maintained.
Some, like Forester, have written from a long and close
study of the seafaring works of others, but most of us who
write about the sea do so because our own personal experience of it demands that we do so, our total involvement and
fascination forever channeling our imaginations in that direction.

The sea means ships of one sort or another, and to
write about ships calls for technical knowledge far beyond
the normal background requirements of fiction--technical
knowledge of tides and weather and charts, of the theory and
practice of navigation.   And if it is sailing ships, then there
is additionally the whole complicated assembly of spars, rigging and sails.   But whether it is sail, steam, motor, or
simply the manpower of oars, there is still a maze of nautical jargon that must come automatically to mind as the pen
slips over the page.

The first great classic of the sea was the Odyssey.
At one time this was thought to be full of myth and legend,
but Schliemann's archaeological discoveries, based on Homer'
Iliad, led to a new assessment of his account of the voyage
of Odysseus.   Now it is accepted that Homer was not recount

ing the tall stories of early Mediterranean seamen, but that he wrote the Odyssey with the aid of the periplus.

Homer's poetic interpretation of this ancient Greek equivalent of our Admiralty Pilot is sometimes a little difficult to comprehend. The best popular study of it is Ernle Bradford's Ulysses Found. The author followed the whole course of the Odyssey in his own small sailing boat, giving sensible nautical explanations to all the hazards Odysseus faced--all except one, that is. The best he could do about the monster Scylla was to suggest that the tidal rush of water through the Messina Straits had dredged up some huge octopus from the seabed close by the whirlpool of Charybdis.

It was not until I had my boat anchored in the old Roman harbor of the small island of Ventotene and saw what the Italians call a "trompo marina" that I realized that Scylla was the maritime equivalent of a gigantic dust devil or tornado. I saw six of them altogether, long fingers, or necks, writhing out of quite high cloud, reaching down into the sea to stir it up like some grizzled head with rows of teeth. And when a Neopolitan fisherman told me that he had once been caught in a trompo marina, had been lifted high in the air, his boat smashed to pieces, and had been sucked deep under water, I knew I had found the reality of Homer's Scylla.

So the first great sea story sets the pattern, and though Homer wrote out of the knowledge of others, as Forester did three thousand years later, still the full flavor of the sea--as opposed to the story itself--only emerges out of experience. How impossible it would have been for Erskine Childers to write that little classic of small boat voyaging, The Riddle of the Sands, without the personal study of the Wadden Zee sands he made in his Vixen.

I was a landsman when I first wrote about the sea, setting a story on the Cornish coast and seeing it through eyes that had never been beyond sight of land. But I could never have written Mary Deare, the story of an elderly freighter beached in the fatal rock reefs of Les Minquiers, without the inshore navigational experience gained in my first ocean racing boat off the northern coasts of France. Atlantic Fury, and more recently North Star, depend for their climaxes on firsthand knowledge of weather patterns and tidal races, Levkas Man on an intimate knowledge of the Ionian Islands gained sailing my own boat in Greek waters.

Long ago I wrote a book called <u>Maddon's Rock,</u> venturing for the first time into the open sea and relying on wartime experience of transports and minesweepers. My knowledge was not enough to do justice to the brief episode of a small boat voyage to Jan Mayen Island. But had I been writing it now, with sixteen years of ocean sailing behind me it would have been very different, probably no longer an episode but the dominant scene of the whole book.

Experience is the raw material of all writing, and once a writer has acquired an intimate personal knowledge of the sea it is bound to influence his work. The greatest short stories in the English language could not have been written had Conrad not spent so many years at sea, nor woul Hemingway have attempted <u>The Old Man and the Sea</u> had he not been hooked on big game fishing. Thus, it is not so mu that sea time gives the stamp of accuracy and the quality of reality to nautical fiction, but that it directs the imagination of the writer into a field where no man dare venture without knowledge.

THE INTEGRITY OF NAUTICAL LITERATURE

Alexander Kent

As a writer of both historical and contemporary sea stories I can well appreciate the value of our maritime heritage. People here speak lightly of "the sea in our blood," but in the British Isles where it is impossible to be born more than eighty miles from salt water it is hardly surprising.

From early times we have been forced to accept the sea as an ally not as a barrier. To enlarge our trade to the ends of the earth, to found and maintain an Empire it took a lot of ships and a lot of determined seamen.

In peace, our freedom to move on the oceans is vital to our environment. In times of war it can measure our very existence in days.

We have had the good fortune of many fine writers on the subject, a lot of whom began their lives at sea or had some special maritime connection.

Unlike the historian, the writer of sea stories must not only inform, he must also entertain. His work must be accurate and technical enough for the "sea buff," but remain smooth and uncluttered for the less professional reader.

Above all he must accept the responsibility and the integrity of his trade, for many more people obtain their knowledge of historical events through reading fiction than they do from more serious studies. This is a trust which is, I believe, for the most part observed.

Watch a ship at sea or in harbor, how she moves and stalks her image on the water. Listen to her people, how they speak, what they think of their hard and often dangerous calling. From the Arctic to the South Pacific on any single day there are men with stories to tell. It is to be hoped that there will always be others to write them.

SEA POWER IN SEA FICTION

F. van Wyck Mason

It is a pity that most Americans, young and old, are so ignorant concerning the naval history of the great nations herein represented. It is an inspiring subject and far from the dull descriptions given in most formal histories.

In the various works of historical fiction that I have written around this theme, it has been my policy to describe characters and battles through the eyes of a number of per-sonages, some of them fictional, some historical.

In the four books I did on the naval side of our War for Independence, I tried to show how utterly dependent Amer-ican forces were on the control of the Seas. Writing from an American viewpoint, these books, Three Harbours, Stars on the Sea, Rivers of Glory, and Eagle in the Sky, demon-strated the same thesis with regard to the British Royal Navy.

I had planned to do four volumes about the naval side of the American Civil War, but was only able to complete three: Proud New Flags, Blue Hurricane, and Our Valiant Few. Concerning the British, The Golden Admiral deals with Sir Francis Drake, and Manila Galleon with Captain George

Anson, both of whom extended British sea power into the Pa
cific long ago.

Nothing is more important than that the public should
understand the essential necessity of real sea power.   I trus
that the information contained in my works will help towards
this end.

LOOMINGS

John D. Seelye

        Five hundred years ago, so far as Europe was con-
cerned, America was only ocean, but then Columbus crossed
his salty Rubicon and the greater fiction began.   If subject
is the definitive object, then the first American literature
was written by the explorers who touched along our coasts,
an eclectic group who shared an abiding faith in the existenc
of a passage to the farther sea.   For nearly a century, the
North American continent was thought of as an obstacle to
westerly progress, but with the Roanoke Colony a different
myth unfolded, as explorers sailed from Elizabeth's Thames
up the savage rivers of the new world into the heart of dark
ness.   The broad Atlantic became a highway of opportunity
for merchants and adventurers, sailors and soldiers, an
arena for the kind of amphibious activity that is epitomized
by Captain John Smith.   Smith was both a proto-frontiers-
man and a putative whaleman, and his adventures at sea and
among wild Indians established the major themes for a national literature, incidentally giving the word "Captain" an
essentially American ambiguity, a title connoting the nobility
which heroic enterprise bestows.

        The Puritan presence in America gave the Atlantic
Ocean yet another meaning, John Winthrop regarding it as ar
equivalent to the Red Sea of Moses, a providential zone of
passage separating the salvational New World from the sinful Old.   This element of schizogenesis is as vital to the
creation of American literature as to the formation of the
Republic, for if James Fenimore Cooper gave fictional form
to the alternatives of adventure provided by Captain John
Smith in America, so his novels were often set in those
zones of conflict which provided the crucible for an emerging
nation-state.   In Cooper's first sea-romance, The Pilot, his
geopolitical emphasis has an amusing biographical-literary

correlative, for Cooper is supposed to have written the novel in response to the faulty seamanship in Sir Walter Scott's The Pirate. He gave a cutting edge to his corrective exercise by setting his romance on the coast of England during the American Revolution and by giving heroic stature to that Scottish renegade, John Paul Jones.

As the English scene had no equivalent to the frontier, so American authors failed to find a domestic setting for the novel of manners, but on the ocean the Queenly Mother and her Liberty-Capped Daughter engaged in rivalry for nearly a century, a literary competition matched by mercantile and naval contests. In volume, certainly, Captain Marryat ranked Mister Midshipman Cooper, but the American remains the greater if the less graceful author, writing, incidentally, more romances about the sea than about the forest and prairie. Moreover, the high seas never inspired the high seriousness in Victorian England that it drew from Cooper and, more particularly, Melville in Andrew Jackson's America. Nor do we find a reforming writer of Dickens' stature exposing the abuses of the quarterdeck in fiction, an important tradition on the other side of the Atlantic inspired by the example (and financial success) of Dana's Two Years Before the Mast. Melville's White Jacket and Redburn are fictional examples in kind, but that he was of two minds regarding the anomaly of hierarchical authority within the frame of a supposed democracy is suggested by Moby Dick, in which he borrowed Cooper's elevated, heroic quarterdeck, and made Captain Ahab a Carlylean "Red Rover" engaged in a transcendental version of the errand in Sea Lions.

Historians of maritime America call the days of Cooper and Melville the Golden Age of Sail, an epithet with imperial and epical connotations, evoking a mercantile equivalent to the colonial design of Great Britain. But the sun soon set on America's sea empire, the emergence of an industrialized nation after the Civil War putting an end to the importance of maritime trade. And with the decline of sea power went the issues and urgency of sea fiction, nor did the renewed energies of American empire at the turn of the century produce a writer of the stature of Cooper or Melville. The Land, that vast Interior, was the premier subject of American literature following the Civil War, and the microcosm provided by the City or the Village seemed to have more validity for the working out of the problems and paradoxes of democracy than did the martial and monastic organization of life at sea. As the popularity of van Wyck

Mason's novels attests, there is still a large audience for
sea romance in America, but save for an occasional sport
like Cozzens' S. S. San Pedro, Goodrich's Delilah, or Hemingway's Old Man and the Sea, the ocean as a transcendental
realm is fast disappearing from our national literature.

American maritime fiction of the past one hundred
years is hardly inconsiderable, the length of this bibliography
and the richness of subject matter evoked by Messrs. Smith
and Weller bearing testimony to both volume and variety.
The Caine Mutiny in its day had popular reverberations ex-
ceeding those of White Jacket and Mister Roberts remains a
minor classic of a distinctive kind. Moreover, if the literature of the sea in the English language after 1900 is domi-
nated by the works of Joseph Conrad, so that deracinated
Pole acknowledged his debt to James Fenimore Cooper. Yet
the fact remains that while Conrad found a symbolic setting
in the exotic outlands of British and Belgian empire, the
heart of the American empire lay inland, and that is the way
our literature has trended, following the mystic line of the
fabled Northwest Passage over an oceanic prairie toward an
ever-retreating West, a chimera that flees like the ghost of
the great White Whale toward an infinite Orient. Still, as
the growing awareness of the dangers of that quest gathers
force, as the notion of Spaceship Earth gains increasing validity, and as the universal threat of totalitarianism takes
nascent shape in America, perhaps, in time, Captain Queeg
and Mr. Roberts will no longer be matters of laughter.
When the American dream takes ship for the waters of
Cathay, then as in the mad vision of Captain Ahab it becomes
the looming menace of nightmare.

Captain Edward L. Beach, U. S. N. (ret.), who skippered an
American submarine in the Pacific during World War II,
took the nuclear sub Triton around the world submerged in
1960. Dr. Edwin M. Hall, now retired, is a Cooper spe-
cialist who was on the Naval Academy faculty for over 30
years. Dr. Wilson Heflin, a Melville scholar, has taught
literature at the U. S. Naval Academy since 1946, and is
past president of the Melville Society. Mr. Ralph Hammond-
Innes is a world-renowned author of nautical fiction; all of
his tales, based on personal research, are written under the
pen name of Hammond Innes. Mr. Alexander Kent writes
his 18th-century sea tales of Royal Navy officer Richard
Bolitho under his own name while penning his equally-excel-

lent World War II yarns under the pseudonym of Douglas Reeman.   Mr. Francis van Wyck Mason is a pioneer in the area
of historical fiction whose naval-oriented works have been
immensely popular.   Dr. John D. Seelye, University of North
Carolina, began the famous "Literature of the Sea" seminar
as part of the Munson Institute of American Maritime History at Mystic Seaport, Conn.

"It is better to live one day as a lion than a hundred years as a sheep."--Italian proverb

1   Aarons, Edward S.   Assignment: Sulu Sea.   Greenwich, Conn.:
      Fawcett, 1964.
          Part of a very large exclusively paperback action series.
      When a fully-armed American nuclear submarine vanishes,
      C. I. A. agent Sam Durell is sent on a savage seahunt with
      a beautiful woman out of his past.

2   Adams, Samuel H.   Canal Town.   New York: Random House,
      1944.
          Life in the small New York village of Palmyra border-
      ing the Erie Canal and very much dependent upon it for
      livelihood.   A good example of the "brown water" novel.

3   Adams, William T.   All Aboard.   By Oliver Optic, pseud.
      Boston: Brown and Bazin, 1865.   y.
          Adams, a school teacher and Sunday School superinten-
      dent, was a prolific, if careless, writer as well known as
      G. Henty (q. v.) or Horatio Alger.   His tales, whose char-
      acters were examplars of inspiration and success, were
      most valuable for their vivid narrative.   They were, how-
      ever, laced with an almost unbelievable amount of cheap
      oratory and an extremely moralistic strain.   Nevertheless,
      his young audiences were devoted, reading and rereading
      his product well into the early years of the 20th century.
      Others by this author, who wrote all of his tales under the
      pan name "Oliver Optic" are entered here for the benefit
      of students of American nautical fiction and while perhaps
      of no interest to modern readers, include:

4   _____.   All Aboard; or, Life on the Lake.   A Sequel to the
      Boat Club.   By Oliver Optic, pseud.   Boston: Lee and
      Shepard, 1847.   y.

5   _____.   At the Front.   By Oliver Optic, pseud.   Boston:
      Lee and Shepard, 1897.   y.

6   _____.   Bear and Forbear; Or, The Young Skipper Ucayaga.
      By Oliver Optic, pseud.   Boston: Lee and Shepard, 1869.
      y.

7   _____.   Bound.   A Story of Travel and Adventure.   By Oli-
      ver Optic, pseud.   Boston: Lee and Shepard, 1877.   y.

8 _____. Brave Old Salt; Or, A Story of The Great Rebellion.
By Oliver Optic, pseud. Boston: Lee and Shepard, 1865.
y.

9 _____. Brave Old Salt; Or, Life on the Quarterdeck. By
Oliver Optic, pseud. Boston: Lee and Shepard, 1894. y.

10 _____. Broke Up; Or, The Young Peacemakers. By Oliver
Optic, pseud. Boston: Lee and Shepard, 1872. y.

11 _____. Building Himself Up; Or, The Cruise of "The Fish
Hawk." By Oliver Optic, pseud. Boston: Lothrop, Lee
and Shepard, 1910. y.

12 _____. The Coming Wave; Or, The Hidden Treasure of
High Rock. By Oliver Optic, pseud. Boston: Lee and
Shepard, 1875; reprinted, 1902. y.

13 _____. Cringe and Crosstree; Or, The Sea Swashes of a
Sailor. By Oliver Optic, pseud. Boston: Lee and Shepard,
1899. y.

14 _____. The Dorcas Club; Or, The Girls Afloat. By Oliver
Optic, pseud. Boston: Lee and Shepard, 1902. y.

15 _____. Down South; Or, Yacht Adventures in Florida. By
Oliver Optic, pseud. Boston: Lee and Shepard, 1881. y.

16 _____. Down the Rhine; Or, Young America in Germany.
By Oliver Optic, pseud. New York: Lee and Shepard and
Dillingham, 1869. y.
Significant water theme, travel genre.

17 _____. Down the River; Or, Buck Bradford and the Tyrants.
By Oliver Optic, pseud. Boston: Lothrop, Lee and Shepard,
1899. y.

18 _____. Going South; Or, Yachting on the Atlantic. By Oliver Optic, pseud. Boston: Lothrop, Lee and Shepard,
1907. y.

19 _____. Isles of the Sea; Or, Young America Homeward
Bound. A Story of Travel and Adventure. By Oliver Optic,
pseud. Boston: Lee and Shepard, 1877. y.

20 _____. Lake Breezes; Or, The Cruise of the Sylvania. By
Oliver Optic, pseud. Boston: Lee and Shepard, 1906. y.

21 _____. Little by Little; Or, The Cruise of the Flyaway.
By Oliver Optic, pseud. Chicago: W. B. Conkey, 189-?
y.

22 _____. Ocean Born. By Oliver Optic, pseud. Boston: Lee

and Shepard, 1875.   y.   Reissued, 1903, as <u>Ocean Born;</u>
<u>Or, The Cruise of the Clubs.</u>

23 _____. <u>Oliver Optic's The Boat Club.</u>   By Oliver Optic,
pseud. New York: Carlton Press, 1968.   y.   "Reprint of
a Nineteenth Century novel. . . ."--subtitle.

24 _____. <u>Out West; Or, Roughing It on The Great Lakes.</u>
By Oliver Optic, pseud. Boston: Lee and Shepard, 1905.
y.

25 _____. <u>Outward Bound.</u>   By Oliver Optic, pseud.   Boston:
Lee and Shepard, 1867.   y.

26 _____. <u>Pacific Shores; Or, Adventures in Eastern Shores.</u>
By Oliver Optic, pseud. Boston: Lee and Shepard, 1898.
y.

27 _____. <u>The Sailor-Boy.</u>   By Oliver Optic, pseud.   Boston:
Lee and Shepard, 1865.

28 _____. <u>Sea and Shore; Or, The Tramps of a Traveller.</u>   By
Oliver Optic, pseud. Boston: Lee and Shepard, 1872.   y.

29 _____. <u>Strange Sights Abroad; Or, A Voyage in European</u>
<u>Waters.</u> By Oliver Optic, pseud. Boston: Lee and Shepard,
1893.   y.

30 _____. <u>Up and Down the Nile; Or, Young Adventures in</u>
<u>Africa.</u> By Oliver Optic, pseud. Boston: Lee and Shepard,
1894.   y.

31 _____. <u>Up the Baltic; Or, Young America in Norway, Swe-</u>
<u>den and Denmark.</u> By Oliver Optic, pseud. Boston: Lee
and Shepard, 1871.   y.

32 _____. <u>The Yacht Club; Or, The Young Boat Builder.</u>   By
Oliver Optic, pseud. Boston: Lee and Shepard, 1875.   y.

33 _____. <u>Yankee Middy; or, The Adventures of a Naval Officer.</u>
By Oliver Optic, pseud. Boston: Lee and Shepard, 1866.
y.

34 Addis, E. E. <u>High Seas Murder.</u> London: Hutchinson, 1940.
Suspense afloat before World War II.

35 Alderman, Clifford L. <u>Silver Keys.</u> New York: Putnam, 1960.
y.
William Phips hunts sunken treasure in the 17th century.
Although well told and aimed at young adults, outclassed by
van Wyck Mason's <u>Log Cabin Noble.</u>

36 _____. <u>Wooden Ships and Iron Men.</u> New York: Walker,

1964. y.
> A young British sailor first fights for King George and then with the Americans during the War of 1812.

37 Aldis, Dorothy. Ride the Wild Waves. New York: Putnam, 1957. y.
> Adventures with the Mayflower pilgrims at sea and in the New World.

38 Aldridge, James. A Captive in the Land. Garden City, N. Y. : Doubleday, 1963.
> After saving an injured Russian in the Arctic, Englishman Rupert Royce visits Moscow to receive a medal--and to carry off a mission for British Naval Intelligence.

39 _____ . The Statesman's Game. Garden City, N. Y. : Doubleday, 1966.
> Rebuffed by the British Admiralty in his efforts to trade ships with the Soviets, Royce must turn to the more "acceptable" Communist Chinese.

40 Allen, Hervey. Anthony Adverse. New York: Farrar, 1933.
> A young 18th century English adventurer travels the globe by land and water seeking adventure.

41 Allis, Marguerite. Water Over the Dam. New York: Putnam, 1947.
> A brown water tale of how a canal changed the lives of the people of Farmington, Connecticut, during the early 19th century.

42 Alter, Robert E. Red Water. New York: Putnam, 1968. y.
> A 17 year old lad is shanghied aboard an American whaler in the 1820's.

43 Ambler, Eric. The Levanter. New York: Atheneum, 1972.
> Adventure and intrigue in the Eastern Mediterranean.

44 American Boy, Editors of. American Boy Sea Stories. Garden City, N. Y. : Doubleday, 1947. y.
> An anthology.

45 The American Cruiser; or, The Two Messmates. A Tale of the Last War. Boston: Waite, Pierce, 1846.
> Students of nautical literature will want to note that this is the sort of James F. Cooper romantic tale which was sweeping America at the time of the Mexican War. While we will be noting other examples of this glorification of the War of 1812, the majority of this kind of yarn appeared in the periodical press, primarily in the New England area.

46 Ames, Nathaniel. An Old Sailor's Yarns. New York: George

Dearborn, 1835.
  A combination of story and memoir. Ames mixed his sentimentality with heavy doses of nautical knowledge, but was extremely inept at plot development. Much of what he wrote in his articles and these two citations was based upon his experiences of long years in the American navy and merchant marine. He was a major figure of the Cooper era.

47 _____. Pirate's Glen and Dungeon Rock. Boston: Redding, 1853.
  Presented in a verse-fiction format.

48 Anderson, Florence M. The Black Sail. New York: Crown, 1948. y.
  Pirate adventure.

49 _____. An Off-Islander: A Story of Wesque by the Sea. Boston: Stratford, 1921. y.

50 Anderson, G. Reid. Boy 1st Class and Other Naval Yarns. London: Muller, 1945. y.
  Royal Navy tales of World War II.

51 Anderson, John R. L. Death on the Rocks. New York: Stein & Day, 1975.
  The first in a projected series featuring a Scotland Yard sleuth solving crimes in a nautical setting. Peter Blair, out yachting, discovers a female body lying on a rocky shore and is drawn into the pursuit of international heroin smugglers afloat.

52 Anderson, Kenneth. In the Grip of the Gale. London: Harrap, 1939.
  A merchantman is caught in a mighty storm.

53 Anderson, U. S. The Smoldering Sea. New York: Wyn, 1953. y.
  American nautical adventure.

54 Andrews, Robert. Burning Gold. Garden City, N. Y.: Doubleday, 1945.
  How an 18th century surgeon manages to survive his adventures aboard a ship filled with pirates.

55 Annixter, Jane and Paul. Vikan the Mighty. New York: Holiday, 1969. y.
  Skilled harpooner Benjy Tetlow encounters an old adversary in Vikan, the killer whale.

56 Ardagh, W. M. The Magada. New York: Lane, 1910.
  The Spanish seaborne conquest of the Canary Islands.

57   Argosy Magazine, Editors of. Book of Sea Stories. New York:
     Barnes, 1953.
          An anthology.

58   Armstrong, Arthur. The Mariner of the Mines; or, The Maid
     of the Monastery: A Tale of the Mexican War. Boston:
     F. Gleason, 1850.
          Of value only to serious students.

59   Armstrong, Frank C. The Cruise of the Daring. 3 vols. in 1.
     London: T. Cantley Newby, 1860.

60   _____. The Young Middy. 2nd ed. London: Marborough,
     1859. y.
          Both of these tales reflect life in the Royal Navy in the
     mid-19th century, but are of little value to the modern
     reader.

61   Armstrong, Richard. Out of the Shallows. London: Dent,
     1961. y.

62   _____. Sailor's Luck. London: Dent, 1959. y.

63   _____. Ship Afire. New York: John Day, 1959. y.
          From which survivors flee after being torpedoed in the
     North Atlantic during World War II.

64   Armstrong, T. Dover Harbour. London: Collins, 1942.
          World War II.

65   Arnold, E. Lester. The Constable of St. Nicholas. London:
     Chatto and Windus, 1894.
          A still-interesting tale of the 15th-century siege of
     Rhodes, that little-known island in the Mediterranean.

66   Arnold, Elliott. Code of Conduct. New York: Scribner's,
     1970.
          Passing as a treasury agent, N.A.S. officer Owen
     Quade travels to Switzerland for another view of the Pueblo
     incident.

67   _____. The Commando. New York: Duell, 1942.
          Similar to Brian Callison's Dawn Attack (q. v.).

68   Ashmead, John. The Mountain and the Feather. Boston:
     Houghton, Mifflin, 1961.
          World War II naval battles in the Pacific, 1943-44,
     including the huge Battle of Leyte Gulf.

69   Ashton, Agnes. The Mark of Safety. London: Epworth Press,
     1961.
          British nautical adventure.

70 Attwill, Kenneth and Orland. Thirteen Sailed Home.   London:
    J. Long, 1935.
         British nautical adventure.

71 Augsburg, P. D. Man the Whale Boats. New York: McBride,
    1959. y.
         American whaling in the South Seas in the 1840's.

72 Austin, F. B. A Saga of the Sea. London: Ernest Benn, 1929.
         British nautical adventure.

73 Austin, John. Battle Dress. By "Gun Buster, " pseud. Lon-
    don: Hodder & Stoughton, 1941.

74 _____. Zero Hours. By "Gun Buster, " pseud. London:
    Hodder & Stoughton, 1942.
         Both of these early wartime nautical adventures concern
    the Royal Navy's ease in handling the German Kreigsmarine.
    Might be compared with the works of Alexander Kent, writing
    under his pen name of Douglas Reeman, cited below.

75 Averill, Charles E. The Avenger; Or, The Fearful Retribution.
    New York: DeWitt, 1868.
         Averill's adventure tales, like those of William T.
    Adams, are rather tame and unromantic by today's stand-
    ards, but were extremely popular and acclaimed in their
    day. Others by this writer include:

76 _____. Blackbeard; Or, The Bloodhound of the Bermudas:
    A Tale of the Ocean's Incidents. New York: DeWitt, 1868.

77 _____. The Corsair King; Or, The Blue Water Rovers: A
    Romance of the Piratical Empire. Boston: F. Gleason, 1847.

78 _____. The Female Fishers; Or, The Beautiful Girl of
    Marblehead. A Thrilling Story of the Sea Coast. Boston:
    T. Wiley, 1848.

79 _____. The Pirates of Cape Ann; Or, The Freebooter's Foe.
    A Tale of Land and Water. Boston: F. Gleason, 1848.
         Features John Paul Jones.

80 _____. The Secret Service Ship; Or, The Fall of San Juan
    d'Ulloa. A Thrilling Tale of the Mexican War. Boston:
    F. Gleason, 1847.

81 _____. The Secrets of the High Seas; Or, The Mysterious
    Wreck in the Gulf Stream. A Tale of the Ocean's Exciting
    Incidents. Boston: Williams, 1849.

82 _____. The Wanderer; Or, The Haunted Nobleman. A Story
    of Sea and Land Adventure. Boston: F. Gleason, 1848.

83 _____. The Wreckers; Or, The Ship Plunderers of Bernegat.
A Startling Story of the Mysteries of the Sea Shore.   Boston: F. Gleason, 1848.

84 Aymar, Gordon C. , ed. Treasury of Sea Stories. New York:
A. S. Barnes, 1948.
Thirty-three selections.

- B -

85 Bachmann, Lawrence P. The Bitter Lake. Boston: Little,
Brown, 1970.
Tensions aboard a ship trapped in the Suez Canal during
the Arab-Israeli Six Day War of 1967.

86 Bagley, Desmond. The Golden Keel. Garden City, N. Y. :
Doubleday, 1964.
Three British adventurers pursue Mussolini's secret gold
by land and sea in the years after the Second World War.

87 _____. Wyatt's Hurricane. Garden City, N. Y. : Doubleday,
1966.
A U. S. Navy meteorologist seeks to alleviate the suffering which will certainly be caused when a great storm hits
a Caribbean island.

88 Bailey, Henry C. Bonaventure. London: Methuen, 1927.
Spain and England in the decade before the sailing of
the Spanish Armada. Bailey is better known for his mysteries than his sea stories.

89 _____. The Gentleman Adventurer. New York: Doran, 1915.
Piracy in the 17th-century West Indies.

90 _____. The Sea Captain. London: Methuen, 1913.
British nautical adventure.

91 Bailey, Ralph E. Sea Hawks of Empire; Eastward to the Indies
for Trade and Treasure, 1500-1700. New York: E. P.
Dutton, 1948.
Fictionalized history which includes a diverse cast of
seabooters and explorers ranging from Columbus to Drake
to Henry Morgan.

92 Balfour, Andrew. By Stroke of Sword. London: Methuen, 1897.
A still-readable tale with location scenes including Fife,
Devon, and the West Indies. Sir Francis Drake is an im-
portant character.

93 Ball, Zachary. Pull Down to New Orleans. New York:
Crown, 1946. y.

Brown water adventure on the Ohio and Mississippi
Rivers during the early 19th century. A nice look at the
Mike Find school of keelboating.

94 Ballantyne, Robert M. <u>Coxswain's Bride</u>. New York: Dodd,
1873.
A few of the authors more than 80 Henty-like stories
include:

95 _____. Fighting the Whales; Or, Doings and Dangers on a
Fishing Cruise. London: J. Nisbet, 187-?

96 _____. In the Track of the Troops. London: J. Nisbet,
1878.

97 _____. The Lifeboat of Our Coast Heroes. London: J.
Nisbet, 1870?

98 _____. Mudman and the Pirate. New York: Dodd, 1874.

99 Ballard, Martin. The Monarch of Juan Fernandez. New York:
Scribner's, 1967. y.
A biographical novel of Alexander Selkirk, the real
"Robinson Crusoe. "

100 Ballinger, William S. The Spy in the Java Sea. New York:
Putnam, 1965.
An agent must locate a computer expert in Djarkarta
and get him to repair a crippled American submarine in the
Java Sea before the Communists discover its whereabouts.

101 Ballou, Maturin Murray. The Adventurer; Or, The Wreck of
the Indian Ocean. By Lt. Murray, pseud. Boston: F.
Gleason, 1848.
Ballou, a traveller who was never a naval officer as
his pen name implies, is probably best remembered today
as the founder of Ballou's Pictorial, one of America's pioneer illustrated newsmagazines.

102 _____. Albert Simmons; Or, The Midshipman's Revenge.
By Frank Forester, pseud. Boston: F. Gleason, 1845. y.

103 _____. The Cabin Boy; Or, Life on the Wing: A Story of
Fortune's Freaks and Fancies. By Lt. Murray, pseud.
Boston: F. Gleason, 1848.

104 _____. Capt. Lovell; Or, The Pirate's Cave, a Tale of the
War of 1812. By Lt. Murray, pseud. New York: F. A.
Brady, 1870.

105 _____. The Child of the Sea; Or, The Smuggler of Colonial
Times. And the Love Test. Boston: U. S. Publishing,
1846.

106 _____. The Circassian Slave; Or, The Sultan's Favorite. A Story of Constantinople and the Caucasus. Boston: F. Gleason, 1851.

107 _____. Fanny Campbell, The Female Pirate Capt. A Tale of the Revolution. Boston: F. Gleason, 1845.

108 _____. The Gipsey; Or, The Robbers of Naples. A Story of Love and Pride by Lieutenant Murray. Boston: F. Gleason, 1847.

109 _____. The Magician of Naples; Or, Love and Necromancy. A Story of Italy and the East. New York: Samuel French, 1850?

110 _____. The Naval Officer; Or, The Pirate's Cave. A Tale of the Last War. Boston: F. Gleason, 1845.
        The War of 1812; not the Mexican conflict, is the back-drop. The American navy, nevertheless, was playing an important role in the Mexican War during the time when Ballou wrote many of his tales. This activity was portrayed visually for millions of citizens in the famous paintings of Lt. Henry Walke.

111 _____. The Pirate Smugglers; Or, The Last Cruise of The Viper. Boston: Elliott, Thomes and Talbot, 1861?

112 _____. Red Rupert; The American Bucanier [sic]. A Tale of the Spanish Indies. Boston: F. Gleason, 1845.

113 _____. Roderick the Rover; Or, The Spirit of the Wave. Boston: Gleason's Publishing House, 1847.

114 _____. The Sea Lark; Or, The Quadroon of Louisiana. A Story of Land and Sea. Boston: Pub. unknown, 186-? "Novelette No. 27. "

115 _____. The Sea Witch; Or, The African Quadroon. A Story of the Slave Coast. New York: Samuel French, 1855?
        American cruisers, heroes of this tale, conducted an unglamorous anti-slavery patrol off the African coast in the 1850's in co-operation with ships of the Royal Navy.

116 _____. The Spanish Musketeer. A Tale of Military Life. Boston: Gleason's Publishing House, 1847.

117 Banks, Polan. Black Ivory. New York: Harper, 1926.
        Pirates; Lafitte's slave trading around New Orleans.

118 Barbour, R. H. Fortunes of War. New York: Century, 1919. y.
        The submarine peril of World War I.

119 Barker, Benjamin. The Bandit of the Ocean; Or, The Female
      Privateer. A Romance of the Sea. New York: R. M.
      DeWitt, 184-?
            Typical of pre-Civil War escapism featuring what be-
      came the archetypal female pirate. Needless to say, sea
      fiction has yet to produce a Modesty Blaise!

120 _____. Corilla; Or, The Indian Enchantress. A Romance
      of the Pacific and Its Islands. Boston: Flag of Our Union
      Office, 1847.
            One of Barker's numerous feminist romances, written
      at a time when American interest in that South Seas and
      China area was "in the news." Remember the Wilkes Ex-
      pedition and Commodere Kearney's activities off China?

121 _____. The Dwarf of the Channel; Or, The Commodore's
      Daughter. A Nautical Romance of the Revolution. Boston:
      F. Gleason, 1846.

122 _____. Francisco; Or, The Pirate. A Tale of Land and
      Sea. Boston: Gleason's Publishing Hall, 1846.

123 _____. The Gold Hunters; Or, The Spectre of the Sea
      King. A Romance of the Sea. Boston: Gleason's Publish-
      ing Hall, 1846.

124 _____. The Land Pirate; Or, The Wild Girl of the Beach.
      A Tale of New Jersey Shore. Boston: F. Gleason, 1847.

125 _____. The Nymph of the Ocean; Or, The Pirate's Be-
      trothal. A Tale of the Sea. Boston: United States Pub-
      lishing Company, 1846.

126 _____. The Sea Serpent; Or, The Queen of the Coral Cave.
      A Romance of the Ocean. Boston: F. Gleason, 1847.

127 Barker, Clarence H. Bold Buccaneer. By "Seafarer," pseud.
      London: Ward, Lock, 1955. y.

128 _____. Captain Firebrace. By "Seafarer," pseud. London:
      Ward, Lock, 1958. y.

129 _____. The Cook's Cruise. By "Seafarer," pseud. London:
      Ward, Lock, 1960. y.

130 _____. Firebrace and the Java Queen. By "Seafarer,"
      pseud. London: Ward, Lock, 1960. y.

131 _____. The Haunted Ship. By "Seafarer," pseud. London:
      Ward, Lock, 1958. y.

132 _____. Make Way for a Sailor. By "Seafarer," pseud.
      London: Ward, Lock, 1947. y.

133 _____. The Sailor and the Widow. By "Seafarer, " pseud.
       London: Ward, Lock, 1957. y.

134 _____. Santa Maria. By "Seafarer, " pseud. London:
       Ward, Lock, 1955. y.

135 _____. Smuggler's Pay for Firebrace. By "Seafarer, "
       pseud. London: Ward, Lock, 1959. y.

136 Barker, Matthew H. Floating Remembrances. By "The
       Old Sailor of Deptford, " pseud. London: Whittaker, 1854.

137 _____. Hamilton King; Or, The Smuggler and the Dwarf.
       By "The Old Sailor of Deptford, " pseud. 3 vols. London:
       Bentley, 1839.

138 _____. Jem Bunt: A Tale of Land and Ocean. By "The
       Old Sailor of Deptford, " pseud. London: Willoughby, 1845.

139 _____. Land and Sea Tales. By "The Old Sailor of Dept-
       ford, " pseud. 2 vols. London: Routledge, 1836.

140 _____. The Log Book; Or, Nautical Miscellany. By "The
       Old Sailor of Deptford, " pseud. London: J. & W. Robins,
       1826.

141 _____. The Naval Club; Or, Reminiscences of Service.
       By "The Old Sailor of Deptford, " pseud. 3 vols. London:
       Henry Colburn, 1843.

142 _____. The Old Sailor's Jolly Boat. By "The Old Sailor
       of Deptford, " pseud. London: Strange, 1844.

143 _____. Topsail-Sheet Blocks; Or, The Naval Foundling.
       By "The Old Sailor of Deptford, " pseud. 3 vols. London:
       Beutlye, 1838.

144 _____. Tough Yarns: A Series of Naval Tales and Sketches
       to Please All Hands from the Swabs on the Shoulders Down
       to the Swabs in the Head. By "The Old Sailor of Deptford, "
       pseud. London: William Marsh, 1835.

145 _____. The Victory; Or, The Ward Room Mess. By "The
       Old Sailor of Deptford, " pseud. 3 vols. London: Henry
       Colburn, 1844.
          Barker was born in Britain in 1792. Although he saw
       service with both the East India Company and the Royal
       Navy, he was never commissioned. His duties did, however,
       provide excellent background for the themes of his stories.

146 Barker, Roland. Jonah's Ark. New York: Carlyle House,
       1940. y.
          One of the last sailing ships out of New York faces

hurricanes, doldrums, illness, etc. All is blamed on a
cursed Jonah figure aboard.

147 _____, and William Doerflinger. The Middle Passage.
New York: Macmillan, 1939. y.
Although innocent, a young Cornishman is found guilty
of wrecking a ship. He escapes his sentence and joins a
slaver, later becoming an important figure in the Black
Ivory trade on the Guinea coast. Tiring of the misery, he
returns to England and secures his freedom.

148 Barker, Shirley. Tomorrow the New Moon. Indianapolis:
Bobbs-Merrill, 1955. y.
A significant water theme forms the backdrop in this
tale of three young girls from the Isle of Man who settle
in early Martha's Vineyard.

149 Barnes, James. The Blockers. New York: Harper, 1905.
y.
The Civil War along the Atlantic seaboard, where the
Union government maintained what eventually became one of
the most successful blockades in maritime history.

150 _____. Drake and His Yeomen. New York: Macmillan,
1899. y.
"A true account of the character and adventures of Sir
Francis Drake as Told by Sir Matthew Maunsell, His Friend
and Follower."--subtitle.

151 _____. For King and Country. New York: Harper, 1896.
y.
Nautical adventure in the American Revolution.

152 _____. A Loyal Traitor. New York: Harper, 1897. y.
A Connecticut waif serving aboard a privateersman during the War of 1812 is taken at sea by a British cruiser,
sent to the infamous Dartmoor Prison, and engineers his
escape.

153 _____. Midshipman Farragut. New York: Appleton, 1902.
y.
Biographical fiction concerning two years of young Farragut's adventures under Commodore Porter, 1812-1814.
Readers might note that families of officers in the 19th-
century American navy were usually very close.

154 _____. With the Flag in the Channel. New York: Appleton, 1902. y.
Barnes' stories are still very readable today. This
particular work concerns the attacks made by John Paul
Jones on shipping in the English Channel during the American Revolution.

155   Barney, Helen C.   Light in the Rigging.   New York: Crown,
      1955.   y.
            The plot centers around an officer of the 17-century
      Royal Navy.

156   Barr, Amelia E.   She Loved a Sailor.   New York: Dodd,
      Mead, 1891.
            A nautical romance set in the days of Andrew Jackson's
      presidency.   A Scottish immigrant to America in 1853, and
      soon widowed, Mrs. Barr was aided by Henry Ward Beecher
      and by her death in 1883, she had published over 75 ro-
      mances.

157   _____.   A Singer from the Sea.   New York: Dodd, Mead,
      1893.
            A night of terror in a sea storm off the British coast
      has a sentimental resolution.

158   Barrows, John S.   A Son of "Old Ironsides." A Story of a
      Boy on the United States Frigate Constitution During the
      War of 1812, When She Was a "Whole Navy."   Boston:
      Lothrop, Lee and Shepard, 1931.   y.

159   Barry, John.   Sea Yarns.   London: W. and R. Chambers, 1910.

160   _____.   A Son of the Sea.   London: Duckworth, 1899.   y.

161   Barth, John.   The Floating Opera.   New York: Appleton,
      1956.

162   Barton, A. H.   With a Flag and a Bucket and a Gun.   Lon-
      don: Hodder & Stoughton, 1959.
            World War II.

163   Bassett, James E.   Cmdr. Prince, USN; A Novel of The Pacif-
      ic War.   New York: Simon and Schuster, 1971.
            American four-stacker destroyers in the Dutch East
      Indies in early 1942.   Good action, little romance.   Based
      on fact, including January 24, 1942, Battle of Makassar
      Strait.

164   _____.   Harm's Way.   Cleveland: World Publishing Co., 1962.
            American cruisers Vs. Japanese battleships late in
      1942.   (John Wayne portrayed the admiral-hero in the mov-
      ie version.)

165   Batchelder, Eugene.   A Romance of the Sea-Serpent; Or, The
      Ichthyosaurus.   By "Wave," pseud.   Cambridge, Mass.:
      John Bartlett, 1849.
            A dinosaur is seen at sea.   Reports of sea serpants
      were still fairly common in the 19th century.

166   Bates, Herbert Ernest.   The Cruise of the Breadwinner.

Boston: Little, Brown, 1947. y.

167 _____ . Rain Bow Fish. New York: E. P. Dutton, 1937.
    y.

168 _____ . The White Admiral. London: Dobson, 1968.

169 Baumann, Hans. The Barque of the Brothers. New York:
    Walck, 1958. y.
        Two boys join one of Prince Henry the Navigator's ex-
    peditions down the coast of Africa.

170 _____ . Son of Columbus. London and New York: Oxford
    University Press, 1957. y.
        The great explorer's 14-year old son records his fa-
    ther's last voyage to the New World.

171 Baume, Frederic E. Yankee Woman. New York: Dodd,
    Mead, 1945.
        A daring New England widow sails her husband's ship
    to California during California Gold Rush days.

172 Beach, Edward Latimer, Sr. An Annapolis First Classman.
    Philadelphia: Frank T. Merrill, 1910.
        The author was the father of the noted submarine com-
    mander/fiction writer cited below. He was cashiered from
    the service for losing his cruiser in a West Indian hurri-
    cane during World War I.

173 _____ . An Annapolis Plebe. Philadelphia: Penn Pub. Co.,
    1907
        A "plebe" would be called a "freshman" by civilians.

174 _____ . An Annapolis Second Classman. Philadelphia:
    Penn Pub. Co., 1909.

175 _____ . An Annapolis Youngster. Philadelphia: Frank T.
    Merrill, 1908.

176 _____ . Dan Quinn of the Navy. Written by Himself and
    Given Out by Captain Beach. New York: Macmillan, 1922.
        Fictional reminiscences of the "Old Navy."

177 _____ . Ensign Ralph Osborn; The Story of His Trials and
    Triumphs in a Battleship Engine Room. Boston: Wilde,
    1911.
        America's battlewagon fleet had advanced to the third
    spot in world navies (after Britain and Germany) by the time
    this patriotic yarn was penned.

178 _____ . Lieutenant Ralph Osborn; Aboard a Torpedo Boat
    Destroyer; Being the Story of How Ralph Osborn Became a
    Lieutenant and of His Cruise in an American Torpedo Boat

Destroyer in West Indian Waters. Boston: Wilde, 1912.
A TBD would today be called a destroyer and remember that from TF's time to FDR's, the USN was deeply involved in Caribbean gunboat diplomacy.

179 _____. Midshipman Ralph Osborn at Sea; A Story of The
U. S. Navy. Boston: Wilde, 1910.
A sequel to Ralph Osborn--Midshipman at Annapolis
(q. v.).

180 _____. Ralph Osborn--Midshipman at Annapolis; A Story
of Life at The U. S. Naval Academy. Boston: Frank T.
Merrill, 1909.

181 _____. Roger Paulding, Apprentice Seaman. Philadelphia:
Penn Pub. Co. , 1911.
Similar to the author's Ralph Osborn saga only involv-
ing, by and large, the life of a sailor on the "lower deck. "

182 _____. Roger Paulding, Ensign. Philadelphia: Penn Pub.
Co. , 1914.

183 _____. Roger Paulding, Gunner. Philadelphia: Penn Pub.
Co. , 1913.

184 _____. Roger Paulding, Gunner's Mate. Philadelphia:
Frank T. Merrill, 1912.

185 Beach, Edward Latimer, [Jr.]. Dust on the Sea. New York:
Holt, 1972.
Submarine wolfpacks against Japan. This writer, who
kindly penned one of the opening statements, was a noted
product of America's World War II submarine campaign
against the Japanese.

186 _____. Run Silent, Run Deep. New York: Holt, 1955.
One of the most famous submarine stories in sea fiction. (Clark Gable played the captain in the movie version.)

187 Beals, Carleton. Adventure of the Western Sea. New York:
Holt, 1956. y.
The 1787 voyage of the Lady Washington to the Orient.

188 Bean, Charles E. W. Flagship Three. London: Alston Rivers,
1913.

189 Beath, I. H. Middle Watch. Boston: Houghton, Mifflin, 1930.

190 Beatty, John and Patricia. Pirate Royal. New York: Macmillan, 1969. y.
The exploits of Sir Henry Morgan's young accountant on
the Spanish Main in the 17th Century.

191 Beaty, David. <u>The Four Winds.</u> New York: William Mor-
     row, 1955.   y.
          Merchant sailing.

192 _____. <u>The Wind Off the Sea.</u> A Novel. New York: Mor-
     row, 1963.
          British R. A. F. vs. German ship in World War II.

193 Beck, Lily A.   <u>The Divine Lady.</u> By E. Barrington, pseud.
     New York: Dodd, 1924.
          Nelson's love, Emma Hamilton. The author's grand-
     father had been a midshipman in Nelson's fleet.

194 _____. <u>The Great Romantic.</u> By E. Barrington, pseud.
     Garden City, N. Y. : Doubleday, 1933.
          A biographical novel of that gadfly and accountant of
     the 17th-century Royal Navy, Samuel Pepys, the diary
     writer.

195 Becke, Louis. <u>By Reef and Palm and the Ebbing of the Tide.</u>
     London: Fisher Unwin, 1914.
          World War I.

196 _____, and Walter Jeffery. <u>A First Fleet Family.</u> London:
     Unwin, 1895.
          The founding of New South Wales, 1788.

197 _____ and _____. <u>The Mutineer.</u> New York: Lippincott,
     1898.
          Fletcher Christian and the <u>Bounty.</u>

198 Bee, Allan G. <u>Swallowing the Anchor: Tales.</u> By "The Id-
     ler, " pseud. London: Blackwood, 1937.
          An anthology of British yarns.

199 Beith, John H. <u>Middle Watch.</u> By Ian Hay, pseud. Boston:
     Houghton, Mifflin, 1930.

200 _____. <u>Midshipmaid: The Tale of a Naval Manoeuvre.</u> By
     Ian Hay, pseud. Boston: Houghton, Mifflin, 1933.
          A farcical tale in which Sir Percy Newbiggin and his
     pretty daughter Celia visit Malta for an official Royal Navy
     inspection. When Sir Percy is called away, the island
     commander is left in charge of the charming girl with or-
     ders to protect her from local officers. How the hero per-
     forms this duty constitutes the remainder of this laughable
     story

201 _____, and S. K. Hall. <u>Admirals All.</u> Boston: Houghton,
     Mifflin, 1934.

202 Belfrage, Cedric. <u>My Master, Columbus.</u> Garden City, N. Y. :
     Doubleday, 1961.

1492 and the Ocean Blue! Should be compared with
Forester's To the Indies cited below. The story is nar-
rated by the explorer's servant, an Indian woman.

203 Bell, J. J. Little Grey Ships. London: Murray, 1916.
World War I.

204 Bell, Kenail. Coast Guard Cadets. New York: Dodd, Mead,
1941. y.
Initiation, rescue adventures. Reflects several real
life exploits of the "Treasury's Navy" during the 1930's.

205 _____. Danger on the Jersey Shore. New York: Dodd,
Mead, 1959. y.
Coast Guard rescue adventures.

206 _____. Ice Patrol; Jim Steele's Adventures with the U.S.
Coast Guard. New York: Dodd, Mead, 1937. y.
The U.S.C.G. became a vital cog in the International
Ice Patrol after the Titanic went down.

207 _____. Jersey Rebel. New York: Dodd, Mead, 1951. y.
A lad's adventures during the 1777 Battle of the Dela-
ware.

208 Bell, Sallie. Marcel Armand. New York: Page, 1935.
Pirates; Lafitte; early 19th century.

209 Bellah, James W. The Journal of Colonel de Tancey. Phila-
delphia: Chilton, 1967.
Filibuster William Walker attempts to take over Central
America in the 1850's only to be thwarted by the U.S. Navy.

210 Belloc, Hilaire, ed. On Sailing the Sea: A Collection of Writings. London: Hart-Davis, 1951.
An anthology.

211 Benchley, Nathaniel. The Off-Islanders. New York: McGraw-
Hill, 1961.
What happens when a Russian submarine is stranded off
Cape Cod. The humorous basis of the hit movie "The Rus-
sians Are Coming!"

212 _____. Sail a Crooked Ship. New York: McGraw-Hill,
1960.
Young naval reservist Peter Bellows and his fiancée
are kidnapped while inspecting an old patrol boat in moth-
balls in the Hudson River. A gang of nasties who have
just knocked over a bank plan to use the vessel for their
get-away and Peter is forced to navigate for them.

213 _____. The Wake of Icarus. New York: Atheneum, 1970.
A small American spy ship is sunk in Caribbean waters

leaving its 15 survivors on a remote little island employed
as a base by Cuban gunrunners.

214   Benjamin, Helen M. and Lewis S. Full Fathom Five: A Sea
      Anthology. London: G. Bell, 1910. y.

215   Bennett, Charles Moon. A Buccaneer's Log. New York: E.
      P. Dutton, 1929. y.
          A pirate story.

216   _____. Mutiny Island. New York: E. P. Dutton, 1928.
      y.
          More pirates.

217   _____. Tim Kane's Treasure. New York: E. P. Dutton,
      1932. y.

218   _____. With Morgan on the Main. New York: E. P. Dut-
      ton, 1930. y.
          Henry Morgan. No comparison with Van Wyck Mason's
      Cutlass Empire cited below.

219   Bennett, Geoffrey M. Falkland Islands Mystery. London:
      Hutchinson, 1951.

220   _____. The Phantom Fleet. London: Collins, 1946.

221   _____. Pirate Destroyer; and Also, The Dockyard Robbery.
      London: Hutchinson, 1951.
          Bennett, a noted British naval historian, set all 3 of
      these tales against the backdrop of the Second World War.

222   Bennett, Jack. Mister Fisherman. Boston: Little, Brown,
      1965. y.
          An unpleasant white kid and a tough old Malay are
      thrown together on a little island when their vessel goes
      down. Faced with little hope of rescue, the boy is forced
      to look upon the man as his protector but cannot bring him-
      self to make the gesture necessary to free himself from his
      prejudice.

223   _____. Ocean Road. Boston: Little, Brown, 1967.
          A nautical attempt to organize a counter-revolution
      against a group of Red Chinese-trained Africans who have
      assassinated a sultan and taken over his island kingdom.

224   Bennett, John. Barnaby Lee. New York: Appleton-Century,
      1902.
          Excellent local color of New Amsterdam in the days
      of the Dutch and more importantly to this work, several
      episodes of piracy are thrown in.

225   Bennett, Mark. Tack Ship. London: Arnold, 1925.

226   _____. Under the Periscope. London: Black, 1919.
            Both of this author's works celebrate World War I.

227   Bennett, Robert A. The Shogun's Daughter. New York:
            McClurg, 1910.
                Set against the backdrop of Commodore Perry's visit
            to Japan.

228   Berger, Josef. Bowleg Bill. New York: Viking, 1939. y.
                A story of a sea-going Wyoming cowboy. Just oppo-
            site of that old yarn of "Windjammer Smith," the mariner
            who ran a freight line of "sailing" wagons.

229   _____. Subchaser Jim. Boston: Little, Brown, 1943. y.
                World War II; Adventure with little American escort
            vessels on anti-submarine patrol.

230   _____. Swordfisherman Jim. Boston: Little, Brown, 1939,
            y.
                Cape Cod schooner fishing; initiation of a landlubber to
            Captain.

231   Berry, Don. To Build a Ship. New York: Viking, 1964.
                Ben Thaler, a settler on the bay of Oregon in the
            1850's, receives word that their provisioning ship will not
            return. Undaunted, Ben and his friends set out to construct
            their own.

232   Besant, Walter. The World Went Very Well Then. New York:
            Harper, 1886.
                Because the 18th-century Royal Navy controlled the
            Thames River and was successful in the South Seas.

233   _____, and James Rice. The Chaplain of the Fleet. Lon-
            don: Chatto, 1881.
                Most of the action in this 18th-century tale takes place
            ashore, rather than afloat, and is designed to show the
            manners, customs, and infighting of the "peace-time"
            Royal Navy.

234   _____, and _____. 'Twas in Trafalgar Bay. London:
            Chatto and Windus, 1879. y.

235   Best, Herbert Nelson. Not Without Danger. New York: Vi-
            king Press, 1951.
                Piracy in 18th-century Jamaica.

236   Beuttler, E. G. O. Humour Afloat: Visualizing Some Imagi-
            nary Episodes in the Royal Navy and Mercantile Marine.
            London: Syren & Shipping, 1919.
                Includes 48 cartoons.

237   Bevan, Tom. Sea Dogs All. London: Nelson, 1908. y.

Sir Francis Drake and the Spanish Armada.

238   Beverley-Giddings, Arthur R.   The Rival Shores.   New York:
         Morrow, 1956.
         Pre-Revolution maneuvering on Chesapeake Bay.

239   Beyer, Audrey W.   Capture at Sea.   New York: Alfred A.
         Knopf, 1959. y.
         Impressment in the Royal Navy at the time of the War
      of 1812.

240   Bickering, Edgar.   In Press-Gang Days.   London: Blackie,
         1894. y.
         The Battle of the Nile, etc.

241   Biemiller, Carl L.   The Hydronauts.   Garden City, N. Y. :
         Doubleday, 1970.
         Depicts a future world in which men live beneath the
      sea after an atomic war has devastated the earth's conti-
      nents and melted the polar ice caps. A cross between nau-
      tical and science fiction.

242   Bill, Alfred H.   Ring of Danger: A Tale of Elizabethan Eng-
         land.   New York: Alfred A. Knopf, 1948.   y.
         Walter Blake and the Captain of the Fair Adventure
      rescue a stranger who, upon arriving in England, leads
      them into many scrapes and escapes.

243   Bindloss, H.   In the Misty Seas.   London: Partridge, 1933.

244   Binns, Archie Fred.   The Enchanted Islands.   New York:
         Duell, Sloan and Pearce, 1956. y.
         Youthful explorations of the mystery-laden San Juan
      Islands off the Seattle coast area.

245   _____.   The Headwaters.   A Novel.   New York: Duell,
      Sloan and Pearce, 1957.
         1890's smuggling adventures between the Pacific North-
      west and Hawaiian Islands.

246   _____.   Lightship.   New York: Reynal and Hitchcock, 1934.
         Mysterious adventures of Lightship 167 off the Oregon
      coast in a "sea of troubles. "

247   _____, and Felix Riesenberg.   The Maiden Voyage.   New
      York: John Day, 1939.
         A tale in collaboration, featuring a captain's wife as a
      major character.

248   _____.   You Rolling River.   New York: Scribner's, 1947.
         Post-Civil War Fort Astoria on the Columbia River;
      Williamette Valley waters of the American Northwest; a tale
      of a Shanghaied bluejacket.

249 Bird, Robert M. The Adventures of Robin Day. 2 vols.
     Philadelphia: Lea and Blanchard, 1839.
          An important early contribution to the development of
     realistic American sea fiction: a satirical and debunking
     attack on the romanticism fostered by James F. Cooper
     and other contemporary Yankee writers.

250 Black, William. White Wings: A Yachting Romance. Lon-
     don: Macmillan, 1880.
          Our Scottish author was a yachting enthusiast.

251 Blackmore, Richard D. Springhaven. London: Sampson,
     Low, 1887.
          Trafalgar. Better known for his classic, Lorna Doone.

252 Blackwood's Magazine, Editors of. Sea Tales from Blackwood.
     London: Blackwood, 1960.
          Some of the best British sea literature of the past two
     centuries has been published within the pages of this grand
     old journal. Readers are advised to check copies of the
     Readers' Guide to Periodical Literature and 19th Century
     Readers' Guide to Periodical Literature for stories indexed
     therein.

253 Blake, George. The Shipbuilders: A Novel. London: Collins,
     1970.

254 Blaker, Richard. The Needle-Watcher. New York: Doubleday,
     1932.
          How a 17th-century English sea captain who knew his
     compass becomes the friend of a Japanese Shogun.

255 Blanc, Suzanne. The Sea Troll. Garden City, N.Y.: Double-
     day, 1969.
          A lady passenger and an old sea captain become roman-
     tically involved on an ancient Norwegian freighter bound for
     Singapore.

256 Blasco-Ibáñez, Vincente. Unknown Lands. New York: E. P.
     Dutton, 1929.
          A look at shipboard life during Columbus' first trip
     over to the New World.

257 Blatchford, Robert. Merrie England. London, 1894.
          Days of Drake.

258 Bloundelle-Burton, John. Fortune's My For. London: Me-
     thuen, 1899.
          Cartegena, 1758.

259 _____. The Hispaniola Plate. London: Cassell, 1895.
          Sir William Phips' search for a lost Spanish treasure.

Van Wyck Mason tells the story much better in his Log Cabin Noble.

260 _____. The Sea Devils. London: White, 1912.
The adventures of a Spanish sailor in the Spanish Armada--who survives, only to face the Inquisition! Gloomy.

261 Blue Book Magazine, Editors of. Best Sea Stories. New York: McBride, 1954.

262 Blundell, Peter. The Confessions of a Seaman. London: Arrowsmith, 1924.

263 Blunder, Godfrey. Charco Harbour: A Novel of Cook's First Tour to Australia. London: Weidenfeld and Nicholson, 1968.

264 No entry

265 Blyth, James. The King's Guerdon. London: Digby & Long, 1906.
A look at the great English-Dutch sea fight off Lowestaft with the great plague and fire of London in the 1660's thrown in.

266 Boden, Clara N. The Cut of Her Jib. New York: Coward-McCann, 1953.
A Mass. grandmother's diary format, reveals the love affairs between sailormen and their lassies in the 1850's.

267 Boff, Charles, ed. A Boys' Book of the Sea. London: Routledge, 1939. y.
An anthology.

268 Bok, William Curtis. Maria: A Tale of the Northeast Coast and of the South Atlantic. New York: Knopf, 1962. y.

269 Boldrewood, Rolf. A Modern Buccaneer. London: Macmillan, 1894.

270 Bolster, David. Roll on My Twelve: Short Stories of the Royal Navy and a Glossary of Naval Slang Terms. London: Sylvan, 1945.

271 Bone, David W. The Brassbounder. London: Duckworth, 1915.
A Scottish sailor-apprentice describes a square-rigger's voyage from Glasgow round the Horn to "Frisco Bay."

272 _____. Broken Stowage. New York: Dutton, 1922.

273 _____. The Queerfella. London: Duckworth, 1952.

274 Bonham, Frank. <u>Deepwater Challenge.</u> New York: Crowell, 1963. y.
   Youthful Cam Walker's outwitting the sea as breadwinner of his family; dangerous adventures in a fishing boat.

275 _____. <u>Storm Tide.</u> New York: Harper, 1965. y.
   Whaling story set during the painful transition of mechanization from sail to steam along the New Bedford coast and in the Pacific Ocean; soon after the Civil War; features a prominent female character.

276 _____. <u>The Submarine Signaled ... Murder!</u> New York: Select Publications, 1942.
   As much a mystery as a sea story.

277 _____. <u>War Beneath the Sea.</u> New York: Crowell, 1962. y.
   A fictional account of the American submarine campaign in the Pacific during World War II.

278 Bordon, Charles A. <u>He Sailed with Captain Cook.</u> New York: Crowell, 1952. y.
   A lad's adventures with the great 18th-century British explorer.

279 Bosworth, Allan R. <u>The Crows of Edwina Hill.</u> New York: Harper, 1961.
   The <u>Bustard</u> was an American navy submarine rescue vessel on duty off Japan after the Korean War. In addition to being the story of the ship and her crew, this yarn concerns a young doctor with a romantic interest in a Japanese girl.

280 _____. <u>Full Crash Dive.</u> New York: Duel, Sloan and Pearce, 1942.
   Sensational crime story of a submarine that took a full dive and never rose again; murder on land and sea.

281 Bottume, Carl Huntington. <u>A Sailor's Choice.</u> Boston: Little, Brown, 1951. y.
   Adventure and intrigue; running illegal goods in the Caribbean.

282 Bourne, Lawrence R. <u>The Adventures of John Carfax, A Gentleman of Devon and Sometimes Seaman in the British Navy.</u> Excelsior Series. London: Oxford University Press, 1933.

283 _____. <u>Captain Coppernob: The Story of a Sailing Voyage.</u> Hawthorn Series. London: Oxford University Press, 1933.

284 _____. <u>Coppernob Omnibus.</u> London: Oxford University Press, 1932.

285 _____. Coppernob, Second Mate: The Story of a Sailing
        Voyage. Hawthorn Series. London: Oxford University
        Press, 1933.

286 _____. Coppernob, Ship-Owner: The Story of a Lost
        Steamer. Excelsior Series. London: Oxford University
        Press, 1934.

287 _____. Eastward Bound: A Story of Present Day Smug-
        gling. London: Oxford University Press, 1933.

288 _____. The Fourth Engineer. London: Oxford University
        Press, 1933.

289 _____. The Voyage of the Lulworth. London: Oxford Uni-
        versity Press, 1932.

290 Bowen, Robert Adger. Uncharted Seas. Boston: Small, May-
        nard, 1913.

291 Bowen, Robert O. The Weight of the Cross. New York:
        Knopf, 1951.
            World War II; Japanese imprisonment reminiscences;
        Navy theme.

292 Bowen, Robert Sidney. Dave Dawson on Convoy Patrol. By
        James Robert Richard, pseud. New York: Crown, 1941.
        y.
            Action in the North Atlantic in World War II.

293 _____. Dave Dawson with the Pacific Fleet. New York:
        Crown, 1942. y.
            Our hero transfers to Halsey's command and "licks"
        the Japanese at the time of the battle of Midway.

294 _____. Red Randall in the Aleutians. New York: Grosset
        and Dunlap, 1945. y.
            World War II in the frozen North Alaskan islands where
        "scrap-iron flotillas" of the American and Japanese fleets
        slugged it out.

295 _____. Red Randall; Or, Pearl Harbor. New York: Gros-
        set and Dunlap, 1944. y.
            The December 7, 1941 attack on America's outpost in
        Hawaii.

296 Bower, John G. H.M.S. --. By "Klaxon," pseud. London:
        Blackwood, 1918.
            First World War.

297 Bowles, G. F. Stewart. A Gun-Room Ditty Box. London:
        Cassell, 1898.
            The Royal Navy at the turn of the century.

298 _____. A Stretch Off the Land. London: Methuen, 1903.

299 Bowling, "Skipper" J. and Gregory. Yarns from a Capt's
     Log. London: Blackwood, 1912.
          Merchant sailing, British style.

300 Bowman, Peter. Red Beach. New York: Random House,
     1945.
          The American assault on a Japanese-held island in the
     Pacific during World War II.

301 Boyd, Alexander J. The Shellback; Or, At Sea in 1860. Lon-
     don: Cassell, 1898.

302 Boyd, Dean. Lighter-than-Air. New York: Harcourt, 1961.
          A humorous examination of the role played by the U.S.
     Navy blimp service in protecting off-shore American con-
     voys in World War II.

303 Boyd, James. Drums. New York: Scribner's, 1925.
          The American Revolution afloat and in North Carolina;
     featuring John Paul Jones.

304 Boynten, B. H., Jr. The White Dart; Or, The Cruiser of the
     Gulf of Mexico. A True Tale of Piracy and War. Boston:
     Star Spangled Banner Office, 1848.
          A naval novel growing out of the Mexican War; relative-
     ly tame, by our standards.

305 Brackenridge, Hugh H. Modern Chivalry; Containing the Ad-
     ventures of John Farrago and Teague O'Regan, His Servant.
     4 Vols. Philadelphia: "Printed and Sold by John M'Cul-
     loch, 1792-97."
          This early example of American sea fiction was re-
     printed in 1962 by the New York firm of Hafner; 1965 ver-
     sion edited for the modern reader by Lewis Leary, New
     Haven: College and U. Press, "Masterworks of Literature
     Series." The author was a Revolutionary War chaplain, a
     close friend of Philip Freneau, a Pennsylvania Supreme
     Court judge, and father of a noted social historian. He
     never served a day at sea in any capacity!

306 Bradford, Richard. Red Sky at Morning. Philadelphia: Lip-
     pincott, 1968.
          Called to duty in World War II, a naval officer sends
     his family to New Mexico to await his return.

307 Brady, Cyrus T. The Blue Ocean's Daughter. New York:
     Moffat, Yard, 1907. y.
          The American Revolution adventures of Susan, the
     captain's daughter, who is caught between a British frigate
     and a Yankee privateer. A nautical romance whose sequel,
     The Adventures of Lady Susan, was published in 1908.

Brady, a familiar sea story writer at the turn of the century and whose tales are still read today, "moonlighted"
as an author; his first "calling" was as an Episcopal clergy-
man.

308   _____ . Bob Dashaway in the Frozen Seas.   New York:
Dodd, Mead, 1913.   y.
A tale based on the Titanic disaster of the previous
year.

309   _____ . Bob Dashaway, Treasure Hunter: A Story of Adventure in the Strange South Seas.   New York: Dodd,
Mead, 1912.   y.
Before 1942 the islands of the South Pacific were for
most Americans very mysterious indeed!

310   _____ . For Love of Country: A Story of Land and Sea in
the Days of the Revolution.   New York: Scribner's, 1898.
y.

311   _____ . For the Freedom of the Sea: A Romance of the
War of 1812.   New York: P. F. Collier, 1899.   y.
The U. S. S. Constitution vs. H. M. S. Guerrière.

312   _____ . The Grip of Honor: A Story of John Paul Jones
and the American Revolution.   New York: Scribner's,
1900.   y.

313   _____ . In the War with Mexico.   New York: Scribner's,
1903.   y.
Includes U. S. naval support of land operations.

314   _____ . In the Wasps's Nest: The Story of a Sea Waif in
the War of 1812.   New York: Scribner's, 1902.   y.
U. S. S. Wasp was a noted cruiser in that war.

315   _____ . The Island of the Stairs; Being a True Account of
Certain Strange and Wonderful Adventures of Master John
Hampdon, Seaman, And Teller of the Tale, and Mistress
Lucy Wilberforce, Gentlewoman of the South Seas.   Chicago:
A. C. McClurg, 1913.   y.
Fiction with only the locale faithfully portrayed.   And
that's the truth!

316   _____ . A Little Traitor to the South.   New York: Mac-
millan, 1904.   y.
The attempted sinking of the U. S. S. Wabash by the
Confederate torpedoboat David.

317   _____ . A Midshipman in the Pacific.   New York: Scribner's, 1904.   y.
The last cruise of the American frigate Essex, lost to
enemy action in the War of 1812.

318 _____ . My Lady's Slipper. New York: Dodd, Mead, 1905.
        y.
            John Paul Jones in Paris before sailing aboard the
        Bonhomme Richard.

319 _____ . On the Old "Kearsarge," A Story of the Civil War.
        New York: Scribner's, 1919.
            A fictional look at the destruction of the C. C. S. Ala-
        bama by the U. S. S. Kearsarge.

320 _____ . The Quiberon Touch: A Romance of the Days
        When "The Great Lord Hawke" Was King of the Sea. New
        York: D. Appleton, 1901. y.

321 _____ . Reuben James, A Hero of the Forecastle. New
        York: Appleton, 1900. y.
            James supposedly saved the life of Stephen Decatur
        during America's first war with the Barbary pirates.

322 _____ . Sir Henry Morgan, Buccaneer: A Romance of the
        Spanish Main. New York: G. W. Dillingham, 1903. y.

323 _____ . The Southerness. New York: Scribner's, 1903.
        y.
            Mobile City and bay during the Civil War.

324 _____ . The Two Captains: A Romance of Bonaparte and
        Nelson. New York: Macmillan, 1905. y.

325 _____ . Waif-o'-the-Sea: A Romance of the Deep. Chica-
        go: A. C. McClurg, 1918. y.

326 _____ . Woven with the Ship: A Novel of 1865, Together
        with Certain Other Voracious Tales of Various Sorts.
        Philadelphia: Lippincott, 1902.
            A look at life afloat late in our Civil War, and earlier,
        during the War of 1812.

327 Brahms, Caryl and Sherrin. Benbow Was His Name. London:
        Hutchinson, 1967. y.
            Pirates.

328 Branch, Houston and Frank Waters. Diamond Head. New
        York: Farrar, 1948.
            A fictional look at the exploits of the raider C. S. S.
        Shenandoah in the Civil War.

329 Brand, Jack. By Wild Waves Tossed. New York: McClures,
        1908.
            Naval action in the War of 1812.

330 Brereton, F. S. A Knight of St. John. London: Blackie,
        1906. y.
            Havre and the siege of Malta, 1564.

331 Breslin, Howard. A Hundred Hills. New York: Crowell,
     1960.
          The Civil War siege of Vicksburg by land and river.
     Very accurate as to factual background.

332 _____. Shad Run. New York: Crowell, 1955. y.
          Hudson River adventures of a fisherman's daughter
     during the Revolution.

333 Bridges, Thomas. Romances and Mysteries of the Sea. Lon-
     don: Newnes, 1940.
          An anthology.

334 Briggs, Charles F. Working a Passage; Or, Life in a Liner.
     New York: John Allen, 1844.
          This fictional account of a packet in the days of sail
     was reprinted by the New York firm of Garnet Press, 1970.

335 Briggs, Philip. North with Pintail. London: 1943.

336 _____. Ocean Redhead. London: Lutterworth Press,
     1949.

337 Brinkley, William. Don't Go Near the Water. New York:
     Random House, 1956.
          A humorous yarn of Navy public relations on a Pacific
     island during World War II.

338 _____. The Ninety and Nine. Garden City, N. Y. : Double-
     day, 1966.
          Life aboard an American LST during the World War II
     invasion of Anzio in Italy.

339 Brooke, W. The Log of a Sailorman. London: Century Press,
     1908.
          Merchant sailing.

340 Brookes, Ewart. Curse of the Trawler Charon. New York:
     Dodd, Mead, 1957.
          When a man dies at the christening of this small British
     vessel, its crew confirms its belief that she is a jinx ship.
     During World War II, she is commissioned as a patrol boat
     in the Royal Navy and sure enough, sinks during a gale in
     the North Atlantic. Originally published by the London
     firm of Jarrolds two years earlier as To Endless Night.

341 _____. The Glass Years. London: Jarrolds, 1957.

342 _____. Glory Passed Them By. London: Jarrolds, 1958.
          Small ships of World War II.

343 _____. Proud Waters. London: Jarrolds, 1954.
          The story of a World War II rescue tug.

344 _____. Ride the Wild Wind. London: Jarrolds, 1958.

345 _____. Turmoil. London: Jarrolds, 1956.
          Published in America the following year as Rescue Tug.

346 Brookfield, Frances M. My Lord of Essex. London: Pitman,
      1907.
          How Essex and Drake singed the King of Spain's beard
      at Cadiz in 1587.

347 Broster, D. K. Ships in the Bay! New York: Coward-
      McCann, 1931. y.
          Naval action in the Napoleonic wars.

348 Brown, Arthur. The French Prisoners of Norman Cross: A
      Tale of the Sea. London: Hodder Bros., 1860?

349 Brown, Hugh. Saturday Island. Garden City, N.Y.: Double-
      day, 1935.

350 Brown, Robert. Spunyard and Spendrift: A Sailor Boy's Log
      of a Voyage Out and Home in a China Tea Clipper. Lon-
      don: Houlston, 1886. y.

351 Brown, Wenzell. They Called Her Charity. New York:
      Appleton-Century, 1951.
          Pirates in the 17th-century Virgin Islands.

352 Bruce, George. Navy Blue and Gold: A Story of The Naval
      Academy. New York: William Caslon Co., 1936. y.
          Supposed life during the Inter-War period; very fanciful
      and on the order of something Pat Boone might have played
      in a movie.

353 _____, and Randal M. White. Salute to the Marines. New
      York: Grosset and Dunlap, 1943.
          U.S. Marine Corps action during World War II.

354 Brysson, James, ed. Plain Sailing. London: Frewin, 1966.
          An anthology of sea yarns.

355 Buchheim, Lothar-Gunther. The Boat. Translated from the
      German by Denver and Helen Lindley. New York: Knopf,
      1975.
          The German U-boat and her youthful crew fight the
      odds after the World War II Battle of the Atlantic has
      turned in favor of the Allies. A German best seller by
      a veteran of Doenitz's underseas wolfpacks, this yarn has
      been compared with Alexander Kent (Douglas Reeman's)
      With Blood and Iron (q.v.).

356 Bulla, Clyde R. The Pirate's Promise. New York: Crowell,
      1958. y.
          A kidnapped youth slated for indentured service in

18th-century America is captured by pirates and thereby
plunged into even greater danger.

357 Bullen, Frank T. Beyond. London: Chapman and Hall, 1909.
          The author spent quite a bit of time on the lecture cir-
     cuit telling stories of the sea, 1869-1883, before doing
     much writing about it.

358 _____. Bounty Boy. London: Marshall Bros. , 1907. y.
          The famous mutiny.

359 _____. The Cruise of the "Cachalot. " New York: Apple-
     ton, 1898.
          Based on the author's experiences as a seaman aboard
     an American whaling ship in the South Seas.

360 _____. Cut Off from the World. London: Unwin, 1909.

361 _____. Deep-Sea Plunderings: A Collection of Stories of
     the Sea. London: Elder, 1901.

362 _____. Frank Brown, Sea Apprentice. Philadelphia: Mc-
     Kay, 1926. y.

363 _____. Idylls of the Sea. London: G. Richard, 1899.

364 _____. The Log of a Sea Waif: Being Recollections of the
     First Four Years of My Sea Life. New York: Appleton,
     1899.
          Fiction, not autobiography.

365 _____. A Sack of Shakings (Shakings Are Odds and Ends
     Accumulated During a Voyage. They Were Formerly the
     Perquisites of the Chief Mate.). New York: McClure,
     1901.

366 _____. The Sea Puritans. London: Hodder & Stoughton,
     1904.
          Admiral Robert Blake and the English Navy at the
     time of the Commonwealth's war with the Dutch.

367 _____. A Whaleman's Wife. 2nd ed. London: Hodder &
     Stoughton, 1902.
          Women's Lib!--she ran an old-time wooden whaler in
     this story.

368 Burchard, Peter. Stranded. New York: Coward, 1967.
          A salt encounters post-Civil War New York.

369 Burgess, J. J. Haldane. The Treasure of Don Andres. Lon-
     don: Matthewson, Lerwick, 1903.
          Shetland and Spain at the time of the Armada.

370 Burgoyne, Alan H. The War Inevitable. London: Nelson, 1908.
Expecting World War I.

371 Burland, Brian. A Fall from Aloft. New York: Random House, 1970.
Follows the activities of one crewman aboard a steamer crossing the submarine-infested Atlantic during World War II.

371a _____. Surprise. New York: Harper, 1975.
An ex-slave's attempt to found an independent black republic on a tiny Caribbean island.

372 Burman, Benjamin L. Blow for a Landing. London: Lutterworth Press, 1948.
Steamboat adventures on the Mississippi.

373 _____. Steamboat Round the Bend. New York: Farrar, 1933.
A pre-Civil War love story set against the background of the rivers and bayous of the South.

374 Burnett, William R. The Goldseekers. Garden City, N.Y.: Doubleday, 1962.
Four men travel afloat via the North Pacific, Bering Sea, and Yukon River to the gold fields of Alaska in the 1890's.

375 Burrage, A. H. Bending the Sails. London: Gardner, 1938.

376 _____. The Captain's Secret. London: Ward, Lock, 1939.
Merchant sailing.

377 Burt, Olive W. I Challenge the Dark Sea. New York: John Day, 1962. y.
A biographical novel of Prince Henry the Navigator.

378 Burton, Hester. Castors Away. Cleveland: World, 1962.
The plot is built around an actual event of 1805 when a British naval seaman was apparently restored to life 13 hours after his death.

379 Burts, Robert. The Scourge of the Ocean: A Story of the Atlantic, by an Officer of the U.S. Navy. 3 Vols. Philadelphia: E. L. Carey and A. Hart, 1837.

380 _____. The Sea King: A Nautical Romance. Philadelphia: A. Hart, 1851.
Both of Burts' efforts concern piracy and privateering. This author was noted for his nautical short stories penned for a number of U.S. magazines. All were

unabashed imitations of James F. Cooper's (q. v.) romantic-narrative style.

381 Bush, E. W. Flowers of the Sea: An Anthology. London: Allen and Unwin, 1962.

382 Bushnell, Oswald A. The Return of the Lono: A Novel of Captain Cook's Last Voyage. Boston: Little, Brown, 1956.
     The death of the great British explorer in the Hawaiian Islands.

383 Butterworth, Hezekiah. The Treasure Ship; A Tale of Sir William Phipps, The Regicides and the Inter-Charter in Massachusetts. New York: D. Appleton, 1899.
     Note the novel by van Wyck Mason, Log Cabin Noble. This writer penned many other novels for young people, mostly with a religious or sentimental bent. His The Story of the Hymns was judged the most important book of 1875.

384 Butterworth, W. E. Stop and Search: A Novel of Small Boat Warfare Off Vietnam. Boston: Little, Brown, 1969. y.
     Relates the activities of U. S. Navy seaman second class Eddie Czernik.

385 Byrne, Donn. The Field of Honor. New York: Appleton-Century, 1929.
     Nelson, Napoleon, and the Napoleonic wars.

386 Bywater, Hector C. The Great Pacific War. London: Constable, 1925.
     Sixteen years before Pearl Harbor, this work of fiction correctly predicted that disaster. The Japanese heeded the author's theories and the book describes other events which actually came to pass. Should be read as a great book of prophecy!

- C -

387 Cahun, Léon. The Adventures of Captain Mayo. New York: Scribner's, 1889.
     Piracy.

388 Caidin, Martin. Cyborg. New York: Arbor House, 1972.
     The first mission of super agent Steven Austin, "The Six Million Dollar Man," is the underwater infiltration of a secret Russian naval base in South America.

389 Calahan, Harold A. Back to Treasure Island. New York: Vanguard Press, 1935. y.
     Long John Silver sails again!

390 Callison, Brian. Dawn Attack. New York: Putnam, 1972.
       A fictional 1941 Commando raid in Norway.

391 _____ . A Flock of Ships. New York: Putnam, 1970.
              Convoy action on the Liverpool to Australia run during
       World War II.

392 _____ . A Plague of Sailors. New York: Putnam, 1972.
              A British sailor-spy is sent to recover a biological
       warfare weapon stolen from a research station and enroute
       by sea to Israel.

393 Calvin, Jack. Fisherman 28. Boston: Little, Brown, 1930.

394 _____ . Square Rigged. Boston: Little, Brown, 1929.
              A futile struggle to save The Queen of Asia and the
       end of the era of square-rigged sails.

395 Cameron, Vernon L. The Cruise of the "Black Prince,"
       Privateer. London: Chatto and Windus, 1886.
              Legalized piracy.

396 Camp, William M. "Retreat, Hell!" New York: Appleton,
       1943.
              The early days of World War II find U.S. Marines
       fighting at Shanghai and in the Philippines.

397 Campbell, V. A. G. Son of the Sea. New York: Frederick
       Warne, 1936.

398 Capes, Bernard. The Extraordinary Confessions of Diana
       Please. London: Methuen, 1904.
              Nelson and Lady Hamilton at Naples, 1798-1799.

399 _____ . Where England Sets Her Feet. London: Collins,
       1918.
              Adventure afloat and shore during the 16th-century.

400 Capron, Louis. "The Blue Witch." New York: Holt, 1957. y.
              A tale concerning the American China trade of the
       1830's and "wreckers" working the Florida coast.

401 Carlisle, Henry. Voyage to the First of December. New York:
       Putnam, 1972.
              A fictional account of the noted 1842 mutiny aboard the
       U.S. Navy brig Sommers; exceptionally interesting.

402 Carpenter, Edward C. Captain Courtesy. New York: Jacobs,
       1906.
              A tale of American naval operations off California dur-
       ing the Mexican War.

403 Carse, Robert. The Beckoning Waters. New York:

Scribner's, 1953.
A story concerning the U.S. merchant marine in World War II.

404 _____. Deep Six. New York: William Morrow, 1946.
Cruiser warfare in the Pacific theater of World War II.

405 _____. The Fabulous Buccaneer. New York: Dell, 1957.
Jean Lafitte.

406 _____. From the Sea and the Jungle. New York: Scribner's, 1951.
Merchantmen vs. U-boats in the Caribbean during World War II.

407 _____. Great Circle. New York: Scribner's, 1956. y.
A yarn concerning a whaling voyage out of Salem, Mass., in the 1840's.

408 _____. Hudson River Hayride. Greenwich, Conn.: New York Graphic Society, 1962. y.
Another 1840's whaling yarn.

409 _____. Pacific. New York: Farrar and Rinehart, 1932.

410 _____. Siren's Song. New York: Farrar and Rinehart, 1930.

411 _____. Winter of the Whale. New York: Putnam, 1961. y.
Whaling in the 1840's.

412 Carter, George G. The Smocksmen: A Story of the Fishermen of the Borough. London: Constable, 1947.

413 Carter, Isabel H. Shipmates. New York: W. R. Scott, 1934.
Maine seafaring in the 1870's; stoic wife aboard a coasting vessel.

414 Case, Josephine. Written in the Sand. Boston: Houghton, Mifflin, 1945.
William Eaton and the invasion of Tripoli in 1805.

415 Casing, James. Submariners. London: Macmillan, 1951.
World War II.

415a Catherall, A. Sea Wraith. London: Lutterworth Press, 1955. y.

416 Cato, Nancy F. North-West by South. London: Heinemann, 1965.
Merchant sailing.

417 Catto, Max. D-Day in Paradise. New York: Morrow, 1964.
An aging Dutch Protestant sea captain in his equally
aging tramp steamer worrying its way among the islands of
the South Pacific picks up a soldier of fortune before making a call at Christ's Island just as an international naval
expedition arrives to prepare for a vast military exercise.
The natives, led by Catholic missionaries and our adventurer, resist the flotilla long enough for a typhoon to over-
take and destroy it.

418 _____. Murphy's War. New York: Simon & Schuster,
1969.
How the sole survivor of a torpedoed Australian merchantman plots to get the U-boat which sank him during the
late days of World War II. Made into a movie.

419 Chalmers, Stephen. The Vanishing Smuggler. London:
Clode, 1909.
British revenue agents vs. smugglers, afloat and
ashore, at the beginning of the 19th-century.

420 Chambers, Robert W. The Happy Parrot. New York: Appleton, 1929.
A schooner trying to sell slaves during the War of 1812.

421 _____. The Man They Hanged. New York: Appleton, 1926.
A sympathetic view of the problems of Captain William
Kidd.

422 _____. The Rake and the Hussy. New York: Appleton,
1930.
Life in New Orleans just before and during the great
battle of 1815.

423 _____. The Reckoning. London: Constable, 1905.
The 1781 battle of Yorktown, which was decided you
will recall by the successful French blockade of the Virginia
capes.

424 Chambliss, William C. Boomerang. New York: Harcourt,
1944.
An American carrier captures a Japanese destroyer
during World War II and employs her as a secret weapon
against her former owners.

425 Chamier, Frederick. The Arethusa: A Naval Story. 3 Vols.
London: Routledge, 1830?
The author was an active Royal Navy captain who served
from 1809-1856. This tale concerns the press gangs.

426 _____. Ben Brace: The Last of Nelson's Agamemnons.
London: Bentley, 1835.
Reprinted by Routledge in 1905, this story was modeled

after the admiral's servant, Allen, and his experiences
from 1770 through the entire Nelson period up to the bom-
bardment of Algiers by Lord Exmouth in 1816.

427 _____. Jack Adams, the Mutineer. 3 Vols. London:
Henry Colburn, 1836.
    The Bounty tragedy. Chamier wrote works as impor-
tant to the development of the sea story as his contemporary, Frederick Marryat (q. v.).

428 _____. The Life of a Sailor. 3 Vols. London: Richard
Bentley, 1832.
    A look at the social side of a naval career in that day.

429 _____. The Perils of Beauty. 3 Vols. London: Henry
Colburn, 1842.

430 _____. The Spitfire, A Tale of the Sea. 3 Vols. London:
Henry Colburn, 1840.

431 _____. Tom Bowling: A Tale of the Sea. London: Henry
Colburn, 1839.
    Based on the life of Lieutenant Richard Bowen, 1761-
1797. A noted literary character, Captain Collingwood,
is introduced as a type for later sea stories by other authors.

432 _____. Walsingham, the Gamester. London: Richard
Bentley, 1837.

433 Champness, Francis Q. Middle Watch Musings. By Guns
Q. F. C. and Phyl Theeluker, pseud. Portsmouth and
London: Simpkin, Marshall, 1912.

434 Charles, T. The Ultimate Surrender. London: Hale, 1958.
y.

435 Charters, Zelda. Barbary Brew. Harrisburg, Pa. : Stackpole, 1937. y.
    A young American doctor is captured at sea by North
African pirates in the 1790's and sold into slavery.

436 Chase, Mary E. The Edge of Darkness. New York: Norton,
1957.
    Coastal Maine characters richly drawn.

437 _____. Mary Peters. New York: Macmillan, 1934.
    Female figure faces the rigors of life ashore from the
1880's onward, after having spent her early years afloat
on her Maine father's ship.

438 _____. Silas Crockett. New York: Macmillan, 1935.

A saga of four generations of Maine seafarers, the Crocketts, from 1830-1933.

439 Chase, Owen. The Loss of the Essex: A Thrilling Tale of the Sea When a Nantucket Ship Was Sunk by a Whale in Mid-Ocean. The Suffering of the Crew as Related by the Survivors of the Tragedy. The Horrors of Cannibalism That Any Might Live. Nantucket Island, Mass. : The Inquirer and Mirror Press, 1935.
     An interesting, if obscure, bit of historical fiction based on a real story of the sinking of the Essex by a whale; an original account was published by the author in 1821.

440 Chastain, Madye L. Magic Island. New York: Harcourt, 1964. y.
     A clipper ship tale set in the West Indies.

441 Chatterton, Edward K. Across the Seven Seas. Philadelphia: Lippincott, 1927.

442 _____. Below the Surface. Philadelphia: Lippincott, 1935. Submarining.

443 _____. In Great Waters. Philadelphia: Lippincott, 1929.

444 _____. On the High Seas. London: Allan, 1931.

445 _____. Sea Raiders. London: Hutchinson, 1940.

446 _____. The Sea Spy. London, 193-?

447 _____. The Secret Ship. London: Hurst, 1939.

448 _____. Through Sea and Sky. Philadelphia: Lippincott, 1929.

449 Cheever, Henry P. The Rival Brothers; Or, The Corsair and the Privateer. A Tale of the Last War. Boston: Gleason's Pub. Hall, 1846.
     War of 1812.

450 _____. The Witch of the Wave; Or, The Corsair's Captive. Boston: F. Gleason, 1847.

451 Chetwood, William R. The Voyages, Dangerous Adventures and Imminent Escapes of Capt. Richard Falconer: Containing the Laws, Customs, and Manners of the Indians in America, etc. etc. 2 Parts. London: The Author, 1720.
     One of the earliest examples of British sea fiction, which should be compared with the works of Daniel Defoe (q. v.).

452 Chevalier, Elizabeth. Drivin' Woman. New York: Macmil-
         lan, 1942.
              Riverboat gambling after the Civil War.

453 Chidsey, Donald B. Captain Adam. New York: Crown, 1953.
              How a former indentured servant becomes a privateer
         and fights for the glory of Queen Anne--and the purse.

454 _____. The Legion of the Lost. New York: Crown, 1967.
              Captain Kidd, the pirate, voyages to Madagascar.

455 _____. Reluctant Cavalier. New York: Crown, 1960.
              A well-bread English lad becomes an unwilling British
         spy and companion of Sir Francis Drake.

456 _____. Stronghold. Garden City, N. Y. : Doubleday, 1948.
              War of 1812; Caribbean naval action; impressment.

457 Childers, Erskine. The Riddle of the Sands: A Record of
         Secret Service. London: Nelson, 1903.
              This tale of adventure afloat and ashore was reprinted
         in 1972.

458 Chipman, W. P. In Ships and Prison. Chicago: Saalfield
         Pub. , 1908. y.

459 _____. Two Yankee Middies. New York: A. L. Burt,
         1904. y.
              A pair of American midshipmen in the days of "The
         Great White Fleet. "

460 Christensen, Willard. Voyage No. 39. New York: Vantage,
         1951.
              Typical voyage on tramp steamer, Sea Witch; a com-
         posite description.

461 Christopher, John. The White Voyage. New York: Simon &
         Schuster, 1961.
              First published in Britain as The Long Voyage, this
         tale chronicles the adventures that befall the people aboard
         a Danish ship that leaves Dublin bound for Western Europe
         and is wrecked on some ice during a storm.

462 Churchill, Winston. The Inside of the Cup. London: Mac-
         millan, 1913.
              Racing afloat off the British Isles.

463 _____. Richard Carvel. 2 Vols. New York: Macmillan,
         1899.
              Richard Carvel, Maryland sailor, serves under John
         Paul Jones during the Revolution. You know, of course,
         that the author was not the British politician.

464   Chute, Arthur Hunt.   The Crested Seas.   New York: J. H.
        Sears, 1928.   y.
            Initiation adventures aboard a fishing boat.

465   _____.   Far Gold.   New York: J. H. Sears, 1927.   y.
            A sealing ship sails after treasure and trouble.

466   _____.   Mutiny of the Flying Spray.   New York: J. H.
        Sears, 1927.
            A grim tale of a clipper's adventures; rounding "The
        Horn."

467   Clagett, John.   The Slot.   New York: Crown, 1958.   y.
            American PT-boats vs. Japanese warships in the
        waters off Guadalcanal during World War II.

468   _____.   Surprise Attack.   New York: Messner, 1968.   y.
            Five men fresh from boot camp experience the 1944
        Battle of Leyte Gulf.

469   _____.   Torpedo Run on Bottomed Bay.   New York:
        Cowles.   1969.   y.
            A Nisei boy is a hero aboard a PT boat off Guadalca-
        nal in 1942.

470   Clapp, Patricia.   Constance.   New York: Lothrop, 1968.   y.
            Trials of a young girl aboard the Mayflower.

471   Clark, Charles.   The Antarctic Queen.   London: Warne, 1902.
            Exploration and adventure.

472   Clarke. Holloway H.   Admiral's Aid.   Boston: D. Lothrop,
        1902.   y.
            Our author was a better historian than novelist and a
        well-known naval officer.

473   _____.   Boy Life in the United States Navy.   Boston: D.
        Lothrop, 1903.   y.

474   _____.   Midshipman Stanford.   Boston: L. and L. Shepard,
        1916.   y.

475   Clarkson, E. Halic.   The Story of a Gray Seal.   New York:
        Dutton, 1970.   y.

476   Clavell, James.   Shogun: A Novel of Japan.   New York: Athe-
        neum, 1975.
            The adventures of English navigator John Blackthorne
        who, in the 17th-century, discovers the sea route to the
        legendary "Japans."

477   _____.   Tai-Pan.   New York: Atheneum, 1966.
            How an English trader overcomes the difficulties of

developing trade in Hong Kong. A massive, but very interesting piece of fiction based on real events.

478 Cleaves, Emery N. Sea Fever: The Making of a Sailor.
Boston: Houghton Mifflin, 1972.
Heavily autobiographical tales of a modern sailor aboard
an American freighter; high adventure.

479 Cleland, John. Memoirs of a Coxcomb. London: R. Frif-
fiths, 1751.
One of England's earliest sea novelists, this former
East India Company sailor is better known for his 1750
erotic publication, Fanny Hill.

480 Clemens, Samuel L. The Adventures of Huckleberry Finn.
By Mark Twain, pseud. New York: C. L. Webster, 1885.
Numerous fine editions available; the picaresque tale
of the Mississippi River adventures of the runaways Huck
and slave Jim is the classic "brown water" tale of America's greatest humorist, whose pen name is derived from
the riverboatman's signal for safe water--"by the mark,
twain!"

481 _____. The Adventures of Tom Sawyer. By Mark Twain,
pseud. San Francisco: A. Roman, 1876.
Picaresque fun with a Mississippi local color setting.
Sequel: Tom Sawyer Abroad, 1894. Reprinted.

482 _____. Following the Equator; A Journey Around the World.
By Mark Twain, pseud. Hartford, Conn.: The American
Pub. Co., 1897.

483 _____. Innocents Abroad; Or, The New Pilgrims' Progress;
Being Some Account of the Steamship "Quaker City's"
Pleasure Excursion to Europe and the Holy Land. By Mark
Twain, pseud. Hartford, Conn.: The American Pub. Co.,
1880.
Iconoclastic travel fiction; yankee innocents afloat.

484 Climenson, Emily J. Strange Adventures in the County of
Dorset, A.D., 1747. London: Poynder, 1907.
Smuggling.

485 Close, Robert S. Dupe. London: Allen, 1958. y.

486 Clowes, William L. The Captain of the Mary Rose. London:
Tower, 1892.
The author of many articles in the Army-Navy Gazette
under the pen name "Nauticus," Sir William is best remembered for his 7-volume The Royal Navy: A History.

487 _____, and Alan H. Burgoyne. Trafalgar Refought. London: Nelson, 1905.

488 _____, and Charles N. Robinson. The Great Naval War of
1887. London: Tower, 1887.

489 Coatsworth, Elizabeth. The Captain's Daughter. New York:
Macmillan, 1950. y.
An American clipper ship skipper objects to the man
his daughter wishes to marry.

490 _____. The Last Fort: A Story of the French Voyageurs.
New York: Holt, 1952. y.
A lad's voyage from Quebec down the dangerous rivers
of the North American interior in the 1760's.

491 Cobb, Sylvanus, Jr. The Golden Eagle; Or, The Privateer
of '76. A Tale of the Revolution. Boston: F. Gleason,
1850.
After serving a hitch with the USN from 1841-1844,
Cobb took up the life of an author becoming noted as the
first American writer to employ "mass-production" methods
to his craft. In 31 years with the New York Ledger, he
wrote 130 novelettes, 834 short stories, and 2,305 brief
sketches!

492 Cochran, Hamilton. The Dram Tree. New York: Bobbs,
1961.
Civil War blockade running.

493 _____. Silver Shoals. Indianapolis: Bobbs-Merrill, 1945.
Treasure hunting in pre-Revolution America.

494 _____. Windward Passage. Indianapolis: Bobbs-Merrill,
1942.
The exploits of Sir Henry Morgan.

496 Cochrell, Boyd. The Barren Beaches of Hell. New York:
Holt, 1959.
A look at the second World War in the Pacific from a
fictional viewpoint, including the assaults by the U.S.
Marines on Tarawa, Saipan, and Tinian, and the naval
support thereof.

496 Codman, John. Sailor's Life and Sailors' Yarns. By Captain
Ringbolt, pseud. New York: C. S. Francis, 1847.
Codman was a true nautical product who spent most of
his life, complete with wife and kiddies, afloat. This is
his best known yarn, although his memoirs as a transport
captain in the Crimean War (An American Transport in the
Crimean War, 1896) are also recalled.

497 Coffin, Robert P. T. John Dawn. New York: Macmillan,
1936.
Maine and her shipbuilding industry a century and more
ago.

498 Colcord, Lincoln. Drifting Diamond. "Landlubberly Fiction."
     New York: Macmillan, 1912.
          Each time "the diamond" surfaces a new terror is close
     behind; typhoon, etc.; Far Eastern romance. Colcord is
     better known for numerous short stories serialized in the
     periodicals of his day, i.e., "The Game of Life and Death;
     Stories of the Sea." New York: Macmillan, 1914.

499 Coleman, William L. The Golden Vanity. New York: Mac-
     millan, 1962.
          During the last weeks of World War II, a power strug-
     gle is waged among the crewmen of an American cargo
     ship in the Pacific.

500 _____. Ship's Company. Boston: Little, Brown, 1955.
          Nine short episodes (stories, really) reflecting life
     aboard the U.S.S. Nellie Crocker in the Mediterranean
     during World War II.

501 Collins, Norman. Black Ivory. New York: Duell, 1948.
          Slaving and pirates.

502 Colton, Arthur. The Belted Seas. London: Chatto and
     Windus, 1907.
          Merchant sailing.

503 Colum, Padraic. The Voyagers: Being Legends and Romances
     of Atlantic Discovery. New York: Macmillan, 1925. y.

504 Colver, Anne. Shamrock Cargo. Philadelphia: Winston,
     1952. y.
          The 1847 famine-relief mission of the U.S.S. James-
     town to Ireland.

505 Compton, Herbert. The Inimitable Mrs. Massingham. London:
     Chatto & Windus, 1900.
          Gretna Green and Botany Bay, 1799.

506 _____. Master Mariner. New York: Macmillan, 1891.
          Life at sea.

507 Connell, Evan S. The Patriot. New York: Viking, 1960.
          The training and deployment of a World War II Ameri-
     can naval aviator.

508 Connolly, James Brendan. Canton Captain. Garden City,
     N.Y.: Doubleday, 1942. y.
          Story of Capt. Robert Forbes. Connolly is best known
     for hundreds of short sea stories which appeared in the
     early 1900's in popular magazines such as Harper's, Scrib-
     ner's and Collier's. Some of his short story anthologies,
     by date, include: Crested Seas (1907); Gloucestermen: Stor-
     ies of the Fishing Fleet (1930); and Out of Gloucester (1902).

509 _____. Coaster Captain; A Tale of the Boston Waterfront.
New York: Macy-Lucius, 1927. y.
A novel joined with two stories, "Jan Tingloff" and
"Down by the Harbor Side," which appeared in Saturday
Evening Post and Redbook in the 1920's.

510 _____. Jeb Hutton. New York: Scribner's, 1902. y.
Connolly's first book, a story for boys, afterwards
entered in the "Boy Scouts Library."

511 _____. Magic of the Sea. St. Louis: B. Herder, 1911.
y.
Commodore John Barry in the making.

512 _____. On Tybee Knoll. New York: A. S. Barnes, 1905.
y.

513 _____. The Seiners. New York: Scribner's, 1904. y.
Aboard a fishing boat out of Gloucester, Mass.

514 _____. Steel Decks. New York: Scribner's, 1925. y.
The adventures of a tramp steamer, The Rapidan.
This novel is an extended version of Connolly's notable
short story, "Don Quixote Kiernan, Pump-Man," which appeared in Wide Courses in 1912, a Scribner's anthology.

515 _____. The Trawler. New York: Scribner's, 1914. y.
A fishing tale for boys; "how Arthur Snow was washed
from deck" and was "lost at sea." Originally appeared in
Collier's Weekly (1914), winning a $2,500 First Prize.
Teddy Roosevelt cherished it's ruggedness.

516 Conrad, Brenda. The Stars Give Warning. New York: Scribner's, 1941.

517 Conrad, Joseph. Collected Edition of the Works of Joseph
Conrad. London: J. M. Dent, 1948-1955.
Conrad was born Josef Teodor Konrad Korzeniowski in
Berdyczew, Poland, in 1857. Orphaned a dozen years later, he was educated at Krakow, but because of his family's anti-Russian leanings, sought greater opportunity by
moving to France in 1874. He did not learn English until
later in that decade.
From 1874-1878, he smuggled arms during the Carlist
uprising in Spain, after which he joined the British merchant
marine. Obtaining his masters papers and English naturali-
zation under the name Joseph Conrad in 1886, he continued
to follow the sea until the early 1890's when a trip up the
Congo River so sapped his health that he was forced ashore.
In 1895, Conrad published his first novel. He visited
his home in Poland in 1914, from whence, with the aid of
the U.S. ambassador, he was able to escape just before
the outbreak of World War I. He lost a son to that conflict,

but in gratitude to his adopted nation, well-served the Admiralty. Late in achieving fame, he made a triumphant tour of America in 1923, the year before his death.

As with Herman Melville, Conrad brought much more to the sea story than the simple Cooper-style narrative. His writings added to the nautical yarn--and the whole concept of the novel as well--by their willingness to experiment with language and form. Most of it concerns protagonists not the nebulous 'T'' ostensibly doing the yarning; much of it is romance spliced with intense realism. More than that, however, his sailor characters, e. g. , <u>Lord Jim</u>, were concerned more with morals and faith than mere adventure. Basing his stories to a large extent on personal experience, experiences still alien to many land-bound readers, the ex-salt was preoccupied with fidelity, man's inner responsibility to himself. His tales abound with themes of guilt and honor, expiation and moral alienation, aimed at encouraging men to review their <u>reason</u> d'être and as importantly, their moral duties in an often immoral world.

Regarded by casual readers, especially high school and college ''lit'' students, as a difficult or ''hard'' writer, Conrad's messages remain highly relative in today's society. To this master such later blue water authors as C. S. Forester (q. v.) have owed much; without his trendsetting works, much that is good in the nautical fiction currently available would never have seen print.

For a full bibliography, readers should see T. G. Ersham's work <u>A Bibliography of Joseph Conrad</u> (Metuchen, N. J. : The Scarecrow Press, 1969.). Most of his yarns are available in paperback from various outlets. Conrad's reminiscences are also interesting and are entitled <u>The Mirror of the Sea: Memories and Impressions</u> (London: Methuen, 1906).

518 _____ . <u>Almayer's Folly</u>. New York: Macmillan, 1895.
The tale of a European married to a Malayan wife, who reverts to her ancestral savagery.

519 _____ . <u>The Arrow of Gold</u>. Garden City, N. Y. : Doubleday, 1919.
The love of an English sea captain smuggling Carlist munitions along the Spanish coast for the beautiful Dona Rita, who is bankrolling his exploits. Based on the writer's personal experiences to a very high degree.

520 _____ . <u>Chance: A Tale in Two Parts</u>. Garden City, N. Y. : Doubleday, 1913.
The daughter of a convicted swindler, believing no one can love her, is saved from suicide by a chivalrous British sea captain.

521 _____ . <u>Lord Jim</u>. New York: Macmillan, 1899.
The author's most famous work is an inner analysis of

a seaman, branded a coward among his colleagues, who ultimately dies the death of a demi-god to the savage natives of Malaya.   Based on the life of Rajah Brooke of Sarawak.   The movie-version starred Richard O'Toole.

522 _____. The Nigger of the Narcissus.   Garden City, N. Y.: Doubleday, 1914.
A character study of a Black sailor and his fellow seamen aboard a sailing vessel which encounters a savage storm enroute from India to Britain.

523 _____. Nostromo: A Tale of the Seaboard.   New York: Macmillan, 1904.
An adventure set in the revolutionary background of a mythical Latin American republic in which a rich Englishman, Nostromo, and his wife, an old Garibaldian, robbers, politicians, and others make a motley crew for a series of interconnected character studies.   The 1951 Modern Library edition contains a useful introduction by Robert Penn Warren.

524 _____. An Outcast of the Island.   New York: Macmillan, 1896.

525 _____. The Rescue: A Romance of the Shallows.   Garden City, N. Y.: Doubleday, 1920.
An English sea captain, in league with Malay natives, plots to keep a youthful ruler on the throne in the face of opposition from a group of shipwrecked Europeans.

526 _____. The Rover.   Garden City, N. Y.: Doubleday, 1923.
Peytol, "The Rover," plans to settle down in an obscure French coastal village during the Napoleonic wars, but becomes involved in a romance and a dangerous secret operation.

527 _____. The Shorter Tales of Joseph Conrad.   Garden City, N. Y.: Doubleday, 1924.
Contents: "Youth," "The Secret Sharer," "The Brute (an Indignant Tale)," "To-morrow," "Typhoon," "Because of the Dollars," "The Partner," and "Falk."

528 _____. Tales of Land and Sea.   New York: Hanover House, 1953.
Contains a valuable introduction by William McFee. Contents: "Youth," "Heart of Darkness," "The Nigger of the Narcissus," "Gaspar Ruiz," "The Brute," "Typhoon," "The Secret Sharer," "Freya of the Seven Isles," "The Duel," "The End of the Thether," and "The Shadow Line."

529 _____. Tales of East and West.   New York: Hanover House, 1958.
Companion volume to the above citation, it contains an excellent introduction by the noted Conrad authority, Morton

Dauwen Zabel.   Contents: "Almayer's Folly," "Karain: A
Memory," "The Planter of Malata," "An Outpost of Prog-
ress," "Falk," "Prince Roman," "The Warrior's Soul,"
"Amy Foster," and 'The Secret Agent."

530 _____. Typhoon and Other Stories.   Garden City, N. Y.:
      Doubleday, 1921.
            Contents: "Typhoon," "Amy Foster," "Falk," and "To-
      morrow."   First published in 1902, the short novel Typhoon
      concerns the difficult encounter of Captain MacWhirr and his
      first officer, Jukes, with a savage China seas hurricane,
      and the 200 coolies aboard ship.

531 _____.   Victory.   Garden City, N. Y.: Doubleday, 1915.
            A Swedish nobleman, living alone on a South Seas
      island, rescues a girl.

532 _____, and Ford Madox Hueffer [i. e., Ford].   Romance.
      London: Smith & Elder, 1903.
            A 19th-century yarn whose action is set ashore and
      afloat in England and the West Indies.

533 Constantin-Weyer, Maurice.   The French Adventurer.   New
      York: Macaulay, 1931.
            Fictionalized tale of the explorer LaSalle.

534 Cook, C. J. R.   The Quarterdeck.   London: Henry Colburn,
      1844.
            A tale of British naval life comparable with the same
      sorts of yarns being printed in America during the pro-
      Civil War years.

535 Cooley, Leland F.   The Run for Home.   Garden City, N. Y.:
      Doubleday, 1959.   y.
            Life aboard the freighter Tropic Trader during the
      1920's was not what new wealthy young deckhand Slim Fred-
      ericks had been led to believe it would.   Nevertheless, he
      makes the best of things and becomes a competent sailor
      during the ensuing voyage from California to New Zealand.

536 Cooper, James Fenimore.   Afloat and Ashore; Or, The Adven-
      tures of Miles Wallingford.   4 Vols. in 2.   Philadelphia:
      published by the author, 1844.
            Subsequent American editions rename the second part
      Miles Wallingford.   Adventuresome Atlantic and Pacific tale
      after the Revolution, including vivid portraits of sea flights.
            James Fenimore Cooper, born into a wealthy New Jer-
      sey family in 1789, entered Yale at 13, only to be expelled
      in 1806 for a prank.   Disappointed, his father bundled him
      off to sea, doubtless hoping the lad might learn some disci-
      pline "before the mast."   After a voyage to Europe, young
      Cooper received a midshipman's commission in 1808 and
      served afloat in the infant U. S. Navy until 1811, when he

resigned, went ashore, married, and began his somewhat stormy literary career. His publication of The Spy in 1821 brought critical acclaim.

Following success with the Leather-Stocking series, and in answer to the famous boast that he could pen a better sea tale than Sir Walter Scott's The Pirate (qv), Cooper discovered his "gift" for romantic and nationalistic nautical fiction, which he would pass down to succeeding generations of writers.

The theme of maritime nationalism was widespread in the eastern United States in the years after the War of 1812 but had not, by and large, been tapped as a fictional source. Employing the idea, Cooper added his own concepts of personal integrity and freedom, stirred them with the mechanics of the romance, and brought forth the blue water tales herein cited. His descriptive narrative of sea life, despite the romanticism of his characters, was the chief ingredient which commanded the attention of readers and was his lasting contribution to the nautical genre. It was a scenic beacon which would be employed in some degree by every blue and brown water author thereafter, including Melville (q. v.) and Conrad (q. v.), and perhaps is viewed most vividly in a modern sense in the works of C. S. Forester (q. v.).

After a long visit in Europe mid-way in his career, Cooper returned home, only to become embroiled in a number of disputes, not the least of which was a bitter feud with the family and friends of Oliver H. Perry. During this unhappy time, the former midshipman turned much of his attention to the sea, producing a number of novels and several excellent naval histories. His fame assured, he died in Cooperstown, New York, in 1851 at the age of 62.

Cooper's nautical fiction, more than a third of his entire production, includes these novels:

537 _____. The Bravo: A Tale. Philadelphia: Carey and Lea, 1831. 2 Vols.

538 _____. The Crater; Or, Vulcan's Peak. A Tale of The Pacific. New York: Burgess, Stinger, 1847.

539 _____. Homeward Bound: Or, The Chase. A Tale of the Sea. Philadelphia: Carey, Lea and Blanchard, 1838.

540 _____. Jack Tier; Or, The Florida Reef. 2 Vols. New York: Burgess, Stringer, 1848.

541 _____. Mercedes of Castile; Or, The Voyage to Cathay. 2 Vols. Philadelphia: Lea and Blanchard, 1840.
Columbus discovers America (1469-93).

542 _____. Miles Wallingford; Sequel to Afloat and Ashore. Boston: Houghton, 1884.
Celebrated for its poignant sea descriptions.

543   _____. The Monikins. Philadelphia: Carey, Lea and
Blanchard, 1835.

544   _____. Ned Myers; Or, A Life before the Mast. Philadelphia: Lea and Blanchard, 1843.

545   _____. The Pilot: A Tale of the Sea. New York: Charles
Wiley, 1824.
           A tale of The Revolution with John Paul Jones in Brit-
ish waters. Features Long Tom Coffin, Cooperesque
American hero of the Natty Bumpo genre. Significant in
its early American authorship, antedating Frederick Marryat's British sea novels by at least five years. Noteworthy
scenes of storms and sea fights, 1778-9.

546   _____. The Red Rover; A Tale. Philadelphia: Carey,
Lea and Carey, 1828.
           How a pirate turns patriot during The Revolution.
Highly regarded along with The Pilot as one of Cooper's
best sea novels.

547   _____. The Sea Lions: Or, The Lost Sealers. 2 Vols.
New York: Stringer and Townsend, 1849.
           A direct attempt by Cooper to create an allegory, or
symbolic narrative, in his last novel--only two years before
the publication of Hermann Melville's Moby Dick. Instead,
Melville reviewed this work in Literary World, IV (1849),
370+.

548   _____. The Two Admirals. A Tale. Philadelphia: Lea
and Blanchard, 1842.
           Deals with second Jacobite rebellion (1745). Fascina-
ting example of where Cooper, perhaps, strayed from his
actual sea experiences and fouled up, as in his fleet ma-
neuvering in this novel.

549   _____. The Water-Witch; Or, The Skimmers of the Seas.
A Tale. Philadelphia: Carey and Lea, 1831.

550   _____. The Wing-and-Wing; Or, Le Feu-Follet: A Tale.
Philadelphia: Lea and Blanchard, 1842.
           French privateers meet Nelson in the Mediterranean
(1798-9).

551   Cooper, Lettice U. The Old Fox. London: Hodder &
Stoughton, 1927.
           A look at smuggling during the American Revolution as
it was practiced in southern England. Much of the plot
centers around a feared French invasion.

552   Corbett, Julian. A Business in Great Waters. London: Methuen, 1895.
           The conspiracy between Sussex smugglers and French

revolutionaries in the 1790's.

553 _____. For God and Gold. London: Macmillan, 1887.
Drake in the West Indies.

554 Corbin, Austin, Jr. The Eagle; Or, The Rover of the Mediterranean. Boston: F. Gleason, 1847.

555 _____. Mneomi; Or, The Indian of the Connecticut. Boston: F. Gleason, 1847.
Significant water setting.

556 Cordell, Alexander. The Deadly Eurasian. New York: Weybright & Talley, 1969.
A Chinese spy story, first published in Britain as The
Bright Cantonese, reveals how a Red Guard and graduate of
the Peking School of Espionage is sent to discover the facts
behind the launching of a U.S. destroyer's atomic missile
which has detonated a low level blast in China's interior.

557 Corder, Eric. Slave Ship. New York: David McKay, 1969.
A rather gory look at the brutal 19th-century slave
trade. Those with tender stomachs might wish to pass this
one by.

558 Cornfold, L. Cope. The Lord High Admiral and Others. London: Hodder & Stoughton, 1915.
First World War.

559 _____. Sons of Adversity. New York: Page, 1898.
British and Dutch exploits at sea in the 16th-century.

560 Costain, Thomas B. For My Great Folly. New York: Putnam,
1942.
Captain John Ward incurs the wrath of England's James
I by trying to prevent the Spanish from wrecking trade in
the Mediterranean. Ward's plan: Out-Drake Drake.

561 _____. High Towers. Garden City, N.Y.: Doubleday,
1949.
Significant water themes set in Canada during the French
years.

562 Costello, F. H. Nelson's Yankee Boy. New York: Holt, 1904.
y.
An impressed seaman (boy) at Trafalgar and later as a
man in the War of 1812.

563 _____. On Fighting Decks in 1812. Boston: Dana Estes,
1899. y.

564 Cottrell, Dorothy. Silent Reefs. New York: Morrow, 1953.
y.

An investigation into the shipwreck of a sailing vessel in the post-war West Indies.

565 Couch, A. T. Quiller. <u>Poison Island</u>. London: Smith, Elder, 1907.
Falmouth and the West Indies, 1813-1814.

566 Couch, G. Northwood. <u>Skipper Morgan</u>. London, 1947. y.
The pirate.

567 Courtland, Harold. <u>The African</u>. New York: Crown, 1967.
Enslaved and transported to the American south 150 years ago, a Black seeks his escape and return home.

568 Cowper, Edith E. <u>Lady Fabia</u>. London: Christian Knowledge Society, 1909.
Smuggling and adventure on England's south coast in 1805.

569 Cox, Cyril. <u>The Navy in Mesopotamia</u>. By Conrad Cato, pseud. London: Constable, 1917.
First World War adventure in the Middle East.

570 Cozzens, James Gould. <u>S. S. San Pedro</u>. New York: Harcourt, Brace, 1931.
Nerve-tingling loss of a passenger liner, matched with allegorical disintegration of crew and officers; novelette first appeared in <u>Scribner's Magazine</u>, August, 1930.

571 Craig, John. <u>In Council Rooms Apart</u>. New York: Putnam, 1971.
During World War II a British officer must learn why the Germans are allowing Allied troop transports free passage across the U-boat infested Atlantic.

572 Crake, E. E. <u>In Mortal Peril</u>. London: Religious Tract Society, 1908.
The Defeat of the Spanish Armada.

573 Crane, Mannin. <u>Yarns from a Windjammer</u>. London: Heath, 1926.
Adventures in a sailing ship.

574 Crane, Stephen. <u>The Open Boat and Other Stories</u>. New York, 1898.
A major American story of men in an open boat vs. Nature after ship explodes during Spanish-American War; based on Crane's actual escape from the wreck of the <u>Commodore</u>. Crane worked as a reporter of the war after being rejected for service by the Navy.

575 Cranston, Edward. <u>A Matter of Duty</u>. London: Longmans, 1943.

World War II afloat with the Royal Navy.

576   Crawford, I.   The Burning Sea.   London: Cassell, 1959.
        Another World War II nautical yarn.

577   Creasey, John.   The Baron on Board.   By Anthony Morton,
        pseud.   New York: Walker, 1967.
          A murder mystery set aboard a ship enroute to Africa
        with the priceless Thai crown jewels along.

578   Crebbin, Edward H.   Six Bells.   London: Rich, 1942.
        A World War II story.

579   Creswick, Paul.   The Ring of Pleasure.   London: Lone, 1911.
          Emma Hamilton and Lord Nelson.   Their "sin" has held
        quite a bit of interest over the years--a movie has even re-
        cently been made about it.

580   Crisp, Frank.   The Sea Robbers.   London: Hamilton, 1963.
        y.
          Pirates and smugglers.

581   _____.   The Treasure of Barby Swin.   New York: Coward-
        McCann, 1955.   y.
          The adventures of a 19th-century English lad in the
        slave trade, on a whaling voyage, and in pursuit of buried
        pirate treasure.

582   Cronin, A. J.   The Stars Look Down.   Boston: Little, Brown,
        1935.
          An American sea story.

583   Cronyn, George W.   '49: A Novel of Gold.   Philadelphia:
        Dorrance, 1925.
          Some mention of clipper ships in the California gold
        rush.

584   Cross, John K.   Blackadder.   New York: E. P. Dutton, 1951.
          Spies and smugglers and sea fights at the time of Tra-
        falgar.

585   Crouch, Archer P.   Nellie of the Eight Bells.   London: Long,
        1908.
          Portsmouth in Nelson's day; Trafalgar.

586   Cule, W. E.   In the Secret Sea.   London: Society for Pro-
        moting Christian Knowledge, 1934.

587   Cullum, Robert.   Sheets in the Wind.   London: Chapman,
        1934.

588   Cupples, George.   The Adventures of a Naval Lieutenant.
        London: Routledge, 1904.

589   _____. The Green Hand: Adventures of a Naval Lieutenant.
       London: Nimmo, 1878.
           The author was one of Blackwood's more active pulp
       writers of sea stories during this time. This was one of
       the first well-written yarns to portray life in the British
       merchant marine.

590   _____. Norrie Seaton Driven to Sea. London: Nimmo,
       1876.
           A romance of that day. The author also wrote Two
       Frigates, Sunken Rock, A Sliced Yarn, and The Deserted
       Ship.

591   Currey, E. Hamilton. Ian Hardy: Naval Cadet. London:
       Hodder & Stoughton, 1914. y.

592   _____. News of Battle. London: Hodder & Stoughton,
       1918. y.
           Both of these concern the First World War.

593   Curtis, A. C. A New Trafalgar. London: Smith, Elder,
       1902.

594   Cussler, Clive. The Mediterranean Caper. New York: Pyra-
       mid, 1973.
           A psychopathic ex-Nazi, an unrelenting narcotics agent,
       a bloodthirsty Greek strongman, a beautiful double agent
       and an amateur egghead commando group keep a U.S. Navy
       troubleshooter "company" as he searches for the cause be-
       hind the sabotage of a U.S. oceanographic research vessel.

                                - D -

595   Dahl, Borghild. Stowaway to America. New York: Dutton,
       1959. y.
           A Norwegian kitchen maid voyages to the U.S. in 1825
       as a stowaway on a sailing packet.

596   Dale, H. , ed. Where Away? London: Jenkins, 1934.
           A nautical anthology.

597   Daly, Robert W. Broadsides: A Novel. London and New
       York: Macmillan, 1940.
           The British title reads Heart of Oak; both concern ad-
       venture in the Napoleonic wars as recalled years later by
       one Captain O'Carboy. As a youth, the good officer skipped
       aboard a Royal Navy warship as a "middie" to avenge his
       father's death and stayed around to climb the ladder of pro-
       motion to a ship-of-the-line at Trafalgar.

598   _____. Soldier of the Sea. New York: William Morrow,
       1942.

Sea fights of the Napoleonic wars as seen by a Royal
Marine.

599 Dana, Richard Henry, Jr. Two Years Before the Mast. New
York: Houghton, 1840.
Primarily autobiographical reporting of Dana's adven-
turesome voyages on merchant ships linking California and
New England. Herein entered due to historical importance
within the context of the evolution of sea fiction.

600 Daniel, Hawthorne. Head Wind. New York: Macmillan, 1936.
Colonial shipping in Connecticut.

601 _____. Whampoa. New York: Crowell, 1941.

602 Darby, Ada C. Keturah Come 'round the Horn. New York:
Stokes, 1935. y.
Travel by clipper to California 125 years ago.

603 Daringer, Helen F. Pilgrim Kate. New York: Harcourt,
1949. y.
A 15-year old girl sales aboard the Mayflower.

604 Dark, Eleanor. Waterway. New York: Macmillan, 1942.

605 David, Evan J. As Runs the Grass. New York: Harper,
1943.
Maine seafarers after the Revolution.

606 Davidson, Louis B. and Edward J. Doherty. Captain Marooner.
New York: Thomas Y. Crowell, 1952.
Mutiny on the whaleship Globe out of Nantucket.

607 Davies, Hugh S. Full Fathom Five. London: Bodley Head,
1956.

608 Davies, John. Lower Deck. London: Macmillan, 1945.

609 _____. Sabotage at Sea. London: Ward, Lock, 1959. y.

610 Davies, Sheila. The Young Marchess. New York: Dodd,
Mead, 1951. y.
Two British naval officers from Lord Nelson's fleet
help a young girl plot the overthrow of Napoleon's regime
on Malta in 1798.

611 Davis, Arthur K. Gentle Captain. New York: Rinehart, 1955.
The story of two English men, the captain of an old cargo ship, the Antares, and his first officer and of the battle
they waged alone to save their vessel from destruction during
a great Atlantic gale.

612 Davis, Clyde B. The Annointed. New York: Farrar, 1937.

A seaman figures God has elected him to solve the secret of the universe.

613 _____. Nebraska Coast. New York: Farrar, 1939.
        An Erie Canal tale.

614 Davis, John. The Post Captain; Or, The Wooden Walls Well
        Manned. London: Thomas Tegg, 1805.
        A modern version of this classic novel was printed in
        London in 1928, edited by R. H. Chase.

615 Davis, John G. Cape of Storms. Garden City, N. Y.: Double-
        day, 1971.
        A novel of British whaling.

616 Davis, Richard Harding. The Lion and Unicorn. New York:
        Scribner's, 1904.
        Davis was well known as a journalist.

617 Dawlish, Peter. Captain Peg-Leg's War. London and New
        York: Oxford University Press, 1939. y.

618 _____. Dauntless Finds Her Crew. London: Oxford Uni-
        versity Press, 1947. y.

619 _____. Peg-Leg and the Invaders. London: Oxford Uni-
        versity Press, 1940. y.
        The above three citations concern World War II.

620 _____. Way for a Sailor. London and New York: Oxford
        University Press, 1955. y.

621 Dawson, Michael. Fathoms Deep. London: Nicholson, 1943.
        Diving.

622 _____. Torpedoes Running. London: Nicholson, 1946.
        World War II.

623 Dean, L. W. Pirate Lair. New York: Rinehart, 1947.
        Adventure on the Spanish Main.

624 Dearden, Robert L. Christopher Parkins, R. N. London, 1925.
        Life in the fleet.

625 _____. Maiden Voyage. London: Jenkins, 1941.

626 Deasy, Mary. The Corioli Affair. Boston: Little, 1954.
        Post Civil War love story and tragedy involving a river-
        boat captain.

627 The Death Ship; Or, The Pirate's Bride and the Maniac of the
        Deep. A Nautical Romance. Boston: George H. Williams,
        1847.

"By the Author of 'The Smuggler King' and Other
Tales. "--Title page.

628 Deck, Mrs. Lily M. A.   Divine Lady: A Romance of Nelson
     and Lady Hamilton.   By E. Barrington, pseud.   New York:
     Dodd, 1924.

629 Defoe, Daniel.   Life, Adventures, and Piracies of Captain
     Singleton.   London: Macmillan, 1720.
            This 18th-century pirate tale still makes interesting
     reading in any of its various reprintings.
            Defoe, born as plain Daniel Foe, son of a London
     butcher about 1660, travelled a good deal, being at one
     time a prisoner of the Barbary pirates.   During the years
     of William III, he was several times in minor government
     positions; during the War of the Spanish Succession, he was
     a British spy--regarded now as the father of British Intelli-
     gence.   Constantly in financial difficulty, he died of a "leth-
     argy" in 1731 while in virtual hiding from his creditors.
            In addition to his political pamphleteering, Defoe also
     wrote fiction and together with Tobias Smollett (q. v.) is re-
     garded as the father of English language nautical literature.
     Today his reputation among casual readers rests almost en-
     tirely on the famous tale of Robinson Crusoe; however, he
     also penned a number of other yarns including: The King
     of Pirates, Being an Account of the Famous Enterprizes of
     Captain Avery, the Mock King of Madagascar; The Four
     Years' Voyages of Captain George Roberts; and A New Voy-
     age Round the World by a Course Never Sailed Before.

630 _____.   The Life and Strange Surprising Adventures of Rob-
     inson Crusoe, of York, Mariner.   London, 1719.
            This famous work has been widely republished in edi-
     tions for both children and adults.

631 Deighton, Len.   Horse Under Water.   New York: Putnam,
     1968.
            A treasure hunt for treasure contained in a Nazi sub-
     marine sunk off the Portuguese coast in World War II.

632 _____.   Spy Story.   New York: Harcourt, 1974.
            An officer in the employ of a joint Anglo-American na-
     val warfare committee has been ordered to spy for his old
     boss and aid in the defection of a Soviet admiral.

633 Dekker, Maurits.   Beggars Revolt.   Translated from the Dutch.
     Garden City, N. Y. : Doubleday, 1938.
            The Dutch "Sea Beggars" in the late 16th-century.

634 Delano, Anthony.   Breathless Diversions.   New York: Harper,
     1973.
            An English midshipman's adventures in China during
     the Boxer Rebellion and his mother's part in a plot to stop

the Russian fleet from engaging the Japanese in 1905 forms
the background. The title comes from some rather erotic
material "liberated" by the boy in China and returned for
sale to Britain. Cynical of Victoria's fleet and a bit raun-
chy in parts--more so than usual for sea stories that is!

635 Delderfield, R. F. The Adventures of Ben Gunn. London:
     Hodder & Stoughton, 1956. y.
         What happens to the marooned sailor found by the he-
     roes of Stevenson's Treasure Island.

636 DeMorgan, John. A Yankee Ship and a Yankee Crew. New
     York: McLoughlin, 1909. y.
         Sea fights in the War of 1812.

637 Denison, Charles Wheeler. "Old Ironsides" and "Old Adams. "
     Stray Leaves from the Log Book of a Man-of-War's Man.
     Boston: W. W. Page, 1846.
         The writer of these tales was a Connecticut clergyman-
     editor-poet who also penned several military biographies
     for young readers.

638 _____. Old Slade; Or, Fifteen Years Adventures of a Sailor.
     Boston: John Putnam, 1844.

639 _____. The Yankee Cruiser: A Story of the War of 1812.
     Boston: J. E. Farwell, 1848.

640 DeSelincourt, A. , ed. The Book of the Sea. London: Eyre
     and Spottiswoode, 1961.

641 Devereux, Mary. Lafitte of Louisiana. Boston: Little, Brown,
     1902.
         The pirate who aided Andy Jackson at New Orleans in
     1815.

642 Devereux, William. Sir Walter Raleigh. London: Greening,
     1909.
         A biographical novel.

643 Devon, John Anthony. O Western Wind. New York: Putnam,
     1957. y.
         Pilgrims aboard the Mayflower.

644 Dewhurst, Peter. The Sea and Sad Voices. London: Low,
     1948.
         British nautical adventure.

645 DeWitt, James. In Pursuit of the Spanish Galleon. New York:
     Criterion, 1961. y.
         Fiction based on the true events surrounding Commo-
     dore George Anson's capture of the "Manila Galleon" in the
     Pacific in the 1740's.

646 Diaz, Argentina L. <u>Mayopan.</u> Indiana Hills, Colorado: The
Falcon's Wing Press, 1955.
Sea adventure with a Latin flavor.

647 Dickens, Charles. <u>Dombey and Son.</u> London, 1848.
This oft-reprinted work, although dealing primarily with
a merchant firm, contains some sketches of interesting sea
characters, especially that of Captain Cuttle.

648 Dickens, Charles, and William Collins. <u>The Wreck of the Gold</u>
<u>en Mary.</u> London: Methuen, 1961.
Not the Dickens of entry 647.

649 Dickey, James. <u>Deliverance.</u> New York: Houghton, 1970.
Man vs. man and nature; a party's survival experiences
on a great American river; subject of recent controversial
movie starring Burt Reynolds.

650 Dibner, Martin. <u>The Deep Six.</u> Garden City, New York:
Doubleday, 1953.
Naval adventure in the Pacific during World War II.

651 _____ . <u>The Trouble with Heroes.</u> Garden City, N. Y.:
Doubleday, 1971.
Something began in that Inchon incident when Paul Damion, a young and ambitious U. S. Navy lieutenant earned a
hero's reputation. It culminated when the famous Captain
Damion of the U. S. S. <u>Chesapeake</u> refused a routine order to
shell a Vietnamese village and relinquished his command to
voluntarily stand court martial.

652 Dingle, A. Edward. <u>Adrift.</u> By "Sinbad," pseud. London:
Paul, 1940.

653 _____ . <u>Moonshine and Moses.</u> By "Sinbad," pseud. London: Hale, 1949.

654 _____ . <u>Old Glory.</u> By "Sinbad," pseud. London: Paul,
1938.

655 _____ . <u>Reckless Hide.</u> By "Sinbad," pseud. London:
Hale, 1947.

656 _____ . <u>Seaworthy.</u> By "Sinbad," pseud. London: Stanley
Paul, 1928.

657 _____ . <u>Spin a Yarn, Sailor.</u> By "Sinbad," pseud. London:
Hale, 1954.

658 Divine, Arthur D. <u>Atom at Spithead.</u> By David Divine, pseud.
New York: Macmillan, 1950.

659 _____ . <u>The Sun Shall Greet Them.</u> By David Rame, pseud.

New York: Macmillan, 1941.
A psychological study of the small-boat skippers who rescued the British Army from the beaches of Dunkirk in 1940.

660 _____. _Thunder on the Chesapeake._ New York: Macmillan, 1961. y.
Naval adventures in the Civil War; meeting of the _Merrimac_ and _Monitor._

661 _____. _Wine of Good Hope._ New York: Macmillan, 1939.

662 Dix, B. M. _Soldier Rigdale._ New York: Macmillan, 1899. y.
A story of the _Mayflower._

663 Dixon, Douglas. _Sail to Lapland._ London: Blackwood, 1938.

664 Dixon, W. Macnelle. _The Fleets Behind the Fleet._ London: Hodder & Stoughton, 1917.
First World War.

665 _____. _Sea Gull and Sea Power._ London: Blackwood, 1937.
A tale of the Royal Navy.

666 Dodge, Constance. _Dark Stranger._ Philadelphia: Penn, 1940.
An escape from Scotland to America at the time of the Revolution.

667 Dodson, Kenneth. _Away All Boats._ Boston: Little, Brown, 1954.
The classic tale of a World War II landing vessel and her crew.

668 _____. _Stranger to the Shore._ Boston: Little, Brown, 1956.
Conflict between a U.S. sailor and a German raider off Chile in 1942.

669 Domville-Fife, Charles W., ed. _I Tell of the Seven Seas._ London: Rankin, 1949.
An anthology.

670 Donovan, Frank R. _The Unlucky Hero._ New York: Duell, 1963.
The British attempt to capture Cuba in the 1760's forms the background of this tale.

671 Doolard, A. Denis. _Roll Back the Sea._ London: Heinemann, 1949.
British nautical adventure.

672 Dorling, Henry Taprell. Carry On! Naval Sketches and Stories. By "Taffrail," pseud. London: Pearson, 1916.
Dorling was a professional Royal Navy officer.

673 _____. Chenies. By "Taffrail," pseud. London: Hodder
& Stoughton, 1943.
Second World War.

674 _____. Cipher K. By "Taffrail," pseud. London: Hodder
& Stoughton, 1932.

675 _____. Dover-Ostend. By "Taffrail," pseud. London:
Hodder & Stoughton, 1938.

676 _____. Endless Story. By "Taffrail," pseud. Black Jacket
Series. London: Hodder & Stoughton, 1938.

677 _____. Eurydice. By "Taffrail," pseud. London: Hodder
& Stoughton, 1956.

678 _____. Fred Travis, A. B. By "Taffrail," pseud. Yellow
Jacket Series. London: Hodder & Stoughton, 1940.
World War II.

679 _____. H. M. S. Anonymous. By "Taffrail," pseud. London: Jenkins, 1919.
World War I.

680 _____. Kerrell. By "Taffrail," pseud. London: Hodder
& Stoughton, 1931.

681 _____. A Little Ship. By "Taffrail," pseud. London:
Chambers, 1918.
World War I.

682 _____. The Man from Scapa Flow. By "Taffrail," pseud.
London: Hodder & Stoughton, 1939.

683 _____. Mid-Atlantic. By "Taffrail," pseud. London: Hodder & Stoughton, 1938.

684 _____. Minor Operations. By "Taffrail," pseud. London:
Pearson, 1917.
World War I.

685 _____. The Mystery at Milford House. By "Taffrail,"
pseud. London: Hodder & Stoughton, 1936.

686 _____. Mystery Cruise. By "Taffrail," pseud. London:
Hodder & Stoughton, 1939.

687 _____. The Navy Is Here: A Convoy of Naval Novels.
By "Taffrail," pseud. London: Hodder & Stoughton, 1940.

World War II.

688 _____. Off Shore. By "Taffrail," pseud. London: Pearson, 1918.
World War I.

689 _____. Oh, Joshua! By "Taffrail," pseud. London: Hodder & Stoughton, 1920.
World War I.

690 _____. Operation M. O. By "Taffrail," pseud. London:
Hodder & Stoughton, 1938.

691 _____. Pincher Martin, O. D.: A Story of the Inner Life
of the Royal Navy. By "Taffrail," pseud. London: Pearson, 1916.
World War I.

692 _____. The Scarlet Stripe. By "Taffrail," pseud. London:
Hodder & Stoughton, 1932.
Dorling was the most prolific of all British naval fiction
writers. Even today, a goodly number of his works make
interesting reading.

693 _____. Sea, Spray, and Spindrift: Naval Yarns. By "Taffrail," pseud. London: Pearson, 1917.
World War I.

694 _____. The Second Officer. By "Taffrail," pseud. London:
Hodder & Stoughton, 1935.

695 _____. Seventy North. By "Taffrail," pseud. London:
Hodder & Stoughton, 1936.

696 _____. The Shetland Plan. By "Taffrail," pseud. London:
Musson, 1939.
World War II

697 _____. Stand By! By "Taffrail," pseud. London: Pearson, 1917.
World War I.

698 _____. The Sub: Being the Autobiography of David Munro,
Sub-Lieutenant, Royal Navy. By "Taffrail," pseud. Lon-
don: Hodder & Stoughton, 1917.
World War I.

699 _____. Swept Channels. By "Taffrail," pseud. London:
Hodder & Stoughton, 1938.

700 _____. The Watch Below. By "Taffrail," pseud. London:
Hodder & Stoughton, 1918.
World War I.

701 _____. White Ensign. By "Taffrail," pseud. London: Putnam, 1943.
World War II.

702 _____, ed. Sea Escapes and Adventures. By "Taffrail,"
pseud. London: Allan, 1929.

703 Douglas, G. Rough Passage. London: Collins, 1938.
British nautical adventure.

704 Douglas, John S. Secret of the Undersea Bell. New York:
Dodd, Mead, 1951. y.
Diving off the California coast.

705 Doyle, Arthur C. The Captain of the Polestar. 7th ed. London: Longmans, 1894.
This writer is better known for his Sherlock Holmes
stories than these few sea yarns.

706 _____. Marcot Deep. New York: Doubleday, 1929.
The use of a strange diving ball.

707 _____. Uncle Bernac. London: Smith, Elder, 1897.
Centers around late 18th-century French schemes for
the invasion of England.

708 Drury, William P. All the King's Men. London: Chapman,
1919.

709 _____. Bearers of the Burden: Being Stories of Land and
Sea. 2nd ed. London: Chapman, 1899.

710 _____. Men at Arms. Stories and Sketches. London:
Chapman, 1917.

711 _____. The Passing of the Flagship and Other Stories.
London: Chapman, 1911.

712 _____. The Peradventures of Private Pagett. London:
Rich, 1933.

713 _____. The Shadow of the Quarter Deck. London: Chapman, 1903.

714 _____. The Tadpole of Archangel, the Petrified Eye, and
Other Naval Stories. London: Chapman, 1904.
The author was an officer in the Royal Marines.

715 Du Bose, L. Aye, Aye, Sir! London: Lothrop, 1958. y.

716 Dumas, Alexandre. The Companions of Jehu. London: 1857.
Napoleon in Egypt, 1799-1800, including the Battle of
the Nile.

717   _____. Love and Liberty; Or, Nelson at Naples. London:
       Stanley Paul, n. d.

718   _____. On Board the Emma. London: Stanley Paul, n. d.

719 Dunnett, Dorothy. The Disorderly Knights. New York: Put-
       nam, 1966.
            The defense of Malta in the 1500's by those great sea
       fighters, the Knights of the Order of St. John.

720 DuSoe, Robert O. The Boatswain's Boy. New York: Long-
       mans, Green, 1950. y.
            The trials of a midshipman fighting under Stephen De-
       catur during America's first war with the Barbary pirates.

721   _____. Detached Command. New York: Longmans, Green,
       1954. y.
            Naval adventure in the War of 1812.

722 The Dutch in the Medway [author unknown]. London, 1845.
            A tale of Robert Blake.

723 Dyer, Brian. The Celtic Queen. New York: Mason & Lips-
       comb, 1974.
            A man hopes to escape from the poverty and second-
       class citizenship of his native Ireland be becoming a crew-
       man aboard the Celtic Queen, the most magnificent luxury
       liner of her day and flagship of England's ill-fated White
       Star Line.

                              - E -

724 Eardley-Wilmot, S. The Battle of the North Sea in 1914. By
       "Searchlight, " pseud. London, 1912.

725   _____. The Next Naval War. London: 1894.
            By a Royal Navy captain.

726 Eaton, Evelyn. Restless Are the Sails. New York: Harper,
       1941.
            Adventure afloat and ashore undertaken in an effort to
       warn of the coming English attack on the fortress of Louis-
       bourg.

727   _____. The Sea Is So Wide. New York: Harper, 1943.
            A saga of the Acadians, banished from Nova Scotia to
       New Orleans.

728 Eberhart, Mignon G. Five Passengers from Lisbon. New
       York: Random House, 1946.
            Romance and murder set around the nurses, doctors
       and ships of the mercy fleet of World War II; "five

passengers unexpected and unwanted" in a lifeboat.

729 Eden, Charles H. <u>Afloat with Nelson</u>. London: Macqueen,
    1897.
        A look at the admiral's career from the Battle of the
    Nile to Trafalgar.

730 Edmonds, H. <u>Death Ship</u>. London: Lane, 1934.
        British mystery afloat.

731 Edmonds, Walter D. <u>Erie Water</u>. Boston: Little, Brown,
    1943.
        A carpenter's adventures during the Pre-Civil War con-
    struction of the Erie Canal.

732 _____. <u>Rome Haul</u>. Boston: Little, Brown, 1929.
        Erie Canal initiation of a farm boy.

733 Edwards, Amelia. <u>Debenham's Vow</u>. New York: Hurst,
    1870.
        Running the blockades off Charleston during the Civil
    War.

734 Edwards, E. J. and Jeanette E. Rattray. <u>"Whale Off!"</u> New
    York: Stokes, 1932. y.
        Chasing the great sperm whale near Long Island in the
    1840's.

735 Eggleston, Edward. <u>Wreck of the Sea Bird</u>. Boston: 1900.
        Story of the Carolina coast. Eggleston is best known
    for his book, <u>The Hoosier School-Master</u>.

736 Eggleston, George C. <u>The Bale Marked X: A Blockade Run-</u>
    <u>ning Adventure</u>. Boston: Lothrop, 1902.
        Action along the coast during the American Civil War.
        Brother of Edward Eggleston (q. v.), this author served
    in that conflict as a Confederate officer. His stories were
    extremely sentimental, but loaded with Southern local color.

737 _____. <u>Joe Lambert's Ferry</u>. Boston: Lothrop, 1883.
        Another Civil War tale.

738 _____. <u>The Last of the Flatboats; A Story of the Mississip-</u>
    <u>pi River and Its Interesting Family of Rivers</u>. Boston:
    Lothrop, 1900.

739 _____. <u>Running the River; A Story of Adventure and Success</u>.
    New York: A. S. Barnes, 1904.

740 _____. <u>What Happened at Quasi; The Story of a Carolina</u>
    <u>Cruise</u>. Boston: Lothrop, Lee and Shepard, 1911.

741 _____. <u>The Wreck of the Red Bird; A Story of the</u>

Carolina Coast. New York: Chatterton-Peck, 1882.

742 Eifert, Virginia. Three River's South. Boston: Dodd, Mead, 1966. y.
     Part of a trilogy on the youth of Abraham Lincoln, this volume concerns his brown water adventures as a riverboat pilot.

743 Eliav, Arie L. The Voyage of the Ulua. Translated from the Hebrew by Israel L Taslitt. New York: Funk & Wagnalls, 1969.
     An Exodus-style yarn concerning 800 young Jewish refugees aboard an ancient American freighter attempting to run the British blockade from Sweden to Palestine in 1947.

744 Eliot, George F. Caleb Pettengill, U. S. N. New York: Julian Messner, 1956.
     Possibly the "best" Civil War naval yarn outside of the trilogy penned by Van Wyck Mason (q. v.). A look at the double-ender gunboat operations of the Union's East Coast Blockading Squadron.

745 Ellis, William D. The Brooks Legend. New York: Crowell, 1958.
     Following the War of 1812, a U. S. Navy surgeon's mate attempts to obtain his M. D.

746 Ellsberg, Edward. Captain Paul. New York: Dodd, Mead, 1941.
     A biographical novel concerning Revolutionary War naval hero John Paul Jones.
     The author, a Rear Admiral in the U. S. Naval Reserve, was a noted salvage expert throughout his professional career, who performed noteworthy service in the Mediterranean and in support of the Normandy invasion in World War II. As a writer, he is noted for his ability to construct exciting plots around his extensive knowledge of submarine diving. Among his other tales are:

747 _____. Hell on Ice; The Saga of "The Jeanette. " New York: Dodd, Mead, 1938.
     Arctic exploration tale; based on fact.

748 _____. "I Have Just Begun to Fight!" The Story of John Paul Jones. New York: Dodd, Mead, 1942. y.
     A biographical novel; Ellsberg's Captain Paul re-written here for the younger reader.

749 _____. Mid Watch. New York: Dodd, Mead, 1945. y.
     A dramatization of events surrounding the boiler explosion aboard the U. S. cruiser Manhattan in 1909.

750 _____. Ocean Gold. New York: Dodd, Mead, 1935. y.

A look at the salvage of treasure from sunken ships.

751 _____. On the Bottom. New York: Dodd, Mead, 1966.
True submarine heroism re-told.

752 _____. Passport for Jennifer. New York: Dodd, Mead,
1952.

753 _____. Pig Boats. New York: Dodd, Mead, 1930.
Submarining, salvage and destroyer work in the U.S.
Navy. Made into the movie "Hell Below."

754 _____. S-54. New York: Dodd, Mead, 1930.
Tale of a submarine, and its crew which succeed
against great odds in raising a sunken treasure from the
floor of the Pacific.

755 _____. Spanish Ingots. New York: Dodd, Mead, 1940.
Treasure hunting. Sequel to Ocean Gold in which our
heroes transport their riches to America.

756 _____. Submarine Treasure. New York: Dodd, Mead,
1936.

757 _____. Submerged; A Novel. London: Hurst and Blackett,
1934.
A look at early USN submarining during the Inter-War
period (1919-1941).

758 _____. Thirty Fathoms Deep. New York: Dodd, Mead, 1929.
More treasure and submarines; an attempt to raise the
booty aboard an ancient Spanish galleon.

759 _____. Treasure Below. New York: Dodd, Mead, 1940.
Similar to no. 758.

760 Elwell, A. At the Sign of the Red Swan. Boston: Small, May-
nard, 1919.
A nautical yarn set around a sailor's bar-and-grill!

761 Engle, Eloise. Sea Challenge. Chicago: Hammond, 1962. y.
Two lads join Magellan's epic adventure.

762 Esler, Anthony. The Blade of Castlemayne. New York: Morrow, 1974.
A romantic adventure in which the father of our heroine
must choose the man to command his ship, The Golden Fortune, which is scheduled to join the armada of Sir Francis
Drake in the spring of 1591. A swashbuckling story of conflict between seamen, all of which takes place on shore.

763 "Etienne," pseud. The Diary of a U-boat Commander. London: Hutchinson, 1920.

World War I.

764 _____. Strange Tales from the Fleet. London: Methuen,
  1919.
      World War I.

765 Evans, E. R. G. R. To Sweep the Spanish Main. London:
  Hodder & Stoughton, 1930.
      By a Royal Navy admiral, a story of pirates.

766 Eyster, Warren. Far from the Customary Skies. New York:
  Random House, 1953.
      Saga of a destroyer from her commissioning to her loss
  off New Guinea during World War II. Packed with action.

- F -

767 Fabricius, J. W. Java Ho! London: Methuen, 1933.
      Adventures afloat in the South Seas.

768 Falkner, J. Meade. Moonfleet. Boston: Little, Brown, 1951.
      A look at smuggling on the 18th-century Dorset coast
  and the hunt for a diamond which legend said Blackbeard
  buried somewhere in Carisbrooke Castle.

769 Farmer, Philip Jose. The Fabulous Riverboat. New York:
  Putnam, 1971.
      A bizarre novel about a planet called Riverworld, "huge
  and mysterious" with one river and mysterious aliens including reincarnated Vikings, and, of all people, Mark
  Twain trying to build a riverboat.

770 Farnol, Jeffery. Adam Penfeather, Buccaneer: His Early
  Exploits. Garden City, N. Y. : Doubleday, 1941.
      "Being a curious and intimate relation of his tribulations,
  joys, and triumphs [on the Spanish Main] taken from Notes
  of His Journal and Pages from His Ship's Log, and here put
  into Complete Narrative"--subtitle.

771 _____. Black Bartlemy's Treasure. Boston: Little, Brown,
  1920.
      Piracy and Treasure in the 17th-century, centering
  around our hero Martin Conisby.

772 _____. Martin Conisby's Vengeance. Boston: Little, Brown,
  1921.
      This sequel to Black Bartlemy's Treasure witnesses the
  further adventures on the 17th-century Spanish Main.

773 _____. Sir John Dering. Boston: Little, Brown, 1923.
      A romantic adventure and pirate tale.

774 _____. Winds of Chance. Boston: Little, Brown, 1934.
        First published in England under the title Winds of For-
        tune, this is the chronicle of an early 18th-century English
        girl, Ursula Revell, on a strange, piratical craft, The Joy-
        ful Deliverance, in danger and adventure on the Spanish
        Main, and in the heat and worry of South American jungles.

775 Fast, Howard M. Patrick Henry and the Frigate's Keel and
        Other Stories of a Young Nation. New York: Duell, 1945.
        y.

776 Faulkner, Nancy. Knights Besieged. Garden City, N. Y. :
        Doubleday, 1964. y.
        The 1522 siege of Rhodes.

777 Felsen, Gregor. Navy Diver. New York: Dutton, 1942. y.
        A youth joins the American Navy in that capacity in
        1939.

778 _____. Struggle Is Our Brother. New York: Dutton, 1944.
        y.
        Turned down by the Navy in 1942, young Chris joins the
        American merchant marine and sails the dangerous North At-
        lantic.

779 _____. Submarine Sailor. New York: Dutton, 1954. y.
        Life aboard an American submarine in the Pacific war,
        young Lt. Cleve Hawkings, commanding.

780 Felton, Harold W. True Tall Tales of Stormalong, Sailor of
        the Seas. Englewood Cliffs, N. Y. : Prentice-Hall, 1968.
        y.
        The Yankee counterpart of Paul Bunyon afloat.

781 Fenner, Phyllis R. , comp. Pirates, Pirates, Pirates. New
        York: Watts, 1951. y.
        A collection of short stories and book excerpts.

782 Fenwick, Kenneth. Coral Seas. London: Hutchinson, 1944.

783 _____. Far Off Ships. London: Hutchinson, 1947.
        Both of the above are Royal Navy romances.

784 _____. Trafalgar. Hamburg, West Germany, 1955.

785 Ferber, Edna. Show Boat. Garden City, N. Y. : Doubleday,
        1926.
        The Hawks-Ravenal family's fortune aboard the Missis-
        sippi show boat "Cotton Blossom" in the 1870's. Basis of
        the noted musical play and movie.

786 Fernald, John. Destroyer From America. London: Macmil-
        lan, 1942.

World War II in the Atlantic.

787 Feuille, Frank. The Cotton Road. New York: Morrow, 1954.
     y.
         Breaking the blockade of cotton to England during the
     Civil War.

788 Field, Bradda. Bride of Glory. New York: Greystone, 1942.
         Published in Great Britain under the title Miledi, this
     is another tale about Nelson, Lady Hamilton, and their re-
     lationship.

789 Fielding, Henry. Jonathan Wild. London, 1743.
         Also available in modern editions, this early work is
     rife with pirates and shipwrecks. The first work to present
     its characters in the "humorous" fashion.

790 Filon, Augustin. Renégat. Paris: Armand Colin, 1894.
         The defeat of the Spanish Armada.

791 Finger, Charles Joseph. Cape Horn Snorter; A Story of the
     War of 1812 and of Gallant Days with Capt. Porter of the
     U.S. Frigate Essex. Boston: Houghton, Mifflin, 1939. y.

792 _____. When Guns Thundered at Tripoli. Boston: Hought-
     on, Mifflin, 1939. y.
         Naval action in the War with Tripoli, 1803-05.

793 Finnemore, John. A Captive of the Corsairs. London: Nel-
     son, 1906. y.
         Tunis and the 1564 siege of Malta.

794 Finney, Jack. Assault on a Queen. New York: Simon &
     Schuster, 1960.
         A group of modern pirates (led by Frank Sinatra in the
     movie version) raise an old World War I U-boat, stop the
     Queen Mary in mid-Atlantic, and proceed to loot the vessel.
     An American destroyer then comes upon the scene to settle
     accounts with the raiders.

795 Fisher, Steve. Destroyer. New York: 1941.
         Rousing early World War II action novel; typical nation-
     alistic tone of the "V-Years."

796 Fleming, Guy. Over the Hills and Far Away. London: Long-
     mans, 1917.
         Romance and adventure, afloat and ashore, in and off
     18th-century Ireland, England, and Scotland.

797 Fletcher, Charles. The Naval Guardian. London: Longmans,
     1805.
         An important early work.

798 Fletcher, Inglis. <u>Bennett's Welcome</u>. Indianapolis: Bobbs-
Merrill, 1950.
"A panel of the Carolina series of historical novels of
the Colonial and Revolutionary period"--jacket; story of the
people of Virginia, their coast, rivers, and sounds in 1651;
historical romance mixed with realism, and in this story, a
look at the Roanoke Island adventure of 1585.

799 _____. <u>Lusty Wind for Carolina</u>. Indianapolis: Bobbs-
Merrill, 1944.
Third in the Fletcher series of novels about Colonial Carolina; the struggle for free trade routes from American
plantations to world markets (1718-25), and the warding off
of the pirates then attacking them.

800 _____. <u>Men of Albemarle</u>. Indianapolis: Bobbs-Merrill,
1942.
On and off the Carolina coast in 1710; the Albemarle
district.

801 _____. <u>Raleigh's Eden</u>. Indianapolis: Bobbs-Merrill, 1940.
First part of Carolina's sequel by Fletcher. Eighteenth
Century setting, with special reference to the years 1765-
1782.

802 _____. <u>Roanoke Hundred</u>. New York: Bobbs, 1948.
Fictionalized version of Grenville's expedition to Roanoke
Island, 1585.

803 _____. <u>Toil of the Brave</u>. Indianapolis: Bobbs-Merrill,
1946.
American Revolution along the Carolinas; fourth in
Fletcher's series along the Albemarle district of North Carolina. A young Britisher and a Continental vie for the affec-
tions of the heroine.

804 Fletcher, J. S. <u>In the Days of Drake</u>. London: Blackie,
1896.

805 Floherty, John Joseph. <u>Sentries of the Sea</u>. New York: Lippincott, 1942. y.
The American Navy in World War II.

806 _____. <u>Youth and the Sea; Our Merchant Marine Calls
American Youth</u>. New York: Lippincott, 1941. y.
As much propaganda for merchant sailor recruitment as
a rousing pre-war sea tale.

807 Foa, Eugenie. <u>Monsieur the Captain of the Carabel</u>. London:
Blackie, 1840.
The Anglo-Dutch war, with De Ruyter a main character.

808 Foley, Fanny (pseud). <u>Romance of the Ocean: A Narrative of</u>

the Voyage of the Wildfire to California.   Philadelphia:
Lindsay and Blakiston, 1850.
   A contemporary clipper ship story.

809   Forbes, Colin.   The Palermo Affair.   New York: Dutton,
      1972.
         Allied raiders move to sink a German train-ferry in
      the straits between Sicily and Italy in 1943.

810   _____.   Target Five.   New York: Dutton, 1973.
         American and Soviet agents, employing everything from
      "choppers" to icebreakers, attempt to obtain the person of
      a Russian scientist making a dash for freedom across the
      Arctic icepack.

811   Forbes, Ester.   The Running of the Tide.   Cambridge, Mass. :
      At the Riverside Press, 1948.
         A fictional look at the great shipbuilding era in Salem,
      Massachusetts, after the Revolution.

812   Forbes, George.   Adventures in Southern Seas.   New York:
      Dodd, Mead, 1920.
         The Dutch navigator Hartog searches for treasure in
      the 17th-century.

813   Forbes-Lindsay, C. H.   John Smith, Gentleman Adventurer.
      Philadelphia: Lippincott, 1907.
         A biographical novel.

814   Ford, Charles.   Death Sails with Magellan.   New York: Ran-
      dom House, 1937.
         The great circumnavigation adventure of the noted
      Spanish seaman.

815   Ford, Ford Madox.   The Half Moon.   New York: Doubleday,
      Page, 1909.
         Henry Hudson's voyage of exploration during the reign
      of James I.

816   Foreman, Russell.   Long Pig.   New York: McGraw-Hill, 1958.
         Thirteen survivors of a shipwreck land on a cannibal-
      infested island in the Fijis a century ago.

817   Forester, Cecil S.   Admiral Hornblower in the West Indies.
      Boston: Little, Brown, 1958.
         Six little adventures set in the Caribbean, with the first
      from the era of Lieutenant Hornblower (q. v.) and the re-
      mainder in the years after the Napoleonic wars.   Rear Ad-
      miral Hornblower, in command of the Royal Navy's West
      Indian station, faces a new Bonapartist uprising, battles
      pirates, suppresses the seaborne slave trade, and maintains
      British diplomacy in the days of the Monroe Doctrine and
      South American revolutionaries.

When the average reader thinks of a sea story, his mind almost always recalls three words: "Captain Horatio Hornblower." Such was the importance of this single character to the development of nautical literature in this century that more than passing attention must be paid to his creator, C. S. Forester.

Born in Cairo, Egypt, in 1899, Forester spent most of his boyhood in London, where from 1910-1917 he attended Dulwich College. A weak heart kept him from active service in "The Great War" and "laziness and indiscipline" caused him to give up medical school for the life of a writer.

Following the publication of his first novel, the mystery Payment Deferred in 1926, Forester married and decided to go sailing aboard a 15 foot dinghy by way of a honeymoon. It was, according to his memoirs Long Before Forty, during the outfitting of the Annie Marble's little library that he happened to purchase three volumes of the old Royal Navy magazine The Naval Chronicle. While exploring the backwaters of England and the Continent, the author spent much time with these fact-filled issues of 1790-1820, reading and rereading the tiny print, becoming familiar with the atmosphere of the 18th-century fleet and the attitude of professional sea fighters of that era. Thus a chance find in an old bookshop "prepared the slime into which the first waterlogged timber [of Hornblower] would be dropped."

Forester did not immediately begin the development of his most enduring naval character; it would come about as an inspiration born of a literary failure. In 1934, the author arrived in America to write the play Nurse Cavell with C. E. Bechhofer Roberts and moved on to Hollywood where success as a screen writer eluded him. Resigning that position, he again went to sea, this time as a passenger bound for Central America. During a rather dull six-weeks cruise, he passed through the history-laden area where Hornblower would conduct his first campaign. Recalling his reading from The Naval Chronicle, and tying it into the local scenery, he began to construct in his mind the plot and character of what would become his first nautical yarn, Beat to Quarters.

Arriving home in England, Forester accepted various correspondent assignments from the London Times and covered, among other things, the Spanish Civil War and the Nazi occupation of Prague. Later, his pen would play an active role in telling the world of Allied naval successes in World War II. During the early part of this newspaper career, he continued to polish Hornblower, giving him the prowess of a Marryat seaman, the psychological complexities of a Conrad captain, and the plots first demonstrated by James Fenimore Cooper. Beat to Quarters was published in 1937 followed in the next two years by its immediate sequels and was combined into the trilogy Captain Horatio Hornblower. Sent to subscribers by both the Book-of-the-Month-Club and the Book Society of England, the work received critical acclaim and instant success on both sides of the Atlantic. The New York Times praised its "fine forthright prose and careful antiquarianism," while the noted nautical writer William McFee was so impressed that he commented that Forester "writes as if nobody had ever written a tale before."

In 1944, the now-successful writer divorced his first wife and settled in his permanent home of Berkeley, California, where three years later he married an American woman. Both Hornblower and another nautical tale, The African Queen, were made into successful motion pictures thereby further ensuring his renown. The main characters in both of these screen adaptions were played to perfection by actors perfectly suited for the roles: Gregory Peck as Hornblower, Humphrey Bogart as Allnut, and Katharine Hepburn as Rose. After V-J Day, Forester sought to supply the increasing demand for his product. Originally planning to retire in 1946, he observed in 1952, several books later, "The odd thing was and is that the Hornblower plots keep coming, without any labor." He continued to pen the successful series and other nautical tales almost up to his death in 1966; a few were salted away in his agent's safe "against some day when I can't pay the rent or am dead."

C. S. Forester, a slight bespectacled man ill most of his life, never saw a day at sea as a maritime warrior and bore no physical resemblance to Hornblower whatsoever. In his mind, however, was a vision of tall ships and gallant men so intense that, when transcribed onto paper, revealed a genius for the nautical yarn so inspired as to leave no reader in doubt that "the master" had passed this way.

In addition to the yarns cited in this work, readers desiring further details on Mr. Forester's writing craft or on the background of the Hornblower saga should see the author's memoirs Long Before Forty (Boston: Little, Brown, 1967) and The Hornblower Companion (Boston: Little, Brown, 1964), which includes an atlas of Horatio's exploits.

818 _____. The African Queen. New York: Modern Library, 1940.
How an English spinster and a little Cockney with a steam launch harass the Germans on an African lake during World War I. The role of Allnut won for Humphrey Bogart his only Oscar.

819 _____. Beat to Quarters. Boston: Little, Brown, 1937.
The first volume of the Hornblower series in which Horatio is sent under sealed orders with the frigate Lydia to the Pacific, where he encounters the mad South American revolutionary El Supremo and his great love, Lady Barbara Wellsey.

820 _____. Brown on Resolution. London, 1919.
An unsuccessful tale of World War I afloat which contains some hint of the author's latent ability then unknown.

821 _____. The Captain from Connecticut. Boston: Little,
Brown, 1941.
An exciting tale of the War of 1812 at sea containing a
mixture of Hornblower and the famed frigate Constitution.

822 _____. Captain Horatio Hornblower. Boston: Little, Brown,
1939.
The famed trilogy containing the above cited Beat to
Quarters, plus Flying Colours and Ship of the Line which
are annotated below.

823 _____. Commodore Hornblower. Boston: Little, Brown,
1945.
Promoted for his heroic escapades in Captain Horatio
Hornblower, the middle-aged hero is sent with a unique
squadron to the Baltic to insure that Russia and Sweden re-
tain their shaky friendship with England. Perhaps the most
interesting section in the tale, drawn almost directly from
the old Naval Chronicle, is the description of a blockade
runner's destruction by balls from his bomb-brig.

824 _____. Flying Colours. Boston: Little, Brown, 1939.
Captured with part of his crew as a result of the exploits in Ship of the Line (q. v.), Hornblower manages a
daring escape across France to eventual freedom on the
English Channel.

825 _____. Gold from Crete. Boston: Little, Brown, 1970.
Ten of the writer's best World War II stories (not all
nautical) revolving around the theme of Allied courage.

826 _____. The Good Shepherd. Boston: Little, Brown, 1955.
The work of an American destroyer captain in sheperd-
ing a convoy across the U-boat infested North Atlantic during the Second World War. Must be compared with Nicholas Monsarrat's The Cruel Sea (q. v.).

827 _____. Hornblower and the Atropos. Boston: Little,
Brown, 1953.
Filling in the three-year gap between Lieutenant Hornblower and Beat to Quarters, this account tells of Horatio's
first marriage, a trip across England's inland waterways by
barge, his participation in Nelson's funeral, and the raising
of a mighty treasure off the coast of Turkey.

828 _____. Hornblower and the Hotspur. Boston: Little,
Brown, 1962.
Another sequel to Lieutenant Hornblower, in which we
again view Horatio's domestic life (quite similar, in fact, to
Lord Nelson's) and his success off the French coast, in
which he wrests control of a Spanish treasure. For this gallant action, he becomes Captain Horatio Hornblower.

829   _____. Hornblower During the Crisis and Two Stories:
Hornblower's Temptation and The Last Encounter. Boston:
Little, Brown, 1967.
        Part of another novel, published posthumously, and two
stories. The novel fragment finds Hornblower assigned to
a spy mission in Spain. One story relates the time during
his days as a midshipman when he is almost taken in by an
Irish seaman about to be hanged. The second tale relates
how Admiral Hornblower helps a stranger in distress--who
turns out to be the future Napoleon III.

830   _____. The Indomitable Hornblower. Boston: Little,
Brown, 1963.
        A trilogy comprising Commodore Hornblower, Lord
Hornblower, and Admiral Hornblower in the West Indies.

831   _____. The Last Nine Days of the Bismarck. Boston:
Little, Brown, 1959.
        A fictitious view of the World War II pursuit of the
German battleship Bismarck. The movie version, complete
with outstanding nautical sequences, starred Kenneth More.

832   _____. Lieutenant Hornblower. Boston: Little, Brown,
1952.
        This account follows his activities as a junior officer
aboard the line-of-battleship H. M. S. Renown.

833   _____. Lord Hornblower. Boston: Little, Brown, 1946.
        In this sequel to Commodore Hornblower, Horatio takes
leave of his beloved Lady Barbara to conclude his private
war with Napoleon, quells a mutiny, and is made a peer of
the realm for his long years of devoted service.

834   _____. The Man in the Yellow Raft. Boston: Little,
Brown, 1969.
        A series of short stories reprinted from The Saturday
Evening Post concerning naval actions in the Pacific during
World War II. Contents: "The Man in the Yellow Raft,"
"Triumph of the Boon," "The Boy Stood on the Burning
Deck," "Dr. Blanke's First Command," "Counterpunch,"
"U. S. S. Cornucopia," "December 6th," and "Rendezvous."
Even more than his other tales, these take a Conradian
view of human nature and the worth of the individual.

835   _____. Mr. Midshipman Hornblower. Boston: Little,
Brown, 1950.
        Ten short stories, reprinted from The Saturday Evening
Post, with a thin connecting line tell how the hero rose
from the lowest commissioned rank to receive his lieutenant's
berth. Contents: "Hornblower and the Even Chance,"
"Hornblower and the Cargo of Rice," "Hornblower and the
Penalty of Failure," "Hornblower and the Man Who Felt
Queer," "Hornblower and the Man Who Saw God,"

'Hornblower, the Frogs, and the Lobsters, " 'Hornblower
and the Spanish Galleys, " 'Hornblower and the Examination, "
'Hornblower and Noah's Ark, " and 'Hornblower, the Dutch-
ess, and the Devil. "

836 _____. The Ship. Boston: Little, Brown, 1943.
The activities of a British light cruiser in defense of
a Malta convoy in the Mediterranean during World War II.

837 _____. Ship of the Line. Boston: Little, Brown, 1938.
Returning from the South Seas of Beat to Quarters,
Horatio is given a "74" and assigned to the blockade of the
Spanish coast. Eventually he takes his vessel into port to
knock out the enemy warships there assembled, losing his
command in the process of success.

838 _____. To the Indies. Boston: Little, Brown, 1940.
A crown lawyer is sent to investigate conditions in the
New World and takes ship as a member of Columbus' tragic
last expedition.

839 _____. Young Hornblower. Boston: Little, Brown, 1960.
A trilogy comprising Mr. Midshipman Hornblower,
Lieutenant Hornblower, and Hornblower and the Atropos.

840 Forman, James. So Ends This Day. New York: Farrar,
1970. y.
A whaling captain takes his children to sea for a bit of
leviathan chasing and a spot of slavery.

841 Forrester, Larry. Battle of the April Storm. New York:
John Day, 1969.
A nonfiction novel portraying the hopeless April 8,
1940, battle between the German heavy cruiser Hipper and
H. M. destroyer Glowworm, in which the latter was sunk
and her commander was nominated for the Victoria Cross
by the enemy captain!

842 Fosdick, Charles A. Marcy, the Blockade Runner. By Harry
Castleman, pseud. Philadelphia, 1891.
The Civil War afloat told with a Southern flavor. The
author served with the Union's Mississippi Flotilla during
the conflict.

843 Foster, H. O. Arnold. In a Conning Tower; Or, How I Took
H. M. S. Majestic Into Action. London, 1900.

844 Foster, John T. Rebel Sea Raider. New York: William Morrow, 1965.
The Civil War, and the C. S. S. Alabama.

845 France, Robert. Race. London: Constable, 1958.
Another British tale of yachting competition.

846 Frank, Bruno. <u>A Man Called Cervantes</u>. New York: Viking,
       1935.
            A biographical novel concerning the life of the creator
       of Don Quixote, who served with the Christian fleet in the
       Battle of Lepanto.

847 Franklin, Augustus. <u>The Sea-Gull; Or, The Pirates League</u>.
       Boston: H. L. Williams, 1846.

848 _____. <u>The Widow's Pirate's Son; Or, Pailine Coustry, the
       Corsair's Mate. A Tale of the Province of Massachusetts</u>.
       Boston: H. L. Williams, 1845.
            Two more 19th-century pirate stories. The American
       interest in buccaneers has been constant throughout out his-
       tory, but especially acute in the years 1840 to 1880.

849 Franklin, Gordon. <u>Another Naval Digression</u>. London: Heath,
       Cranton, 1920.
            World War I.

850 _____. <u>A Naval Digression</u>. London: Blackwood, 1916.
            World War I.

851 Freedgood, Stanley and Morton. <u>Yankee Trader</u>. By Stanley
       Morton, pseud. New York: Sheridan, 1947.
            The adventures of a money-mad American sea captain
       of the Revolutionary War era.

852 Freeman, M. <u>A Diary of the Great War</u>. By Samuel Pepys,
       Jr. pseud. London: Hodder & Stoughton, 1916.

853 _____. <u>A Last Diary of the Great War</u>. By Samuel Pepys,
       Jr., pseud. London: Hodder & Stoughton, 1919.

854 _____. <u>A Second Diary of the Great War</u>. By Samuel
       Pepys, Jr., pseud. London: Hodder & Stoughton, 1917.

855 French, Joseph L., ed. <u>Great Pirate Stories</u>. 2 Vols. Lon-
       don: Brentanos, 1922-1925.

856 _____. <u>Great Sea Stories</u>. 2 Vols. London: Brentanos,
       1921-1925.

857 Frith, Henry. <u>Aboard the Atlanta</u>. Publisher unknown, 1900.
            A look at life aboard the new armored cruisers of the
       American fleet.

858 _____. <u>The Cruise of the Wasp; A Romance of the North
       Atlantic</u>. Publisher unknown, 1890.
            A tale of the War of 1812.

859 _____. <u>Jack O'Lanthorn</u>. New York: Scribner's, n. d.

860 _____. The Lost Trader. London: Chambers, 1894.

861 _____. Search for the Talisman. London: Blackie, n. d.

862 Frost, Elizabeth H. This Side of Land. New York: Coward,
        1942.
            Post Revolutionary Nantucket Island tale.

863 Frothingham, Jessie P. Running the Gauntlet. New York:
        Appleton, 1906.
            Civil War; C. C. S. Albemarle vs. the Union's William
        Cushing.

864 Frye, Pearl. Gallant Captain: A Biographical Novel Based
        on the Life of John Paul Jones. Boston: Little, Brown,
        1955.

865 _____. A Game for Empires. Boston: Little, Brown,
        1950.
            Lord Nelson and his exploits afloat.

866 _____. The Narrow Bridge. Boston: Little, Brown, 1947.
            Honolulu during and after the Japanese raid on Pearl
        Harbor.

867 _____. The Sleeping Sword. Boston: Little, Brown, 1953.
            Nelson and Lady Hamilton.

868 Fuller, Iola. The Gilded Touch. New York: Putnam, 1957.
        y.
            LaSalle and the discovery of the Mississippi River.

869 Fulton, Reed. Davy Jones' Locker. New York: Doran, 1928.
        y.
            Nautical adventure in the Astorian expedition, 1810-1812.

870 Fyfe, J. G. , ed. Stories of Ships and the Sea. London:
        Blackie, 1933.
            An anthology.

- G -

871 Gabriel, Gilbert W. I, James Lewis. Garden City, N. Y. :
        Doubleday, 1932.
            John Jacob Astor and Astoria, 1810-12.

871a Gage, Nicholas. The Bourlotas Fortune. New York: Holt,
        1975.
            Tale of a Greek shipping magnet from his first service
        as a deck boy in 1913 to the creation of his New York-based
        world wide fleet after World War II.

872   Gage, William H.   The Cruel Coast.   New York: New Ameri-
      can Library, 1966.

873   Gallery, Daniel V.   "Away Boarders."   New York: Norton,
      1971.
            Most of this author's writing concerns humor in the
      contemporary U.S. Navy.

874   _____.   The Brink.   Garden City, N.Y.:   Doubleday, 1968.
            An American nuclear submarine confronts a Soviet de-
      stroyer in the Arctic and the world is at the brink of
      World War III (not one of his humorous tales).

875   _____.   Cap'n Fatso.   New York: Norton, 1969.

876   _____.   Now, Hear This!   New York: Norton, 1965.

877   _____.   Stand by-y-y to Start Engines.   New York: Norton,
      1966.
            The author of these often humorous yarns of the modern
      Navy was a World War II escort carrier commander in the
      Atlantic.

878   Gallico, Paul.   The Poseidon Adventure.   New York: Coward-
      McCann, 1969.
            The giant ocean liner S.S. Poseidon is caught in a tidal
      wave eminating from an underwater earthquake in the Medi-
      terranean, and capsizes, remaining afloat upside down and
      slowly sinking.   A few passengers manage to make their
      way up to the keel and eventual safety.   Basis of the Irwin
      Allen catastrophe movie.

879   Gann, Ernest.   Fiddler's Green.   New York: William Sloane,
      1950.
            Norwegian-American fisherman out of San Francisco;
      set along Pacific coast; drama of a son's rebellion and love.

880   _____.   Song of the Sirens.   New York: Ballantine, 1968.
            High adventure amongst seventeen "wonderful sirens,"
      beloved vessels.   Classic dilemmas afloat.

881   _____.   Twilight for the Gods.   New York: Sloane, 1956.
            Aboard the Cannibal, a three-master barquentine bound
      across the Pacific to Mexico in the 1920's; drama among a
      cross-section of passenger.

882   Gardiner, F. M.   Dynamite Duncan, USN.   New York: Dodd,
      Mead, 1943.   y.
            World War II.

883   _____.   Standby-Mark.   New York: Dodd, Mead, 1943.   y.
            World War II, Submarine action.

884   Gardiner, Leslie. Call the Captain. London: Blackwood's,
      1964.

885   Gardner, John. Understrike. New York: Viking, 1965.
           British agent Boysie Oakes is sent to San Diego to wit-
      ness a hush-hush American submarine trial and the Rus-
      sians thoughtfully send along a carefully-trained double to
      take his place.

886   Gardner, Mona. Hong Kong. Garden City, N.Y.: Doubleday,
      1958.
           Fiction centered around the Opium Wars.

886a Garfield, Brian. Act of Piracy. By Frank O'Brian, pseud.
      New York: Dell, 1975.
           In 1850 a paddiewheel steamer is hijacked out of New
      York harbor and sailed to California in the record time of
      144 days. Based on an actual event.

887   Garfield, Leon. Jack Holborn. New York: Pantheon, 1966.
      y.
           London orphan Jack Holborn stows away aboard a pirate
      ship and his adventures take him to Africa where he is in-
      volved with the early 18th-century slave trade.

888   Garner, G. Mystery Men-of-War. London: Nelson, 1932.

889   Garnet, Clew. Hammered Shipshape. London: Methuen,
      1935.

890   Garrett, George. The Death of the Fox. Garden City, N.Y.:
      Doubleday, 1971.
           How Sir Walter Raleigh, the "Fox," fell out of favor
      with James I and lost his head. Interesting, but sad!

891   Garstin, Crosbie. China Seas. New York: Stokes, 1931.
           Life aboard an English merchantman plying the waters
      between Singapore and Hong Kong.

892   _____. High Noon. New York: Stokes, 1925.
           The first sequel to the Owl's House in which Ortho
      Penhale is taken and escapes from a British warship, re-
      joins the fleet in time for a battle with the French, and re-
      turns to England where he enters into a marriage which be-
      comes so unhappy that he is forced back to sea.

893   _____. The Owl's House. New York: Stokes, 1924.
           Ortho, the elder of two sons of a Cornish farmer and
      gipsy wife, becomes involved in smuggling and is eventually
      carried off by Barbary pirates.

894   _____. West Wind. New York: Stokes, 1926.
           The final sequel to the Owl's House in which Ortho

finishes his glorious life afloat in a final spurt of noble
self-sacrifice.

895   Garth, David.   Three Roads to a Star.   New York: Putnam,
        1955.
              Nautical intrigue of an international flavor featuring a
        post-war American cruiser in the powder-keg of the Medi-
        terranean.

896   Gaskell, Elizabeth C.   Sylvia's Lovers.   London: Smith,
        Elder, 1863.
              Whaling and the press gang in the late 18th-century.

897   Gaskin, Catherine.   Sara Dane.   Philadelphia: Lippincott,
        1955.
              The life and romance of a former British naval officer
        condemned as a prisoner to late 18th-century Australia.

898   Gathorne-Hardy, Robert.   Other Seas.   London: Collins, 1934.
              British nautical adventures.

899   Gavin, Catherine I.   The Fortress.   Garden City, N. Y. :
        Doubleday, 1964.
              The romance of a Yankee sea captain and a Russo-
        Finnish noblewoman set against the backdrop of Baltic oper-
        ations in the Crimean War.

900   Gebler, Ernest.   The Plymouth Adventure.   Garden City,
        N. Y. :   Doubleday, 1950.
              Fictionalized voyage of the Mayflower.   Spencer Tracy
        starred in the movie version; both versions are very close
        to the mark historically.

901   Geer, A. C.   Sea Chase.   New York: Harper, 1948.
              A World War II German cargo vessel is pursued by the
        Royal Navy.   John Wayne played the non-Nazi sea captain
        in the movie version.

902   Gendron, Val.   Outlaw Voyage.   Cleveland: World, 1955.   y.
              How a young man works aboard a slaver to earn a spot
        on a better ship and security for his mother.

903   George, S. Charles.   Midshipman's Luck.   London: Warne,
        1955.   y.

904   Gerould, G. H.   Filibuster.   New York: Appleton, 1924.   y.
              Spanish-American War naval action.

905   Gerson, Noel B.   Clear for Action.   By Carter Vaughan,
        pseud.   New York: Doubleday, 1970.
              A biographical novel concerning David G. Farragut.

906   _____.   Dragon Cove.   Garden City, N. Y. :   Doubleday, 1964.

Privateering exploits around Newport during the American Revolution; notable female characters; climaxes in a fierce running sea battle between British and American privateers over the fate of Rhode Island.

907   _____. Forest Ford. By Samuel Edwards, pseud. Garden City, N.Y.: Doubleday, 1955.
An English nobleman is shanghaied aboard a ship and transported to colonial America.

908   _____. The Nelson Touch. By Paul Lewis, pseud. New York: Holt, 1960.
A biographical novel of the heroic little admiral, his loves and victories.

909   _____. River Devils. Garden City, N.Y.: Doubleday, 1968.
Foiling the dangerous Mississippi River pirates of the 1830's.

910   _____. Warhead. A Novel about the Men Who Make Nuclear Submarines, Their Town and Their Women. Garden City, N.Y.: Doubleday, 1970.
The Hawk, advanced nuclear prototype, is lost, unleashing wrath upon her builders.

911   _____. The Yankee Brig. By Carter A. Vaughan, pseud. Garden City, N.Y.: Doubleday, 1960.
How an American sea captain, seeking to earn sufficient cash to purchase part ownership in his own brig, involuntarily gives up the life of a privateer's quarterdeck for that of an 18th-century British warship's forecastle. In short, he was impressed!

912   Gibbons, Thomas. Tales That Were Told. Chicago: The Chicago Press, 1892.
Sea fights and pirate operations.

913   Gibbs, Mary A. The Admiral's Lady. New York: Mason, Charter, 1975.
Due to retire, Admiral Sir John Farebrother is sent on a secret mission by Queen Victoria. His twin brother Will is sent home to keep up the masquerade and the family black sheep conducts himself well enough to secure the love of the admiral's niece.

914   Gibson, T. Ware. The Priest of the Black Cross: A Tale of the Sea. Cincinnati: "Great West", 1848.
A pirate tale written by an American naval officer.

915   Gilbert, William. King George's Middy. London, 1869.
An imitation of Marryat.

916   Giles, Janice, H. <u>Run Me a River</u>. Boston: Houghton, Mif-
        flin, 1964. y.
              Civil War along the Mississippi.

917   Gillies, Robert P. <u>Tales of a Voyager to the Arctic Ocean</u>.
        Vols. 13-18 of The Naval and Military Library of Entertain-
        ment. 6 Vols. London: Henry Colburn, 1834.
              The author was an important sea fiction contributor to
        <u>Blackwood's Magazine</u> in the early part of the 19th-century.

918   Gilligan, Edmund. <u>Gaunt Woman</u>. New York: Scribner's,
        1943.
              A square-rigger, the <u>Gaunt Woman</u>, is fitted out as a
        U-boat supply vessel by the Nazis and is hunted down and
        sunk by a single small American warship operating off New-
        foundland.

919   _____. <u>I Name Thee Maria</u>. New York: Scribner's, 1946.
              Two brothers captain their father's vessel on the Grand
        Banks in the age of sail and lend a helping hand to Captain
        Delehanty, who is suspected of murder.

920   _____. <u>My Earth, My Sea</u>. New York: Norton, 1960.
              Tale of a young man growing up at sea off Gloucester,
        Nova Scotia, and Newfoundland.   Contains a vivid descrip-
        tion of the wreck of a sailing yacht on the treacherous shift-
        ing sands of the Grand Banks region.

921   _____. <u>Ringed Horizon</u>. New York: Scribner's, 1943.
              In this sequel to <u>Gaunt Woman</u>, the Yankee heroes con-
        tinue their war on German U-boats.

922   _____. <u>Voyage of the Golden Hind</u>. New York: Scribner's,
        1945.
              A look at Drake's voyage of circumnavigation which
        should be compared with Van Wyck Mason's <u>The Golden
        Admiral</u> (q. v.).

923   _____. <u>White Sails Crowding</u>. New York: Scribner's,
        1939.
              A clipper ship yarn.

924   Gilpatrick, Guy. <u>Action in the North Atlantic</u>. New York:
        Dutton, 1943.
              A wartime tale of Arctic convoys harassed by German
        U-boats and the Luftwaffe.

925   _____. <u>The Glencannon Omnibus, Including "Scotch and
        Water," "Half-Seas Over" [and] "Three Sheets in the Wind</u>. "
        3 Vols. in 1. New York: Dodd, 1938.

926   _____. <u>The Last Glencannon Omnibus, Including "The Can-
        ny Mr. Glencannon" [and] "Glencannon Ignores the War</u>. "

2 Vols. in 1. New York: Dodd, 1953.

927 _____. The Second Glencannon Omnibus, Including "Mr.
Glencannon," "The Gentleman with the Walrus Mustache"
[and] "Glencannon Afloat." 3 Vols. in 1. New York:
Dodd, 1942.
Each of the eight volumes was also published separate-
ly.

928 Gilson, Charles. The Lost Empire. London: Frowde and
Hodder, 1909.
Contains a section on the Battle of the Nile.

929 Gladd, Arthur A. Galleys East. New York: Dodd, Mead,
1961. y.
A young sponge diver serves as a galley slave during
the great 1571 Battle of Lepanto.

930 Glascock, William N. Land Sharks and Sea Gulls. 3 Vols.
London: Richard Bentley, 1838.
Writing from personal experience, the author, a captain in the Royal Navy, has in these four works left an accurate picture of the seamans' life in Nelson's fleet. For
this accuracy, however, the serious reader must accept
deadly dull prose.

931 _____. The Naval Sketch Book; Or, The Service Afloat and
Ashore, With Characteristic Reminiscences, Fragments,
and Opinions. 2 Vols. London: Henry Colburn, 1826.
Reprinted in 1843.

932 _____. Sailors and Saints; Or, Matrimonial Manoeuvres.
London: Henry Colburn, 1829.
A romance.

933 _____. Tales of a Tar. London: Whittaker, 1836.

934 Gleig, Charles. The Middy of the Blunderbore. London:
Chambers, n. d. y.

935 _____. When All Men Starve. London, 1898.
The author also wrote two other stories with a Royal
Navy flavor: Bunter's Cruise and The Nancy Manoeuvres.

936 Gleig, George. The Chelsea Pensioners. Vols. 10-12 of The
Naval and Military Library of Entertainment. 3 Vols.
London: Colburn, 1834.
Gleig was a British army officer present in America
during the War of 1812 for the battles at Baltimore and
New Orleans. This set is based on his experiences at the
Chelsea Hospital as a chaplain.

937 Godtsenhoven, Oscar van. The Sable Lion. New York:

Putnam, 1954.
How Flemish pirates preyed on English shipping in the
Channel during the reign of James I.

938   Golding, Louis.   Little Old Admiral.   New York: Vanguard,
      1958.
            Our hero is a part-time bum and navy buff who fre-
      quents the watering holes of sailors.   One day he encoun-
      ters an orphan named Terry; the two adopt one another,
      and attempt to work out their lonely problems.

939   Golding, William G.   Two Deaths of Christopher Martin.   New
      York: Harcourt, 1957.
            First published in Britain as simply Pincher Martin,
      this yarn concerns the fate of that naval officer whose ship
      having been torpedoed in the North Atlantic finds shelter on
      a small almost barren island and there mounts a lonely
      vigil awaiting rescue.

940   Goldston, Robert.   The Shore Dimly Seen.   New York: Ran-
      dom House, 1963.
            From scattered bits of evidence and the fact that a
      passenger overhauls a faulty rocket computer aboard an
      American nuclear submarine, in midocean, passengers
      aboard the luxury yacht Columbia, en route to New York
      from Spain suspect that atomic war may have broken out
      and that the whole Atlantic coastline of the U.S. may be a
      blackened radioactive rubble.

941   Golon, Serge and Anne.   Angélique in Barbary.   By Sergeanne
      Golon, pseud.   New York: Bantam Books, 1968.
            First published in England in 1960 under the title,
      Angélique and the Sultan, this account finds the Countess
      twice captured by North African pirates and sold into slav-
      ery.   Rest assured she manages to escape in the end.

942   _____.   Angélique in Love.   By Sergeanne Golon, pseud.
      New York: Bantam, 1968.
            First published in 1961, this account of the famous
      17th-century French countess finds her falling in love with
      her Canada-bound ship's captain.

943   Goodrich, Marcus.   Delilah.   New York: Farrar and Rine-
      hart, 1941.
            Saga of a U.S. destroyer in the undeclared naval war
      against Hitler's Atlantic U-boats, summer-fall, 1941.

944   Goodrich, Samuel Griswold.   A Home in the Sea; Or, The Ad-
      ventures of Philip Brusque--Designed to the Nature and
      Necessity of Government.   Philadelphia: Sorin and Ball,
      1845.
            Remembered--if at all--for his priggish "Parley" books
      written at a time when little juvenile literature was

available, Goodrich edited a gift-book annual in the 1820's
and "discovered" Hawthorne.

945   Goodridge-Roberts, Theodore.   Brothers of Peril.   By Theo-
      dore Roberts, pseud.   New York: Doubleday, Page, 1905.
          British fishermen struggle for control of early New-
      foundland.

946   Goudge, Elizabeth.   Green Dolphin Street.   New York: Coward,
      1944.
          A sailor loves a Lady.

947   Gould, John W.   Forecastle Yarns, by the Late John W. Gould.
      Edited by His Brother, Edward S. Gould.   Baltimore: Wil-
      liam Taylor, 1845.
          A product of the American merchant marine, Gould's
      stories, soggy with nautical lingo, were penned mostly be-
      fore his 21st birthday.   Published posthumously, this vol-
      ume brings some of these from the pages of leading Ameri-
      can magazines into a single collection.

948   Graham, Winston.   The Grove of Eagles.   Garden City, N. Y. :
      Doubleday, 1964.   y.
          The son of an English governor is captured by the
      Spanish in the early 17th-century and returns to share the
      fate of his friend Sir Walter Raleigh.

949   Gray, Ernest.   Surgeon's Mate: The Diary of John Knyveton,
      Surgeon in the British Fleet During the Seven Years' War,
      1756-1763.   London: Hale, 1942.
          Known in America as "The French and Indian War. "

950   Gray, Stanley.   Half That Glory.   New York: Macmillan,
      1941.   y.
          Initiation of a young runaway Virginian at sea during the
      Revolution.

951   Grayson, Charles, ed.   New Stories for Men.   Garden City,
      N. Y. :   Doubleday, 1940.
          Some nautical fiction here.

952   Greeley, Robert F.   The Child of the Islands; Or, The Ship-
      wrecked Gold Seekers.   New York: Stringer and Townsend,
      1850.

953   Green, E. Everett.   The Faith of Hilary Lovel.   London: Re-
      ligious Tract Society, 1904.
          The Spanish Armada.

954   _____.   Loyal Hearts and True.   London: Nelson, 1891.
          Elizabeth, her court, and the Armada.

955   Green, Fitzhugh.   Anchors Aweigh.   New York: D. Appleton,

1927. y.
    A story of the USN in the years immediately after World War I.

956   _____. Bob Bartlett, Master Mariner. New York: G. P. Putnam's Sons, 1929. y.

957   _____. Fitz, Jr. With the Fleet. New York: Brewer, Warren and Putnam, 1931. y.

958   _____. Fought for Annapolis. New York: D. Appleton, 1925. y.
    This, and the next two citations are a tale of student life at the U.S. Naval Academy.

959   _____. Hold 'em Navy. New York: D. Appleton, 1926. y.

960   _____. Midshipmen All. New York: D. Appleton, 1925. y.

961   _____. The Mystery of the Erik. New York: Appleton, 1923. y.
    The story of a missing ship.

962   _____. Won for the Fleet: A Story of Annapolis. New York: E. P. Dutton, 1922. y.
    A Naval Academy yarn.

963   Gregory, Charles. His Sovereign Lady. London: Melrose, 1919.
    Drake's pre-Armada adventures, including his circum-navigation with the Golden Hind.

964   Gregory, Jackson. Lords of the Coast. New York: Dodd, 1935.
    Tale of the settlement days along California coast.

965   Gregory, James. Nag's Head; Or, Two Months Among "The Bankers." A Story of Sea-Shore Life and Manners. Philadelphia: A. Hart, 1850.
    A look at the New England fishing industry before the Civil War. Valuable for its contemporary view.

966   Gribble, Leonard, ed. Famous Stories of the Sea and Ships. London: Barker, 1962.
    An anthology.

967   Grieve, A. H. G. Bilbao Blockade. London: Jenkins, 1939.
    A tale of the Royal Navy.

968   Griffin, Gwyn. Master of This Vessel. New York: Holt, 1961.
    A young British merchant marine officer suddenly finds

himself Acting Captain--in a hurricane no less!

969 _____. An Operational Necessity. New York: Putnam, 1967.
    What happens to the survivors of a freighter torpedoed in the Atlantic by a German U-boat during World War II.

970 Griffin, Henry F. The White Cockade. New York: Greystor 1941.
    How a Yankee sea captain saves a Frenchman at the time of the French Revolution.

971 Griffith, George. John Brown, Buccaneer. London: White, 1908.
    Pirates at work on the Spanish Main.

972 Griggs, P. G. Treachery at 40 Knots. Sydney, Australia: Shakespeare, 1946.
    World War II.

973 Grogan, Walter E. The King's Cause. London: Milne, 1909
    Prince Rupert's capture of Bristol and his later surrender to Fairfax during the English Civil War.

974 Groom, A. John P. Devil Fish. London: Ward, Lock, 195 y.
    Treasure and giant octopi.

975 Grubb, Davis. The Golden Sickle. New York: World, 1968.
    Ohio River pirates in search of treasure before the Civil War.

976 Gruppe, Henry. Truxton Cipher. New York: Simon and Schuster, 1973.
    A yarn concerning a shipwreck of 200 people, a secret naval code, and the commander of the Yankee destroyer Somerset.

977 Guillot, Robert. The Sea Rover. London: Oxford University Press, 1956.
    Pirates and privateers.

978 Gunn, James. Gibraltar Sabotage. London: Lutterworth, 1957.

979 Gunn, Neil M. Silver Darlings. London: Stewart, 1945.
    Scottish fishermen struggle to make a living in the North Sea.

- H -

980 Hackforth-Jones, Gilbert. The Greatest Fool. London:

Hodder & Stoughton, 1948.

981   _____. Green Sailors in the Caribbean. London: Hodder
        & Stoughton, 1958.

982   _____. One-One-One: Stories of the Navy. London: Hod-
        der & Stoughton, 1942.

983   _____. Sixteen Bells: Stories of The Royal Navy in Peace
        and War. London: Hodder & Stoughton, 1946.

984   _____. Submarine Alone: A Story of H. M. S. Steadfast.
        London: Hodder & Stoughton, 1943.

985   _____. Submarine Flotilla: A Chapter in the Life of an
        Obedient Servant. London: Hodder & Stoughton, 1940.

986   Hadath, John E. G. The Mystery of Black Pearl Island.
        New York: Stokes, 1933.

987   _____. Twenty Good Ships. London: Cassell, 1933.

988   Hains, Thornton Jenkins. Bahama Bill, Mate of the Wrecking
        Sloop "Sea Horse. " By Captain Mayn Clew Garnet, pseud.
        New York, ca. 1890. y.
            Hains, grandson of the distinguished Admiral Thornton
        Jenkins, wrote most of his novels under pseudonyms. This
        tale is set in 1812.
            Others by this author are:

989   _____. The Black Barque; A Tale of the Pirate Slave Ship
        "Gentle Hand" on Her Last African Cruise. Boston: L. C.
        Page, 1905. y.
            Reprinted in 1971 by Books for Libraries Press, Free-
        port, N. Y. ; "The Black Heritage Library Collection. "

990   _____. Capt. Gore's Courtship: His Narrative of the Af-
        fair of the Clipper "Conemaugh" and Loss of the "Countess
        of Warwick. " Philadelphia: J. B. Lippincott, 1896. y.

991   _____. The Chief Mate's Yarns. New York: Dillingham,
        1912. y.

992   _____. Cruise of the Petrel; A Story of 1812. New York:
        McClure, Phillips, 1901. y.

993   _____. Mr. Trunnell, Mate of the Ship Pirate. Boston:
        Lothrop, 1900. y.

994   _____. The Strife of the Sea. New York: Baker and
        Taylor, 1903. y.

995   _____. Tales of the South Seas. Portland, Me. : Brown

Thurston, 1894. y.

996 _____. The Voyage of the "Arrow" to the China Seas. It
Adventures and Perils, Including Its Capture by Sea Vultur
from the "Countess of Warwick," As Set Down by William
Gore, Chief Mate. By William Gore, pseud. Boston: L.
C. Page, 1906. y.
    This novel can be compared with the works of Clark
Russell.

997 _____. The White Ghost of Disaster; The Chief Mate's
Yarn. New York: G. W. Dillingham, 1912.

998 _____. The Windjammers. Philadelphia: J. B. Lippinco⬤
1899.

999 _____. The Wreck of the Conemaugh; Being a Record of
Some Events Set Down from the Notes of An English Baron
During the American War with Spain. Philadelphia: J. B
Lippincott, 1900.

1000 Hainsselin, Montagu T. The Curtain to Steel. London: Hod⬤
der & Stoughton, 1918.
    Adventure afloat in World War I.

1001 _____. Grand Fleet Days. London: Hodder & Stoughton,
1917.
    World War I.

1002 _____. In Peril of the Sea. London: Hodder & Stoughto⬤
1919.
    World War I.

1003 _____. In the Northern Mists: A Grand Fleet Chaplain's
Note Book. London: Hodder & Stoughton, 1916.
    World War I.

1004 _____. Naval Intelligence. London: Hodder & Stoughton,
1918.
    World War I.

1005 Haislip, Harvey. Escape from Java. Garden City, N. Y. :
Doubleday, 1962.
    Getting out of the Dutch East Indies in the early days
of World War II.

1016 _____. The Prize Master. Garden City, N. Y. : Doubleday
1959. y.
    A midshipman's success at bringing in a British ship
during the Revolution. Part Two of the "Haislip Trilogy.
Sequel to entry below, A Sailor Named Jones.

1007 _____. A Sailor Named Jones. Garden City, N. Y. : Dou-

bleday, 1957. y.
    Another tale of John Paul, and the Revolution afloat.

008   _____ . The Sea Road to Yorktown. Garden City, N. Y. :
    Doubleday, 1960. y.
        Revolutionary war naval operations culminating in the
    Yorktown campaign. Thomas Potter, a young patriot amongst
    the French in the Caribbean and Atlantic coast. Part Three
    of the "Haislip Trilogy. "

009   Hale, Edward Everett. The Man Without a Country. Boston:
    Ticknor and Fields, 1861.
        An ex-soldier is granted his wish, a curse that he
    never hear of America again, by being condemned to sail
    the seven seas aboard American warships, never being told
    of events in America. (Actor Cliff Robertson appeared in a
    memorable film version.)

010   Haley, George E. Cormorant Sails Again. London: Blackie,
    1955. y.

011   Hall, Basil. Fragments of Voyages and Travels. New edi-
    tion. London: Edward Moxon, 1856.
        First published by this Royal Navy captain in 1831.

012   Hall, Cyril. Sea Stories of Today. London: Blackie, 1943.
    An anthology.

013   Hall, J. F. Atlantic Interlude. London: Hutchinson, 1950.

014   Hall, James Norman. Doctor Dogbody's Leg. Boston: Little,
    Brown, 1940.
        Ten tales of a seagoing Munchausen, Doctor Dogbody,
    who was a surgeon for 50 years in His Majesty's Navy.

015   _____ . The Far Lands. Boston: Little, Brown, 1950.
        Story of the ancestors of Polynesian islands. Hall is
    best known for his collaborations with Nordoff on the Mu-
    tiny on the Bounty trilogy, listed below.

016   _____ . The Forgotten One. Boston: Little, Brown, 1952.

017   _____ . Lost Island. Boston: Little, Brown, 1944.
        What happens when the Americans decide to build an air
    base on a Pacific island during World War II.

018   _____ . The Tale of a Shipwreck. Boston: Houghton, Mif-
    flin, 1934.

019   Hall, Rubylea. The Great Tide. New York: Duell, 1947.
        Hurricane hits Florida; Pre-Civil War setting.

1020 _____ . Trial by Fire; A Tale of the Great Lakes.   Bos-
          ton: Small, Maynard, 1916.

1021 Halyard, Harry (pseud.).   The Doom of the Dolphin; Or, The
          Sorceress of the Sea. A Tale of Love, Intrigue, and Mys-
          tery.   Boston: F. Gleason, 1848.
               This author was an important figure in American pre-
          Civil War sea fiction.   His real name is yet unknown.

1022 _____ .   The Ocean Monarch; Or, The Ranger of the Gulf.
          A Mexican Romance.   Boston: F. Gleason, 1848.

1023 _____ .   The Peruvian Nun; Or, The Empress of the Ocean
          A Maritime Romance.   Boston: F. Gleason, 1848.

1024 _____ .   The Rover of the Reef; Or, The Nymph of the
          Nightingale.   A Romance of Massachusetts Bay.   Boston:
          F. Gleason, 1848.

1025 _____ .   The Warrior Queen; Or, The Buccaneer of the
          Brazos! A Romance of Mexico.   Boston: F. Gleason,
          1848.

1026 _____ .   Wharton the Whale-Killer! Or, The Pride of The
          Pacific. A Tale of the Ocean.   Boston: F. Gleason, 1848

1027 Hamilton, Bernard.   His Queen.   London: Hutchinson, 1927.
               The friendship of Queen Isabella and Christopher Colum
          bus.

1028 Hammond-Innes, Ralph.   Atlantic Fury.   By Hammond Innes,
          pseud.   New York: Knopf, 1962.
               Against the onslought of a hurricane, seamen must
          evacuate a British guide missile unit from Laerg in the
          Outer Hebrides.

1029 _____ .   Blue Ice.   By Hammond Innes, pseud.   New York
          Harper, 1949.
               A wild chase after a fugitive possessing vital secrets
          is carried on by yacht and overland into the mountains of
          Norway.

1030 _____ .   Gale Warning.   By Hammond Innes, pseud.   New
          York: Harper, 1948.
               Modern piracy predominates when three men, who esca
          death at the hands of Captain Halsey race the evil skipper
          and his men to find the lost cargo of silver aboard the ill-
          fated Trikkala.

1030a _____ .   Levkas Man.   New York: Knopf, 1971.   By Ham-
          mond Innes, pseud.
               A son seeks his father in the islands of the Indian Sea

1031 _____. The North Star. By Hammond Innes, pseud.
New York: Knopf, 1975.
A tale of passion and intrigue set aboard an obsolete
oil drilling rig in the North Sea.

1032 _____. The Strode Venturer. By Hammond Innes, pseud.
New York: Knopf, 1965.
The conflict of a London shipping company with the
people of the Maldives in the Indian Ocean.

1033 _____. The Survivors. By Hammond Innes, pseud. New
York: Harper, 1950.
A ship is run aground on an iceberg off Antarctica and
its survivors struggle to stay alive until they can be rescued.

1034 _____. The Wreck of the Mary Deare. By Hammond Innes,
pseud. New York: Knopf, 1956.
John Sands saw the Mary Deare briefly that dark night,
but going aboard the next morning, he found her deserted
and drifting dangerously close to the great reef area of the
Channel Islands. What was her great secret?

1035 Hampden, John, ed. Sea Stories. London: Nelson, 1933.
An anthology.

1036 Hanley, James. Half an Eye. London: Lane, 1937.

1037 _____. Sailor's Song. London: Nicholson, 1943.
Two tales of British nautical adventure.

1038 Hannay, J. O. Sea Battle. London: Methuen, 1948.
A sea story of World War II.

1039 Hannay, James. Biscuits and Grog: The Personal Remins-
cences of Percival Plug, R. N. , Late Midshipman of H. M. S.
Preposterous. By Percival Plug, pseud. 2nd ed. London:
John and D. A. Darling, 1848.
After his dismissal from the Royal Navy for insubordi-
nation, Hannay wrote the following tales in an effort to im-
mitate the stories of Marryat. Finding he could not achieve
success, he gave up nautical literature in favor of literary
criticism, a career in which he did quite well.

1040 _____. A Claret Cup. London [185?]
All of Hannay's tales, like Marryat's (q. v.), are based
on personal experiences, in these cases, the Mediterranean,
1840-1845.

1041 _____. Eustace Congers. London [185?]

1042 _____. King Dobbs: Sketches in Ultramarine. London:
Darling, 1849.
A humorous story dedicated to W. Thackeray.

1043   _____. Sand and Shells: Nautical Sketches. London:
        Darling, 1854.

1044   _____. Singleton Fontenoy. London [185?]

1045   Hardy, Adam. The Fox. New York: Pinacle, 1973.
                Seven volumes in this paperback series about 18th-cen
        tury British naval stinker George A. Fox are in print as
        of this writing: (1) The Press Gang, (2) Prize Money, (3
        Savage Siege, (4) Treasure Map, (5) Sailor's Blood, (6) Se
        of Gold, and (7) Court-Martial.

1046   Hardy, Thomas. The Trumpet Major. London: Macmillan,
        1880.
                Set at the time of the Napoleonic wars and includes
        Lord Nelson. A giant of literature, Hardy is known for
        much better writing than this!

1047   Hardy, William M. The Ship They Called the Fat Lady. Ne
        York: Dodd, Mead, 1969.
                The exploits of an old passenger liner, used as a sub-
        marine tender in Manila Bay during the early months of
        World War II.

1048   _____. Submarine Wolfpack. New York: Dodd, Mead,
        1061.
                American submarines attack a Japanese convoy in ear
        1942 deep in the Imperial Navy's home waters.

1049   _____. U. S. S. Mudskipper: The Submarine That Wrecke
        a Train. A Novel. New York: Dodd, Mead, 1960.
                An American submarine off the coast of Japan plots the
        destruction of an important freight train during the Second
        World War.

1050   Harper, Robert S. Trumpet in the Wilderness. New York:
        Mill, 1940.
                The building and operations of Commodore O. H. Perr
        Lake Erie squadron.

1051   Harrington, M. F. Sea Stories from Newfoundland. London:
        Bailey, 1959.
                An anthology.

1052   Harris, John. Close to the Wind. New York: Sloane, 1956.
                A debt-ridden Australian family, plus a murderer, flee
        Sydney for the islands.

1053   Harris, Laura B. Bride of the River. New York: Crowell,
        1956. y.
                Ante-bellum plantation bride changes her life style
        aboard Mississippi riverboat.

1054 Harrison, Frederick. <u>England Expects</u>. London: Christian
        Knowledge Society, 1904.
               Trafalgar.

1055 Hart, Joseph C. <u>Miriam Coffin; Or, The Whalefishermen</u>.
        2 Vols. New York: G. and C. Carvill, 1834.
               Valuable as a contemporary view of the American
        square-rigged whaling industry.

1056 Hartog, Jan de. <u>The Captain</u>. New York: Atheneum, 1966.
               The activities of a Dutch rescue tug assigned to sail
        with a British convoy on the World War II Murmansk run.
               Hartog, the son of a Dutch theologian, ran away to sea
        at age 10, served on ocean-going tugboats, and as a sub-
        inspector with the Amsterdam Harbor Police. One of Hol-
        land's earliest World War II resistance fighters, he escaped
        to England in 1940. After marrying the oldest daughter of
        J. B. Priestley, he settled down upon a houseboat to write
        these well-known tales of Netherlands nautical glory.

1057 _____. <u>The Lost Sea</u>. New York: Harper, 1951. y.
               A small Dutch boy is carried off by the "Black Skipper,"
        to become a "sea-mouse," a boy too small to go to sea
        legally.

1058 Haugaard, Erik C. <u>Orphans of the Wind</u>. Boston: Houghton,
        Mifflin, 1966. y.
               The adventures of a boy serving aboard an English brig
        during the American Civil War.

1059 Hawes, Charles B. <u>The Dark Frigate: Wherein Is Told the
        Story of Philip Marsham Who Lived in the Time of King
        Charles and Was Bred a Sailor</u>. Boston: Little, Brown,
        1923. y.
               The prize-winning story of a well-to-do 17th-century
        English lad who runs away to sea, is captured by pirates,
        and barely avoids hanging.
               Hawes was a noted writer of sea fiction for "boys" who
        in his work of magazine editorship took the time to be quite
        thorough in his research and writing. He died in 1923 at the
        early age of 33.

1060 _____. <u>The Great Quest; A Romance of 1826, Wherein Are
        Recorded the Experiences of Jonah Woods [who] Sailed for
        Cuba and the Gulf of Guinea</u>. Boston: Atlantic Monthly,
        1921. y.
               Excitement aboard American ships in the Caribbean and
        along the African coast.

1061 _____. <u>The Mutineers; A Tale of the Old Days at Sea and
        of Adventures in the Far East as Benjamin Lothrop Set It
        Down Some Sixty Years Ago</u>. Boston: Atlantic Monthly,
        1920. y.

An American merchantman sails from Salem to Canton in 1809 for trade and adventure.

1062 Haycox, Ernest. Long Storm. Boston: Little, Brown, 1946.
Long hastle to keep a boat operating along the Oregon coast.

1063 Hayes, Frederick W. Captain Kirke Webbe. London: Hutchinson, 1907.
A jolly good fellow who holds privateering commissions from the English and French during the Napoleonic wars; as the letters of marque were issued about the same time, he naturally sees no wrong in preying on the commerce of both sides at the same time!

1064 Hayes, John F. The Dangerous Cove. New York: Messner, 1960. y.
Two lads help an early Newfoundland village escape damage at the hands of visiting fishermen.

1065 Hayes, Nelson. Blockade. London: Lovat Dickson & Thompson, 1935.
Blockade running in the U.S. Civil War.

1066 _____. The Roof of the Wind. Garden City, N.Y.: Doubleday, 1961.
A man and his wife battle a storm at sea in their small boat off the Bahamas.

1067 Hays, Wilma P. Noko, Captive of Columbus. New York: Coward-McCann, 1967. y.
The early conflict between the Indians and the Spaniards.

1068 Haywood, O.F. Eastward the Sea. Boston: Nichols-Ellis, 1959. y.

1069 Heagney, H.J. Blockade Runner. New York: Longmans, Green, 1939. y.
Life aboard the C.S.S. Robert E. Lee.

1070 Heandi, pseud. From Snotty to Sub. London: Heinemann, 1918. y.
How a young British midshipman becomes a sub-lieutenant, circa World War I.

1071 Hebden, Mark. A Pride of Dolphins. New York: Harcourt, 1975.
Someone wants ex-Navy men for an about-to-be-hijacked submarine and James Venner infiltrates the crew for British Intelligence just as the Royal Navy discovers that the sub is carrying dangerous nerve gas.

1072 Heckert, Eleanor. The Golden Rock. Garden City, N.Y.:

Doubleday, 1971. y.
        A Continental supply agent tries to save St. Eustatious
island from destruction by the Royal Navy in 1781.

1073 Heckman, Richard D. , ed. Yankees Under Sail. Dublin,
        N. H. : Yankee Magazine, 1968.
            Forty sea tales from Yankee Magazine.

1074 Heggin, Thomas. Mister Roberts. Boston: Houghton, Mif-
        flin, 1946.
            Humorous tale of life on a Pacific fleet supply vessel
        during World War II, with a dramatic twist. (James Cag-
        ney and Henry Fonda starred in the movie version.) See
        Lederer's Ensign O'Toole and Me, below, for sequel.

1075 Heldman, B. Mutiny on Board the Leander. London: Low,
        1934.

1075a Hemingway, Ernest. Islands in the Stream. New York:
        Scribner's, 1970.
            The last part of this 3-part posthumous tale, "At Sea, "
        details the nautical search for some World War II German
        U-boat survivors.

1076 _____ . The Old Man and the Sea. New York: Scribner's,
        1952.
            Santiago, old man of heroic proportions, catches the
        great fish and loses it. Heavily allegorical statement of the
        tragic irony of man's fate. (Spencer Tracy starred in the
        movie version.)

1077 _____ . To Have and Have Not. New York: Scribner's,
        1940.
            Set amongst the 1930's charter-boat marlin-fishing
        crowd around Key West; artist-protagonist who had given in
        to wealth.

1078 Hendry, F. C. From All the Seas. London: Blackwood,
        1933.

1079 _____ . Land and Sea. London: Blackwood, 1939.

1080 _____ . Sail Ho! London: Oxford University Press, 1947.

1081 _____ . Ships and Men. London: Blackwood, 1946.

1082 Henty, George A. At Aboukir and Acre. London: Blackie,
        1899. y.
            Nelson and Abercrombie.
            Following several careers, Henty became a contributor
        to magazines in the late 1870's and from there reached out
        to become a leading adventure story writer for "boys. "
        His works are noted for their clear style, sobriety, and

what he himself called their "manly tone." His works are still widely read, primarily by older adults seeking to re-discover some of the better yarns they recall having en-joyed in their youth.

1083 _____. *By Conduct and Courage*. London: Blackie, 1905. y.
    Camperdown and the Battle of Cape St. Vincent, 1790-1798.

1084 _____. *Held Fast for England*. New York: Scribner's, 1891. y.
    The siege of Gibraltar, 1779-1783.

1085 _____. *In Greek Waters*. New York: Scribner's, 1892. y.
    The Greek War of Independence, 1821-1823.

1086 _____. *Under Drake's Flag*. London: Blackie, 1883. y.
    The circumnavigation with the *Golden Hind* and the de-feat of the Spanish Armada.

1087 _____. *When London Burned*. London: Blackie, 1895. y.
    The Anglo-Dutch naval wars and the Great Fire of Lon-don, 1664-1666.

1088 _____. *With Cochrane the Dauntless*. London: Blackie, 1897. y.
    Admiral Lord Cochrane's South American activities, 1819-1825.

1089 _____. *Yarns on the Beach*. London: Blackie, n. d. y.

1090 Hentz, Mrs. Caroline Lee (Whiting). *Linda; Or, The Young Pilot of the Belle Creole. A Tale of Southern Life.* Phila-delphia: A. Hart, 1850.
    Steamboat romance. Mrs. Hentz was a well-known and prolific romance writer of the 1850's.

1091 Hepburn, Andrew. *Letter of Marque*. Boston: Little, Brown, 1959.
    Privateering action during the War of 1812.

1092 Herber, William. *Tomorrow to Live*. New York: Coward, 1958.
    U.S. Marines in the Pacific in 1944, and their naval support.

1093 Herbert, Henry W. *Tales of the Spanish Seas*. New York: Burgess, Stringer, 1847.
    Pirates. An English emigrant to America in 1831, Herbert was an eccentric (he made public appearances

oddly dressed) who is still recalled for his sports writing,
especially his 1857 manual of horsemanship.

1094   Hergesheimer, Joseph.   Java Head.   New York: Grosset
       and Dunlap, 1919.
              Tale of China trading out of Nineteenth Century Salem,
       Mass. ; heydays of square-rigger shipping and a wife brought
       to Salem from the Far East.

1095   Hersey, John.   A Single Pebble.   New York: Alfred A.
       Knopf, 1956.
              An American engineer is sent to China in the 1920's to
       inspect the terrible Yangtze River for dam constructions.
       Remember China's rivers were at that time patrolled by an
       international fleet of gunboats, some of which are mentioned
       herein.

1096   _____.   Under the Eye of the Storm.   New York: Knopf,
       1967.
              Gripping tale of two men and their wives on a yawl en-
       countering a great storm.   High drama.

1097   Herzberg, Mas J. , comp.   Treasure Chest of Sea Stories.
       New York: Julian Messner, 1948.   y.
              A collection of short stories and book excerpts.

1098   Hewes, Agnes D.   Glory of the Seas.   New York: Knopf,
       1933.
              The clipper ship rivalry between Boston and New York
       in the mid-19th-century.

1099   _____.   Spice and the Devil's Cave.   New York: Knopf,
       1930.
              Vasco da Gama's route to India.

1100   _____.   Spice Ho! A Story of Discovery.   New York:
       Knopf, 1941.

1101   Hewett, George.   In Nelson's Day.   London: Wells Gardner,
       1891.

1102   Heyer, Georgette.   Beauvallet.   New York: Longmans, 1930.
              The English corsairs of Elizabeth I and the defeat of the
       Spanish Armada.

1103   Hibbert, Eleanor.   Spain for the Sovereigns.   By Jean Plaidy,
       pseud.   London: Hale, 1960.
              Isabella and Columbus.

1104   Hickling, Hugh.   Falconer's Voyage.   Boston: Houghton, Mif-
       flin, 1956.
              During the winter preceding the Normandy invasion, a
       group of landing craft is at practice in the tidal inlets of

Scotland.   This is the story of the captain of one of these,
Alexander Falconer, and of the last six months of his life
through D-Day.   First published in Britain as English Flotilla.

1105   Hicks, John B.   With the R.N.R.   By "Windlass," pseud.
       London: Hodder & Stoughton, 1917.
       World War I.

1106   Higginbotham, Robert E.   Wine for My Brothers.   New York:
       Rinehart, 1946.
            Life on a tanker plying between Texas and New York in
       January, 1942.

1107   Hill, Kay.   And Tomorrow the Stars: The Story of John Cabot.
       New York: Dodd, Mead, 1968.   y.
            A biographical novel exploring the life of the man who
       discovered North America in 1497 and was eventually lost
       at sea.

1108   Hill, R. A.   First Mate of the Henry Glass.   New York:
       Vantage, 1959.   y.
            A look at life in the American merchant marine.

1109   Hilton, James.   The Story of Dr. Wassell.   Boston: Little,
       Brown, 1943.
            A fictionalized account of the good physician's attempt
       to lead a body of wounded from Java to Australia in 1942.
       Gary Cooper portrayed the hero in the movie version.

1110   Hine, E. Curtiss.   Orlando Melville; Or, The Victims of the
       Pressgang.   A Tale of the Sea.   Boston: F. Gleason, 1848.
            A look at British impressment of American seamen, a
       contributor to the coming of war between America and Brit-
       ain in 1812.

1111   _____.   The Signal; Or, The King of Blue Isle, A Sea
       Tale.   Boston: F. Gleason, 1848.
            A pirate story.

1112   Hinkson, H. A.   The Splendid Knight.   London: White, 1905.
       Sir Walter Raleigh.

1113   Hiscock, Robin.   The Last Run South.   New York: Knopf,
       1958.
            Our title is the problem facing Canadian seaman James
       Collins as his ship sails for South America after his union
       looses a crippling strike.

1114   Hobart, Alice Tisdale.   Pidgin Cargo.   New York: Century,
       1929.
            A tale set along the unconquerable Yangtze River.
       Hobart is noted for several novels about China of the 1920's

with significant river themes, i. e. , Venture into Darkness,
1955, et al.

1115   Hobson, Richard Pearson.   Buck Jones at Annapolis.   New
       York: D. Appleton, 1907.   y.

1116   _____.   In Line of Duty.   New York: D. Appleton, 1910.
       y.

1117   Hocking, Charles.   Tommy Trevannion, Sea Cadet.   London:
       Stanmore, 1953.   y.

1118   Hocking, Joseph.   The Birthright.   New York: Dodd, 1897.
       Smuggling in 18th-century Cornwall.

1119   _____.   A Flame of Fire.   London: Cassell, 1903.
       Spain and England at the time of the Armada.

1120   Hodges, C. Walter.   The Overland Launch.   New York:
       Coward-McCann, 1970.
       A story centered around life boats and life-saving at
       sea off the English coast during the 19th-century.

1121   Hodgson, W. H.   The Boats of the Glen-Carrig.   London:
       Chapman, 1907.
       Adventures in the Pacific in the 16th-century as related
       by a retired mariner.

1122   Hoffman, Margaret J.   My Dear Cousin.   By Peggy Hoffman,
       pseud.   New York: Harcourt, 1970.   y.
       Baltimore and the War of 1812.   The romance between
       an American lady and a British diplomat based on an actual
       episode.

1123   Hogeboom, Amy, comp.   Tales from the High Seas.   New
       York: Lothrop, 1948.
       Contains a useful introduction by Charles Lee Lewis.

1124   Holland, C. G.   Perilous Seas.   London: Nelson, 1958.

1125   Holland, Rupert S.   The Boy Who Lived on London Bridge.
       Philadelphia: Macrae-Smith, 1938.   y.
       Another look at the Spanish Armada.

1126   _____.   Drake's Lad.   New York: Century, 1929.   y.
       The exploits of a boy who joined Drake for his circum-
       navigation aboard the Golden Hind.

1127   _____.   Yankee Ships in Pirate Waters.   Philadelphia:
       Macrae-Smith, 1931.   y.
       Early 19th-century trading voyages to the Orient and
       Great South Seas.

1128   Holling, Holling Clancy. <u>Paddle to-the-Sea</u>. New York:
       Houghton, 1941.

1129   Hollis, Gertrude. <u>Two Dover Boys</u>. London: Blackie, 1910.
       y.
             Two English lads adventure with Barbarossa in the
       Mediterranean, 1534-1535.

1130   Holmes, F. M. <u>Brave Sidney Somers</u>. London: Blackie,
       1910.   y.
             The adventures of a 16th-century English youth during
       a voyage to the Far East in a spice ship.

1131   Holmes, Robert. <u>Walter Greenway, Spy and Hero: His Life
       Story</u>. London: Blackwood, 1917.
             First World War exploits afloat and ashore.

1132   Holmes, Wilfred J. <u>Battle Stations</u>! By Alec Hudson, pseud.
       London and New York: Macmillan, 1939.
             When two of a squadron of five British submarines are
       sunk shortly after the opening of hostilities, the remaining
       three find themselves in the midst of a great naval battle.

1133   _____. <u>Enemy Sighted</u>! By Alec Hudson, pseud.   Lon-
       don and New York: Macmillan, 1940.
             For two months the British light cruiser <u>Perseus</u> and
       the submarine <u>Petard</u> cruised the Indian Ocean waiting to
       engage a pocket battleship. With the signal "Enemy Sighted,"
       the battle is on.

1134   _____. <u>Open Fire</u>. By Alec Hudson, pseud.   4 Vols. in 1.
       New York: Macmillan, 1942.
             In addition to the two novels cited above, the following
       two tales are included: <u>Rendezvous</u> (1941) and <u>Night Action</u>
       (1942).

1135   Hope, Robert. <u>Seamen and the Sea</u>. London: Harrap, 1965.

1136   Hopkins, William John. <u>The Clammer and the Submarine</u>.
       Boston: Houghton, Mifflin, 1917. y.
             World War I.

1137   _____. <u>She Blows</u>! And Sparm at That. Boston: Houghton
       Mifflin, 1922. y.
             Adventure on a three-year whaling voyage to the South
       Pacific in the 1870's.

1138   Horan, James D. <u>Seek Out and Destroy</u>. New York: Crown,
       1958. y.
             How the <u>C. S. S. Lee</u> attempted to destroy the Yankee
       whaling industry during the Civil War. Based on the feat
       of the real <u>C. S. S. Shenandoah</u>.

1139 Hough, Henry Beetle. <u>Long Anchorage</u>. New York: Apple-
      ton, 1947.
            A story set in New Bedford's whaling industry before
      the Civil War.

1140 _____. <u>The Port</u>. New York: Atheneum, 1963.

1141 Hough, S. B. <u>Seas South</u>. London: Hodder & Stoughton,
      1953.

1142 Houman, William. <u>Guns Along the Big Muddy</u>. New York:
      Arcadia House, 1962.
            A tale of mystery involving a Civil War river gunboat
      sent to meet a Yankee general.

1143 Household, Geoffrey. <u>Prisoner of the Indies: The Adventures
      of Miles Philips</u>. An Atlantic Press Book. Boston: Little,
      Brown, 1967.
            True-life adventures, based on facts related in the fa-
      mous travel books by Richard Hakluyt in the late 16th-cen-
      tury.

1144 Hovighurst, Walter. <u>The Quiet Shore</u>. New York: Macmil-
      lan, 1937.
            Fiction based on the changes of the Lake Erie shoreline
      during the late Nineteenth Century. Significant water im-
      pact.

1145 Howard, Clark. <u>The Doomsday Squad</u>. New York: Weybright
      & Talley, 1970.
            A six-man squad from an American submarine stages a
      suicidal attack on a strategic Japanese-held island during
      MacArthur's sweep to the Philippines in 1944.

1146 Howard, Edward G. G. <u>The Old Commodore</u>. 3 Vols. Lon-
      don: Bentley, 1837.

1147 _____. <u>Rattlin' the Reefer</u>. 3 Vols. London: Bentley,
      1836.
            The author's work was edited by Frederick Marryat.

1148 Howard, J. Hamilton. <u>In the Shadow of the Pines</u>. New
      York: Eaton and Mains, 1906.
            Civil War story about Virginia's Great Dismal Swamp.

1149 Howell, John. <u>The Man-o-War's Man</u>. By Bill Truck, pseud.
      London: Blackwood's, 1843.
            Royal Navy, circa 1830's.

1150 Hubbard, Lucien. <u>Rivers to the Sea</u>. New York: Simon and
      Schuster, 1942.
            Steamboating adventures along the Mississippi before
      the Civil War.

1151 Hughes, Richard. In Hazard. New York: Harper, 1938.
A ship and its crew are helpless in the fury of a hurricane.

1152 _____. The Innocent Voyage; Or, A High Wind in Jamaica.
New York: Harper, 1929. y.
How some pirates nearly go bananas due to a group of
children they have captured. A movie has been made of
this not all together pleasant tale.

1153 Hulme, Kathryn. Annie's Captain. Boston: Little, Brown,
1961. y.
The late 19th-century introduction of steam to merchantmen forms this story's background.

1154 Humes, Harold L. Men Die. New York: Random House,
1960.
After an explosion which kills everyone on an island
used by the USN as an ammunition dump except six Black
prisoners and their white guard, the author takes us back
through a series of flashbacks to tell us how those seven
came to be in their present situation.

1155 Hungerford, Edward B. Fighting Frigate. New York: Will-
cox & Follett, 1947. y.
The U.S.S. Constitution in the War of 1812.

1156 Hunt, Howard. East of Farewell. New York: Knopf, 1942.
Convoys and their escort in the World War II North Atlantic.

1157 Hunt, J. H. Leigh. Sir Ralph Esher. London: Henry Col-
burn, 1832.
An early British sea novel concerning the 17th-century
Anglo-Dutch wars at sea.

1158 Hunter, C. The Adventures of a Naval Officer. London:
Long, 1905.
Written by a Royal Navy captain.

1159 Hunter, Evan. Murder in the Navy. By Ed McBain, pseud.
New York: Fawcett, 1955.
Hunter is best known for numerous "Inner Sanctum
Mystery Novelettes."

1160 _____. The Sentries. By Ed McBain, pseud. New York:
Simon and Schuster, 1965.

1161 Hunter, Fred. The Spaniard; Or, The Cruiser of Long Island.
A Story of Sunshine and Sorrow. Boston: F. Gleason,
1849.
Another pirate yarn.

1162   Hunter, John. Captain Dack. London: Hurst, 1940.
       World War II.

1162a Huntford, Roland. Sea of Darkness. New York: Scribner's
       1975.
       A tale of Columbus written in a pseudo-15th-century
       style.

1163   Huntington, H. S. His Majesty's Sloop Diamond Head. Bos-
       ton: Houghton, Mifflin, 1904.
       An islet near Martinique which was armed by the Brit-
       ish as a sloop-of-war, 1802-1803.

1164   Huntley, H. V. The Memoirs of Peregrine Scramble. 2 Vols.
       London: Henry Colburn, 1849.
       Written by a Royal Navy captain.

1165   Hutchinson, Horace G. A Friend of Nelson. London: Long-
       mans, 1902.
       How Nelson turned a "blind eye" towards Copenhagen in
       1801 and thereby turned in another victory. Lady Hamilton
       does not appear enough to interfere with this good action
       story!

1166   Hyde, Lawrence. Captain Deadlock. Boston: Houghton, Mif-
       flin, 1968. y.
       A young fellow who simply cannot stay out of trouble en-
       counters pirates, road agents, and smugglers before being
       arrested as a spy in the days just after Trafalgar.

1167   _____. Under the Pirate Flag. Boston: Houghton, Mif-
       flin, 1965. y.
       A Nova Scotian lad finds himself a stowaway on board
       a dastardly pirate ship.

1168   Hyne, C. J. Cutcliffe. The Adventures of Captain Kettle.
       London: Blackie, 1898.
       The author wrote nine other Kettle stories. These in-
       clude, by date: The Further Adventures of Captain Kettle
       (1899); The Little Red Captain (1902); Captain Kettle, K. C. B.
       (1903); The Marriage of Captain Kettle (1912); Captain Ket-
       tle on the Warpath (1916); The Reverend Captain Kettle
       (1925); President Kettle (1928); Mister Kettle, Third Mate
       (1931); and Captain Kettle, Ambassador (1932).

1169   _____. The Captured Cruiser. London: Blackie [189?]

1170   _____. The Lost Continent. London: Blackie, 1900.
       The destruction of Atlantis well told.

1171   _____. McTodd. New York: Grosset & Dunlap, 1903.

1172   _____. Master of Fortune. New York: Dillingham, 1898.

1173 _____. Prince Rupert the Buccaneer. New York: Stokes, 1900.
    17th-century piracy on the Spanish Main.

1174 _____. Sandy Carmichael. London: Low, 1908.
    The South Seas adventures of two Englishmen who es-
    caped the 1745 Battle of Culloden.

1175 _____. The Trials of Commander McTurk. New York:
    Dutton, 1906.

- I -

1176 Icenhower, Joseph B. Mr. Midshipman Murdock and the
    Barbary Pirates. New York: Winston, 195?. y.
        An American midshipman, contemporary of Stephen
    Decatur, Jr., battles the Corsairs in 1803.

1177 _____. Mr. Murdock Takes Command. New York: Win-
    ston, 1958. y.
        When David Porter's flotilla captures a West Indian
    pirate ship, young Jim is made prizemaster with orders
    to sail the ship and her imprisoned crew home.

1178 _____. Submarine Rendezvous. New York: Winston, 195?.
    y.
        Three youths must get a scientist away from Manila to
    an American submarine hiding from the Japanese in Manila
    Bay.

1179 Inchfawn, F. Who Goes Over the Sea. London: Lutterworth,
    1953.

1180 The Indiaman. By a Bluejacket. 2 Vols. London: Richard
    Bentley, 1840.

1181 Ingraham, Joseph H. Black Ralph; Or, The Helmsman of
    Hurlgate. Boston: Edward P. Williams, 1844.
        Grandson of a noted shipbuilder, Ingraham spent much
    of his youth in the American merchant service before taking
    Holy Orders as an Episcopal minister. Better known for
    his religious romances, he nevertheless produced several
    sea stories and novels featuring swashbuckling pirates, heroic
    ladies, and young mates outstripping salty villains. His
    works should be compared with those by Justin Jones (q.v.)
    in their application of the Coopersonian yarn-spinning formu-
    la.

1182 _____. Bonfield; Or, The Outlaw of the Bermudas. New
    York: H. L. Williams, 1846.

1183 _____. The Brigantine; Or, Guitierro and the Castilian:

A Tale Both of Boston and Cuba. New York: Williams, 1847.

1184　_____. Captain Kyd: Or, The Wizard of the Sea. New York: Harper, 1839.

1185　_____. The Clipper-Yacht; Or, Moloch, The Money-Lender: A Tale of London and The Thames. Boston: H. L. Williams, 1845.

1186　_____. The Corsair of Casco Bay; Or, The Pilot's Daughter. Gardiner, Me: G. M. Atwood, 1844.

1187　_____. The Cruiser of the Mist. New York: Burgess, Stringer, 1845.

1188　_____. The Dancing Feather; Or, The Amateur Freebooters. A Romance of New York. Boston: George Roberts, 1842.
　　　　See Morris Graeme, below, for sequel.

1189　_____. Forrestal; Or, The Light of the Reef. A Romance of the Blue Waters. Boston: H. L. Williams, 1845.

1190　_____. Freemantle; Or, The Privateersman: A Nautical Romance of the Last War. Boston: George W. Redding, 1845.
　　　　See Norman; Or, The Privateersman's Bride, below, for sequel.

1191　_____. The Free-Trader; Or, The Cruiser of Narragansett Bay. New York: Williams Brothers, 1847.

1192　_____. Grace Weldon; Or, Frederica, The Bonnet-Girl. A Tale of Boston and Its Bay. Boston: H. L. Williams, 1845.

1193　_____. Jennette Alison; Or, The Young Strawberry Girl. A Tale of the Sea and the Shore. Boston: F. Gleason, 1848.

1194　_____. The Lady of the Gulf: A Romance of the City and the Seas. Boston: H. L. Williams, 1846.

1195　_____. Lafitte: The Pirate of the Gulf. New York: Harper and Brothers, 1836.
　　　　See Theodore, below, for sequel.

1196　_____. Mark Manly; Or, The Skipper's Lad. Boston: Publisher unknown, 1843?

1197　_____. Mate Burke; Or, The Foundlings of the Sea. New York: Burgess, Stringer, 1846.

1198   . The Midshipman; Or, The Corvette and Brigantine.
A Tale of Sea and Land. Boston: F. Gleason, 1844.

1199   . Morris Graeme; Or, The Cruise of the Sea-Slipper.
Boston: E. P. Williams, 1843.
A sequel to Dancing Feather, above.

1200   . The Mysterious State-Room. A Tale of the Mississippi. Boston: Gleason's, 1846.

1201   . Norman; Or, The Privateersman's Bride. Boston:
Yankee Office, 1845.
A sequel to Freemantle, above.

1202   . Rafael; Or, The Twice Condemned. A Tale of
Key West. Boston: H. L. Williams, 1845.

1203   . Ringold Graffit; Or, The Raftsman of the Susque-
hannah. A Tale of Pennsylvania. Boston: F. Gleason,
1847.

1204   . The Silver Ship. New York: H. L. Williams,
1846.

1205   . The Spanish Galleon; Or, The Pirate of the Mediterranean. A Romance of the Corsair Kidd. Boston: F.
Gleason, 1844.

1206   . The Spectre Steamer, and Other Tales. Boston:
United States Publishing Company, 1846.

1207   . Steel Belt; Or, The Three Masted Goleta. A Tale
of Boston Bay. Boston: Yankee Office, 1844.

1208   . The Surf Skiff; Or, The Heroine of the Kennebec.
New York: Williams Brothers, 1847.

1209   . Theodore; Or, The "Child of the Sea. " Being a
Sequel to the Novel of "Lafitte, The Pirate of the Gulf. "
E. P. Williams, 1844.
See Lafitte, above.

1210   . The Truce; Or, One and Off Soundings. A Tale of
the Coast of Maine. New York: Williams Brothers, 1847.

1211   . Wildash; Or, The Cruiser of the Capes. New
York: Williams Brothers, 1847.

1212   . The Wing of the Wind: A Novelette of the Sea.
New York: Burgess, Stringer, 1845.

1213   . Winwood; Or, The Fugitive of the Seas. New
York: H. L. Williams, 1846.

1214   Ingram, Archibald K.   The Greater Triumph: A Story of
       Osborne and Dartmouth.   London, 1911.
              Napoleonic Wars.

1215   Ingram, J. K.   The Pirate's Revenge; Or, A Tale of Don
       Pedro and Miss Lois Maynard.   Boston: Wright's Steam
       Power Press, 1845.

                                - J -

1216   Jack Tench, Or, The Midshipman Turned Idler.   By "Blow-
       hard," pseud.   London: W. Brittain, 1842.
              The Royal Navy of that day.

1217   Jack's Edition of Life at Sea; Or, The Jervian System in
       183-.   Being a Series of Letters by an Old Irish Captain
       of the Head to His Nephew.   Dublin: Samuel J. Machen,
       1843.
              Some humorous and some not-so-humorous accounts.
       The "Jervian System" comes from Sir John Jervis, an im-
       portant admiral of the Napoleonic period, known for fair
       but rather harsh discipline.

1218   Jackson, Basil.   Rage Under the Arctic.   New York: Norton,
       1974.
              The world's first submarine oil tanker, the North Star,
       voyaging from the north slope of Alaska to Boston under the
       polar ice is sabotaged and the resulting oil spill is catas-
       trophic.

1219   Jacobs, William W.   Castaways.   London: Methuen, 1934.
              A yachting trip around the world by a suddenly-rich
       bachelor.   The author's short story collections, with dates,
       include: Lady of the Barge (1902); Many Cargoes (1903);
       and the next four citations:

1220   _____ .   Cruises and Cargos.   London: Methuen, 1934.

1221   _____ .   Light Freights.   London: Methuen, 1951.

1222   _____ .   Sea Whispers.   London: Methuen, 1934.

1223   _____ .   Ship's Company.   London: Methuen, 1934.
              Tales of merchantmen.

1224   Jameson, Storm.   Lovely Ship.   New York: Alfred Knopf,
       1927.
              The story centers around the romances of the niece of
       a 19th-century British shipbuilder, who is himself attempt-
       ing to produce a "lovely ship." It's two sequels are Richer
       Dust (1931) and Voyage Home (1930).

1225   Jamieson, M. Attack. New York: William Morrow, 1940.
          A fictitious American aircraft carrier in action against
       a fictitious enemy bearing a strong resemblance to the
       Germans.

1226   Jane, Fred T.   Blake of the Rattlesnake.   London: Thacker,
       1895.

1227   _____. The Port Guard Ship: A Romance of the Present
       Day Navy.   London, 1900.

1228   _____. A Royal Bluejacket.   London, 1908.

1229   Janvier, Thomas Allibone. In Great Waters.   New York:
       Harper and Brothers, 1901.
          Longer tales; haunting romanticism presented as real-
       ism.

1230   _____. In the Sargasso Sea. A Novel.   New York:
       Harper and Brothers, 1898.
          A young sailor is trapped in a mass of old wrecks
       within the mysterious, entirely imaginative, Sargasso Sea.
       Has been compared to the lonely adventures of Robinson
       Crusoe.

1231   Jeans, T. T.   A Naval 'Venture': The War Story of an
       Armored Cruiser.   London: Blackie, 1917.
          World War I.

1232   Jeffries, R. G.   Brandy Ahoy! London: Hutchinson, 1954.
       y.

1233   _____. Brandy Goes a Cruising.   London: Hutchinson,
       1954.   y.

1234   Jenkins, Geoffrey.   A Bridge of Magpies.   New York: Put-
       nam, 1975.
          Three unusual characters attempt to retrieve a treasure
       from the hulk of an ocean liner sunk off the coast of south-
       west Africa.

1235   _____. A Grue of Ice.   New York: Viking, 1962.
          Captain Bruce Wetherby, former World War II Royal
       Navy officer, is kidnapped by a British whaling magnate who
       is bent upon the rediscovery of the "lost" Thompson Island,
       some 1600 miles south of Cape Town.

1236   _____. The Hollow Sea.   New York: Putnam, 1972.
          In 1909 the crack liner Waratah disappeared off the
       South African coast without a trace. In this Bermuda-
       Triangle type story, the grandson of the ship's first officer
       launches a dangerous quest for the mystery's solution.

1237 _____ . Hunter Killer. New York: Putnam, 1967.
      Bosses of the U.S. Seventh Fleet oppose the testing of
a new secret missile.

1238 _____ . The River of Diamonds. New York: Viking,
      1965.
      A group of mining experts plan to dredge diamonds from
the seafloor off the storm-ridden South African coast, but
are frustrated by a mysterious old prospector, who seems
to be in league with nature.

1239 _____ . Twist of Sand. New York: Viking, 1960.
      Off the southwest coast of Africa during World War II,
a Royal Navy submarine tracks down a secret new Nazi
U-boat propelled by nuclear energy.

1240 Jennings, John E. Banners Against the Wind. Boston:
      Little, Brown, 1954.
      Biographical novel of Dr. Samuel G. Howe.

1241 _____ . Chronicle of the Calypso, Clipper: A Novel of
      the Golden Days of the California Trade, of the Great
Ocean Race Around Cape Horn, of Clipper Ships, and of
Men--and Women--Who Sailed in Them. Boston: Little,
Brown, 1955.

1242 _____ . Coasts of Folly. By Joel Williams, pseud. New
      York: Reynal and Hitchcock, 1942.
      A tale of revolution in and off the shores of South
America in the early 19th-century.

1243 _____ . The Raider. New York: William Morrow, 1963.
      How the Royal Navy tracks down a raider, modeled
after S.M.S. Emden, during World War I.

1244 _____ . River to the West. Garden City, N.Y.: Double-
      day, 1948.
      A tale of John Jacob Astor's fur empire in the Pacific
Northwest.

1245 _____ . Rogue's Yarn. Boston: Little, Brown, 1953.
      American privateering in our Quasi-War with France.

1246 _____ . The Salem Frigate, A Novel. Garden City, N.Y.:
      Doubleday, 1946.
      War of 1812, and the War with Tripoli as the U.S.S.
Essex battles Barbary pirates.

1247 _____ . The Sea Eagles: A Story of the American Navy
      During the Revolution. Garden City, N.Y.: Doubleday,
1950.
      Centers around the activities of Joshua Barney.

1248 _____. The Tall Ships. New York: McGraw-Hill, 1959.
      Naval action in the War of 1812, blocking the British.

1249 _____. The Tide of Empire. By Bates Baldwin, pseud.
      New York: Holt, 1952.
           A young Irishman voyages to California in the days of
      the great gold rush.

1250 _____. The Wind in His Fists. New York: Holt, 1956.
           From galley slave to harem lord in 1571, the year of
      the great Christian/Moslem sea fight at Lepanto.

1251 Jennings, William D. The Sinking of the Sarah Diamond.
      New York: Erikkson, 1974.
           A young man inherits an old sailing barque at the time
      of the Civil War, charms an acerbic old sea captain into
      sailing her 5000 miles from South America to Boston, and
      survives numerous commerce raiders, storms, and escaped
      convicts from Devil's Island enroute.

1252 Jesse, F. Tennyson. Moonraker; Or, The Female Pirate and
      Her Friends. New York: Knopf, 1927.
           The author's Tom Fool (New York: Knopf, 1926), is an
      interesting tale of life in the contemporary Australian mer-
      chant service.

1253 Jessup, Richard. Sailor, A Novel. Boston: Little, Brown,
      1969.
           The career of an American bluejacket from his boyhood
      in Savannah, Ga., through World War I, and on into World
      War II, during which his ship is sunk by a U-boat in the
      Atlantic.

1254 Jewett, Sara Orne. The Tory Lover. Boston: Houghton,
      Mifflin, 1902.
           Features John Paul Jones, in the Revolution.

1255 John, Elliott. An Old Sailor's Legacy. By The Reformer,
      pseud. Boston: Usher and Strickland, 1841.

1256 Johns, Cecil S. With Gold and Steel. New York: Lane,
      1917.
           A French-sponsored treasure hunt for a wrecked Spanish
      galleon in the 1500's.

1257 Johnson, Victor H. Strike the Lutine Bell. New York: Duell,
      1958.
           A merchantman under American registry is overloaded
      with ore and in serious danger of not reaching her Baltimore
      landing when a serious storm comes up along the Atlantic
      coast.

1258 Johnston, Mary. Croatan. Boston: Little, Brown, 1923.

A tale woven around the voyage to and settlement of
Roanoke Island under the direction of Sir Walter Raleigh
and John White.

1259   _____. 1492. Boston: Little, Brown, 1922.
            A Christopher Columbus story based on an account of
his famous 3-ship expedition to the New World.

1260   _____. Sir Mortimer. New York: Houghton, Mifflin,
            1903.
            English naval supremacy in the time of Elizabeth I.

1261   _____. Slave Ship. Boston: Little, Brown, 1924.
            How a young Jacobite, David Scott, becomes involved
in the 18th-century slave trade between Africa and Virginia.

1262   _____. To Have and To Hold. New York: Houghton,
            Mifflin, 1900.
            Published in England under the title By Order of the
Company, this tale recounts the story of a young English
maid-of-honor who flees to Virginia in 1621, marries an
adventuresome swordsman, and becomes involved in all
sorts of occurrences afloat and ashore.

1263   Johnston, Ronald. The Angry Ocean. New York: Harcourt,
       1966.

1264   _____. Collision Ahead. Garden City, N.Y.: Doubleday,
            1965.
            Two tankers collide--one on her maiden voyage. Pub-
lished in Britain the previous year by the London firm of
Collins under the title, Disaster at Dungeness.

1265   _____. The Wrecking of Offshore Five. New York: Har-
            court, 1968.
            When a North Sea oil rig is hit by a company tanker
and collapses into the brimey, two men are trapped inside
beneath the waves.

1266   Jonas, Carl. Beachhead on the Wind. Boston: Little, Brown,
       1945.
       World War II in the Aleutians.

1267   Jones, Justin. Big Dick, The King of the Negroes; Or, Vir-
       tue and Vice Contrasted. A Romance of High and Low Life
       in Boston. By Harry Hazel, pseud. Boston: The "Star
       Spangled" Office, 1846.
       Jones created numerous romantic novels during the
mid-19th-century, heavy in adventure with moralizing
touches; excellent examples of period melodrama. Compare
with Joseph Holt Ingraham's works, above. Other stories
include:

1268 _____. The Corsair; Or, The Foundling of the Sea; An American Romance. By Harry Hazel, pseud. Boston: F. Gleason, 1846.

1269 _____. The Doomed Ship; Or, The Wreck of the Arctic Regions. By Harry Hazel, pseud. Philadelphia: T. B. Peterson and Bros., 1864?

1270 _____. The Flying Yankee; Or, The Cruise of the Clippers. A Tale of Privateering in the War of 1812-15. By Harry Hazel, pseud. New York: H. Long, c.1853.

1271 _____. Fourpe Tap; Or, The Middy of the Macedonian. In Which Is Contained the Concluding Incidents in the Career of "Big Dick," The King of the Negroes. By Harry Hazel, pseud. Boston: Jones, 1847.
 See Big Dick, above.

1272 _____. Gallant Tom; Or, The Perils of a Sailor, Ashore and Afloat. By Thomas Peckett, pseud. Boston, 1850.

1273 _____. Harry Helm; Or, The Cruise of the Bloodhound. By Harry Hazel, pseud. Philadelphia: T. B. Peterson, c.1870.

1274 _____. Harry Tempest; Or, The Pirate's Protege. An American Nautical Romance. By Harry Hazel, pseud. New York: H. Long and Brothers, c.1853.

1275 _____. The King's Cruisers; Or, The Rebel and the Rover. By Harry Hazel, pseud. New York: E. D. Long, 1845.

1276 _____. Mad Jack and Gentleman Jack; Or, The Last Cruise of Old Ironsides Around the World. A Tale of Adventures by Sea and Land. By Harry Hazel, pseud. Boston: The "Star Spangled Banner" Office, 1850.

1277 _____. The Pirate's Daughter; Or, The Rovers of the Atlantic. By Harry Hazel, pseud. Boston: The "Star Spangled Banner" Office, 1847.

1278 _____. The Pirate's Son, A Sea Novel of Great Interest. By Harry Hazel, pseud. Philadelphia: T. B. Peterson, 1855.

1279 _____. The Rebel and the Rover; Or, The King's Cruisers. A Thrilling Tale of the Sea. By Harry Hazel, pseud. Philadelphia: T. B. Peterson and Brothers, 1865.

1280 _____. Yankee Jack; Or, The Perils of a Privateersman. By Harry Hazel, pseud. New York: H. Long and Brother, c.1852.

1281   Jones, Nard. Swift Flows the River. New York: Dodd,
       1940.
              Ante-bellum taming of the Columbia River area.

1282   Jordan, H. R. Anchor Comes Back. London: Musson, 1939.

1283   _____. Blue Water Dwelling. London: Hodder & Stoughton,
       1949.

1284   _____. Found at Sea. London: Hodder & Stoughton, 1957.

1285   _____. No Charts for the Job. London: Hodder &
       Stoughton, 1958.

1286   _____. Overdue--Arrived. London: Hodder & Stoughton,
       1953.

1287   _____. Sea Way Only. London: Hodder & Stoughton, 1941.

1288   _____. Ship by Herself. London: Hodder & Stoughton,
       1938.

1289   _____. Spoiling for Mischief. London: Hodder & Stought-
       on, 1958.
              All of this author's adventure stories take place in the
       20th-century.

1290   Judah, Charles B. Tom Bone. New York: William Morrow,
       1944.
              Romance is mixed with the 17th-century slave trade.

1291   Judson, Edward Z. C. Andros, the Free Rover; Or, The
       Pirate's Daughter. By Ned Buntline, pseud. New York:
       Beadle and Adams, 1883.
              "Ned Buntline" Judson ran away to sea as a small boy
       and joined the U. S. Navy. He received a commission from
       the lower deck in 1838 for his rescue efforts in an East
       River drowning. Resigning from the fleet in 1842, he trav-
       elled in the West and eventually elected for the career of
       an "author," becoming the primary figure in the development
       of the sensational "dime novel."
              Borrowing from Cooper, Marryat, and contemporary
       magazine pulp-fiction writers (to say nothing of the showman-
       likes of P. T. Barnum), Judson synthesized prototypes of
       the "American Hero" in both his nautical and western tales.
       His mass production "formula style" and the low cost of his
       product created an important new reading market among
       Civil War soldiers.
              After the "unpleasantness," Judson introduced and pop-
       ularized "Buffalo Bill" Cody and as noted in the Wyatt Earp
       saga, handed out his famous "Buntline Special" revolvers
       for a maximum of publicity. His yarns were as popular in
       their day as the male-oriented paperback adventure series

is today and in fact, there is a direct relationship between
the two.   Both Judson and Aarons (q. v.) for example, have
relied on formula plots and characters, low-cost production,
and mass-marketing.

Only a few large libraries today possess copies of Judson's pen, but if you should happen across one of these,
perhaps in an attic or an antique shop, it would be worth
your time to peruse it.   While "racy" and sensational for
the times, you will undoubtedly soon reach the conclusion
that it is rather dull by present standards.   You would undoubtedly find it interesting in comparison with, say,
Cooper's The Pilot (q. v.).

A rascal of the first order, Judson's eccentricity in
and out of print secures his place in literature.   For serious
students and "nostalgia buffs" we cite a number of his many
nautical tales here:

1292   _____.   The Black Avenger of the Spanish Main; Or, The
Fiend of Blood.   A Thrilling Tale of Buccaneer Times.   By
Ned Buntline, pseud.   Boston: F. Gleason, 1847.

1293   _____.   The Buccaneer's Daughter.   By Ned Buntline,
pseud.   New York: Dick and Fitzgerald, 1850.

1294   _____.   Captain Sea Waif, The Privateer.   By Ned Bunt-
line, pseud.   New York: Beadle and Adams, 1879.
"Beadle's Dime Library. "
Reprinted as Seawaif.

1295   _____.   Clarence Rhett; Or, The Cruise of a Privateer:
An American Sea Story.   By Ned Buntline, pseud.   New
York: Brady, 1866.
Appeared later in the "New York Boys' Library Series, "
1878.

1296   _____.   Cruisings, Afloat and Ashore, from the Private
Log of Ned Buntline.   By Ned Buntline, pseud.   New York:
Robert Craighead, 1848.
Featuring "The Captain's Pig, " or "Eating the Captain's
Pig, " a popular tale of the mid-19th-century.   Also issued
as Navigator Ned; see below.

1297   _____.   Darrow the Floating Detective; Or, The Shadowed
Buccaneer.   By Ned Buntline, pseud.   New York: Street
and Smith, 1889.
Numerous variations appeared in magazines of the time.

1298   _____.   Dashing Charlie, The Texas Whirlwind.   By Ned
Buntline, pseud.   New York: Street and Smith, 1890.
Published in an earlier form in Street and Smith's New
York Weekly, 1872.

1299   _____.   Elfrida, The Red Rover's Daughter, A New

Mystery of New York. By Ned Buntline, pseud. New
York: F. Brady, 1860.
   Re-published in 1883 as Andros; see above.

1300   . English Tom; Or, The Smuggler's Secret: A Tale
of Ship and Shore. By Ned Buntline, pseud. New York:
Cauldwell, Southworth and Whitney, 1862.

1301   . Ethelbert, The Shell-Hunter; Or, The Ocean Chase.
By Ned Buntline, pseud. New York: Beadle and Adams,
1884.
   See The Shell-Hunter, below, for earlier version.

1302   . Fire Feather, The Buccaneer King. By Ned Buntline, pseud. New York: Beadle and Adams, 1890.
   Had been serialized in Beadle's Weekly, 1885.

1303   . Hank Cringle, The One Armed Buccaneer. By Ned
Buntline, pseud. New York: Street and Smith, 1890.
   Had been serialized in Street and Smith's New York
Weekly, 1871.

1304   . Harry Bluff, The Reefer; Or, Love and Glory on
the Sea. By Ned Buntline, pseud. New York: Street and
Smith, 1890.
   Had been serialized in Street and Smith's New York
Weekly, 1882.

1305   . Harry Halyard's Ruin: A True Tale for the In-
temperate to Read. By Ned Buntline, pseud. Boston:
Star Spangled Banner Office, c. 1850-70.
   Appeared under various titles during this period.

1306   . The Ice-King; Or, The Fate of the Lost Steamer.
A Fanciful Tale of the Far North. By Ned Buntline, pseud.
Boston: Williams, 1848.
   Later re-issued as a "DeWitt Ten-Cent Romance,"
1869.

1307   . The King of the Sea: A Tale of the Fearless and
Free. By Ned Buntline, pseud. Boston: Flag of Our
Union Office, 1847.
   Numerous versions and reprintings during the Civil War
period.

1308   . The Last of the Buccaneers: A Yarn of the Eighteenth Century. By Ned Buntline, pseud. New York: Dick
and Fitzgerald, c. 1850.
   Evidence exists that it appeared in other forms in the
1840's.

1309   . Long Tom Dart, The Yankee Privateer: A New
Naval Story of the War of 1812. By Ned Buntline, pseud.

New York: Beadle and Adams, 1891.

1310 _____. The Man-O'Wars Man's Grudge: A Romance of the Revolution. By Ned Buntline, pseud. New York: Brady, 1858.

1311 _____. Matanzas: Or, A Brother's Revenge: A Tale of Florida. By Ned Buntline, pseud. Boston: Williams, 1848.

1312 _____. Morgan; Or, The Knight of the Black Flag: A Strange Story of Bygone Times. By Ned Buntline, pseud. New York: Brady, 1860.

1313 _____. The Naval Detective's Chase; Or, Nick, The Steeple Climber. A Thrilling Tale of Real Life. By Ned Buntline, pseud. New York: Street and Smith, 1889.
      Had been serialized earlier in Street and Smith's New York Weekly, 1886.

1314 _____. Navigator Ned; Or, He Would Be Captain. By Ned Buntline, pseud. New York: Street and Smith, 1890.
      Had been serialized in Street and Smith's New York Weekly, 1876.

1315 _____. Old Nick of the Swamp. By Ned Buntline, pseud. New York: George Munro, c. 1870.

1316 _____. The Queen of the Sea; Or, Our Lady of the Ocean. A Tale of Life, Strife and Chivalry. By Ned Buntline, pseud. Boston: F. Gleason, 1848.

1317 _____. Rattlesnake Ned, The Terror of the Sea. By Ned Buntline, pseud. New York: Street and Smith, 1890.
      Privateers and the American Navy.

1318 _____. The Red Privateer; Or, The Midshipman Rover: A Romance of 1812. By Ned Buntline, pseud. New York: Beadle and Adams, 1890.

1319 _____. Red Ralph, The River Rover; Or, The Brother's Revenge. By Ned Buntline, pseud. New York: Beadle and Adams, 1884.

1320 _____. The Red Revenger; Or, The Pirate King of the Floridas: A Romance of the Gulf and Its Islands. By Ned Buntline, pseud. Boston: Gleason, 1847.
      Appeared under various titles throughout the 1840-80 period.

1321 _____. The Revenge Officer's Triumph; Or, The Sunken Treasure. By Ned Buntline, pseud. New York: Street and Smith, 1891.
      Had appeared as serial in Street and Smith's Weekly,

1884, under "The Smuggler's Daughter. "

1322 _____. The Sea Bandit; Or, The Queen of the Isles: A Tale of the Antilles. By Ned Buntline, pseud. New York: Beadle and Adams, 1870.

1323 _____. The Sea Spy; Or, Mortimor Monk, The Hunchback Millionaire. A Tale of Sea and Land Fifty Years Ago. By Ned Buntline, pseud. New York: Beadle and Adams, 1890.

1324 _____. Seawaif; Or, The Terror of the Coast: A Tale of Privateering in 1776. By Ned Buntline, pseud. New York: Brady, 1859.
Had appeared in the New York Mercury, 1859.

1325 _____. The Shell-Hunter; Or, An Ocean Love-Chase: A Romance of Love and Sea. By Ned Buntline, pseud. New York: Brady, c. 1858.
See Ethelbert, the Shell-Hunter, above, for later version.

1326 _____. The Smuggler; Or, The Skipper's Crime: A Tale of Ship and Shore. By Ned Buntline, pseud. New York: F. Starr, 1871.

1327 _____. The White Cruiser; Or, The Fate of the Unheard-of: A Tale of Land and Sea; of Crime and Mystery. By Ned Buntline, pseud. New York: Garrett, 1853.

- K -

1328 Kaler, James O. Armed Ship America; Or, When We Sailed from Salem. Boston: Estes, 1900. y.
A tale of privateering in the War of 1812. Kaler, who also wrote under the pen names of Otis James or Jack Brace, marketed over 100 novels for "young people" based on historical themes.

1329 _____. Captain Tom, the Privateersman of the Armed Brig Chasseur, As Set Down by Stephen Burton of Baltimore. Boston: Estes, 1899. y.
There was a Captain Tom [Boyle] and a privateer Chasseur both operating out of Baltimore during the War of 1812; the story is much better told in Kenneth Roberts' The Lively Lady (q. v.).

1330 _____. A Cruise with Paul Jones. New York: Burt, 1898. y.
The commerce-raiding voyages of 1778.

1331 _____. Lobster Catchers: A Story of the Coast of Maine. New York: Dutton, 1900. y.

Useful presentation of the lobsterman's craft under sail.

1332 _____. A Struggle for Freedom. New York: Burt, 1909.
      y.
      Washington's "whaleboat navy" in 1776.

1333 _____. With Porter in the Essex. New York: Wilde,
      1901. y.
      The commodore's famous voyage to the South Pacific
      during the War of 1812.

1334 _____. With Preble at Tripoli. New York: Wilde, 1900.
      y.
      As much a tale of Stephen Decatur, Jr., and the frigate
      Constitution as crusty old Edward Preble, who was in charg
      during much of our first war with the Barbary Pirates.

1335 _____. With Rodgers on the President: The Story of the
      Cruise Wherein the Flagship Fired the First Hostile Shot
      in the War with Great Britain for the Rights of American
      Seamen. Boston: Wilde, 1903. y.
      The U.S.S. President badly damaged H.M.S. Little Belt
      in unofficial reprisal for the 1807 Chesapeake Affair. Both
      incidents greatly contributed to the bad feelings leading to
      the War of 1812.

1336 Karig, Walter and Horace V. Bird. Don't Tread on Me. New
      York: Rinehart, 1954. y.
      A fictional view of the American Revolution afloat; much
      on John Paul Jones.

1337 Kauffman, R. W. Barbary Bo. Philadelphia: Penn, 1929.
      y.
      Adventure afloat during our first war with Tripoli.

1338 Kaye, Margaret M. Trade Wind. New York: Coward-Mc-
      Cann, 1964.
      An American girl in early 19th-century Zanzibar falls
      in love with a renegade English slave trader.

1339 Keaton, George W. Mutiny in the Caribbean. London: Bell,
      1940.
      British nautical adventure.

1340 Kelsey, Frederick. Prowlers of the Deep. London: Harrap,
      1942.
      British underseas operations in World War II.

1341 Kemp, Peter, ed. A Hundred Years of Sea Stories. London:
      Cassell, 1955.
      An anthology.

1341a Kendall, Oswald. Romance of the Martin Connor. Boston:

Houghton, Mifflin, 1916.
      An American tramp steamer makes an adventurous
voyage up the Amazon, in defiance of a tyrannical rubber
barron.

1342 Kennedy, Sara B. <u>Joscelyn Cheshire</u>. Garden City, N. Y.:
      Doubleday, 1901. y.
            During the Revolution the hero is captured and sent
      to a British prison ship, from whence he escapes.

1343 Kent, Alexander. <u>Blaze of Glory</u>. By Douglas Reeman,
      pseud. London: Hutchinson, 1975.
            A tale of a World War II British escort carrier on the
      Murmansk run and of a young Royal Navy pilot assigned to
      her. American title below, no. 1366a.

1344 _____. <u>Command a King's Ship</u>. New York: Putnam,
      1973.
            Capt. Richard Bolitho is given command of the firgate
      Undine and sent to the Indian Ocean to protect British inter-
      ests in the years after the American Revolution.   Kent,
      whose craft comments appear elsewhere in this compilation,
      writes all of his 18th-century tales under his own name and
      has adopted the pen name of Douglas Reeman for those set
      in the 20th-century. His Bolitho series follows closely in
      the wake of Forester's Hornblower set quality-wise and
      when completed should stand beside it.

1345 _____. <u>The Deep Silence</u>. By Douglas Reeman, pseud.
      New York: Putnam, 1968.
            The British nuclear submarine <u>Termeraire</u> is sent to
      find a damaged American SSN "somewhere" in the Far East.
      In the process, her skipper manages to run afoul of the
      Chinese Communists.

1346 _____. <u>The Destroyers</u>. By Douglas Reeman, pseud.
      New York: Putnam, 1974.
            How a "scrapyard flotilla" of recommissioned British
      World War I destroyers batter the defenses of Nazi-occupied
      Europe on the eve of D-Day.

1347 _____. <u>Dive in the Sun</u>. By Douglas Reeman, pseud. Lon-
      don: Hutchinson, 1961.
            A British midget submarine attacks a giant floating dock
      in the Adriatic during World War II.

1348 _____. <u>Enemy in Sight</u>. New York: Putnam, 1970.
            Commanding a British 74-gun ship-of-the-line, Bolitho
      fights a mighty engagement in the Caribbean in 1794.

1349 _____. <u>The Flag Captain</u>. New York: Putnam, 1971.
            As flag captain to a crusty old admiral in 1797, Bolitho
      must find a way to get his squadron into the Mediterranean.

1350   _____. Form Line of Battle. New York: Putnam, 1969.
Captain Bolitho operates under Lord Hood off Toulon in the
epic days of the Napoleonic Wars.

1351   _____. Go In and Sink. By Douglas Reeman, psued.
London: Hutchinson, 1973.
         Published in America simultaneously by the New York
firm of Putnam under the title His Majesty's U-boat, this
novel, based on a true story, tells how a British captain,
employing a captured German submarine, lands Allied agent
in Italy, sinks German supply submarines, and destroys an
Axis weapons factory during World War II.

1352   _____. The Greatest Enemy. By Douglas Reeman, pseud.
New York: Putnam, 1971.
         The trials of a British frigate during the World War II
Battle of the Atlantic.

1353   _____. H. M. S. Saracen. By Douglas Reeman, pseud.
New York: Putnam, 1966.
         A British officer and a monitor see service in both
World Wars.

1354   _____. High Water. By Douglas Reeman, pseud. London: Hutchinson, 1959.
         An ex-Royal Navy officer becomes more deeply involved
in a smuggling operation than originally planned.

1355   _____. The Hostile Shore. By Douglas Reeman, pseud.
London: Hutchinson, 1962.
         Employing a pearling schooner, a man searches for his
sister lost in the New Hebrides.

1356   _____. The Last Raider. By Douglas Reeman, pseud.
London: Hutchinson, 1963.
         A disguised German cruiser is loose on the high seas
preying on British shipping at the close of World War I.

1357   _____. The Path of the Storm. By Douglas Reeman,
pseud. New York: Putnam, 1968.
         The captain of H. S. S. Hibiscus is unwelcome at Payen-
ham, where he is supposed to prepare a naval base.

1358   _____. A Prayer for the Ship. By Douglas Reeman, pseud.
London: Hutchinson, 1958.
         The author's first novel; a semi-autobiographical account
of British MTB's in the English Channel during World War
II.   Published in America by Putnam in 1973.

1359   _____. The Pride and the Anguish. By Douglas Reeman,
pseud. New York: Putnam, 1969.
         The daring exploits of H. M. river gunboat Porcupine,
fighting against overwhelming odds to escape the 1942

Singapore disaster.

1360 _____. Rendezvous--South Atlantic. By Douglas Reeman, pseud. New York: Putnam, 1972.
How the S. S. Benbecula was converted into an Armed Merchant Cruiser and while guarding a convoy in World War II is forced to engage a heavy German surface ship. Based on a true incident from the early days of the Big War.

1361 _____. Richard Bolitho--Midshipman. London: Hutchinson, 1975.
The adventures of the hero aboard H. M. S. Gorgon, his second ship, at age 16, off the coast of West Africa. Slavers, pirates, and a wild attack on a fortress.

1362 _____. Send a Gunboat. By Douglas Reeman, pseud. New York: Putnam, 1960.
How Captain Justin Rolfe, R. N. , redeemed the honor of an old China river gunboat on its last dangerous mission in the post-World War II China Seas.

1363 _____. Signal-Close Action. New York: Putnam, 1974.
In 1798 Commodore Richard Bolitho hoists his broad pendant over a small squadron and is sent to the Mediterranean to check on rumors of a huge French armada armed with the latest type of artillery.

1364 _____. Sloop of War. New York: Putnam, 1972.
How Richard Bolitho, in command of H. M. S. Sparrow, participates in the American Revolution at sea, including the Battle of the Chesapeake.

1365 _____. To Glory We Steer. New York: Putnam, 1968.
How young Captain Richard Bolitho wins the loyalty of his crew and takes part in the Battle of the Saintes in 1783.

1366 _____. To Risks Unknown. By Douglas Reeman, pseud. London: Hutchinson, 1969.
A battle-weary British officer must shape up the Corvette Thistle for the World War II Battle of the Atlantic; somewhat similar to Nicholas Mensarrat's The Cruel Sea (q. v.).

1366a _____. Winged Escort. By Douglas Reeman, pseud. New York: Putnam, 1975.
Expected to perform miracles, H. M. escort carrier Growler sails the seas of World War II from grueling runs to Murmansk to the horrors of Kamikaze attacks in the Indian Ocean.

1367 _____. With Blood and Iron. By Douglas Reeman, pseud. New York: Putnam, 1965.
A look at the closing days of the World War II Battle

of the Atlantic from the viewpoint of a German U-boat commander.

1368   Kent, Louise A. He Went with Champlain. Boston: Houghton, Mifflin, 1959. y.
An English interpreter sails with Samuel de Champlain on his Quebec-founding expedition of 1604.

1369   . He Went with Christopher Columbus. Boston: Houghton, Mifflin, 1940. y.
An English deckboy on the first great voyage.

1370   . He Went with Drake. Boston: Houghton, Mifflin, 1961. y.
"Piracy, " spies, and the Spanish Armada.

1371   . He Went with John Paul Jones. Boston: Houghton, Mifflin, 1958. y.
Based on the diary of a young lad actually kept aboard the Bonhomme Richard.

1372   . He Went with Magellan. Boston: Houghton, Mifflin, 1943. y.
A young sailor takes part in the Spaniard's epic first circumnavigation of the globe.

1373   . He Went with Vasco de Gama. Boston: Houghton, Mifflin, 1938. y.
Two boys join in the first Portuguese voyage around Africa to India.

1374   Kent, Madeleine F. The Corsair. Garden City, N. Y. : Doubleday, 1955.
Jean Lafitte, pirate and patriot. Yul Brynner played the title role in the movie version with Charlton Heston as Andrew Jackson.

1375   Kentfield, Calvin. Alchemist's Voyage: An Adventure. New York: Harcourt, 1955.
Two young men sign aboard a liberty ship looking for excitement during the dark early days of American involvement in World War II.

1376   . All Men Are Mariners, A Novel. New York: McGraw-Hill, 1962.

1377   . The Angel and the Sailor. New York: McGraw-Hill, 1957.

1378   . The Great Wandering Goony Bird: Ten Short Stories. New York: Random House, 1963.
Each of these yarns concerns a person or event aboard the rusty old freighter S. S. Lever's Wife as she wallows

down the sea lanes of the world.

1379 Kenyon, Frank W. Emma. New York: Crowell, 1955.
      Lady Hamilton and Lord Nelson.

1380 Kerr, Lawrence. The Dauntless Goes Home. London: Ox-
      ford University Press, 1960.

1381 _____. Dauntless in Danger. London: Oxford University
      Press, 1954.

1382 _____, ed. On (and Under) the Ocean Wave. London:
      Nelson, 1933.

1383 Kingsley, Charles. Westward Ho! New York: Macmillan,
      1896.
            The rivalry of England and Spain during the reign of
      Elizabeth I and the exploits of the British "pirates, "
      Drake, Raleigh, Hawkins, and Grenville. This author's
      Hereward the Wake and Two Years Ago also contain glimpses
      of the sea.
            Kingsley, the son of a Devonshire vicar, was a militant
      Christian Socialist whose purpose in writing this work, born
      of the Crimean War, was to "preach muscular Christianity. "
      Westward Ho is not read for that purpose anymore, but
      rather as a good sea yarn.

1384 Kingston, William H. G. The Cruise of the Frolic. London:
      1860. y.
            British merchant adventure. This writer, one of the
      most popular "boy" adventure authors of the late 19th-cen-
      tury, wrote the same kinds of things in almost the same
      style as George Henty (q. v.). Unlike Henty, however, he is
      almost forgotten today. Of his more than 150 books, we
      have selected these sea tales for citation here:

1385 _____. Kidnapping in the Pacific. London: Griffith,
      1879. y.

1386 _____. Mark Seaworth. London: Griffith [189?]

1387 _____. The Missing Ship. London: Griffith [189?]

1388 _____. Peter the Whaler. London: Griffith [189?]

1389 _____. Salt Water. London: Griffith [189?]

1390 _____. The Three Admirals. London: Griffith [189?]

1391 _____. The Three Commanders. London: Griffith [189?]

1392 _____. The Three Lieutenants. London: Griffith [189?]

1393 _____ . The Three Midshipmen. London: Griffith [189?]

1394 _____ . Will Weatherhelm. London: Griffith [189?]

1395 Kipling, Rudyard. Captains Courageous. New York: 1897.
High adventures of New England fishermen, featuring
the initiation of a spoiled millionaire into manhood at sea.

1396 _____ . From Sea to Sea. 2 Vols. London: Macmillan,
1900.

1397 _____ . With the Night Mail. New York: Doubleday, Page
1909.
The author wrote a number of short stories dealing with
the sea.

1398 Kirk, Michael. All Other Perils. Garden City, N. Y.:
Doubleday, 1975.
Someone attempts to keep the S. S. Pelamis from sailing
with a load of vital oil pipeline.

1399 Kitchen, Frederick H. The Lost Naval Papers. By Bennet
Copplestone, pseud. London: Murray, 1917.

1400 _____ . The Secret of the Navy. By Bennet Copplestone,
pseud. London: Murray, 1918.

1401 Klingman, L. and G. Green. His Majesty Okeefe. New
York: Charles Scribner's Sons, 1950.
A nautical adventure of 19th-century seamen set in the
Great South Seas.

1402 Klitgaard, K. The Deep. New York: Doubleday, Doran,
1941.

1403 Knight, A. L. A Sea-King's Midshipmen. London: Murray,
1900. y.
Napoleonic era.

1404 Knight, Frank E. Albatross Comes Home. London: Hollis
& Carter, 1949. y.

1405 _____ . Clippers to China. Adapted ed. London: Macmillan, 1960. y.

1406 _____ . Remember Vera Cruz! New York: Dial Press,
1966. y.
How a young 16th-century English sailor-boy grows up
amidst sea fights, pirates, slaving, and sundry escapes.

1407 _____ . The Sea Chest. London: Collins, 1965. y.
A collection of tales.

1408   _____. The Slaver's Apprentice. New York: St. Martin's,
            1961. y.
                 A moralistic yarn of slavery between Africa and Ameri-
            ca as carried on by English merchants in the late 18th-cen-
            tury.

1409   Knight, Ruth A. The Search for Galleon's Gold. New York:
            McGraw-Hill, 1960. y.
                 A 1950's search for sunken treasure supposedly aboard
            the Florencia, flagship of the Spanish Armada which was
            wrecked in Tobemory Harbour, Scotland.

1410   Knopp, Lloyd. The Drift. Garden City, N. Y. : Doubleday,
            1969.
                 Adventure in the Sargasso Sea.

1411   Knox, William "Bill." Blueback. Garden City, N. Y. : Double-
            day, 1969.
                 Carrick of Scotland's Fishery Protection Service finds
            himself involved with a pretty girl, poachers, moonshiners,
            and a killer using an ultra-modern hydrafoil.

1412   _____. Devilweed. Garden City, N. Y. : Doubleday, 1966.
                 Carrick investigates the mystery of an abandoned cabin
            cruiser with her safe untouched and £ 15, 000.

1413   _____. Figurehead. Garden City, N. Y. : Doubleday, 1968.
                 A lady scientist leads Officer Carrick and the men of
            the Marlin in search of a sea serpent.

1414   _____. Seafire. Garden City, N. Y. : Doubleday, 1971.
                 Carrick takes command of his first ship, the research
            vessel Clavella, and must seek the solution to a strange,
            small form of sea life destroying everything in its path.

1415   _____. Stormtide. Garden City, N. Y. : Doubleday, 1973.
                 The feud between a rough gang of shark hunters and
            local fishermen over the mysterious death of a young girl
            must be smoothed over by Carrick and co.

1416   _____. Whitewater. Garden City, N. Y. : Doubleday, 1974.
                 The wedding flag at Port MacFarlane opens an investiga-
            tion into blackmail and murder for Carrick and the men of
            the Fishery Protection cruiser Marlin.

1417   Konigsberger, Hans. The Golden Keys. Chicago: Rand-
            McNally, 1956. y.
                 A courageous Dutch lad takes part in the 16th-century
            Barents sea expedition aimed at finding a northwest passage
            to the Indies.

1418   Krey, Otto. Ship's Cook and Baker. New York: Cornell
            Maritime, 1941.

1419 Kringle, Matthew. Borrower of the Deep; Or, Master of Salty Spray. A Romance. Boston: H. Williams, 1849.

1420 _____. Captain Saturday; Or, The Rise of the Waif. A Nautical Tale. Boston: Williams, 1847.

1421 _____. Ride Out; Or, Lost at Sea. A Nautical Romance of the Caribbean. Boston: Williams, 1845.

1422 Kristobel, John. Flotilla Sam; Or, The Pirate's Daughter Announces a Turnabout. A Tale of the Sea. New York: Hulme, 1868.

1423 _____. Widening Courses; Or, Re-taking the Caribbean. New York: Hulme, 1869.
        More pirates.

1424 Kropp, Lloyd. The Drift. Garden City, N. Y.: Doubleday, 1969.

1425 Kubeck, James. The Calendar Epic. New York: Putnam, 1956.
        The lives and loves of merchantman's crews during World War II.

1426 Kyle, Duncan. A Raft of Swords. New York: St. Martin's, 1974.
        A desperate race is on to defuse six nuclear missiles on the ocean floor.

1427 _____. The Suvarov Adventure. New York: St. Martin's, 1974.
        The Russians wish to recover a long-immersed but still lethal missile off Vancouver Island and a British torpedo recovery expert is forced to do the work.

1428 Kyne, Peter Bernard. Cappy Ricks Comes Back. New York: Grosset and Dunlap, c. 1934. y.
        Sequel to no. 1430.

1429 _____. Cappy Ricks; Or, The Subjugation of Matt Peasley. New York: Grosset and Dunlap, c. 1916. y.
        The struggle for mastery between the head of a large Pacific coast shipping concern and a young skipper in his employ.

1430 _____. Cappy Ricks Retires. New York: Cosmopolitan, 1922. y.
        Retired from the Blue Star Navigation Company, the hero is unable to keep out of the shipping game.

1431 _____. Cappy Ricks Special. New York: H. O. Kinsey, 1935. y.

1432   _____. Captain Scroggs; Or, The Green Pea Pirates.
        New York: Grosset and Dunlap, c. 1919. y.

1433   _____. Comrades of the Storm. New York: Grosset and
        Dunlap, c. 1933. y.

1434   _____. The Gringo Privateer and Island of Desire. New
        York: Cosmopolitan, 1931. y.

1435   _____. Tide of Empire. New York: Cosmopolitan, 1928.
        y.
            Adventure during the California Gold Rush days.

                              - L -

1436   LaFarge, Oliver. Long Pennant. Boston: Houghton, Mifflin,
        1933.
            War of 1812; privateering in the Caribbean.

1437   Laing, Alexander Kinnan. Dr. Scarlett; A Narrative of His
        Mysterious Behavior in the East. New York: Farrar and
        Rinehart, c. 1936.

1438   _____. Jonathan Eagle. Boston: Little, Brown, 1955.
            Saga of a lone youth cast ashore somewhere along the
        Connecticut seacoast in November 1785 and who grows up
        on land and at sea finally commanding his own sloop, tak-
        ing a load of cannon to aid in the 1801 election of Tom
        Jefferson.

1439   _____. Matthew Early. New York: Duell, 1957.
            A sea romance in which a 19th-century New England sea
        captain pursues his love, Barbara, as far as London and
        Malta before giving up the chase.

1440   _____. Sea Witch; A Narrative of the Experiences of
        Roger Murray and Others in an American Clipper Ship
        During the Years 1846-56. New York: Farrar and Rine-
        hart, 1933.

1441   Lake, James. No Ordinary Seaman. London: Barker, 1957.

1442   Lamb, G. F. Modern Adventures at Sea. London: Harrap,
        1970.
            An anthology.

1443   Lancaster, Bruce. Blind Journey. Boston: Little, Brown,
        1953.
            A nautical secret mission is ordered by Ben Franklin
        during the Revolution involving the transport of French gold
        from Paris to America.

1444 _____, and Lowell Brentano. <u>Bride of a Thousand Cedars</u>. New York: Stokes, 1939.
Bermuda and the blockade runners of the American Civil War.

1445 Lancaster, William J. C. <u>Across the Spanish Main</u>. By Harry Collingwood, pseud. London: Blackie, 1906. y.
West Indian adventures in the days of Drake.

1446 _____. <u>Blue and Grey</u>. By Harry Collingwood, pseud. London: Cassell, 1908. y.
<u>Alabama</u> vs. <u>Kersarge</u>.

1447 _____. <u>Congo Rovers</u>. By Harry Collingwood, pseud. New York: Scribner's, [189?]

1448 _____. <u>The Log of a Privateersman</u>. By Harry Collingwood, pseud. London: Blackie, 1897. y.

1449 _____. <u>The Log of the Flying Fish</u>. By Harry Collingwood, pseud. New York: Scribner's [189?]

1450 _____. <u>A Middy of the Slave Squadron</u>. By Harry Collingwood, pseud. London: Blackie, 1910. y.
A British midshipman's adventures ashore and afloat chasing slavers in Africa in 1822.

1451 _____. <u>The Missing Merchantman</u>. By Harry Collingwood, pseud. New York: Scribner's [189?] y.

1452 _____. <u>Pirate Island</u>. By Harry Collingwood, pseud. New York: Scribner's [189?] y.

1453 _____. <u>The Rover's Secret</u>. By Harry Collingwood, pseud. New York: Scribner's [189?] y.

1454 _____. <u>The Strange Cruise</u>. By Harry Collingwood, pseud. London: Blackie, 1938. y.

1455 _____. <u>The Voyage of the Aurora</u>. By Harry Collingwood, pseud. London: Low, 1934. y.

1456 Lane, Carl D. <u>The Fire Raft</u>. Boston: Little, Brown, 1951. y.
A youth accompanies his uncle down the Mississippi in 1811 aboard the first steamboat on those waters.

1457 _____. <u>The Fleet in the Forest</u>. New York: Coward, 1943. y.
War of 1812, Battle of Lake Erie; how Admiral Perry got his ships.

1458 Lane, Margaret. <u>A Night at Sea</u>. New York: Knopf, 1964.

1459 Lang, William. A Sea-Lawyer's Log. London: Methuen,
      1919.

1460 Langdon, Franklin C. S.S. Silverspray. By John Langdon,
      pseud. New York: Macmillan, 1958.
            A description of an American C-2's routine voyage be-
      tween San Francisco and Manila written in "semi-documen-
      tary" style and giving a useful picture of the day-to-day
      operation of a modern cargo vessel.

1461 Larson, Jean R. Jack Tar. New York: Macrae-Smith,
      1970. y.
            A seaman in Victoria's navy is discharged--for, of all
      things, serving salt in his captain's tea! Bloody funny read-
      ing.

1462 Laskier, Frank. Log Book. New York: Scribner's, 1943.
            Life sketch of a British merchant sailor from his early
      days through early World War II, when loss of a leg forces
      him ashore.

1463 _____. The Siren Sea. London: Allen, 1953.
            Action in 'The Devil's Triangle. "

1464 Lathem, Jean L. Drake, the Man They Called Pirate. New
      York: Harper & Row, 1960. y.
            A biographical novel concerning the English sea captain,
      1540-1596.

1465 _____. The Voyager: The Story of James Cook. New
      York: Harper & Row, 1970. y.
            A biographical novel.

1466 Lathrop, West. Unwilling Pirate. New York: Random House,
      1951.
            Pirates on Cape Cod in 1720.

1467 Lavallee, David. Event 1000. New York: Holt, 1971.
            Rescuing the crew of an atomic submarine sunk on the
      bottom off New London.

1468 Law, C. R. Tales of the Old Ocean. London: Warne, 1942.

1468a Lawson, Robert N. Beloved Shipmates. London, 1924.

1469 _____. Capt. Kidd's Cat: Being the True and Dolorous
      Chronicle of Wm. Kidd, Gent. , and Merchant of New York,
      Late Captain [of] The Adventure Galley .... Boston: Little,
      Brown, 1956. y.
            Piracy; talking cat. Excellent for children.

1470 _____. I Discover Columbus; A True Chronicle of the
      Great Admiral and His Finding of the New World, Narrated

by the Venerable Parrot Aurelio, Who Shared the Glorious
Venture.   Boston: Little, Brown, 1941.   y.

1471   Lederer, William J.   Ensign O'Toole and Me.   New York:
       Morrow, 1957.
              Sequel to T. Heggin's Mister Roberts, entered above.

1472   Lee, Jonathan.   The Fate of the Grosvenor.   New York:
       Covici, 1938.
              Published in Britain as The Wreck of the Grosvenor,
       this novel tells of the loss of an East Indiaman on the coast
       of South Africa and how her survivors make their way over-
       land to Capetown.

1473   Lee-Hamilton, Eugene.   The Romance of the Fountain.   New
       York: Fisher Unwin, 1905.
              Historical fiction of the story of Ponce de Leon, the
       discovery of Florida and the pursuit of the fountain of youth.

1474   LeGallienne, Richard.   Pieces of Eight.   New York: Double-
       day, Page, 1918.
              Similar in themes to Robert Louis Stevenson's Treasure
       Island, (q. v.).

1475   _____.   There Was a Ship.   New York: Doubleday, 1930.
       y.
              Young Dionysus Lancaster, after wasting time at the
       court of Charles II, joins the jovial Captain Thunder in a
       voyage to the West Indies in search of sunken Spanish
       treasure.

1476   Leggett, William.   Naval Stories.   New York: G. and C.
       Carvill, 1834.
              Leggett was a USN midshipman from 1822-1826 and
       later an associate editor of William Cullen Bryant's New
       York Evening Post.   He was the first of the Dana breed of
       well-educated men who, having gone to sea, returned to
       expose for correction the harsh life of American merchant
       and naval sailors.   Read in this light, his works are yet
       useful as damning social history.

1477   _____.   Tales and Sketches.   By a Country Schoolmaster.
       New York: Harper, 1929.
              Contains three of his early sea stories.

1478   Leighton, Robert.   Cap'n Nat's Treasure.   London: S. W.
       Partridge, 1902.
              A tale of Liverpool harbor in 1776.

1479   _____.   The Golden Galleon.   London: Blackie, 1898.
              Sir Richard Grenville and the famous fight of the
       Revenge.

1480   .   Hurrah for the Spanish Main. London: Melrose,
        1904.
            Drake's third voyage to Darien, starting from Plymouth
        in 1572.

1481   .   With Nelson in Command. London: Melrose, 1905.

1482 Leighton, Margaret. The Sword and the Compass: The Far-
        flung Adventures of Captain John Smith.   Boston: Houghton,
        Mifflin, 1951. y.
            Biographical novel of Jamestown's champion.

1483 LeMay, Alan. Pelican Coast. New York: Doubleday, 1929.
            New Orleans piracy before the War of 1812.

1484 Lenski, Lois. Ocean-Born Marcy. Philadelphia: Lippincott,
        1939. y.
            A girl born on a pirate ship is spared, along with her
        mother, by the swashbuckling captain. As she grows older,
        Marcy and Mom settle ashore at Londonderry, New Hamp-
        shire, where the author then proceeds to present a panoramic
        picture of that city's 18th-century waterfront.

1485 Leslie, Mrs. Doris (Oppenheim). Royal William: The Story
        of a Democrat. London and New York: Macmillan, 1941.
            A biographical novel concerning the life of William IV,
        England's "sailor-king. "

1486 Lesterman, John. The Adventures of a Trafalgar Lad. New
        York: Harcourt, 1927. y.

1487   .   A Sailor of Napoleon. New York: Harcourt, 1927.
            A look at Nelson and Trafalgar from the French view-
        point.

1488 Lever, Charles. Charles O'Malley. London: Routledge [189?]

1489   .   The O'Donoghue. London: Routledge, 1845.
            This tale virtually ends with the Bantry Bay disaster to
        the French Fleet in 1796.

1490 Levy, Mimi C. Whaleboat Warriors. New York: Viking
        Press, 1963. y.
            The Revolution; whaleboats pressed into patriotic serv-
        ice.

1491 Lewis, Alfred Henry. The Story of John Paul Jones, An His-
        torical Romance. By Don Quinn, pseud. New York: Dill-
        ingham, c. 1906.

1492 Leyland, E. Jolly Roger Sails Again. London: Hutchinson,
        1955. y.
            Piracy.

1493 Lieber, Joel. How the Fishes Live. New York: McKay,
      1967.
            A rather grisly tale in which ten survivors of an At-
      lantic shipwreck drift about without food or water and are
      eventually forced to murder and eat each other until only
      two are left.

1494 "Lieut. Hatchway, R. N. , " pseud. The Greenwich Pensioners.
      3 Vols. London: Henry Colburn, 1834.
            Grennwich was the Royal Navy home.

1495 Life in a Whale Ship; Or, The Sports and Adventures of a
      Leading Oarsman. Written by an American Author and
      Based Upon the Cruise of an American Whale Ship in the
      South Atlantic and Indian Ocean, During the Years 1836-7-8.
      Boston: Redding, 1846.
            Believed to have been first published in 1841 at the
      Boston firm of J. N. Bradley and Co. with printing at the
      Office of the Daily Mail and Universal Yankee Station.

1496 The Life of a Midshipman: A Tale Founded on Facts and
      Intended to Correct and Injudicious Predilection in Boys
      For the Life of a Sailor. London: Henry Colburn, 1829.

1497 Lincoln, Joseph Crosby. Blowing Clear. New York: Apple-
      ton, 1930. y.
            Lincoln's novels, primarily set along Cape Cod, pre-
      sent accurate portraits of local color characters. Others
      include:

1498 _____. Cap'n Dan's Daughter. New York: Appleton,
      1914. y.
            A fortune inherited by this Cape Cod seaman arouses the
      social ambitions of his superficial wife, bringing about prob-
      lems which his daughter must solve.

1499 _____. Cap'n Eric: A Story of the Coast. New York:
      Appleton, c. 1920. y.
            A tale of Cape Cod, in which three jolly sea captains
      are forced into matrimony to escape the hardships of their
      own housekeeping.

1500 _____. Cap'n Warren's Wards. New York: Burt, c. 1911.
      y.
            A Cape Cod skipper inherits some children.

1501 _____. Christmas Days. New York: Coward, 1938. y.
            A Cape Cod family at sea from 1850-70.

1502 _____. Doctor Nye of North Constable. A Novel. New
      York: Appleton, 1923. y.
            A tale of heroic high-mindedness.

1503   _____.   Extricating Obadiah.   New York: Appleton, 1917.
            A kindly and simple sea cook inherits $12,000 and
            trouble therewith.

1504   _____.   Fair Harbor; A Novel.   New York: D. Appleton,
            1922.   y.

1505   _____.   Head Tide.   New York: D. Appleton, 1932.   y.

1506   _____.   Keziah Coffin.   New York: Appleton, 1909.   y.

1507   _____.   Mr. Pratt, A Novel.   New York: Burt, c. 1900.
            y.
            Two boys elect to live by "The Nautical Code."

1508   _____.   Mr. Pratt's Patients.   New York: Appleton,
            1913.   y.

1509   _____.   Out of the Fog.   New York: Appleton, 1940.   y.

1510   _____.   Partners of the Tide.   New York: A. S. Barnes,
            1905.   y.
            A boy adopted by two maiden kinswomen adventures on
            a coasting schooner and in the wrecking business.

1511   _____.   Portygee.   A Novel.   New York: D. Appleton,
            1920.   y.

1512   _____.   Queer Judson.   New York: Appleton, 1925.   y.

1513   _____.   The Rise of Roscoe Paine.   New York: Appleton,
            1912.   y.

1514   _____.   Rugged Water.   New York: Appleton, c. 1924.   y.
            A boy's rise from obscurity to chief of the life saving
            station at Setuckit on Cape Cod.

1515   _____.   "Shavings!" A Novel.   New York: Appleton,
            1918.   y.

1516   _____.   Silas Bradford's Boy.   New York: Appleton,
            1928.   y.

1517   _____.   Storm Signals.   New York: Appleton, 1935.   y.
            Cape Cod during the Civil War.

1518   _____, and Freeman.   The New Hope.   New York:
            Coward, 1941.   y.
            The story of a Cape Cod privateer in the War of 1812.

1519   Little, George.   The American Cruiser; Or, The Two Mess-
            mates.   A Tale of the Last War.   Boston: Waite, Pierce,
            1846.

Another mid-19th-century pro-American view of the War of 1812. Little was a privateersman during that conflict.

1520 Livingstone, D. S. Full and By. New York: Dodge, 1936.
Sailing ship adventures at the turn of the century.

1521 Lloyd, Christopher, ed. The Englishmen and the Sea: An Anthology. London: Allen, 1946.

1522 Lobdell, Helen. The King's Snare. Boston: Houghton, Mifflin, 1955.
Sir Walter Raleigh's expedition to the Orinoco in South America and his subsequent fall from the grace of James I --a fall which proved fatal.

1523 Lockhart, John G., ed. The Mary Celeste and Other Strange Tales of the Sea. London: Hart-Davis, 1963.

1524 _____. Strange Tales of the Seven Seas. London: Allen, 1934.

1524a Lockley, Ronald. The Seal-Woman. New York: Bradbury, 1975.
While searching for U-boats off Ireland during World War II, a naval intelligence officer spots a girl swimming with a school of seals.

1525 Lodwick, John. The Cradle of Neptune. London: Heinemann, 1946.

1526 Lofts, Norah Robinson. Colin Lowrie. New York: A. A. Knopf, 1939.

1527 _____. Here Was a Man: A Romantic History of Sir Walter Raleigh, His Voyages, His Discoveries, and His Queen. New York: Alfred A. Knopf, 1936.

1528 Lomask, Milton. Ships Boy with Magellan. Garden City, N.Y.: Doubleday, 1960. y.
A lad escapes a nasty uncle only to find himself embarked on the famous three-year sea voyage of circumnavigation.

1529 London, Jack. The Cruise of the Dazzler. New York: Century, 1902. New York: Platt and Munk, 1960.
Excellent tale of juvenile initiation. London himself had gone to sea at age 16. His tales are heavily autobiographical.

1530 _____. Jerry of the Islands. New York: Macmillan, 1917.
Noteworthy dog story based on "real adventures" in the Solomon Islands.

1531   _____ . The Mutiny of the Elsinore. New York: Macmil-
          lan, 1914.
               A landlubber initiated into rough sea life of the Pacific
          leaves to sail a ship, quell a mutiny.

1532   _____ . The Sea Wolf. New York: Macmillan, 1903.
               Numerous editions. Passionate and savage tale--in the
          London style--of rugged men of the sea based on author's
          own stark sailor life. A superman Norwegian sealer is
          portrayed here. Often reprinted.

1533   _____ . South Sea Tales. New York: Macmillan, 1925.
               Although planning a circumnavigation in his handmade
          boat, our author got only as far as the Solomon Islands,
          and reveals in fictional form the life he lived in that primi-
          tive paradise under the Southern Cross.

1534   Long, Edward L. David Farragut, Boy Midshipman. New
          York: Bobbs Merrill, 1950. y.

1535   _____ . Gold Ballast. New York: Ward Lock, 1952.

1536   Long, Ernest L. Abaft 'Midships. London: Ward, Lock,
          1949. y.

1537   _____ . Anchor's Aweigh. London: Ward, Lock, 1941.
          y.

1538   _____ . As They Rise. London: Ward, Lock, 1938. y.

1539   _____ . Captain Flynn. London: Ward, Lock, 1939. y.
               Naval action in the 18th-century.

1540   _____ . Captain Flynn Returns. London: Ward, Lock,
          1950. y.

1541   _____ . Carried Away. London: Ward, Lock, 1945. y.

1542   _____ . Clear Round. London: Ward, Lock, 1946. y.

1543   _____ . Crew of L. C. London: Ward, Lock, 1947. y.

1544   _____ . Cumsha Cruise. London: Ward, Lock, 1941. y.

1545   _____ . Curtailed Voyage. London: Ward, Lock, 1957.
          y.

1546   _____ . Deep Channels. London: Ward, Lock, 1944. y.

1547   _____ . Double Banked. London: Ward, Lock, 1941. y.

1548   _____ . Flynn. London: Ward, Lock, 1940. y.

1549 _____. Flynn of the Martagon. London: Ward, Lock,
      1941. y.

1550 _____. Flynn's Sampler. London: Ward, Lock, 1945.
      y.

1551 _____. The Fortunes of Flynn. London: Ward, Lock,
      1938. y.

1552 _____. Foul Hawsers. London: Ward, Lock, 1940. y.

1553 _____. Four in a Fairlead. London: Ward, Lock, 1950.
      y.

1554 _____. Gabbart Destiny. London: Ward, Lock, 1956.
      y.

1555 _____. Galleys of St. John. London: Ward, Lock, 1943.
      y.

1556 _____. Gauges Steady: A Romance of the Early P. & O.
      Days. London: Ward, Lock, 1946. y.

1557 _____. Ghost of the Dunsany. London: Ward, Lock,
      1942. y.

1558 _____. Live Lumber. London: Ward, Lock, 1938. y.

1559 _____. Luggar Audace. London: Ward, Lock, 1956. y.

1560 _____. Lumber Ship. London: Ward, Lock, 1949. y.

1561 _____. On Schedule. London: Ward, Lock, 1939. y.

1562 _____. Opium Clipper. London: Ward, Lock, 1942. y.

1563 _____. Ould Flynn. London: Ward, Lock, 1955. y.

1564 _____. Port of Destination. London: Ward, Lock, 1938.
      y.

1565 _____. The Purser's Mate. London: Ward, Lock, 1939.
      y.

1566 _____. Saga of the Cliffs. London: Ward, Lock, 1944.
      y.

1567 _____. The Schooner Sybil. London: Ward, Lock, 1939.
      y.

1568 _____. Sea Dust. London: Ward, Lock, 1938. y.

1569 _____. Sea Range. London: Ward, Lock, 1939. y.

1570 _____. Seconds and Thirds. London: Ward, Lock, 1941.
         y.

1571 _____. Son of Flynn. London: Ward, Lock, 1940. y.

1572 _____. Storm Canvas. London: Ward, Lock, 1940. y.

1573 _____. Strong Room of the Sutro. London: Ward, Lock,
         1948. y.

1574 _____. Trials of the Phideas. London: Ward, Lock,
         1944. y.

1575 _____. Two Little Ships. London: Ward, Lock, 1938.
         y.

1576 _____. The Vengeance of Flynn. London: Ward, Lock,
         1943. y.
         Flynn was a Hornblower-type character of the same
      period.

1577 _____. 'Way Aloft. London: Ward, Lock, 1949. y.

1578 _____. Young Flynn. London: Ward, Lock, 1938. y.
         All of the works by this prolific author are worth the
      trouble of reading.

1579 Long, Gabrielle C. A Knight of Spain. By Marjorie Bowen,
      pseud. London: Methuen, 1913. y.
         Don Juan of Austria in the 1571 Battle of Lepanto.

1580 Longstreet, Stephen. Masts to Spear the Stars. Garden City,
      N. Y. : Doubleday, 1967. y.
         A chronicle of the tea trade and clippers in the 1840's.

1581 Lorenz, H. The Sunken Fleet. Boston: Little, Brown, 1930.
         A tale of treasure-hunting for sunken Spanish galleons
      off the Florida coast.

1582 Love, Edmund G. A Shipment of Tarts. Garden City, N. Y. :
      Doubleday, 1967.
         Mississippi River during the Civil War.

1583 Lovelace, J. A. The Charming Sally. New York: John Day,
      1932.

1584 Lowden, Desmond. Bandersnatch. New York: Holt, 1969.
         Retired Royal Navy Commander Alec Sheldon and his
      wartime crew plan to extract a cool £2 million from a
      Greek shipping magnate whom they've kidnapped. Unfortu-
      nately for them, their plan commences to unravel and they
      find that things are not as easy now as they were against
      the Germans in the Adriatic almost 30 years earlier.

1585 _____. The Boondocks. New York: Holt, Rinehart and
        Winston, 1972.
            World War II in the Pacific.

1586 Lowry, Malcolm. Ultramarine, A Novel. New York: Lip-
        pincott, 1962.
            Famous first work of the son of an English wind-jamming
        sea captain; an autobiographical effort concerning the life of
        a youth on a tramp steamer.

1587 Luard, Lawrence. Conquering the Sea. London: Longmans,
        Green, 1935.

1588 Lund, Robert. Daishi-San. New York: Stein & Day, 1961.
            A biographical novel of Will Adams, the first English
        shipbuilder to settle in Japan, circa 1600.

1589 _____. Horn of Glory. New York: John Day, 1950.

1589a Lyall, Gavin. Blame the Dead. New York: Viking, 1973.
            A fiery collision at sea.

1590 Lynn, E. S. The Luck of the Bertrams. London: Chambers,
        1928.
            Merchant sailing.

- M -

1591 Maass, Edgar. Magnificent Enemies. New York: Scribner's,
        1955.
            Piracy and adventure set against the background of the
        Hanseatic League of Northern Europe.

1592 MacArthur, David Wilson. Lola of the Isles. London: Cas-
        sals, 1926.
            A tale of the South Seas.

1593 _____. The Mystery of the "David M;" A Yachting Mys-
        tery Story of Rothesay and Kyles of Bute. London: Mel-
        rose, 1932.

1594 _____. They Sailed for Senegal. An Historical Novel.
        New York: Frederick A. Stokes, 1938.
            Troubles based on the wrecked frigate H. M. S. Medusa.

1595 McChesney, Dora G. The Wounds of a Friend. London:
        Smith, Elder, 1908.
            The Spanish Armada.

1596 McCutchen, Philip. Beware, Beware the Bight of Benin.
        New York: St. Martin's Press, 1975.
            Royal Navy Lieutenant Halfhyde is sent to the west
        coast of Africa in Victorian days to learn if British

trading interests are in danger from Russian naval presence.

1597 McDonnell, J. E. <u>Commander Brady</u>. London: Constable, 1956.

1598 _____. <u>Gimme the Boats</u>. London: Constable, 1953.

1599 _____. <u>Subsmash</u>. London: Collins, 1960.

1600 _____. <u>Wings of the Sea</u>. London: Constable, 1956.
       All four of this author's works deal with the Royal Navy.

1601 McFadden, Gertrude V. <u>The Preventive Man</u>. London: Lane, 1920.
       The name given to a custom's official who is sent to the Dorset coast sometime during Victoria's reign to stamp out smuggling.

1602 McFarland, Raymond. <u>The Masts of Gloucester</u>. New York: Publisher unknown, c. 1937.
       This author penned a number of tales concerning merchant sailing men. Others include:

1603 _____. <u>Sea Adventure</u>. New York: Harper and Bros., c. 1938.

1604 _____. <u>The Sea Panther</u>. New York: F. A. Stokes, 1928.

1605 _____. <u>Skipper John of the Nimbus</u>. New York: Macmillan, 1918.

1606 _____. <u>Sons of the Sea</u>. New York: G. P. Putnam, 1921.

1607 McFee, William M. P. <u>Aliens</u>. Garden City, N. Y. : Doubleday, 1918.
       McFee was born afloat in 1881 and spent most of his sea career as an engineer in the American merchant service. When he came ashore in Westport, Conn., in 1922 to launch his full-time writing, he retained all of his native British mannerisms, including an aversion to "sex" in sea fiction and a passion for realism. Some of the other tales which made him an important figure in nautical literature are:

1608 _____. <u>The Beachcomber</u>. Garden City, N. Y. : Doubleday, 1935.

1609 _____. <u>Captain Macedoine's Daughter</u>. Garden City, N. Y. : Doubleday, 1920.
       A girl is used as a pawn of her father's Anglo-Hellenic Development Co.

1610 _____. <u>Casuals of the Sea: The Voyage of a Soul</u>. Garden

City, N. Y.: Doubleday, 1936.
A London brother and sister adrift on a liferaft at sea.

1611 _____. Command. Garden City, N. Y.: Doubleday, 1922.
Action afloat in World War I.

1612 _____. Derelicts, a Novel. Garden City, N. Y.: Doubleday, 1938.

1613 _____. Harbourmaster, a Novel. Garden City, N. Y.:
Doubleday, 1931.
The death of a couple in a Caribbean port as related
by the cruiseship engineer who knew them.

1614 _____. In the First Watch. New York: Random House,
1946.

1615 _____. North of Suez. Garden City, N. Y.: Doubleday,
1930.
The activities of a young British naval officer in First
World War Port Said.

1616 _____. Pilgrims of Adversity. Garden City, N. Y.: Doubleday, 1928.
The crew of the British tramp steamer Candleshoe becomes involved in a South American revolution.

1617 _____. Sailor's Bane. Philadelphia: Rittenhouse, 1936.

1618 _____. Sailors of Fortune. Garden City, N. Y.: Doubleday, 1926.
An anthology.

1619 _____. Ship to Shore. New York: Random House, 1944.

1620 _____. Watch Below: A Reconstruction in Narrative Form
of the Golden Age of Steam When Coal Took the Place of
Wind and the Tramp Steamer's Smoke Covered the Seven
Seas. New York: Random House, 1940.

1621 _____., ed. Stories of the Sea. London: Faber, 1955.

1622 _____., ed. World's Great Tales of the Sea. Cleveland:
World Pub. Co., 1944.

1623 MacGibbon, Jean. A Special Providence. New York: Coward-
McCann, 1964. y.
The final third of this tale relates the passage of the
Mayflower.

1624 McGinnis, Paul. Lost Eden. New York: McBride, 1947. y.
The Hawaiian adventures of one of Captain James Cook's
sailors, who was voluntarily left behind.

1625 Macgregor, J. M. When the Ship Sank. Garden City, N. Y. :
      Doubleday, 1959.

1626 Machen, Walter. Rain on the Wind. New York: Macmillan,
      1950.
          The lives of a group of Irish fishing families.

1627 McInnes, C. M. Give Me Two Ships. London: Odhams,
      1963.

1628 McIntyre, John T. Blowing Weather. New York: Century,
      1923. y.
          A storm at sea.

1629 _____. The Boy Tars of 1812. Philadelphia: Penn, 1907.
      y.
          Constitution vs. Guerriere.

1630 _____. Drums in the Dawn. N. Y. : Doran, 1932.   y.
          The decisive role of the French Navy in the 1781 Bat-
      tle of the Chesapeake.

1631 _____. Stained Sails. New York: Stokes, 1928. y.
          A clipper ship yarn.

1632 _____. With Fighting Jack Barry. Philadelphia: Lippin-
      cott, 1907. y.
          A tale of the Revolution.   John Barry has been called
      "the Father of the American Navy. "

1633 _____. With John Paul Jones. Philadelphia: Penn, 1906.
      y.

1634 McIntyre, K. L. Child of the Seas. New York: Scribner's,
      1881. y.

1635 _____. Crimson Sails. New York: Scribner's, 1880.   y.
          War of 1812.

1636 _____. Good Ship Wave. New York: Scribner's, 1887.
      y.

1637 _____. Storm Voyage. New York: Scribner's 1885. y.
          Another tale of typhoons vs. wooden sailing ships and
      "iron" sailors.

1638 McIntyre, Marjorie. The River Watch. New York: Crown,
      1955. y.
          Mississippi riverboat adventures of a young girl before
      the Civil War.

1639 McKee, Ruth E. The Lord's Annointed. Garden City, N. Y. :
      Doubleday, 1934.

Missionaries sail to Hawaii.

1640   McKemy, Kay.   Samuel Pepys of the Navy.   London: Warne,
       1970. y.
            A biographical novel.

1641   McKenna, Richard.   The Sand Pebbles.   New York: Harper,
       1963.
            An American gunboat in China during the 1920's.
       (Steve McQueen starred in the movie version.)

1642   Mackenzie, Compton.   South Wind of Love.   New York: Dodd,
       1937.
            Part of a larger series, this volume concerns naval ac-
       tion in the First World War.

1643   Mackintosh, Elizabeth.   The Privateer.   By Gordon Daviot,
       pseud.   New York: Macmillan, 1952. y.
            Sir Henry Morgan.

1644   McLaughlin, William R.   Antarctic Raider.   London: Harrup,
       1960.
            The search for and exploits of a World War II dis-
       guised merchant cruiser.

1645   McLaws, Emile Lafayette.   When the Land Was Young.   New
       York: Lothrop, 1902.
            Caribbean buccaneers.

1646   MacLean, Alistair.   The Golden Rendezvous.   Garden City,
       N. Y. : Doubleday, 1962.
            An espionage story set aboard a tramp steamer cruising
       the Mediterranean in the early 1960's.

1647   _____ .   The Guns of Navarone.   Garden City, N. Y. :
       Doubleday, 1957.
            Action afloat and ashore as a five-man Commando team
       attempts to knock out some German guns commanding a
       strategic site in the eastern Mediterranean during World
       War II.

1648   _____ .   H. M. S. Ulysses.   Garden City, N. Y. : Doubleday,
       1956.
            Action aboard a light cruiser of the Royal Navy on the
       World War II Murmansk run.

1649   _____ .   Ice Station Zebra.   Garden City, N. Y. : Double-
       day, 1963.
            How a British agent and an American submarine attempt
       to rescue the crew of a British meteorological station in the
       Arctic, running into the Russians in the process.

1650   _____ .   South by Java Head.   Garden City, N. Y. : Doubleday

1958.
　　Tale of an escape from Singapore in 1942 aboard an
old slaving vessel.

1651 _____. When Eight Bells Toll. Garden City, N. Y. :
　　Doubleday, 1966.
　　Hijacking off the modern Scottish coast present certain
problems for the British agent sent to investigate.

1652 Maclennan, Hugh. Barometer Rising. New York: Duell,
　　Sloan and Pearce, 1941.
　　Seamen encounter a fierce storm at sea.

1653 McManus, C. Hades Belle. London: Harrap, 1955.

1654 _____. Whiskey Johnny. London: Harrap, 1956.

1655 McMeekin, Isabel and Dorothy Clark. Red Raskall. By
　　Clark McMeekin, pseud. New York: Appleton, 1943.
　　A Virginia coast shipwreck before the Civil War.

1656 McNeilly, Mildred M. Heaven Is Too High. New York:
　　Morrow, 1944.
　　Adventures on the Pacific Northwest in the 1780's when
the Russians were attempting to found a colony.

1657 _____. Praise at Morning. New York: Morrow, 1947.
　　Features the Russian fleet visit to America during the
Civil War.

1658 MacOrlan, Pierre. The Anchor of Mercy. New York: Pan-
　　theon, 1967.
　　How the French attempt to capture an 18th-century pirate before he can join the British and spill the beans.

1659 Maher, Thomas F. Swoop of the Falcon. London: Dent,
　　1953.

1660 Mailer, Norman. The Naked and the Dead. New York:
　　Rinehart, 1948.
　　An action tale of the amphibious operations of the Allies
in the Pacific during World War II.

1661 "Main Royal, " pseud. Second Dog Watch. London: Thor-
　　son's, 1949.

1662 Makgill, G. Outside and Overseas. London: Methuen, 1903.
　　18th-century English colonialization of New Zealand.

1663 Malcolmson, Anne and Dell J. McCormick. Mister Storma-
　　long. Boston: Houghton, Mifflin, 1952. y.
　　Another look at the Paul Bunyon of the seven seas.

1664   Malkus, A. S. Pirates' Port. New York: Harper, 1929. y.
       New Amsterdam (New York) in the 1600's.

1665   Mallalieu, Joseph P. W. Very Ordinary Seamen. London:
       Gollancz, 1944.
       World War II.

1666   Mandel, Paul. The Black Ship. New York: Random House,
       1969.
              British and American PT-Boat action against a World
       War II German destroyer nicknamed "the Black Ship. "

1667   _____ . Mainside. New York: Random House, 1962.

1668   Mansford, Charles J. Fags and the King. London: Jarrold,
       1909. y.
       A schoolboy's adventures at the time of Nelson.

1669   Margerison, John S. Action! London: Hodder and Stoughton,
       1917.
       World War I.

1670   _____ . Destroyer Doings. London: Pearson, 1918.
              Yarns concerning First World War "four stackers" of
       the Royal Navy.

1671   _____ . Hunters of the U-boat. London: Pearson, 1918.
       More anti-submarine warfare yarns.

1672   _____ . The Navy's Way. London: Duckworth, 1916.
       World War I.

1673   _____ . Periscope and Propeller: More Tales of the Navy
       Trade. London: Pearson, 1917.
       World War I.

1674   _____ . Petrol Patrols. London: Hodder & Stoughton,
       1918.
       World War I.

1675   _____ . Torpedo vs. Gun: The Story of a Naval Bet.
       London: Pearson, 1919.
       World War I.

1676   _____ . Turret and Torpedo: Tales of the Navy Trade.
       London: Pearson, 1917.
       World War I.

1677   _____ . Von Tirpitz: The True Story of a Submarine
       Hunt. London: Chambers, 1918.
              Relax reader, this really is fiction; an anti-submarine
       warfare tale based on the unsophisticated techniques of
       World War I.

1678   Marmur, Jacland. <u>Andromeda</u>. New York: Holt, 1947.
       An American freighter escapes Singapore just before it
       falls to the Japanese in 1942.

1679   _____. <u>The Sea and the Shore</u>. New York: Holt, 1941.

1680   Marryat, Frederick. <u>Frank Mildmay; Or, The Naval Officer</u>.
       London, 1829.
           A native Londoner, Marryat entered the Royal Navy in
       1806 at the age of 14, saw continued action through the
       Napoleonic Wars (most notably under Lord Cochrane), and
       by 1815 had risen to the rank of commander. He was on
       duty at St. Helena in 1821 when Napoleon died and per-
       formed valiantly during the Burmese War of 1824-1825. In
       1830, Marryat resigned his commission and came ashore to
       devote his remaining 18 years to writing realistic novels
       about "the old navy," attempting to inject some humor to
       the narrative style of Cooper (q.v.) and cut-down the bla-
       tant savagery introduced to sea fiction by Tobias Smollett
       (q.v.).
           Unlike Conrad (q.v.) and other modern nautical-yarn
       spinners, "Captain" Marryat was important to the genre not
       for his psychological insights, but for his narrative fluency,
       his ability to depict the stirring action he encountered with
       Cochrane, and a vigor of dash powdered with humor and
       camaraderie. Ford Madox Ford once over-generously
       termed him "the greatest of English novelists"; this opinion
       was widely shared by many generations of young English
       and American readers and the durability of his product,
       some of which is still read today, make him a pillar in the
       development of British nautical literature. Oliver Warner
       has written a useful biography, <u>Captain Marryat: A Redis-
       covery</u> (London, 1953), for those interested in a closer
       work at his life and writing.

1681   _____. <u>Jacob Faithful</u>. London: Routledge, 1896.
       Reprinting of an earlier edition.

1682   _____. <u>Japhet in Search of a Father</u>. New York: Apple-
       ton, 1894.
       Reprinting of the earlier London edition.

1683   _____. <u>The King's Own</u>. New York: Dutton, 1834.
           A tale of adventure, piracy, naval battles, and the 1797
       Nore uprising as experience by men aboard several Royal
       Navy vessels.

1684   _____. <u>Masterman Ready</u>. New York: Grosset & Dunlap,
       1926.
           Reprinting of the London edition of 1840. A naval ad-
       venture in the Swiss Family Robinson vein follows a lad's
       abandonment on a deserted island.

1685 _____. Mr. Midshipman Easy. New York: Appleton,
     1892.
          One of many reprintings of the author's most famous
     work first published in London in 1836. The exploits of
     Easy are based on the author's actual experiences with Lord
     Cochrane off the coasts of France and Spain during the
     Napoleonic wars.

1686 _____. Olla Podrida. 3 Vols. London: Longmans, 1840.

1687 _____. Pacha of Many Tales. New York: Appleton, 1882.
     Reprinting of the earlier London edition.

1688 _____. Percival Koene. 3 Vols. London: Henry Colburn,
     1842.

1689 _____. Peter Simple. New York: Appleton, 1895.
          Reprinting of the earlier London edition. The journal
     of a British sailor from the day he entered the Royal Navy
     as a midshipman to the day he retires as Lord Privilege.

1690 _____. The Phantom Ship. 3 Vols. London: Colburn,
     1839.

1691 _____. The Pirate and the Three Cutters. London, 1836.

1692 _____. _____. New edition, With a Memoir of the Author.
     London, 1861.

1692a _____. The Poacher. New York: Appleton, 1891.

1693 _____. Poor Jack. London: Longmans, 1846.

1694 _____. The Privateers Man One Hundred Years Ago. 2
     Vols. London, 1846.

1695 _____. Snarleyvow. New York: Appleton, 1892.

1696 Marsh, Frances. A Romance of Old Folkestone. London:
     Fifield, 1906.
          A romantic tale of the love held by an English admiral
     of Nelson's day for a goddaughter of Marie Antoinette.
     More romance than fighting.

1697 Marsh, George T. Ask No Quarter. New York: Morrow,
     1945.
          Piracy at the end of the 17th-century.

1698 Marsh, John. The Cruise of the Carefree. London: Ward,
     Lock, 1955. y.

1699 Marshall, Beatrice. The Queen's Knight Errant. London:
     Seeley, 1904.

Sir Walter Raleigh.

1700 Marshall, Edison. American Captain. New York: Farrar,
      Straus and Young, 1954.
           War of 1812.

1701   _____. The Great Smith. New York: Farrar, 1943.
           A biographical novel concerning Captain John Smith.

1702   _____. Yankee Pasha. New York: Farrar, 1947.
           Privateering in the War of 1812.

1703 Marshall, Emma. The First Light on the Eddystone. Lon-
      don: Seeley, 1894.
           The lighthouse built at Plymouth, 1696-1703.

1704 Marshall, James V. My Boy John That Went to Sea. Lon-
      don: Hodder & Stoughton, 1966. y.
           A modern tale of whaling in the Antarctic. First pub-
      lished by the New York firm of Morrow in 1963.

1705   _____. A River Ran Out of Eden. New York: Morrow,
      1963.

1706 Masefield, John. Bird of Dawning. London and New York:
      Macmillan, 1933.
           The race between two English tea clippers from Canton
      and Liverpool. England's late Poet Laureate is as well
      known for his salty verse as his nautical prose.

1707   _____. Captain Margaret. London: Grant Richards, 1908.
           A story of south Devon and Cornwall, as well as the
      Spanish Main, about 1685-1688.

1708   _____. Dead Ned: The Autobiography of a Corpse Who
      Recovered Life Within the Coast of Dead Ned and Came to
      What Fortune You Shall Read. New York and London:
      Macmillan, 1938.
           A tale of an 18th-century doctor accused of killing his
      sea captain, is hanged at Newgate, but resurrected by two
      other doctors, and escapes to Africa aboard a slaver.

1709   _____. Jim Davis. New York: Stokes, 1911.
           Smuggling on the Devonshire coast 150 years ago.

1710   _____. Live and Kicking Ned. 2 Vols. in 1. London and
      New York: Macmillan, 1939.
           In which our hero arrives at the Coast of Dead Ned
      aboard the slaver Albicore, where he proceeds to meet new
      adventures linking him with a past he thought long dead.

1711   _____. Lost Endeavor. New York and London: Macmillan,
      1910. y.

A 17th-century English youth is kidnapped, sold into slavery in America, and escapes only to meet strange piratical exploits in the waters off the Spanish Main.

1712 _____. Mainsail Haul. London and New York: Macmillan, 1905.

1713 _____. Martin Hyde. London: Gardner, 1910. y.
Service afloat for a lad during the Monmouth Rebellion, 1684-1685.

1714 _____. Sard Harker. London and New York: Macmillan, 1924.
Ships, the sea, and the jungle, burning deserts, and icy mountains, murder, lust and intrigue on a tropical stage.

1715 _____. The Taking of the Gry. London: Heinemann, 1934.

1716 _____. A Tarpaulin Muster. London, 1907.
Short stories in a collection.

1717 Mason, Arthur. Come Easy, Go Easy. New York: John Day, c.1933.
Heavy autobiographical emphasis by an Irish-born, naturalized American salt. Other yarns by this writer include:

1718 _____. Fire Over England. New York: Doubleday, Doran, 1936.
Spanish Armada.

1719 _____. The Flying Bo'sun. New York: H. Holt, 1920.
Mystery.

1720 _____. An Ocean Boyhood. New York: J. H. Sears, c.1927.
Heavily autobiographical tale.

1721 _____. The Roving Lobster. Garden City, N.Y.: Doubleday, 1931.

1722 _____. Salt Horse. London: Cape, 1928.
Heavily autobiographical tale.

1723 _____. The Ship That Waited. Publisher unknown, c.1925.

1724 _____. Swansea Dan. New York: Cosmopolitan, 1929.

1725 Mason, Colin. Hostage. New York: Walker, 1973.
A shaky peace in the Middle East is shattered when a right-wing gang of Israelis steal some American strategic

A-bombs stockpiled in Tel Aviv and use them to blow up
Cairo.   The Russians respond by sending a nuclear-missile
sub to Australia and holding the city of Sydney hostage until the U.S. and Britain give up their allegiance to Israel.

1726   Mason, Francis van Wyck, ed.   American Men at Arms.
       Boston: Little, 1964.
           Excellent anthology of 56 extracts of American fiction
       about the two World Wars and Korea.

1727   _____. Blue Hurricane.   Philadelphia: Lippincott, 1954.
           A tale of the Mississippi River during the Civil War,
       told from the viewpoint of the sailors under Captain Henry
       Walke commanding the U.S. Steam Gunboat Carondelet.

1728   _____. Captain Nemesis.   New York: Pocket Books, 1957.
           First published in 1931, this is the story of a cashiered
       18th-century Royal Navy officer who turned pirate.   Swash-
       buckling!

1729   _____. Cutlass Empire.   Garden City, N.Y.: Doubleday,
       1949.
           The best fictional account of Sir Henry Morgan.

1730   _____. Eagle in the Sky.   By Geoffrey Coffin, pseud.
       Philadelphia: Lippincott, 1948.
           Sea battles during The Revolution; featuring the York-
       town campaign; patriotic doctors.

1731   _____. Golden Admiral.   Garden City, N.Y.: Doubleday,
       1953.
           A very realistic portrayal of Sir Francis Drake.

1732   _____. Harpoon in Eden.   Garden City, N.Y.: Doubleday,
       1969.
           Whaling adventures in the South Seas in the 1840's.

1733   _____. Log Cabin Noble.   Garden City, N.Y.: Doubleday,
       1973.
           William Phips' search for sunken treasure.

1734   _____. Manila Galleon.   Boston: Little, Brown, 1961.
           A graphic and extremely accurate retelling of the tre-
       mendous suffering and success sustained by Commodore
       George Anson during his circumnavigation of 1740-1744.
       Upon his return from the Pacific, where he captured the
       Spanish treasure ship from Manila, he gained the title of
       "Father of the British Navy."

1735   _____. Our Valiant Few.   Boston: Little, Brown, 1956.
           The blockade of the Confederate East Coast as seen by
       a Charleston newspaperman.

1736 _____. Proud New Flags. Philadelphia: Lippincott, 1951
A Confederate naval officer's attempts to bolster the de-
fenses of New Orleans before the arrival of Farragut's
fleet; the Confederate Navy's materialization.

1737 _____. Rivers of Glory. By Geoffrey Coffin, pseud.
Philadelphia: Lippincott, 1942.
Siege of Savannah, Georgia during the Revolution, 1778-
9.

1738 _____. Roads to Liberty. Boston: Little, Brown, 1972.
Contains the author's four earlier and successful sea
stories Three Harbors, Stars on the Sea, Wild Horizon,
and Eagle in the Sky.

1739 _____. The "Sea 'Venture." Garden City, N.Y.: Doubleday, 1961.
How a Virginia Company ship is blown off route and
strands its company on Bermuda, which it commences to
populate.

1740 _____. Stars on the Sea. By Geoffrey Coffin, pseud.
Philadelphia: Lippincott, 1940.
Featuring John Paul Jones during The Revolution sea
battles, Rhode Island, Charleston, and the American powder
expedition to the Bahamas.

1741 _____. Three Harbours. By Geoffrey Coffin, pseud.
Philadelphia: Lippincott, 1938.
Sea fights during The Revolution; Boston, Norfolk, Va.,
etc. Mason removed use of pseudonym in later editions.

1742 _____. Trumpets Sound No More. Boston: Little, Brown
1975.
An ex-Confederate cavalry officer searches for shipwrecked gold in order to save his homestead.

1743 _____. Young Titan. Garden City, N.Y.: Doubleday,
1959.
A story of the French and Indian War, of settlement on
Penobscot Bay, and of the Colonists adventure against Louis-
burg.

1744 Mather, Berkeley. The Road and the Star. New York: Scribner's, 1965.
Lord Bemforth, with the help of Cloda St. Bride, escapes from Cromwell's men and joins the "Men of the Middle Passage," a group of pirates operating around the tip of
Africa.

1745 Mathews, Basil. The Quest of Liberty. New York: Doran,
1920. y.
The Mayflower and the Pilgrims.

1746   Matthiessen, Peter. Far Tortuga. New York: Random
      House, 1975.
         The Ahab-like Captain Raib Avers skippers the decrepit
      turtling schooner Lillias Eden on her last voyage from Grand
      Cayman Island.

1747   _____. Raditzer. New York: Viking, 1961.
         World War II in Honolulu as viewed by a pair of Ameri-
      can sailors.

1748   Mayer, Albert I. Follow the River. New York: Doubleday,
      1969. y.
         A Philadelphia schoolteacher's frontier river jaunt; past
      Civil War.

1749   Mayrant, Drayton. The Land Beyond the Tempest. New
      York: Coward-McCann, 1960.
         A storm-tossed trip via sailing ship to the new world
      of Virginia, via Bermuda.

1750   Mays, Victor. Action Starboard. Boston: Houghton, Mifflin,
      1956. y.
         Young Toby Ives learns his seamanship aboard a Yankee
      privateer in the War of 1812.

1751   Meacham, Ellis K. The East Indiaman. Boston: Little,
      Brown, 1968.
         An interesting view of naval service with the privately-
      owned warships of "The Company. "

1752   _____. On the Company's Service. Boston: Little,
      Brown, 1971.
         Naval action with ships of the British East India com-
      pany in the Indian Ocean in the late 18th-century.

1753   Meader, Stephen W. Away to Sea. New York: Harcourt,
      Brace, 1931. y.
         American merchant sailing.

1754   _____. The Black Buccaneer. New York: Harcourt,
      Brace and Howe, 1920. y.
         Pirates.

1755   _____. The Cape May Packet. New York: Harcourt,
      1969. y.
         A tale of privateering in Delaware Bay during the War
      of 1812.

1756   _____. Clear for Action. New York: Harcourt, Brace,
      1940. y.
         Action afloat during the War of 1812.

1757   _____. The Commodore's Cup. New York: Harcourt, 1958.
      Yacht racing.

1758 _____. Down the Big River. New York: Harcourt, 1924. y.
A brown water tale of the Mississippi in the days of the keelboat.

1759 _____. Everglades Adventure. New York: Harcourt, 1957. y.
A tale of Florida after the Civil War.

1760 _____. Guns for the Saratoga. New York: Harcourt, 1955. y.
Privateering in the American Revolution.

1761 _____. Phantom of the Blockade. New York: Harcourt, 1962. y.
The blockade-runner Gray Witch makes several perilous voyages through the Yankee cordon drawn off Wilmington.

1762 _____. The Sea Snake. New York: Harcourt, 1943. y.
A young fishing lad attempts to put a South American U-boat base out of action during World War II.

1763 _____. Topsail Island Treasure. New York: Harcourt, 1966. y.
Pirates and booty.

1764 _____. The Voyage of the Javelin. New York: Harcourt, 1959. y.
The rise of a lad from seaman to 4th mate aboard an American clipper ship in the 1850's.

1765 _____. Whaler 'Round the Horn. New York: Harcourt, 1950. y.
Square-rigged whaling adventures in the 1840's.

1766 Meigs, Cornelia L. Clearing Weather. Boston: Little, Brown, 1928.
American merchant sailing.

1767 _____. The Pirate of Jasper Peak. By Aldair Aldon, pseud. New York: Macmillan, 1918.

1768 _____. Swift Rivers. Boston: Little, Brown, 1932.
Logging on the Upper Mississippi down to St. Louis, circa 1835-1848.

1769 _____. The Trade Wind. Boston: Little, Brown, 1927.
Revolutionary War sea engagements.

1770-79. No entry

1780 _____. Vanished Island. New York: Macmillan, 1914.

781 Melville, Herman. Billy Budd, Foretopman. New York:
     Various publishers, 1891--.
          What might now be called a "novelette, " concerning the
     unfortunate fate of a kindly sailor charged with striking an
     officer in the Royal Navy at the time of the Spithead and
     Nore mutinies of 1797.   Peter Ustinov played the captain
     who, though sympathetic to Budd's plight, was forced to
     hang him in the movie version just before a French attack.
          Born in New York City in 1819, Herman Melville had a
     varied early life, attending school at short intervals, attempt-
     ing several trades, and finally seeking employment as a cab-
     in boy aboard a New York to Liverpool trading ship in 1839.
     Upon his return, he taught school briefly and travelled west
     as far as Illinois.   Planting no roots, he returned east and
     signed on as a seaman aboard the whaling ship Acushnet at
     Fair Haven.
          After 18 months in the South Seas, Melville deserted
     the whaler at Nukuhiva in the Marquesas Islands, spent a
     month with the cannibalistic natives in the Typee Valley,
     and escaped to Tahiti by signing aboard an Australian whaler.
     He remained with this ship until it touched Honolulu where
     he "ran" again, signed aboard the U.S. frigate United States,
     and returned to America in 1844 where he was "paid off. "
          Needless to say, this nautical experience would prove the
     well from which he would draw forth his many tales of the
     sea, the first being Typee (q.v.) which met grand acclaim
     when published in 1846.   It was so successful that the ex-
     bluejacket elected the career of an author on dry land, and
     to help establish roots, he married in 1847, the year of his
     second tale, Omoo (q.v.).
          Despite this early success, Melville was in financial
     trouble from the 1840's onward.   After the publication of
     Mardi (q.v.), Redburn (q.v.), and White-Jacket (q.v.), he
     moved to a farm ("Arrowhead") near Pittsfield, Massachu-
     setts, where he wrote Moby Dick.   The story of the white
     whale was not an immediate "hit" (nor would it be in his
     lifetime) and after several more tales, voyages, and sev-
     eral seasons on the lecture circuit, he arrived in New York
     City in 1863 where he would serve for nearly twenty years
     as district inspector of customs.
          After the initial success of his first works, Melville
     was pretty much neglected during the remainder of his ca-
     reer, although he continued to turn out a number of excellent
     essays, short novels, and some poetry.   His beautiful short
     novel Billy Budd (q.v.) was not published until 1924, 33
     years after his death.   Indeed, students of literature did not
     "discover" the greatness of his writings until after the First
     World War when another pioneering nautical writer, Joseph
     Conrad, was obtaining prominence.   Now Melville is con-
     sidered among the half dozen greatest authors ever produced
     in America, and copies of his works are available in many
     editions from expensive hardbounds to cheap paperbacks.

1782   . The Confidence-Man: His Masquerade. Publisher unknown, 1857.
      A satirical novel that caricatures passengers on a boat bound for New Orleans down the Mississippi from St. Louis. Melville was as far out of his element writing about the river as Samuel Clemens was when writing about the sea.

1783   . Israel Potter: His Fifty Years of Exile. New York: Putnam, 1855.
      John Paul Jones and Benjamin Franklin figure in this tale of the American Revolution at sea.

1784   . Mardi: And a Voyage Thither. 2 Vols. New York: Harper, 1849.
      Travel fiction with faithful South Seas descriptions, wherein Mardi is a strange archipelago reminiscent of Gulliver's findings. Should be related to Omoo and Typee, below.

1785   . Moby Dick; Or, The White Whale. New York: Harper, 1851.
      Without a doubt, the famed tale of the killer white whale is one of the most important sea stories ever written and indeed, one of the greatest literary masterpieces written by any American. It is made up of three separate but related elements which are combined to provide a master yarn: (1) a contemporary view of the 1840's American whaling industry and a natural history of the sperm whale; (2) an exciting narrative of a sea hunt by a deranged skipper named Ahab; and (3) most importantly, a philosophical and psychological commentary upon human life and fate. It is the third element which has received the widest interpretation and re-evaluation during this century, being seen as an allegory, a struggle against consumate evil, or the ability of a single man to take on the forces of nature. The work is rich in symbolism to a point where each reader must eventually interpret it according to his own prejudices--a favorite high school or college English assignment. When people talk about the classics of American literature, Moby Dick for these reasons must always top the list. Gregory Peck portrayed Ahab in the movie version.

1786   . Omoo: A Narrative of Adventures in the South Seas. New York: Harper, 1847.
      Faithful descriptions of Polynesian seas. Along with Typee, below, heavily autobiographical travel-fiction.

1787   . Redburn: His First Voyage. Being the Sailor-Boy Confessions and Reminiscences of the Son-of-a-Gentleman, in the Merchant Service. New York: Harper, 1849.
      Autobiographical-fiction; tells how Melville entered the merchant service (1837) as a youth, sailed to England.

1788   _____. Typee: A Peep at Polynesia Life. During a Four
Month's Residence in a Valley of the Marquesas with Notices
of the French Occupation of Tahiti and the Provisional Ces-
sion of the Sandwich Islands to Lord Paulet. New York:
Wiley and Putnam, 1846.
        Probably the earliest published descriptions of these
islands. Heavily autobiographical-fiction (1842-3) of a sailor
amongst the cannibals of the Marquesas. Melville is concerned with demoralization due to exposure to missionaries
and Western ideas.

1789   _____. White Jacket; Or, The World in a Man-of-War
New York: Harper, 1850.
        Melville had served aboard several merchant vessels
and sailed for a year aboard the United States, an American
man-of-war. This autobiographical novel tells of Jack
Chase. White Jacket was instrumental in abolishing corporal
punishment in naval service, as a copy was sent to each
member of Congress during debates on the issue.

1790   Meredith, George. Evan Harrington. London, 1860.
        The author was the son of a Portsmouth naval outfitter
and the story reflects this background.

1790a Merrell, E. L. Tenoch. London: Nelson, 1954.

1791   Merrett, John. From Faeroes to Finisterre. London: Muller, 1952.

1792   Meyer, Edith P. Pirate Queen. Boston: Little, Brown, 1961.
y.
        An Irish lass named Graina O'Malley finds adventure
afloat during the days of Good Queen Bess.

1792a Michaels, Barbara. The Sea King's Daughter. New York:
Dodd, Mead, 1975.
        An American girl hunts the lost continent of Atlantis
and sunken treasure off the coast of Greece.

1793   Michener, James A. The Bridges at Toko-Ri. New York:
Random House, 1953.
        Korean War naval air attacks on an enemy logistics key,
with insight into the thinking of the pilots involved.

1794   _____. Hawaii. New York: Random House, 1959.
        A fictional history based on fact, with considerable em-
phasis on the sea in the life of the islands. Two movies
have been based on this chronicle.

1795   _____. Tales of the South Pacific. New York: Macmillan,
1947.
        An excellent collection of salty yarns.

1796   Miers, Earl S. Pirate Chase. Williamsburg, Va.: Colonial
        Williamsburg, 1965. y.
                The career and fate of Edward Teach, called "Black-
        beard. "

1797   Miller, Helen. Dark Sails. Indianapolis: Bobbs-Merrill,
        1945.
                General Oglethorpe leads a group of English settlers to
        St. Simon's Island.

1798   _____. Slow Dies the Thunder. Indianapolis: Bobbs-
        Merrill, 1955.
                Romance set against the Royal Navy's bombardment of
        Charleston in 1780.

1799   Miller, John D. Adventures Afloat. London: Black, 1949.

1800   Miller, Merle. Island 49. New York: Crowell, 1945.
                The Marine capture of a Pacific island during World
        War II. Much on the naval-backed amphibious phase of
        the operation.

1801   Miller, Robert. Voyage of the Sea Curse. New York: Van-
        tage, 1958.

1802   Miller, Stanley. Mr. Christian: The Journal of Fletcher
        Christian, Former Lieutenant of His Majesty's Armed Ves-
        sel Bounty. New York: John Day, 1973.

1803   Mirvish, Robert F. Eternal Voyagers. New York: Sloane,
        1953.

1804   _____. Holy Loch. New York: Sloan, 1964.
                A nautical romance set in Scotland.

1805   _____. Midshipman Stuart. New York: Scribner's, 1889.

1806   _____. Red Sky at Midnight. New York: Sloan, 1955.

1807   _____. White Conquerors. New York: Scribner's, 1893.
                Sailing ships in the exploration of the Arctic.

1808   Monjo, F. M. Pirates of Panama. New York: Simon and
        Schuster, 1970. y.
                A tale of Henry Morgan.

1809   Monroe, Kirk. Midshipman Stuart. New York: Scribner's,
        1889. y.
                The last cruise of the frigate Essex in the War of 1812.

1810   _____. Through Swamp and Glade. London: Blackie,
        1896. y.
                Adventure afloat during the Second Seminole War.

1811 Monsarrat, Nicholas. Corvette Command. London: Cassell,
      1944.

1812 _____. The Cruel Sea. New York: Knopf, 1951.
            Probably the best naval novel to emerge from World
      War II. The commander of the hero ship Compass Rose,
      a corvette plying the North Atlantic, was well played by
      Jack Hawkins in the movie version.

1813 _____. Depends What You Mean By Love. 3 Vols. in 1.
      New York: Knopf, 1948.
            Contains three novels: Heavy Rescue, Leave Cancelled,
      and H.M.S. Marlborough Will Enter Harbour.

1814 _____. East Coast Corvette. London: Cassell, 1943.

1815 _____. H.M. Frigate. London: Cassell, 1946.

1816 _____. The Kappillan of Malta. New York: William
      Morrow, 1974.
            A novel of unending heroism set against the siege of
      Malta during the Second World War.

1817 _____. The Ship That Died of Shame, and Other Stories.
      New York: Sloane, 1960.
            The lead title in this collection concerns a small Brit-
      ish motor gunboat of World War II which is later used for
      smuggling.

1818 _____. Three Corvettes. London: Cassell, 1945.
            Contains three novels: H.M Corvette, East Coast
      Corvette, and Corvette Command.

1819 _____. The White Rajah. New York: Sloane, 1961.
            How the son of a British baronet turns pirate, marries
      the daughter of an eastern Rajah, and comes in time to in-
      herit his father-in-law's throne as well.

1820 Montgomery, James Stuart. Tall Man. New York: Green-
      berg, 1927.
            Confederate blockade running during Civil War; battle
      between C.S.S. Alabama and U.S.S. Kearsarge.

1821 Montgomery, Rutherford G. Hurricane Yank. Philadelphia:
      McKay, 1942.
            A tale of the second World War.

1822 _____. The Last Cruise of the Jeanette. Philadelphia:
      Westminster Press, 1944.
            A tale based on fact as this vessel was lost in the
      Arctic late in the last century.

1823 _____. McGonnigle's Lake. Garden City, N.Y.:

Doubleday, 1953.

1824 _____. Men Against the Ice. Philadelphia: Westminster,
1946.

1825 _____. Sea Raiders, Ho! Philadelphia: David McKay,
1945.
World War II.

1826 _____. Thar She Blows. Philadelphia: Westminster,
1945.
Whaling.

1827 Moon, A. R. , ed. Adventures on the High Seas. London:
Longmans, 1943.

1828 Moore, David W. The End of Long John Silver. New York:
Crowell, 1946. y.
Based on the R. L. Stevenson novel Treasure Island.

1829 Moore, F. Frankfort. Captain Latymer. London: Cassell,
1907.
Barbadoes and Ireland at the time of the English Civil
War; Prince Rupert appears regularly.

1830 _____. Coral and Coconut. London: Blackie, 1885.

1831 _____. The Great Orion. London: Blackie, 1886.

1832 _____. Highways and High Seas. New York: Scribner's,
[189?]

1833 _____. Mutiny on the "Albatross. " London: Blackie,
1885.

1834 _____. Tre, Pol, and Pen. London: Christian Knowledge
Society, 1887.
Smuggling in Cornwall and Nelson's victories, 1798-1800.

1835 _____. Under Hatches. London: Blackie, 1888.

1836 Moore, Hamilton J. Nautical Sketches. London: William
Edward, Printer, 1840.

1837 Moore, Ruth. A Fair Wind Home. New York: Morrow,
1953.
Coastal Maine seafaring during the early days when
that area was a part of Massachusetts.

1838 Mordaunt, E. M. C. To Sea! To Sea! London: Muller,
1943.

1839 Morgan, Charles L. The Gunroom. London: Black, 1919.

World War I.

1840 _____. The Voyage. New York and London: Macmillan, 1940.
World War II.

1841 Morgan, G. Convoys Ahoy! London: Lutterworth, 1955. y.
World War II.

1841a Morley, Frank V. East South East. New York: Harcourt, 1929. y.
A boy from Baltimore runs away in 1806 to England, goes whaling, and finally treasure hunting on an island somewhere south of New Zealand.

1842 Morrison, John. Sailors Belong to Ships. Melbourne, Australia: Dolphin, 1947.

1843 Morrow, Honoré W. Yonder Sails the Mayflower. New York: Morrow, 1934.
Pilgrim adventure afloat.

1844 Morton, Benjamin A. The Veiled Empress. New York: Putnam, 1923.
A 19th-century Creole girl is captured at sea by Barbary pirates and sent to Constantinople as a wife for the Sultan.

1845 Moseley, Sydney A. The Fleet from Within: Being the Impressions of a RNVR Officer. London: Sampson, Low, 1919.

1846 Mottram, R. H. Traders' Dream. New York: Appleton, 1939.
A look at the British East India Company, 1599-1664.

1847 Mowat, Farley. The Black Joke. Boston: Little, Brown, 1962. y.
A group of boys go adventuring on the rum-runner Black Joke during Prohibition days.

1848 Mudgett, Helen P. The Seas Stand Watch. New York: Knopf, 1944.
New England sea life from 1783-1815, with emphasis on the new China trade, Jefferson's embargo, and the War of 1812.

1849 Muller, Charles G. Hero of Champlain. New York: Stein & Day, 1961.
An accurate biographical novel concerning Thomas Macdonough, victor in the Battle of Lake Champlain.

1850 Munoz, Charles C. Stowaway. New York: Random House,

1957.
   An allegorical novel about the crew of a tramp steamer
and the effect of a stowaway on the different men in the
ship's company.

1851   Murphy, John.   The Gunrunners.   New York: Macmillan,
       1966.
          A story of Caribbean adventure featuring an old freight-
       er, a motley crew of World War II veterans and a dangerous
       mission.

1852   Myers, John.   The Wild Yazoo.   New York: Dutton, 1947.
       Ante-bellum Mississippi and Yazoo River adventures.

1853   Myrer, Anton.   The Big War.   New York: Appleton, 1957.
       World War II and the Marines in the Pacific.

                              - N -

1854   Nason, Leonard H.   The Incomplete Mariner.   Garden City,
       N. Y. : Doubleday, 1929.

1855   Naval Anecdotes Illustrating the Character of the British Sea-
       man.   London: Cundee, 1806.

1856   "Navarchus, " pseud.   When the Great War Came.   London:
       1909.
          A look to World War I.

1857   The Navy at Home.   By a Captain in the Navy.   3 Vols.
       London: William Marsh, 1831.

1858   Neale, W. Johnson.   Cavendish, Or, The Patrician at Sea.
       2nd ed.   London: Richard Bentley, 1832.
          This author was born in 1812 and served from 1824-
       1830 in the Royal Navy without obtaining a commission.

1859   _____.   Gentleman Jack: A Naval Story.   3 Vols.   Lon-
       don: Richard Bentley, 1841.

1860   _____.   The Naval Surgeon.   3 Vols. London: Richard
       Bentley, 1841.

1861   _____.   Paul Periwinkle; Or, The Pressgang.   London:
       [1831?]
          Considered the author's best work.

1862   _____.   The Port Admiral.   London: Richard Bentley,
       1833.
          Frederick Marryat called this a "Villainous libel upon
       one of our very best officers, the gallant Troubridge. "

1863 _____ . Will Watch, From the Autobiography of a British
Officer. 3 Vols. London, 1834.

1864 Neill, Robert. The Shocking Miss Anstey. Garden City,
N. Y. : Doubleday, 1965.
Naval action ashore as a British naval captain pursues
his lady love--a high ranking courtesan--from London to
Cheltenham during the early 19th-century. Her name was
'Miss Anstey. "

1865 Nelson, C. M. With Nelson at Trafalgar. New York: Reilly
and Lee, 1961.
The Battle of the Nile, the admiral's activities in Italy,
and Trafalgar are all witnessed by a Royal Navy midshipman.

1866 Newbolt, Henry. Taken from the Enemy. London: Chatto &
Windus, 1892.
An attempt to rescue Napoleon from St. Helena via the
sea.

1867 Newell, Charles W. The Cruise of the Graceful; Or, The
Robbers of Carracas. By "Captain Barnacle, " pseud.
Boston: "Star Spangled Banner" Office, 1847.
Newell also wrote, by date, A Sailor's Love (1849);
The Voyage of the Fleetwing (1886); The Wreck of the
Greyhound (1889), etc.

1868 Newhafer, Richard L. The Last Tallyho. A Novel. New
York: Putnam, 1964.
World War II in the air, as seen by U.S. carrier pilots.

1869 Nicholls, Frederick F. The Log of the Sardis. New York:
Norton, 1963.
Damage to a piece of navagational equipment causes
problems aboard an American clipper ship.

1869a Nicole, Christopher. The Devil's Own. New York: St.
Martin's Press, 1975.
An Antiguan lad ships out with Sir Henry Morgan.

1870 Nielsen, Virginia. The Whistling Winds. New York: McKay,
1964.
Adventures of a young whaler who is left to recuperate
among missionaries after a fight on Hawaiian Islands.

1871 The Night Watch. Vols. 18-20 of The Naval and Military Library of Entertainment. 2 Vols. London: Henry Colburn,
1834.

1872 Niles, Blair. East by Day. New York: Farrar, 1941.
Ante-bellum slaves take over a ship; based on the
Amistad event.

1873 Nisbet, William H. Lone Survivor. London: Cape, 1955.

1874 Niven, Frederick. The Island Providence. London: Lane, 1910.
 Englishmen face their trials on the 17th-century Spanish Main and in Cartagena.

1875 Noble, Edward. Outposts of the Fleet. London: Heinemann, 1917.
 World War I.

1876 Noble, Hollister. Woman with a Sword. Garden City, N.Y.: Doubleday, 1948.
 Anna Ella Carroll and her role in shaping the Union river strategy which brought success at Forts Henry and Donelson in 1862.

1877 Nordhoff, Charles B. Derelict. Boston: Little, Brown, 1928. y.
 The adventures of a boy captured by a German raider during World War I--a raider whom the author modeled after the famous Count Luckner, "The Sea Devil."

1878 _____. Pearl Lagoon. Boston: Little, Brown, 1924. y.
 A California lad on a pearl expedition in the South Seas encounters sharks and pirates.

1879 _____, and James N. Hall. Botany Bay. Boston: Little, Brown, 1941.
 A romance of early Australia.

1880 _____. The Bounty Trilogy. Boston: Little, Brown, 1936.
 Composed of the works next cited.

1881 _____. Men Against the Sea. Boston: Little, Brown, 1934.
 How Captain William Bligh and those sailors faithful to him are set adrift and sail their way several thousands of miles to safety.

1882 _____. Mutiny on the Bounty. Boston: Little, Brown, 1932.
 The famous uprising aboard the Bounty caused by bread-fruit and harsh discipline. The original movie version starred Clark Gable and Charles Laughton; the remake, with beautiful location shots, featured Marlon Brando as Christian and Trevor Howard as Bligh.

1883 _____. Pitcairn's Island. Boston: Little, Brown, 1934.
 How the Bounty mutineers and their Polynesian friends reach a deserted island, dispose of the ship, and settle into a violent life.

1884 Norris, Frank. Shanghaied. A Story of Adventure off

California Coast. New York: De La More, 1904.
Realistic sea romance.

1885 Norton, Alice M. Scarface: Being the Story of One Justin
Blade, Late of Pirate Isle of Tortuga, and How Fate Did
Justly Deal With Him, to His Great Profit. By André
Norton, pseud. New York: Harcourt, 1948.

1886 Norvel Hastings; Or, The Frigate in the Offing. A Nautical
Tale of the War of 1812. Philadelphia: A. Hart, 1850.
"By a Distinguished [but unknown] Novelist. "

- O -

1887 O'Brian, Patrick. The Golden Ocean. New York: John Day,
1957.
The exploits of Commodore George Anson.

1888 _____. Master and Commander. Philadelphia: Lippincott,
1969.
Captain Jack Aubrey and the crew of his brig the Sophie
battle the French in the Mediterranean during the Napoleonic
wars.

1889 _____. Post Captain. Philadelphia: Lippincott, 1972.
This sequel to Master and Commander finds Jack
Aubrey and his friend Stephen Maturin in action in the far
seas and in love with beautiful girls.

1890 _____. The Unknown Shore. London: Hart-Davis, 1959.

1891 O'Brien, Charles. Atlantic Adventure. London: Harrap,
1943.
World War II afloat.

1892 O'Connor, P. F. Mungo Starke. New York: Norton, 1955.

1893 O'Connor, Patrick. Gunpowder for Washington. New York:
Washburn, 1956. y.
A young sea captain encounters all sorts of difficulties
in the West Indies attempting to capture ammunition during
the Revolution.

1894 O'Connor, Richard. Officers and Ladies. Garden City, N. Y. :
Doubleday, 1958.
American occupation of the Philippines in 1898.

1895 O'Dell, Scott. The Dark Canoe. Boston: Houghton, Mifflin,
1968. y.
An investigation of a ship's sinking brings Captain Ahab
of Moby Dick fame back to life.

1896   Ogilvie, Elizabeth. Ebbing Tide. New York: Crowell, 1947.

1897   _____. Storm Tide. New York: Crowell, 1945.
          Both works by this author concern Maine fishermen
       during World War II.

1898   Ollivant, Alfred. Devil Dare. New York: Doubleday, 1924.
          The action surrounds a traitor in the war between Nel-
       son and Napoleon.

1899   _____. The Gentleman. New York: Macmillan, 1908.
          Is a French agent who attempts to kidnap Nelson be-
       fore the Battle of Trafalgar.

1900   Olsen, Robert I. and David Porter. Torpedoes Away! New
       York: Dodd, Mead, 1957.   y.
          World War II submarine action in the Pacific.

1900a O'Neill, Ed. The Rotterdam Delivery. New York: Coward,
       McCann, 1975.
          Arab terrorists hold a Dutch supertanker for ransom.

1901   O'Rierdon, Conal C. The Young Days of Admiral Quilliam.
          By F. Norreys Connell, pseud. London: Blackwood, 1906.
          Trafalgar.

1902   O'Rorke, B. G. In the Hands of the Enemy. London: Hod-
          der & Stoughton, 1915.
          World War I.

1903   Osgood, Grace R. At the Sign of the Blue Anchor. New
          York: Clark, 1909.
          A nautical tale of 1776.

1904   Ostlere, Gordon. Captain's Table. By Richard Gordon, pseud
       New York: Harcourt, 1955.
          An English cruise liner on the London to Sydney run re-
       ceives a new captain, a man who had spent his 25 years of
       service aboard freighters.   The plot concerns his adjustment
       to the life of a passengership in which, after several run-ins
       with guests and crew, proves successful.

1905   Owen, John. The Shadow in the Sea. New York: Dutton,
       1972.
          An unidentified submarine lurks off the British coast
       awaiting a freighter bound for Israel.

1906   Oxley, J. MacDonald. Diamond Rock. London: Nelson,
       1904.
          The British sloop-rigged island off Martinique and the
       Battle of Trafalgar.

1907   _____. Terry's Trials and Triumphs. London: Nelson,

1900. y.
Features the Civil War battle between the <u>Monitor</u> and <u>Merrimac</u>.

- P -

1908 Page, Thomas N. <u>Among the Banks</u>. New York: Scribner's, 1892.
Fisherman off New England.

1909 _____. <u>On Newfound River</u>. New York: Scribner's, 1894.
Another tale of the Grand Banks fisherman. Page's romances were extremely popular in their day; he served as U.S. ambassador to Italy 1913-1919.

1910 Paine, Ralph D. <u>Blackbeard</u>. New York: Penn, 1922. y.
A tale of the noted pirate as told by a young Charleston, S.C., youth, Jack Cockrell. This highly prolific author of nautical fare, fact and fiction, wrote these additional tales of interest:

1911 _____. <u>A Cadet of the Black Star Line</u>. New York: Scribner's, 1910.
A young officer in the Atlantic passenger business before World War I.

1912 _____. <u>The Call of the Offshore Wind</u>. New York: Houghton, Mifflin, 1918.

1912a _____. <u>Comrades of the Rolling Ocean</u>. Boston: Houghton, Mifflin, 1923. y.
The adventures of three young men in a succession of experiences at sea.

1913 _____. <u>Four Bells: A Tale of the Caribbean</u>. Boston: Houghton, Mifflin, 1924. y.
Young Richard Cary adventures after treasure to the seas off the Spanish Main.

1914 _____. <u>In Zanzibar</u>. Boston: Houghton, Mifflin, 1925.
The shore-leave adventures of a machinist's mate from an American cruiser.

1914a _____. <u>The Judgments of the Sea</u>. New York: Sturgis and Walton, 1912.

1915 _____. <u>Midshipman Wickham</u>. New York: Houghton, Mifflin, 1926.

1916 _____. <u>The Penford Adventure</u>. New York: Houghton, Mifflin, 1926.

1917 _____. The Praying Skipper. New York: Outing Pub. Co.,
          1906.

1918 _____. Privateers of '76. Philadelphia: The Penn Pub.
          Co., 1923.
          The Revolution afloat.

1919 _____. Ships Across the Sea. Boston: Houghton, Mifflin,
          1920.

1920 _____. A Tale of the Caribbean. Boston: Houghton, Mif-
          flin, 1924.
          Pirates.

1921 _____. The Wrecking Master. New York: Scribner's,
          1911.

1922 Pakington, Humphrey. Roving Eye. New York: Norton,
          1932.
          A young British naval officer suddenly finds himself
          with a wedding proposal on his hands--but not from the girl
          he truly loves. Pictures of social life afloat and ashore in
          the Victorian naval establishment complete a volume of
          twinkling humor.

1923 Pangborn, Edgar. Wilderness of Spring. New York: Rine-
          hart, 1958.
          Two brothers--a sailor and a doctor--increase their
          fortunes; 18th-century setting.

1924 Parkinson, C. Northcote. Devil to Pay. Boston: Houghton,
          Mifflin, 1973.
          Lt. Richard Delancey, on half pay, assumes command
          of a revenue cutter and then a privateer. In his last ad-
          venture, he obtains proof that Spain is taking sides with
          France for the upcoming Napoleonic wars.

1925 _____. The Fireship. Boston: Houghton, Mifflin, 1975.
          Denied promotion after Camperdown, Richard Delancey
          is given an antiquated fireship with which to sink a French
          ship-of-the-line off the Irish coast.

1926 _____. The Life and Times of Horatio Hornblower. Bos-
          ton: Little, Brown, 1970.
          A unique piece of literature which claims to be the
          "biography" of C. S. Forester's epic hero. The author
          imaginatively fills in the gaps between and amidst the great
          sea captain's published adventures.

1927 Parrish, Randall. Wolves of the Sea. New York: McClure,
          1918.
          How a man escapes slavery in 17th-century Virginia
          to become a pirate.

1928   Partington, Norman.   The Sunshine Patriot; A Novel of the
        American War of Independence.   New York: St. Martin's,
        1975.
              Benedict Arnold and the Valcour Island naval battle.

1928a The Patriotic Sailor; Or, Sketches of the Humors, Cares and
        Adventures of Naval Life, Partially founded on Facts.   2
        Vols. Baltimore: H. W. Bool, 1829.
              Similar to several other works on British sea life being
        written by officers of the Royal Navy about this time.

1929   Patterson, J. E.   The Sea's Anthology.   London: Heinemann,
        1913.

1930   Pattinson, James.   Last in Convoy.   New York: Astor-Honor,
        1958.   y.
              Action in the North Atlantic during World War II.

1931   _____.   Silent Voyage.   New York: McDowell, 1959.   y.
              Brett Manning and Grill Butler are rescued by the
        Soviet mystery ship which has rammed their Scottish mer-
        chantman in the Barents Sea.   They are taken on a voyage
        to Antarctica and there plot their desperate escape.

1932   Payne, Donald G.   Midnight Sea.   By Ian Cameron, pseud.
        London: Hutchinson, 1958.

1933   Peacocke, I. M.   The Cruise of the Crazy Jane.   London:
        Ward, Lock, 1932.   y.

1934   Pearce, Donn.   Pier Head Jump.   Indianapolis: Bobbs-Mer-
        rill, 1972.
              When the battered crew of a battered World War II
        American liberty ship discovers a body floating in the water
        they rescue it.   When they find out it is not a body at all,
        but a life-sized female doll--well, then the fun begins.

1935   Peard, Frances M.   Scapegrace Dick.   London: National So-
        ciety, 1886.
              Admiral Blake vs. the Dutch fleet under Van Tromp
        during the period of the English Commonwealth.

1936   Pease, Clarence Howard.   The Black Tanker; The Adventures
        of a Landlubber on the Illfated Last Voyage of the Oil Tank
        Steamer, "Zambora. " New York: Doubleday, 1942.   y.
              Our title concerns an American vessel transporting crude
        oil to the Japanese fighting in China in the 1930's.   Other
        merchant marine yarns by this writer are:

1937   _____.   Bound for Singapore; Being a True and Faithful Ac-
        count of the Making of an Adventurer.   Garden City, N. Y. :
        Doubleday, 1948.   y.
              A youth joins the crew of a tramp steamer.

1938 _____.   Capt. Binnacle.   New York: Dodd, Mead, 1938.
        y.

1939 _____.   Capt. of the Araby; The Story of a Voyage.
        Garden City, N. Y. : Doubleday, 1953. y.

1940 _____.   The Dark Adventurer.   Garden City, N. Y. : Double-
        day, 1950. y.

1941 _____.   Foghorns; A Story of the San Francisco Waterfront.
        Garden City, N. Y. : Doubleday, 1937. y.

1942 _____.   Heart of Danger; A Tale of Adventure on Land and
        Sea with Tod Moran, Third Mate of the Tramp Steamer,
        "Araby. "   Garden City, N. Y. : Doubleday, 1946. y.
        The third mate of a tramp steamer becomes involved in
        wartime nautical intrigue.

1943 _____.   Hurricane Weather: How Stan Ridley Met Adven-
        ture on the Trading Schooner "Windrider. "   Garden City,
        N. Y. : Doubleday, 1936. y.
        Pearl diving adventure aboard a stolen ship.

1944 _____.   Jinx Ship: The Dark Adventure That Befell Tod
        Moran When He Shipped as Fireman Aboard the Tramp
        Steamer "Congo" Bound Out of New York for Caribbean
        Ports.   Garden City, N. Y. : Doubleday, 1946. y.

1945 _____.   Jungle River.   Garden City, N. Y. : Doubleday,
        1938. y.
        A youth encounters difficulties while attempting to pene-
        trate New Guinea's inland rivers.

1946 _____.   Long Wharf; A Story of Young San Francisco.
        Garden City, N. Y. : Doubleday, 1947. y.
        A look at that California city's harbor and waterfront
        life in the 1850's.

1947 _____.   Night Boat.   Garden City, N. Y. : Doubleday, 1942.
        y.

1948 _____.   Secret Cargo; The Story of Lorry Mathews and
        His Dog Sambo....   Garden City, N. Y. : Doubleday, 1931.
        y.

1949 _____.   Shanghai Passage.   Garden City, N. Y. : Double-
        day, 1929. y.

1950 _____.   The Ship Without a Crew.   Garden City, N. Y. :
        Doubleday, 1934. y.

1951 _____.   Shipwreck; The Strange Adventures of Renny
        Mitchum, Mess Boy....   Garden City, N. Y. : Doubleday,

1957. y.

1952 _____ . The Tattooed Man; A Tale of Strange Adventures
Befalling Tod Moran of the Tramp Steamer "Araby. "
Garden City, N. Y. : Doubleday, 1926.
The strange adventures of a messboy on his first voyage
from San Francisco to Genoa.

1953 _____ . Wind in the Rigging: An Adventurous Voyage of
Tod Moran on the Tramp Steamer "Sumatra" New York to
North Africa. Garden City, N. Y. : Doubleday, 1935

1954 Peck, William H. The Confederate Flag on the Ocean. New
York: Publisher unknown, 1868.
A strongly biased view of Rebel commerce raiding dur-
ing the Civil War. An educator, Peck was President of the
Masonic Female College in Greenville, Ga.

1955 Peisson, Edouard. Outward Bound from Liverpool. London:
Methuen, 1934.
Merchant sailing adventures.

1956 Pendexter, Hugh. Wife-Ship Woman. Indianapolis, Ind. :
Bobbs-Merrill, 1926.
A girl voyages from France to marry in colonial New
Orleans. Significant water/waterfront setting.

1957 Perrault, E. G. The Twelfth Mile. Garden City, N. Y. :
Doubleday, 1972.
A big tug out of Vancouver to retrieve a big off-shore
drilling rig is struck by a hurricane. The skipper finds a
liferaft with three Americans (one dead) and throws a line
to a crippled ship nearby, even though his own rig has dis-
appeared. What he has discovered is a Russian vessel
whose Captain has orders not to be captured at any cost--
even if the cost involves defying the Canadian Navy, the
U. S. Air Force and an American battleship, and taking the
world to the brink of nuclear war.

1958 Peterson, Charles J. Cruising in the Last War. Philadelphia:
T. B. Peterson, 1850.
A tale of the war of 1812. Peterson wrote a biographical history of American sea captains in the conflict, but is
best known for his extremely popular Peterson's Magazine,
which came to overshadow its prototype, Godey's Lady's
Book. His fiction is all but forgotten today.

1959 Pfarrer, Donald. Cold River. New York: St. Martin's,
1962.
The sinking of a tug has tragic effects on the officers
of the American destroyer which rammed her.

1960 Phelps, E. W.   Jack the Fisherman. Boston: Houghton,
      Mifflin, 1894.

1961 _____. Sealed Orders and Other Stories. Boston:
      Houghton, Mifflin, 1892.

1962 Philip, Hugh.   Two Rings and a Red: A Naval Surgeon's Log.
      London: International Pub. Co. , 1945.

1963 Phillpotts, Eden.   The American Prisoner. London: Me-
      thuen, 1904.
           A study of U. S. privateersmen captured and imprisoned
      at Dartmoor during the War of 1812.

1964 Pickering, Edgar.   The Cruise of the Angel. London: Warne,
      1907. y.
           The Dutch Sea Beggars and the 1585 siege of Antwerp.

1965 _____. An Old Time Yarn. London: Blackie, 1893.
           Drake and Hawkins in the West Indies in 1567.

1966 Pilkington, Roger.   I Sailed on the Mayflower: A Boy's Dis-
      covery of the New World. New York: St. Martin's, 1966.
      y.
           A Pilgrim's adventures at sea.

1967 Pinkerton, Thomas A.   The French Prisoner. London: Son-
      nenschein, 1894.
           Captured as a spy and pirate during the time Napoleon
      was planning to invade England.

1968 The Pirate Boy; Or, Adventures of Henry Warrington.   A
      Story of the Sea. New York: Nafis and Cornish, 1844.
           "By the Author of 'The Cabin Boy, ' 'Ambrose and
      Eleanor, ' 'Valley of the Mohawk, ' etc. "

1969 The Pirate Doctor; Or, The Extraordinary Career of a New
      York Physician. By a Naval Officer. New York: Garrett,
      1850.

1970 Plagemann, Bentz.   The Steel Cocoon. New York: Viking,
      1958.
           Life aboard a Pacific Fleet warship during World War
      II.

1971 Poe, Edgar Allan.   The Narrative of Arthur Gordon Pym of
      of Nantucket. New York: Harper, 1838.
           See Sidney Kaplan's edition, 1960, Hill and Wang pub-
      lishers.   Poe writes a gripping tale in the then-popular
      authentic travel narrative genre. A grisly crew encounters
      extraordinary adventures in Antarctica. Recent criticism
      explores heavy metaphorical implications. Compare with
      Seaborn's Symzonia, below.

1972   Pole, James T. <u>Midshipman Plowright</u>. New York: Dodd,
        Mead, 1969. y.
            Adventures of a Naval Academy graduate captured dur-
        ing the Mexican War.

1973   Pollard, Eliza F. <u>A Girl of the Eighteenth Century</u>. London:
        Nelson, 1907. y.
            Nelson and the Battle of the Nile.

1974   Polonsky, Abraham. <u>The Enemy Sea</u>. Boston: Little, Brown,
        1943.
            World War II.

1975   Pope, Dudley. <u>Drumbeat.</u> Garden City, N. Y. : Doubleday,
        1968.
            In this sequel to Ramage, Nicholas continues his career
        in the time of the Napoleonic wars by rescuing a marchioness,
        capturing a Spanish frigate, losing his <u>Kathleen</u> and becoming
        a POW, but escaping to warn England of invasion.

1976   _____. <u>Governor Ramage.</u> Garden City, N. Y. : Doubleday,
        1973.
            Dogged by a hateful admiral who wishes him hanged to
        cover a blot on his own record, Ramage sails to the West
        Indies and there recovers a treasure sufficient to aid in his
        defense when finally court-martialled.

1977   _____. <u>Ramage.</u> Philadelphia: Lippincott, 1965.
            Acting under Nelson's orders, the young lieutenant res-
        cues a beautiful Italian Marchesa sympathetic to the British
        cause.

1978   _____. <u>Ramage's Prize.</u> New York: Simon and Schuster,
        1974.
            Lieutenant Lord Ramage is given the dangerous task of
        finding out why all of His Majesty's mail packets sailing be-
        tween England and the West Indies are all of a sudden being
        snapped up by French privateers.

1979   _____. <u>The Triton Brig</u>. Garden City, N. Y. : Doubleday,
        1969.
            Assigned to a new warship, the lieutenant is sent to the
        West Indies to solve a mystery of disappearing trading
        schooners. Enroute he is faced with and puts down an in-
        cipient mutiny.

1980   Popham, Hugh. <u>The Fabulous Voyage of the Pegasus.</u> New
        York: William Morrow, 1959. y.

1981   _____. <u>The Sea Beggers.</u> New York: William Morrow,
        1962. y.
            Holland, 1500's.

1982 Porteous, Richard S. Sailing Orders. London: Dymock, 1949.

1983 _____. Salvage and Other Stories. London: Harrap, 1963.
An anthology.

1984 Porter, David Dixon. The Adventures of Harry Marline; Or, Notes from An American Midshipman's Lucky Bag. New York: Appleton, 1885.
Porter, who created a number of lively tales, was the famous Civil War admiral whom many considered a study in fiction himself.

1985 _____. Allan Dare and Robert le Diable. A Novel. New York: Appleton, 1885.

1986 _____. Arthur Merton, A Romance. New York: Appleton, 1889.

1987 Porter, Jane. Sir Edward Seaward's Narrative of His Shipwreck, and Consequent Discovery of Certain Islands in the Caribbean Sea. London, 1831.
Published as a literary hoax in the style of Defoe.

1988 Porter, Katherine Anne. Ship of Fools. Boston: Little, 1962.
A look at some of the passengers aboard a cruise ship.

1989 Porteus, Stanley D. The Restless Voyage. New York: Prentice-Hall, 1948.

1990 Post, Melville Davisson. The Revolt of the Birds. New York: Appleton, 1927.
Adventures in the China seas.

1991 Post, Waldron Kintzing. Smith Brunt: A Story of the Old Navy. G. P. Putnam's Sons, 1899. y.
A story of how Capt. James Lawrence came to utter, 'Don't give up the ship!" A fight between Shannon and Chesapeake and defense of the Essex (1811-15).

1992 Poyer, Joe. North Cape. Garden City, N.Y.: Doubleday, 1969.
An American spy plane is diverted from her mission to a mid-Atlantic meeting with an American nuclear destroyer, which is fighting its way through the worst storm of the century; high above, the pilot discovers that the Russians are out to get him at all cost.

1993 Poynter, H. May. Scarlet Town. London: S. P. C. K., 1894.
Reminiscent of Forester's Hornblower in Flying Colours,

a young English naval officer escapes from one of Napoleon's jails.

1994 Pratt, Tinsley. <u>When Hawkins Sailed the Sea.</u> London: Grant Richards, 1907.
       Elizabethan.

1995 Prokosch, Frederic. <u>The Wreck of the Cassandra.</u> New York: Farrar, 1966.
       Saved from catastrophe at sea, nine people of different backgrounds are cast onto a savage island between Hong Kong and Australia. There, after cooperative existence which their situation requires, they unexpectedly set about creating their own private tragedies. A very brutal "Gilligan's Island."

1995a Putnam, Henry. <u>The Land Where the Sun Dies.</u> New York: Putnam, 1975.
       Action ashore and afloat during the Second Seminole War.

1996 Putt, S. Gorley. <u>Men Dressed as Seamen.</u> London: Christophers, 1943.
       World War II.

1997 Pyle, Howard. <u>Book of Pirates: Fiction, Fact, and Fancy.</u> New York: Harper, 1921.

1998 _____. <u>The Story of Jack Ballister's Fortunes.</u> New York: Appleton-Century, 1895. y.
       The exploits of a young English boy of good family who was kidnapped from England to Virginia in 1719, only to fall into the hands of the infamous Blackbeard.

1999 _____. <u>Within the Capes.</u> New York: Scribner's, 1885.
       Love and adventure set along early 19th-century American coast during the War of 1812. Pyle was one of America's best known illustrators. His other sea/pirate tales include, by date, <u>The Rose of Paradise</u> (1888); <u>The Ghost of Captain Brand</u> (1896); <u>The Price of Blood</u> (1899); <u>Stolen Treasure</u> (1907); and <u>The Ruby of Kishmoor</u> (1908).

- Q -

2000 Quick, Herbert. <u>Vandemark's Folly.</u> New York: Bobbs, 1922. y.
       Story of early 19th-century Erie Canal mystery and adventure.

2001 Quiller-Couch, Arthur T. <u>The Blue Pavilions.</u> By "Q," pseud. New York: Scribner's, 1891. y.
       The title refers to a pair of ancient 17th-century sea captains who once loved the hero's mother and look after

the boy once he is orphaned.

- R -

2002 Raddall, Thomas H. Governor's Lady. Garden City, N. Y. :
      Doubleday, 1960.
           Nautical adventure and political maneuvering in old
      Nova Scotia.

2003 _____. The Hangman's Beach. Garden City, N. Y. :
      Doubleday, 1966.
           Friction between a Nova Scotian shipping tycoon and
      the Royal Navy during the Napoleonic wars.

2004 _____. His Majesty's Yankees. Garden City, N. Y. :
      Doubleday, 1942.
           The American Revolution's effects on Nova Scotia.

2005 _____. Pride's Fancy. Garden City, N. Y. : Doubleday,
      1946.
           A Nova Scotian privateer in the West Indies.

2006 _____. Roger Sudden. Garden City, N. Y. : Doubleday,
      1945.
           The rivalry between French and British seamen over
      the settlement of Nova Scotia.

2007 _____. Rover: The Story of a Canadian Privateer. New
      York: St. Martin's Press, 1959.

2008 Ramon, The Rover of Cuba (pseud.). The Personal Narra-
      tive of that Celebrated Pirate. Translated from the Original
      Spanish. Boston: Richardson, Lord and Holbrooke, 1829.
           An early American pirate story.

2009 Rascovich, Mark. The Bedford Incident. New York: Athe-
      neum, 1963.
           Cold War naval action, similar to Gallery's The Brink
      (q. v.).

2010 Ratigan, William. The Adventures of Captain McCargo. New
      York: Random House, 1956.
           Spirited tales of a Great Lake's captain; ante-bellum
      setting.

2011 Rawlings, Alfred. A Sea Anthology. London: Hay and Han-
      cock, 1913.

2012 Rayford, Julian Lee. Child of the Snapping Turtle, Mike
      Fink. New York: Abelard, 1951.
           Boating adventures along frontier rivers in the early
      19th-century. Mike Fink was the Paul Bunyon of keelboat-
      men.

2013   Raymond, George S.   The Nautilus; Or, The American Priva-
       teer.   A Tale of Land and Sea During the Last War.   Bos-
       ton: F. Gleason, 1847.

2014   Rayne, Theodore, ed.   Sea Stories.   London: Aaronson,
       1943.

2015   Rayner, Denys A.   The Enemy Below.   New York: Holt,
       1957.
             This story of a World War II battle between a U-boat
       and the British destroyer Hecate was made into a movie
       starring Robert Mitchum and Curt Jurgens.   The movie
       version casts the British destroyer and her crew as an
       American destroyer escort and the unnamed Captain as a
       hard-driving Yank.

2016   _____.   Long Flight.   London: Collins, 1958.

2017   _____.   The Long Haul.   New York: McGraw-Hill, 1960.
             The trials of a British destroyer in hauling a torpedoed,
       but seaworthy, tanker to port during World War II.

2018   Reach, Angus B.   Leonard Lindsay.   London: Routledge,
       1850.
             English and Scottish buccaneers dominate the Spanish
       Main at the end of the 17th-century and in this rather dry
       tale.

2019   Reed, D.   Rule of Three.   London: Cape, 1950.
       Mutiny.

2020   Reed, T. Baines.   Sir Ludar.   London: Sampson, Low, 1889.
       England, Ireland, and the Spanish Armada.

2021   Reyner, F.   David Farragut, Sailor.   Philadelphia: Lippin-
       cott, 1953.

2022   Reynolds, J. M.   The Guns of Yorktown.   New York: Apple-
       ton, 1932.
             The climactic Revolutionary War battle by land and sea.

2023   Rhodes, James A. and Dean Jauchius.   The Court Martial of
       Commodore Perry.   Indianapolis: Bobbs-Merrill, 1961.
             Based on an incident in the life of Oliver H. Perry.

2024   Rhys, Ernest.   The Man at Odds.   London: Hurst, 1904.
       Piratical smuggling off the Welsh coast in 1745.

2025   Rickert, Edith.   Out of the Cypress Swamp.   New York:
       Baker and Taylor, 1902.
             1812 setting; New Orleans pirates; inter-racial marriage
       problems.

RIDEOUT

178

2026 Rideout, Henry Milner. Admiral's Light. Boston: Houghton,
Mifflin, 1907. y.
Rideout, ex-Harvard English professor turns his experi-
ences into fiction. This tale deals with New Brunswick and
Maine salty types.

2027 _____. Barbry. New York: Duffield, 1923. y.
Americans in adventure off the North African coast.

2028 _____. The Far Cry. New York: Duffield, 1916. y.
Gripping story of youths' survival against the sea and
rascals in the South Seas. Comparable to themes found in
Joseph Conrad's stories (q.v.).

2029 _____. The Twisted Foot. Boston: Houghton, Mifflin,
1910. y.
Originally appearing in sequel in Saturday Evening Post,
this tale of the East Indies is reminiscent of the bizarre
themes found in Robert Louis Stevenson (q.v.).

2030 Riesenberg, David. Under Sail; A Boy's Voyage Around Cape
Horn. New York: Harcourt, Brace, c.1924. y.

2031 Riesenberg, Felix. Full Ahead! A Career Story of the
American Merchant Marine. New York: Dodd, Mead, 1941.

2032 _____. Man on the Raft. New York: Dodd, Mead, 1945.
y.
A young American merchant cadet makes his first voyage in wartime.

2033 _____. Mother Sea. New York: Claude Kendall, 1933.
y.
Story of a sea captain's adventures in the late 1890's.

2034 _____. The Phantom Freighter. New York: Dodd, Mead,
1944.
The mysterious voyage of a white-painted transport to
a South Seas island in 1943.

2035 _____. Salvage. New York: Dodd, Mead, 1942. y.
Action in the Sargasso Sea in December 1941.

2036 _____. Shipmates. New York: Harcourt, 1928. y.

2037 Ripley, Clements. Clear for Action; A Novel about John Paul
Jones. New York: Appleton, Century, 1940.
About the Bon Homme Richard.

2038 Ritchie, Lewis A. Action Stations! By "Bartimus," pseud.
Boston: Little, Brown, 1941.
Naval action in early World War II.

2039   _____ . An Awefully Big Adventure. By "Bartimus,"
        pseud. London: Cassell, 1919.

2040   _____ . The Bartimus Omnibus. By "Bartimus," pseud.
        London: Rich, 1938.

2041   _____ . The Ditty Box. By "Bartimus," pseud. London:
        Hutchinson, 1940.

2042   _____ . The Long Trick. By "Bartimus," pseud. Lon-
        don: Cassell, 1917.

2043   _____ . Naval Occasions. By "Bartimus," pseud. Lon-
        don: Collins, 1944.

2044   _____ . The Navy Eternal. By "Bartimus," pseud. Lon-
        don: Hodder & Stoughton, 1918.

2045   _____ . Seaways. By "Bartimus," pseud. London: Cas-
        sell, 1923.

2046   _____ . Steady as You Go. By "Bartimus," pseud. Lon-
        don: Collins, 1942.

2047   _____ . A Tall Ship and Other Naval Occasions. By
        "Bartimus," pseud. Famous Books. London: Penguin,
        1937.
            First published in 1915.

2048   _____ . The Turn of the Road. By "Bartimus," pseud.
        London: Collins, 1946.

2049   Rivette, Marc. The Incident. Cleveland: World, 1957.
            In the far Pacific off the usual shipping lanes, an un-
        identified submarine sinks an American merchantman in
        peacetime. Thus begins a terrifying quest for survival
        among the Yankee crewmen.

2050   Roark, Garland. Bay of Traitors. Garden City, N.Y.:
        Doubleday, 1966.
            The story of a freighter caught in a terrific hurricane.

2051   _____ . Captain Thomas Fenion, Master Mariner. New
        York: Messner, 1958. y.
            Biographical fiction which explores the life of this
        American and his early adventures on the Erie Canal, a
        Chesapeake Bay oyster boat, and an Atlantic coastal schoon-
        er. Later we see his experiences with tankers and tugs in
        the oil business and throughout we hear of his fabulous
        feats of seamanship.

2052   _____ . Fair Wind to Java. Garden City, N.Y.: Double-
        day, 1948.

Square-rigging in the 1880's.

2053   _____ . The Lady and the Deep Blue Sea. Garden City,
        N. Y. : Doubleday, 1958.
        A clipper ship race.

2054   _____ . The Outlawed Banner. Garden City, N. Y. :
        Doubleday, 1956.
        Running blockades during the Civil War at sea.

2055   _____ . Rainbow in the Royals. Garden City, N. Y. :
        Doubleday, 1950.
        California Gold Rush sailing adventures; set in the
        1850's.

2056   _____ . Slant of the Wild Wind. Garden City, N. Y. :
        Doubleday, 1952.
        Government schooner Upstart in treacherous seas and
        business; Far Eastern islands; gold; a naval court; and love.

2057   _____ . Star in the Rigging. A Novel of the Texas Navy.
        Garden City, N. Y. : Doubleday, 1954.
        1835 on the waters of the Gulf of Mexico. The best
        fictional introduction to that little-known fleet.

2058   _____ . Wake of the Red Witch. Boston: Little, Brown,
        1946.

2059   _____ . The Wreck of the Running Gale. Garden City,
        N. Y. : Doubleday, 1953.
        A white man on forbidden islands evens the score after
        wrong done him by a Confederate privateer; a strange annal.

2060   Roberts, Charles G. D. The Forge in the Forest. New
        York: Silver, 1897.
        Building and fighting Oliver H. Perry's flotilla.

2061   _____ . A Prisoner of Mademoiselle. New York: Page,
        1905.
        A Yankee seaman and a French girl fall in love in
        early Acadia.

2062   _____ . A Sister to Evangeline. New York: Silver, 1898.
        Nova Scotia in the mid-18th-century. Reminiscent of
        the tales by Thomas Raddall (q. v.).

2063   Roberts, Kenneth Lewis. Arundel; A Chronicle of the Prov-
        ince of Maine and the Secret Expedition Against Quebec.
        New York: Doubleday, c. 1933, 1956.
        One of several Roberts' works set around Cape Arun-
        del, Maine. This tale concerns Arnold's expedition against
        Quebec.

2064 _____. Boon Island. Garden City, N. Y. : Doubleday,
       1956.
       In 1710, the Nottingham struck Boon Island, a hump-
back boulder-strewn ledge off the Maine coast; against great
odds, men refused to give in to Nature, but the shipwreck
was still complete.

2065 _____. Captain Caution; A Chronicle of Arundel. Garden
       City, N. Y. : Doubleday, c. 1934.
       Set around Arundel, Maine, during War of 1812.
French privateer and American mariners vs. British; much
action.

2066 _____. The Lively Lady; A Chronicle of Arundel, of
       Privateering, and of the Circular Prison on Dartmoor.
       Garden City, N. Y. : Doubleday, c. 1931, 1959.
       Begins at Arundel, at the mouth of the Arundel River
in the Province of Maine, during the War of 1812, in which
privateers were America's chief substitute for a navy. An
American captain is imprisoned.

2067 _____. Lydia Bailey. Garden City, N. Y. : Doubleday,
       1947.
       Sea and land adventures during the Haitian revolution
and the War with Tripoli.

2068 _____. Northwest Passage. Garden City, N. Y. : Double-
       day, c. 1937.
       Book I of this novel appeared serially as 'Rogers'
Rangers. " The story of Robert Rogers' overland and ice
excursion looking for the Pacific.

2069 _____. Oliver Wiswell. Garden City, N. Y. : Doubleday,
       1940.
       Presents the Tory or Loyalist point of view of the
Revolution; significant sea setting.

2070 _____. Rabble in Arms; A Chronicle of Arundel and the
       Burgoyne Invasion. Garden City, N. Y. : Doubleday, c.
       1933.
       The Battle of Valcour Island during the Revolution is
featured; Maine coastal settings; sequel to Arundel, above.

2071 Roberts, Morely. Sea Dogs. London: George Newnes,
       1910.
       Drake and company.

2072 Roberts, Theodore. A Cavalier of Virginia. New York:
       Page, 1910.
       Virginia and the sea in Georgian days.

2073 Robertson, Keith. Ice to India. New York: Viking, 1955.
       The Mason family of Philadelphia gambles on

transporting ice after the War of 1812.

2074 _____. Wreck of the Saginaw. New York: Viking, 1954.
How a shipwrecked crew attempts to voyage 1500 miles to the safety of Hawaii.

2075 Robertson, Morgan. Down to the Sea. New York: Harper, 1905.
Hairbreadth escapism based on fantastic autobiographical adventures at sea. Robertson is often compared with Jack London in that genre of virile salts who turned to writing to keep alive. Others of his stories include:

2076 _____. Land Ho! New York: Harper, 1905.

2077 _____. Masters of Men; A Romance of the New Navy. New York: Doubleday, 1901.
A tale of Teddy Roosevelt's "Great White Fleet."

2078 _____. Shipmates. New York: Appleton, 1901.

2079 _____. Sinful Peck; A Novel. New York: Harper, 1903.

2080 _____. The Wreck of the Tilton; Or, Futility. New York: McClures, 1914.

2081 Robeson, Kenneth. The Sea Angel. New York: Bantam Books, 1970.
The famed 1930's bronze crimefighter had several adventures afloat, all of which have been reprinted in paperback by this firm: The Polar Treasure; The Fantastic Island; The Sargasso Ogre; The Mystery Under the Sea; The Terror in the Navy; and The Sea Magician.

2082 Robinson, Charles N., and John Leyland. In the Queen's Navee: The Adventures of a Colonial Cadet on His Way to Britannia. London: Tower, 1892. y.

2083 Robinson, Gertrude. Sign of the Golden Fish. New York: Winston, 1949.
A fishing adventure along the Maine coast in which an 18th-century boy sails and works with hardy Cornish fishermen.

2084 Robinson, Hercules. Harry Evelyn; Or, The Romance of the Atlantic: A Naval Novel, Founded on Facts. London: John and D. A. Darling, 1859.
Treasure hunting.

2085 _____. Sea Drift. London, 1858.
Naval sketches and stories. The author fought at Trafalgar as a young midshipman.

2086   Roche, James J. Story of the Filibusterers. New York:
       Macmillan, 1891. "Adventure Series."
            Filibusterers were Caribbean adventurers often involved
       in gunrunning sorties to Cuba. Reissued in 1901 as By-
       Ways of War; The Story of the Filibusterers and lauded by
       Richard Harding Davis.

2087   Rogers, Cameron. Drake's Quest. New York: Doubleday,
       Page, 1927.
            Elizabethan voyages of discovery and exploration with
       action on the Spanish Main.

2088   Rogers, Robert C. Will o' the Wasp. New York: Putnam,
       1896.
            Adventures of the War of 1812.

2089   Rogers, S. R. H. Ships and Sailors. London: Harrap, 1934.

2090   Roth, Robert, Sand in the Wind. Boston: Little, Brown,
       1973.
            U. S. Marines in Vietnam; tough Corps, trained for
       land and sea.

2091   Rolt-Wheeler, Francis. The Wonder of War at Sea. Boston:
       Lothrop, Lea, & Shepard, 1918.
            Tales of the First World War afloat.

2092   Rooney, Philip. Golden Coast. New York: Duell, Sloane
       & Pearce, 1949.
            Early 19th-century encounters with the Barbary Pirates.

2093   Rose, Alec. My Favorite Tales of the Sea. London: Har-
       rap, 1969.

2094   Ross, Sutherland. Freedom Is the Prize. New York: Walk-
       er, 1964. y.
            The naval action of the War of 1812 as seen by a young
       American lad pressed into the Royal Navy.

2095   Rourke, Lawrence, ed. Men Only at Sea. London: Pearson,
       1940.

2096   Rowe, G. In Nelson's Day. London: Scott, 1905.

2097   Rowe, John G. , ed. Thrilling Tales of Adventure on the High
       Seas. London: Crowther, 1945.

2098   Rowland, Henry C. Hirondelle. New York: Harper, 1922.
            The adventures of an Irish lord engaged in the slave
       trade, with a spot of piracy on the side, during the War of
       1812.

2099   Rucker, Helen. Cargo of Brides. New York: Brown, 1956.

A bevy of women set sail for the Northwest in pursuit
of husbands; late 19th-century tale.

2100 Rumanes, George N.   The Man with the Black Worry Beads.
New York: E. P. Dutton, 1973.
Concerns the Anglo-Greek attempt to break Rommel's
seaborne life-line during World War II.

2101 Russ, Martin. War Memorial. New York: Atheneum, 1967.
World War II.

2101a _____ . Searchers at the Gulf. New York: Norton, 1970.

2102 Russell, W. Clark. The Death Ship. London, n. d.
Russell, born in New York City of English parents,
was one of the most important sea novelists at the turn of
the century, a man also well known for his verse. After
eight years in the rough British merchant service, he came
ashore to begin writing in an effort to correct its many
ills. He was as successful, or more so, in eliminating
privation from the British Merchant Marine as Dana (q. v.)
was earlier in the American. His only son became the
famous British naval philosopher Admiral Sir Herbert Russell.

2103 _____ . Jack's Courtship. London: Low, 1885.

2104 _____ . John Holdsworth, Chief Mate. London: Low, 1875.

2105 _____ . List Ye Landsmen. London: Cassell, n. d.

2106 _____ . Marooned. New York: Macmillan, 1895.

2107 _____ . My Danish Sweetheart. 3rd ed. London: Methuen
1895.

2108 _____ . My Shipmate Louise. London: Chatto & Windus,
1894.

2109 _____ . My Watch Below. London: Low, 1882.
Republished from a serial running in the London Daily
Telegraph. A collection of fictitious tales which helped to
improve life in the British Merchant Navy.

2110 _____ . The Mystery of the Ocean Star. New York: Appleton, 1888.

2111 _____ . An Ocean of Free Lance. New York: Macmillan,
1881.
Privateering during the Napoleonic wars.

2112 _____ . An Ocean Tragedy. London: Chatto & Windus,
1893

2113 _____. The Romance of a Midshipman. London: Chatto & Windus, 1898.

2114 _____. The Romance of Jenny Harlowe. London: Chatto & Windus, 1887.

2115 _____. Rose Island. Chicago: Herberts, 1899.
All American editions of this author's works were reprinted from the British originals.

2116 _____. Round the Galley Fire. London: Low, 1883.
More tales of the British merchant marine.

2117 _____. A Sailor's Sweetheart. London: Low, 1886.

2118 _____. The Sea Queen. New York: Harper, 1883.

2119 _____. Strange Voyage. London: Low, 1886.

2120 _____. The Tragedy of Ida Noble. New York: Appleton, 1892.

2121 _____. A Voyage to the Cape. London: Chatto & Windus, 1889.

2122 _____. The Wreck of the Grosvener. London: Low, 1877.
The author's most important work, designed to improve conditions for British merchant seamen.

2123 _____. The Yarn of Old Harbour Town. London: Jacobs, 1900.
A story of Lord Nelson at work in the English Channel. Even during his lifetime, Russell had a reputation as one of England's leading sea novelists. His works are still interesting today.

- S -

2124 Sabatini, Rafael. The Black Swan. Boston: Houghton, Mifflin, 1932.
A virtuous hero opposes the infamous Tom Leach, skipper of the pirate ship Black Swan off the 17th-century Spanish Main.
Master of the historical/pirate tale, Sabatini was born of an English mother in Central Italy in 1875. He went to Britain on business as a young man and there became a citizen, settling down to write these well-known yarns.

2125 _____. Captain Blood: His Odyssey. Boston: Houghton, Mifflin, 1922.
The famous story of Dr. Peter Blood, soldier, country

doctor, slave, pirate, and finally Governor of Jamaica in
the bloody days after Monmouth. Played by Errol Flynn in
the 1935 movie version.

2126 _____. Captain Blood Returns. Boston: Houghton, Mifflin, 1931.

2127 _____. The Carolinian. Boston: Houghton, Mifflin, 1925.
Set along the Carolinas before and during the Revolution.

2128 _____. Columbus, A Romance. Boston: Houghton, Mifflin, 1942.
A biographical novel concerning the great explorer.

2129 _____. The Fortunes of Captain Blood. Boston: Houghton
Mifflin, 1936.
Sequel to Blood Returns; further adventures are related.

2130 _____. Saga of the Sea. 3 Vols in 1. London: Hutchinson, 1953.
The Peter Blood series.

2131 _____. The Sea Hawk. Boston: Houghton, Mifflin, 1915.
How Sir Oliver Tressilian, Cornish gentleman and some
time commander of one of Her Majesty's ships which dis-
persed the Spanish Armada, became a follower of Mahmud
and a barbary corsair--winning for himself the title "Sakr-
el-Bahr, " or "Hawk of the Sea. "

2132 _____. The Sword of Islam. Boston: Houghton, Mifflin,
1939.
Genoese admiral Andrea Doria takes on that superior
Turkish admiral-pirate Barbarossa in the early 16th-century.

2133 _____, ed. A Century of Great Sea Stories. London:
Hutchinson, n. d.

2134 _____, ed. Romances of the Sea. London: Hutchinson,
1933.

2135 Sabin, E. L. Mississippi River Boy. Philadelphia: Lippin-
cott, 1932. y.
Early steamboats and social life along the "Father of
Waters. "

2136 Sackville-West, Victoria. No Signposts in the Sea. Garden
City, N. Y. : Doubleday, 1961.
A famous journalist accompanies an attractive widow on
a leisurely sea voyage and discovers love.

2137 Sadler, S. Whitechurch. The African Cruiser. New York:
E. P. Dutton, date unknown.
Patrolling the slave trade.

2138 Safford, Henry B.   <u>Tory Tavern.</u> Philadelphia: Penn, 1942.
      y.
           Action in the Revolution in which a Tory lad, after
      serving three years in the Royal Navy, becomes a Yankee
      spy.

2139 Sagon, Amyot.   <u>When George III Was King</u>. London: Sands,
      1899.
           Smuggling was epidemic in Cornwall.

2140 St. John, H.   <u>The Voyage of the Avenger</u>.   London: Jarrold,
      1898.
           Drake's last expedition.

2141 St. Ledger, H.   <u>Ocean Outlaw</u>. London: Blackie, 1934.

2142 Sale, Richard.   <u>Is a Ship Burning</u>? New York: Dodd, Mead,
      1938.
           Disaster to a passenger ship.

2143 Sallaska, Georgia.   <u>Three Ships and Three Kings</u>.   Garden
      City, N. Y. : Doubleday, 1969.   y.

2144 Sargent, Lucius Manlius.   <u>A Word in Season; Or, The Sailor's</u>
      <u>Widow.   Founded on Fact</u>.   Boston: William S. Damrell,
      1835.
           This author (1786-1867) was better known as an anti-
      quarian and temperance leader than a novelist.

2145 <u>Saturday Evening Post</u>, Editors of.   <u>The Saturday Evening</u>
      <u>Post Reader of Sea Stories</u>.   Edited by Day Edgar.   Garden
      City, N. Y. : Doubleday, 1962.

2146 Saxton, Alexander P.   <u>Bright Web in the Darkness</u>. New
      York: St. Martin's, 1959.
           The story of Black welder Joyce Allen in a San Fran-
      cisco shipyard during World War II.

2147 Schauwecker, Frederick.   <u>The Armored Cruiser: A Naval</u>
      <u>Romance of the Great War</u>.   Translated by Katherine Barlow.
      London: Massie, 1938.
           World War I.

2148 Schmeltzer, Kurt.   <u>Long Arctic Night</u>. New York: Watts,
      1952.   y.
           The Barents expedition left Amsterdam in 1594 on an
      ill-fated mission to find an Arctic route to the Orient.

2149 Schoonover, Lawrence L.   <u>Central Passage</u>.   New York:
      Sloane, 1962.
           Action in the West Indies in the days of the buccaneers.

2150 _____.   <u>The Queen's Cross</u>. New York: Sloane, 1955.

Isabella and Columbus.

2151 _____. The Revolutionary. Boston: Little, Brown, 1958.
John Paul Jones aboard the Bon Homme Richard.

2152 Schumacher, Henry. Nelson's Last Love. London: Hutchinson, 1913.
The relationship between the admiral, Lady Hamilton and Queen Maria Caroline.

2153 Scott, James M. Heather Mary. New York: Dutton, 1953.
A yacht race from England to Bermuda.

2154 _____. The Lady and the Corsair. New York: Dutton, 1958.
A Sicilian pirate captures and harasses a British merchantman thereby arousing the ire of an indomitable lady passenger.

2155 _____. Sea-Wyf. New York: Dutton, 1956.
A mysterious woman and several men are shipwrecked on a tropic island.

2156 Scott, Michael. The Cruise of the Midge. London, 1835.
Appeared first as a Blackwood's Magazine serial, 1834-1835. Born in 1789, Scott did much travelling afloat, but as a passenger, not a sailor.

2157 _____. Tom Cringle's Log. New York: Dodd, 1927. y.
First published in Blackwood's Magazine in 1829-1830 and in book form in 1834, this quick story tells in diary form of the adventures of a British midshipman in the West Indies during 1813-1814. Encounters with privateers and smugglers and life aboard Royal Navy warships are accurately portrayed.

2158 Scott, Sir Walter. The Pirate. A Waverly Novel. Various publishers, 1821.
A tale of a piratical career ended by the hangman in 1725. Scott, the famous author of Ivanhoe, visited the Orkney and Shetland Islands in 1814 and there learned of the early 18th-century pirate John Gaw. He attempted to create a romance around his adventures, but except for his scenic descriptions, failed. James Fenimore Cooper (q.v.) was so upset by this tale that he undertook the writing of The Pilot (q.v.) to show his friends (and the world) how a real sea novel should be done!

2159 "Sea Lion," pseud. Cargo for Crooks. London: Collins, 1948.

2160 _____. Phantom Fleet. London: Collins, 1946.

2161 _____ . Sea of Troubles. London: Collins, 1947.

2162 _____ . Sink Me a Ship. London: Collins, 1947.

2163 Seaborn, Captain Adam (pseud.). Symzonia: A Voyage of
      Discovery. By Captain Adam Seaborn. New York: J.
      Seymour, 1820.
          Travel genre popular at the time; relate to Poe's Nar-
      rative of Arthur Gordon Pym, above.

2164 Searls, Henry. The Hero Ship. New York: World, 1969.
          World War II in the Pacific; based on true ordeals of
      the U.S. carrier Franklin.

2165 Seawell, Molly E. The Imprisoned Midshipman. New York:
      Appleton, 1908. y.
          Capture of the U.S. frigate Philadelphia during the war
      with the Barbary Pirates.

2166 _____ . Little Jarvis. New York: D. Appleton, 1894. y.
          This tale of the war with Tripoli features the Constitu-
      tion and the hero, a midshipman.

2167 _____ . Midshipman Paulding. New York: D. Appleton,
      1895. y.
          A story of Midshipman Hiram Paulding (to become
      Commodore) at the Battle of Lake Champlain (1814).

2168 _____ . The Rock of the Lion. New York: Harper, 1899.
      y.
          The siege of Gibraltar, 1779-1783.

2169 Seelye, John. The True Adventure of Huckleberry Finn, As
      Told by the Author. Evanston, Ill.: Northwestern Univer-
      sity Press, 1970.
          Huck answers all the critical and scholarly objections
      to the original version.

2170 Seifert, Shirley. River Out of Eden. New York: Mills,
      1940. y.
          The adventures of a young boatman on the lower Mis-
      sissippi in 1763.

2171 _____ . Those Who Go Against the Current. New York:
      Lippincott, 1943. y.
          Mapping the Missouri River in the early 19th-century.

2172 _____ . The Wayfarer. New York: Mill, 1938. y.
          A tale of whaling and women during the Civil War
      period.

2173 Seligman, Adrian. Thunder in the Bay. London: Hodder &
      Stoughton, 1951.

2174 Sels, Owen. The Portugese Fragment. New York: Pantheon,
      1973.
           Agreeing to visit Asia for a bit of "harmless smug-
      gling, " Nicholas Maaston ends up battling for a treasure in
      the waters off the coast of Ceylon.

2175 Senseney, Daniel. Scanlon of the Sub Service. Garden City,
      N. Y. : Doubleday, 1963. y.
           Will Pete Scanlon's secret fear permit him to make good
      in the Silent Service?

2176 Serraillier, I. Captain Bounsaboard and the Pirates. Lon-
      don: Cape, 1949. y.

2177 Service Afloat, Comprising the Personal Narrative of a Naval
      Officer Employed During the Late [Napoleonic] War. Lon-
      don: Richard Bentley, 1833.

2178 Setlowe, Rick. The Brink. New York: Fields, 1975.
           A look at the Cold War generation of the 1950's, and
      most especially those men of the Navy Air Force trapped be-
      tween the ghosts of "winning" World War II and the grim
      realities of nuclear destruction.

2179 Shaw, Charles. Heaven Knows Mr. Allison. New York:
      Crown, 1952.
           World War II; Marine and a nun in the Pacific.

2180 Shaw, Frank H. Eastward Ho! London: Low, 1949.
           Reprinted from an earlier edition.

2181 _____. Exultant Danger. London: Paul, 1948.

2182 _____. In the Days of Nelson. London: Cassell, 1910.

2183 _____. The Reluctant Pirate. London: Blackie, 1939.

2184 _____. Sea-Fret. London: Arnold, 1938.

2185 Shay, Edith. Private Adventure of Captain Shaw. Boston:
      Houghton, Mifflin, 1945.
           Exploits of a Cape Cod skipper in France in 1793 when
      Robespierre was running the French Revolution.

2186 Sheean, Vincent. Sanfelice: A Novel. New York: Doubleday,
      1936.
           A story of the Neapolitan uprising of 1799 with considera
      ble mention of the love affair between Lady Hamilton and
      Horatio Nelson.

2187 Shellabarger, Samuel. Captain from Castile. Boston: Little,
      Brown, 1945.
           Biographical fiction of the Spanish conquest of Mexico;

significant sea episodes.

2188   Sheppard, Francis H.   Love Afloat: A Story of the American
       Navy.   New York: Publisher unknown, 1875.
              Buccaneers.

2189   Sherman, D. R.   Brothers of the Sea.   Boston: Little,
       Brown, 1966.   y.
              A fisherman's son's moving adventure with a dolphin
       results in tragedy.

2190   Shirreffs, Gordon D.   The Cold Seas Beyond.   Philadelphia:
       Westminster, 1959.   y.
              Two young Yankee tars man a PT-boat in the Aleutians
       during the Second World War.

2191   _____.   The Enemy Seas.   Philadelphia: Westminster,
       1965.   y.
              A pair of young sailors are rescued by an American
       submarine and then take part in the boat's perilous mission
       against the Japanese.

2192   _____.   The Hostile Beaches.   Philadelphia: Westminster,
       1961.   y.
              The lads above join a destroyer in hazardous fighting
       during the Solomons campaign.

2193   Shortfellow, Tom, pseud.   The Lady of the Cabin.   Boston:
       F. Gleason, 1850.
              This popular romance writer of the 1840's is yet un-
       known by his or her real name.   An interesting literary
       mystery.

2194   Shute, Nevil.   Most Secret.   New York: William Morrow,
       1945.
              A British-sponsored naval expedition, commanded by
       Free French officers, is sent to bolster the morale of the
       inhabitants of an isolated Breton channel town and do in the
       nasty Germans stationed there in 1941.

2195   Simons, Katherine D. M.   The Land Beyond the Tempest.
       By Drayton Mayrant, pseud.   New York: Coward-McCann,
       1960.
              Another telling of the "Sea Venture" story and Bermuda.

2196   Sladen, Douglas.   The Admiral.   London: Pearson, 1898.
              Nelson and Lady Hamilton love again.

2197   Slaughter, Frank G.   Buccaneer Surgeon.   By C. V. Terry,
       pseud.   New York: Hanover, 1954.
              A pirate ship doctor and his adventures on the 17th-
       century Spanish Main.

2198 _____. The Deadly Lady of Madagascar. By C. V. Terry, pseud.
What happens to a nest of 17th-century pirates when a
British East India Company ship is commissioned to hunt
them down.

2199 _____. Flight from Natchez. Garden City, N. Y. : Doubleday, 1955.
A group of Loyalists flee that city via river in 1781.

2200 _____. Fort Everglades. Garden City, N. Y. : Doubleday,
1951.
Motion in the Seminole war, which was fought to a large
extent by small U. S. Navy and marine boat parties.

2201 _____. The Golden Ones. By C. V. Terry, pseud.
Garden City, N. Y. : Doubleday, 1957.
"From the lusty court of Queen Bess to the treasure-
laden jungles of the New World, Shawn MacManus pursued
adventure, fortune, and a treacherous Spanish beauty, Doña
Elvira. . . . "

2202 _____. The Mapmaker. Garden City, N. Y. : Doubleday,
1957.
A Venetian cartographer working for Prince Henry the
Navigator.

2203 _____. The Warrior. Garden City, N. Y. : Doubleday,
1956.
Another look at the Seminole wars of the 1830's.

2204 Sleeper, John S. Tales of the Ocean, and Essays for the
Forecastle: Containing Matters and Incidents Humorous,
Pathetic, Romantic, and Sentimental. By Hawser Martin-
gale, pseud. Boston: S. A. Dickinson, 1841.
A mariner by trade, Sleeper also wrote, by date: Salt-
Water Bubbles (1854); Ocean Adventure (1857); Jack in the
Forecastle (1860); and Mark Rowland (1867).

2205 Smith, Arthur D. H. Porto Bello Gold. London: Brentanos,
1924.
More or less a sequel to Stevenson's Treasure Island,
telling how captains Flint and Murray sacked a Spanish galleon and buried their treasure on Treasure Island.

2206 Smith, Arthur G. Jack Scott, Midshipman: His Log. By
"Aurora, " pseud. London, 1912. y.

2207 Smith, Cicely F. A Sea Chest: An Anthology of Ships and
Sailormen. London: Methuen, 1927.

2208 _____. Ship Aground. London: Oxford University Press,
1940.

2209 _____, ed. True Tales of the Sea. London: Oxford University Press, 1932.

2210 Smith, Francis H. Arm Chair at the Inn. New York: Scribner's, 1910.
John Paul Jones makes an appearance.
Smith, a lighthouse keeper and painter, created numerous works popular in his day, entering upon his literary career late in life as a result of his famous "after dinner" stories. Most of these next citations are based on anecdotes from his engineering career (lighthouse and breakwater construction, etc) and are noteworthy for their picturesque colloquialism.

2211 _____. Caleb West, Master Diver. New York: Houghton, Mifflin, 1898. y.
New England mariners build and secure a lighthouse.

2212 _____. Tides of Barnegat. New York: Scribner's, 1906.
Fisherman along the New Jersey coast during the Civil War.

2213 Smith, Freelove. Trading East. Boston: Little, Brown, 1930. y.
Based on Hakluyt's voyages, 1580-1600.

2214 Smith, G. C. The Boatswains' Mate; Or, An Interesting Dialogue Between Two British Seamen. London: W. Whittemore, n. d.
A fictitious religious dialogue by a former Royal Navy chaplain, c. 1830.

2215 _____. The Quartermaster; Or, The Second Part of the Boatswains' Mate. London: W. Whittemore, n. d.

2216 Smith, Herbert H. His Majesty's Sloop Diamond Rock. By H. S. Huntington, pseud. New York: Houghton, 1905.
Sea battles in defense of Martinique during the Napoleonic era.

2217 Smith, Ralph. The Dragon in New Albion. By S. H. Paxton, pseud. Boston: Little, Brown, 1953. y.
"Dragon" was the Spanish name for Sir Francis Drake, around whom this adventure unfolds.

2218 Smith, Ruel P. Prisoners of Fortune. New York: Page, 1907.
Pirates and treasure in the Massachusetts Bay Colony.

2219 Smollett, Tobias G. The Miscellaneous Works. 8 Vols. Edinburgh, Scotland, 1809.
Titles important to this work include:

2220   . The Adventures of Peregrine Pickle (1751).
            Deemed the best picaresque novel in English, Pickle,
      an infamous practical joker, takes shelter with a retired
      Royal Navy Commodore.   Filled with wild absurdities and
      brutal obscenities.

2221   . The Adventures of Roderick Random (1748).
            The first autobiographical novel in the English lan-
      guage and is based almost entirely on events in the author's
      naval career.   Pungent in style and loaded with detail, it
      lacks the grace of other tales.
            Tobias G. Smollett, born in Scotland in 1721, was a
      surgeon's mate aboard H. M. S. Chicester during the Royal
      Navy's 1741 assault on the Spanish stronghold of Cartegena
      in present-day Colombia.   Sickened by the horrors atten-
      dant to his post, he quit the sea in 1744 to enter upon a
      surgeon's career in London.   His latent interest in writing
      eventually blossomed into a new profession and he gave up
      "healing" to become a terror of the late 18th-century lit-
      erary world.
            Although it is nearly impossible for the casual modern
      reader to enjoy Smollett, much of whose product was
      "bloody awful, " his debt to the ex-surgeon is immense.
      Smollett as much or more so than Defoe was the father
      of the sea novel, a debt acknowledged by many later writ-
      ers including Frederic Marryat (q. v.) and Charles Dickens.
      The two works cited above are classics which should be re-
      quired reading of all serious students of nautical literature.
            Smollett, who also began the genre called Gothic today,
      was not a kindly man, either in his personal life or with
      regards to fellow writers.   His atrabilious nature was ac-
      centuated by an illness which caused him to seek a new
      life in Italy.   He died near Leghorn (Livorno) in 1771.

2222 Smythe, Theodore. Atlantic Tramp. London: Jarrolds, 1942.
      Battle of the Atlantic in World War II.

2223 Snaith, John C. The Sailor. New York: Appleton, 1916.
            A lad from the London slums serves six years at sea
      before achieving literary success.   Suggested by the life of
      John Masefield.

2224 South, Henry E. The Destroyers, and Other Stories of the
      Royal Navy. London: Simpkin, Marshall, 1918.
            World War I.

2225 Spain, Nancy. Thank You, Nelson. London: Hutchinson,
      1945.
            A tale of the Napoleonic wars at sea.

2226 Spanner, E. F. The Broken Trident. London, 1926.

2227 Spence, Hartzell. Vain Shadow. New York: McGraw-Hill,

1947.
    The 1541 discovery of the Amazon River by Don Fran-
cisco Orellana.

2228 Sperry, Armstrong. <u>All Sails Set</u>. Philadelphia: Winston,
      1935. y.
      Nautical adventure off the New England coast, 1800-1825.

2229 _____. <u>The Black Falcon</u>. Philadelphia: Winston, 1949.
      y.
      Escaping a British frigate, a lad joins the pirate band
of Jean Lafitte.

2230 _____. <u>Hull-Down for Action</u>. Garden City, N. Y. : Double-
      day, 1945.
      Nazi sympathizers mutiny aboard an American ship, put-
ting loyal crewmen adrift on a raft.

2231 _____. <u>Storm Canvas.</u> New York and Philadelphia: Win-
      ston, 1944. y.
      Adventures of the U. S. frigate <u>Thunderbolt</u> in the War
of 1812. Modeled after the U. S. S. <u>Constitution.</u>

2232 Stables, Gordon. <u>As We Sweep Through the Deep.</u> London:
      Nelson, 1894.
      Camperdown and the Battle of the Nile.

2233 _____. <u>Chris Cunningham.</u> London: Show, 1903.
      Nelson and the Battle of Cape St. Vincent.

2234 _____. <u>Westward with Columbus.</u> London: Blackie, 1894.
      The first great expedition.

2235 Stackpole, Edouard A. <u>Nantucket Rebel</u>. New York: Wash-
      burn, 1953. y.
      Patriotic Quakers on Nantucket impede British ships
during the Revolution by turning from whaling to privateering.

2236 _____. <u>Privateer Ahoy.</u> New York: Morrow, 1937. y.
      Action in the War of 1812.

2237 _____. <u>Smuggler's Luck.</u> New York: Morrow, 1931. y.
      Nantucket in the Revolution.

2238 _____. <u>You Fight for Treasure.</u> New York: Morrow,
      1932. y.
      America's early 19th-century war with the Barbary
Pirates.

2239 Stacton, David. <u>A Signal Victory.</u> New York: Pantheon,
      1962.
      A tale of the Napoleonic wars.

2240 _____ . Sir William. New York: Putnam, 1963.
     The husband of Lady Emma Hamilton, who was the Brit-
     ish ambassador to Naples and a friend of Lord Nelson's, did
     not seem to mind the triangle of their relationship.

2241 Stafford, Frank. Heritage Undimmed. London: Hurst, 1942.

2242 _____ . Tattered Ensign. London: Hurst, 1940.

2243 _____ . Weather Shore. London: Hurst, 1949.
     Three tales of the Royal Navy in World War II

2244 Stanford, Alfred B. The Navigator. New York: Morrow,
     1927.
     Nathaniel Bowditch's famous navigating accomplishments.

2245 Stanton, Kenneth "Ken." Cold Blue Death. New York: Mc-
     fadden-Bartell, 1970.
     The "Aquanauts" are a top-secret American navy intelli-
     gence group made up of a crusty old admiral in command, a
     daring diver-agent, Cmdr. William Martin the "Tiger Shark,"
     and a highly sofisticated mini-submarine. Others in the
     series thus far include:

2246 _____ . Evil Cargo. New York: Mcfadden-Bartell, 1973.

2247 _____ . Operation Deep Six. New York: Mcfadden-Bartell,
     1972.

2248 _____ . Operation Mermaid. New York: Mcfadden-Bartell,
     1974.

2249 _____ . Operation Sea Monster. New York: Mcfadden-
     Bartell, 1974.

2250 _____ . Operation Steelfish. New York: Mcfadden-Bartell,
     1972.
2251 _____ . Sargasso Secret. New York: Mcfadden-Bartell,
     1971.

2252 _____ . Seek, Strike, and Destroy. New York: Mcfadden-
     Bartell, 1971.

2253 _____ . Stalkers of the Sea. New York: Mcfadden-Bartell,
     1972.

2254 _____ . Ten Seconds to Zero. New York: Mcfadden-Bar-
     tell, 1970.

2255 _____ . Whirlwind Beneath the Sea. New York: Mcfadden-
     Bartell, 1972.

2256 Steelman, Robert. Call of the Arctic. New York: Coward-

McCann, 1960. y.
A biographical novel concerning USN Arctic explorer
Charles F. Hall.

2257 Steen, Marguerite. The Sun Is My Undoing. New York:
      Viking Press, 1941.
      How an 18th-century English slave trader is captured
      and escapes from the Barbary Pirates.

2258 Stephens, Edward. Blow Negative! Garden City, N.Y.:
      Doubleday, 1962.
      Basically a study of the struggle within the American
      navy (and it was quite a battle!) for the adoption of nuclear-
      powered submarines that culminated in the U.S.S. Nautilus.

2259 _____. The Submariner. Garden City, N.Y.: Doubleday,
      1973.
      Mystery and top secret assignment after two precious
      nuclear submarines vanish.

2260 Sterling, Charles F. Buff and Blue; Or, The Privateers of
      the Revolution. A Tale of Long Island Sound. New York:
      William H. Graham, 1847.

2261 Stevens, William O. and Barclay McKee. The Young Priva-
      teersman. New York: Appleton, 1910. y.
      Three Baltimore lads in the War of 1812 are taken at
      sea and sent to Dartmoor Prison.

2262 Stevenson, Robert L. Kidnapped. Various publishers, 1886.
      How the orphaned David Balfour's own uncle had him
      shanghaied aboard a brig to be sold as a bonded servant to
      an 18th-century Carolina plantation. The sequel, first pub-
      lished in 1892, is David Balfour.
      Robert Louis Stevenson came from a long line of Scotch
      Calvinist engineers. Forced to travel for his health, he met
      violent family opposition when he elected for the career of a
      writer rather than an engineer. His journeys led him to
      California (where he married an attractive American divorcée
      in 1880), around the world, and finally in 1888 to what be-
      came his permanent home, Apia in the Samoan Islands.
      There he continued his writing until his death from cerebral
      hemorrhage in 1894.
      Stevenson was a master of the adventure story, in which
      men of the sea often played leading roles. His narrative
      was usually of the joyous romantic quest, the triumph of
      good over evil, and the solving of enchanting mystery. All
      of his tales, including Ebb Tide (1895) and In the South Seas
      (1896), are much in demand by current readers.

2263 _____. Treasure Island. Various publishers.
      The classic tale of piracy in which a boy and his friends
      seek Captain Flint's gold only to be "stalled" by Long John

Silver and company. One of the most perfect character por-
trayals of movie history grew out of this story when Walt
Disney cast Robert Newton as the one-legged pirate in the
movie version of this story.

2264   _____, and Lloyd Osbourne. Adventure Island. New York:
        Scribner's, 1894.
            Another yarn about pirates and treasure.

2265 Stewart, Davenport. Black Spice. New York: Dutton, 1959.
          After the War of 1812, an unemployed privateersman
        turns to trading in the Spice Islands.

2266 Stewart, George R. East of the Giants. New York: Holt,
        1938.
            A tale of the California gold rush.

2267   _____. Storm. New York: Random House, 1941.
            Impact of a devastating storm along the California coast;
        threats to water supplies, dams, etc. Significant water
        themes.

2268 Stewart, James A. The Branching Coral. By James Meade,
        pseud. New York: Viking, 1961.
            Set in present-day Fiji, this yarn concerns a half-caste
        young Australian, Dan Menard, who is well up the ladder of
        success as the skipper and owner of a 32-foot charter launch
        --until he faces economic disaster.

2269 Stirling, Yates. A United States Midshipman Afloat. Phila-
        delphia: Penn Publishing, 1908. y.
            Sea stories were extremely popular in the early part of
        this century, as was the American Navy, and just as spy
        stories were big in the 1960's, so these were cranked out
        then. Many naval officers, like this one, turned them out
        for the royalties they offered. Four more by Stirling are:

2270   _____. A United States Midshipman in China. Philadelphia:
        Penn Publishing, 1909. y.

2271   _____. A United States Midshipman in Japan. Philadelphia:
        Penn Publishing, 1911. y.

2272   _____. A United States Midshipman in the Philippines.
        Philadelphia: Penn Publishing, 1901. y.

2273   _____. A United States Midshipman in the South Seas.
        Philadelphia: Penn Publishing, 1913. y.

2274 Stitt, George. H. M. S. Wideawake. London: Allen, 1943.
        World War II.

2275 Stockton, Francis R. The Adventures of Captain Horn. New

York: Scribner's, 1895.
A fanciful, entertaining yarn of Inca treasure hunting.
A noted short story writer ("The Lady and the Tiger"),
Stockton was a most prolific sea tale teller as these next
citations demonstrate.

2276 _____ . _Afield and Afloat_. New York: Scribner's, 1900.

2277 _____ . _Captain Chap; Or, The Rolling Stones_. Philadelphia: J. B. Lippincott, 1897.

2278 _____ . _The Captain's Toll-Gate_. New York: D. Appleton, 1903.

2279 _____ . _The Casting Away of Mrs. Lecks and Mrs. Aleshire_. New York: Century, c. 1886.
Robinsoe Crusoe-like story of two matrons surviving a
deserted island. See sequel below, _The Dusantes_.

2280 _____ . _The Clocks of Randaine_. New York: Scribner's, 1892.

2281 _____ . _The Dusantes; A Sequel to "The Casting Away of Mrs. Lecks and Mrs. Aleshire."_ New York: Century, 1888.
Clever, Defoe-like parody. See preliminary story above,
The Casting Away of....

2282 _____ . _The Floating Prince, etc._ New York: Scribner's, 1894.

2283 _____ . _The Great Stone of Sardis. A Novel_. New York: Harper, 1898.
Reflecting on the actual ill-fated explorations of the Sir
Hubert Wilkens-Ellsworth expedition to the North Pole (1891)
in the _Nautilus_, Stockton has written a humorous tale of a
submarine, _Dipsey_, laden with fantastic mechanical devices;
the futuristic tale is set in 1947, including a woman among
a crew of thirteen.

2284 _____ . _Kate Bonnet, The Romance of a Pirate's Daughter_. New York: Appleton, c. 1902.

2285 _____ . _Mrs. Cliff's Yacht_. New York: Scribner's, 1896.
Sequel to _The Adventures of Capt. Horn_, above. Mrs.
Cliff spends her millions made from treasure hunting on a
steam yacht; pirates and clergymen abound.

2286 _____ . _The Reformed Pirate_. New York: Scribner's, 1936.

2287 _____ . _Rudder Grange_. New York: Scribner's, 1879.
Comic escapades on a derelict barge. The author's

most noted work, which began his humorist career. Its
sequels, by date, were The Rudder Grangers Abroad (1891)
and Pomona's Travels (1894).

2288 Stone, William S.   Thunder Island. New York: Mordinoff,
      1942.
           World War II in the Pacific.

2289 Stover, Herbert Elisha.   Powder Mission. New York: Dodd,
      1951.
           Down the Mississippi during the Revolution in search
      of powder for General Washington.

2290 Strang, Herbert.   The Adventures of Dick Trevanion. Lon-
      don: Frowde, 1906.
           Smuggling in Cornwall in 1804.

2291 _____. Humphrey Bold. London: Frowde, 1908.
           How Admiral Benbow chased the fleet of Du Casse in
      1702.

2292 _____. Jack Hardy. London: Frowde, 1906.
           Adventure on the south coast of England in 1804; Nelson;
      smuggling.

2293 _____. With Drake on the Spanish Main. London: Frowde,
      1904.

2294 _____, and Richard Stead. A Mariner of England. Lon-
      don: Frowde, 1910.
           Sir Francis Drake.

2295 Street, James Howell.   By Valour and Arms. Garden City,
      N. Y.: Sun Dial Press, 1945.
           The exploits of the Confederate ironclad Arkansas on
      the Mississippi during the Civil War. A very well-written
      and gripping account.

2296 _____. The Velvet Doublet. Garden City, N. Y.: Double-
      day, 1953.
           Another tale of Columbus.

2297 Stuart, Esmé.   Carried Off. London: National Society, 1888.
      y.
           A boy is taken captive by pirates under Henry Morgan
      in 1670.

2298 Stuart, Vivian A.   The Brave Captains. London: Hale, 1968.
           Part of a larger saga concerning British naval captain
      Philip Horatio Hazard in the Crimean War. Other titles in
      this Hornblower-type series, published by this firm and re-
      printed in America by the New York paperback firm of
      Pinnacle Books, include: The Valiant Sailors; Hazard's

Command, Hazard of Huntress; Victory at Sebastopol; and
Hazard to the Rescue.

2299 Styles, Showell. The Admiral's Fancy. London: Faber,
1958.
Nelson and Lady Hamilton, as seen by Captain Ben
Hallowell, one of the admiral's friends.

2300 _____. Frigate Captain. New York: Vanguard, 1955.
The adventures of Captain Lord Cochrane during the
Napoleonic wars.

2301 _____. Midshipman Quinn. London: Faber, 1956.
Action afloat in Nelson's day.

2302 _____. Mr. Nelson's Ladies. London: Faber, 1953.

2303 _____. Quinn of the Fury. London: Faber, 1958.

2304 _____. The Sea Officer. New York: Macmillan, 1961.
A biographical novel concerning that intrepid British
frigate commander of the Napoleonic Wars, Edward Pellew.

2305 Subercaseaux, Benjamin. Jemmy Button. New York: Mac-
millan, 1954. y.
A look at Darwin's expeditions in the British warship
Beagle.

2306 Sublette, Clifford M. The Scarlet Cockerel. Boston: Little,
Brown, 1925.
A look at the French Huguenot colonization along the
Carolinas during the 1690's.

2307 Surrey, George S. Adrift in the South Seas. London: Oxford
University Press, 1940.

2308 Sutcliffe, Rosemary. The Armourer's House. London and
New York: Oxford University Press, 1951. y.
Two children in Tudor England yearn for a life at sea.

2309 Swallow, Henry J. Love While Ye May. London: Jarrold,
1907.
Adventure along the Durham coast, 1569-1572.

2310 Swanson, Neil. The Star-Spangled Banner. New York: Holt,
1958.
Francis Scott Key and the national anthem, written
afloat near Ft. McHenry. A good look at Baltimore under
siege.

2311 Swift, Jonathan. Gulliver's Travels. London, 1726.
This, the British author's most famous work, has been
widely republished.

2312   Swinson, Charles, ed.   Twenty Tales of the Sea.   London:
       Black, 1942.
              An anthology.

2313   Syers, William E.   The Seven: Navy Subchaser.   New York:
       Duell, 1961. y.
              When Lt. Sam Chance, a newsman and 90-day wonder,
       takes over the USN gunboat Seven in 1943, everyone aboard
       is as green as he is.   But in the great tradition of World
       War II, they are toughened up fighting U-boats off South
       America and Japs in the far Pacific.

2314   Syme, Robert, ed.   Hakluyt's Sea Stories.   London: Heine-
       mann, 1948.
              From the collections of the great 16th-century travel
       author.

- T -

2315   Tales of Military Life.   Vols. 7-9 of the Naval and Military
       Library of Entertainment.   London: Henry Colburn, 1834.
              Part of a noted series cited throughout this compilation.

2316   "Tankey, " pseud.   Men Only in the Navy.   Men Only Series.
       London: Pearson, 1942.

2317   Taylor, Theodore.   The Cay.   Garden City, N. Y.: Double-
       day, 1969.   y
              A young American boy and an old West Indian Black are
       marooned on a tiny Caribbean island after a U-boat sinks
       their ship.   Subject of a recent tv special.

2318   Tearle, Christian.   Holborn Hill.   London: Mills & Boon,
       1909.
              The London of Nelson's day.

2319   Tebbel, John W.   Touched with Fire.   New York: Dutton,
       1953.   y.
              LaSalle's riverborne explorations in the Mississippi
       Valley.

2320   Teilhet, Darwin.   Lion's Skin.   New York: Sloane, 1955.
              Another view of William Walker's schemes of Central
       American empire in the 1850's.

2321   _____.   Retreat from the Dolphin.   Boston: Little, Brown,
       1943.
              That ship's role in the early 19th-century South Ameri-
       can wars of independence.

2322   _____.   Steamboat on the River.   New York: Sloan, 1952.
              How young Abe Lincoln pilots the first steamer on

Illinois' Sangamon River during the 1830's.

2323 Telenga, Suzette. <u>Freighter</u>. By Susan Yorke, pseud. New
      York: Stein & Day, 1957.
          An Atlantic crossing aboard the battered <u>Lady Cunning-
      ton</u> redirects the lives of several of the passengers aboard.

2324 Thane, Elsworth. <u>Ever After</u>. New York: Duell, Sloan and
      Pearce, 1945.
          Spanish-American War action.

2325 Thatcher, Russell. <u>The Captain</u>. New York: Macmillan,
      1951.
          The trials of triumphs of a landing craft commander in
      the Pacific during World War II.

2326 Thelwall, John. <u>Trident of Albion</u>. London, 1805.
          One of the earliest novels on British naval supremacy.

2327 Thomas, David, ed. <u>Teen-Age Underwater Adventure Stories</u>.
      New York: Pocket Books, 1965.
          An anthology concerning divers, rescue work, and buried
      treasure.

2328 Thomas, William H. <u>Running the Blockade</u>. New York, 1874.
          The Civil War on the Atlantic seaboard.   In 1842,
      Thomas worked his way around the Horn to California and
      later returned there during the Gold Rush on a clipper.
      Two earlier nautical romances are <u>A Whaleman's Adventures</u>
      and <u>A Slaver's Adventures</u>, both published in 1872.

2329 Thompson, Thomas. <u>Lost</u>. New York: Atheneum, 1975.
          The harrowing true story of three boaters who must
      survive at sea after their pleasure craft capsizes in a Pacif-
      ic storm in 1973.

2330 _____. <u>Square-Rigger</u>. London: Warne, 1955.

2331 Thomson, B. <u>South Sea Yarns</u>. London: Blackwood, 1894.

2332 Thorndike, Russell. <u>Dr. Syn on the High Seas</u>. London:
      Hutchinson, 1936.

2333 _____. <u>Dr. Syn Returns</u>. London: Hutchinson, 1937.

2334 _____. <u>The Further Adventures of Dr. Syn</u>. London:
      Hutchinson, 1938.
          How the Vicar of Dymchurch becomes a pirate, and in
      a segment portrayed by Patric McGoohan in the Walt Disney
      series, the Scarecrow of Romney Marsh.

2335 Thorne, Anthony. <u>I'm a Stranger Here Myself</u>. London:
      Heineman, 1943.

World War II.

2336   Thruston, Lucy M.   Jack and His Island.   Boston: Little,
       Brown, 1902.   y.
          The British attack on Baltimore in 1814.

2337   Tickell, Jerrard.   High Water at Four.   Garden City, N. Y. :
       Doubleday, 1966.
          Court-martialed and cashiered, Commander Millerton
       is given a berth aboard the yacht of a Greek millionaire
       and is led into a tight chase involving a cast of international
       nasties.

2338   Tilsley, Frank.   Mutiny.   New York: Reynal & Hitchcock,
       1959.
          How a kindly captain and sadistic first lieutenant are
       placed in opposition over the treatment of seamen aboard
       H. M S. Regenerate in the days of Nelson.   The book was
       made into a movie, "H. M. S. Defiant," starring Alec
       Guinness, Dirk Bogarde, and Anthony Quayle.   Both are worth
       your time.

2339   Titcomb, Margaret.   The Voyage of the Flying Bird.   New
       York: Dodd, Mead, 1963.   y.
          The Polynesian discovery of Hawaii.

2340   Tomlinson, Henry M.   All Hands.   London: Heinemann, 1938.

2341   _____.   London River.   London: Cassell, 1921.

2342   _____.   Galleons Reach.   London: Hart-Davis, 1949.
          A shipping clerk escapes to sea, is shipwrecked in the
       Indian Ocean, picked up, and finally reaches his destination
       in Malaya.   Modeled on Conrad, the author's chief concern
       is the spiritual odyssey of his hero.

2342   _____, ed.   Great Sea Stories of All Nations.   New York:
       Doubleday, 1930.

2344   _____.   _____.   London: Spring Books, 1967.
          The author also wrote at least two other sea stories,
       The Day Before and Pipe All Hands.

2345   Tourgée, Albion W.   Out of the Sunset Sea.   New York: Mer-
       rill & Baker, 1893.
          Supposed yarn of an English sailor on Columbus' 1492
       voyage.

2346   Townend, William.   Fingal's Passenger.   London: Rich, 1948.
       y.

2347   _____.   The Long Voyage.   London: Chapman, 1943.   y.

2348 _____. The Lovely Ship. London: Rich, 1950. y.

2349 _____. Red Ensign, White Ensign. London: Chapman,
        1942.
             World War II.

2350 _____. Sailors Must Yarn. London: Chapman, 1939. y.

2351 _____. Ship in the Fanlight. London: Jenkins, 1934. y.

2352 _____. The Ship That No One Owned. London: Rich,
        1956. y.

2353 _____. South of Forty-Five. London: Rich, 1948. y.

2354 _____. Yonder Is the Sea. London: Rich, 1949. y.

2355 Tracy, Donald. Carolina Corsair. New York: Dial Press,
        1955.
             Blackbeard.

2356 _____. Crimson Is the Eastern Shore. New York: Dial
        Press, 1953.
             British raids and patriot resistance on Maryland's East-
        ern Shore during the War of 1812.

2357 _____. Roanoke Renegade. New York: Dial Press, 1954.
             Raleigh's lost colony.

2357a Tracy, Louis. Wings of the Morning. New York: Clode,
        1903.
             Following a shipwreck, the survivors land on a deserted
        Pacific island, find a treasure, and have to fight off fierce
        Malay pirates to keep it.

2358 Tranter, N. G. The Man Behind the Curtain. London: Hod-
        der & Stoughton, 1959.

2359 Traven, B. The Death Ship. New York: Knopf, 1934.
             An American sailor stranded in Antwerp minus his pass-
        port finally gets a berth as a stoker aboard the good ship
        Yorikke, which her owners want sunk for the insurance.

2360 Trevor, Elleston. Gale Force. New York: Macmillan, 1957.
             A cargo ship and its passengers are caught in a huge
        storm some 200 miles off Cornwall.

2361 Trew, Antony. Kleber's Convoy. New York: St. Martin's
        Press, 1973.
             Escorts vs. U-boats in World War II.

2362 _____. Two Hours to Darkness. New York: Random
        House, 1963.

The skipper of a British polaris submarine conspires
with his communications officer to receive false dispatches
instructing the submarine to launch its atomic missiles
towards Russian targets.

2362a _____. The Zukov Briefing. New York: St. Martin's
Press, 1975.
A Soviet nuclear submarine flounders near a desolate
island within Norway's territorial waters.

2363 Trimble, H. J. Return from the Deep. New York: McGraw-
Hill, 1958.

2364 Tute, Warren. The Admiral. London: Cassell, 1963.

2365 _____. The Cruiser. New York: Ballantine Books, 1956.
A look at life aboard H. M. S. Antigone in the years as
the peace turned into the Second World War. An excellent
job of interpreting for the layman what life was like in the
British Navy in 1938-1942. First published by Cassell in
1955.

2366 _____. Leviathan. Boston: Little, Brown, 1959.
The building and operation of a great passenger liner
from her launching in the 1930's to her sinking as a troop-
ship during the Second World War.

2367 Tyler, Royal. Algerian Captive. Publisher unknown, 1797.
In the manner of Smollett, this is a tale of horror on
slave ship voyages; significant only as one of the Republic's
first sea stories.

- U -

2368 Ullman, James Ramsey. Fia Fia, A Novel of the South Pacific. New York: World, 1962.

2369 Uris, Leon. Battle Cry. New York: Putnam, 1953.
World War II in the Pacific.

- V -

2370 Vaczek, Louis C. River and Empty Sea. Boston: Houghton,
Mifflin, 1950. y.
An early canoe trip to Hudson's Bay via the rivers of
the Canadian wilderness.

2371 Vail, Philip (pseud.). The Sea Panther; A Novel about the
Commander of the U. S. S. Constitution. New York: Dodd,
1962. y.
A biographical novel concerning Captain William

Bainbridge; also Stephen Decatur's operation against Algiers
in 1815.

2372   Van der Post, Laurens.   The Hunter and the Whale.   New
       York: Morrow, 1967.
              South African whaling just after World War I.

2373   Vance, Marguerite.   Courage at Sea.   New York: Dutton,
       1963. y.
              A boy's heroism during the sinking of the Titanic.

2374   Vaughan, Owen.   The Jewel of Ynys Galon.   By Owen Rhos-
       comyl, pseud.   London: Longmans, 1895.
              The adventures of Sir Henry Morgan.

2375   Vaux, Patrick.   Gadgets.   London: Hodder & Stoughton, 1917.

2376   Vercell, Roger.   Ride Out the Storm.   New York: Putnam,
       1953.
              A sailing ship captain battles the sea and the advent of
       steamers at the turn of the century.

2377   Verne, Jules.   Mysterious Island.   New York: Scribner's,
       [189?].
              The oft-reprinted sequel to the next citation.

2378   _____.   Twenty Thousand Leagues Under the Sea.   Garden
       City, N. Y.: Doubleday, 1963.
              One of countless reprints.   Captain Nemo and his sub
       Nautilus threaten world shipping.

2379   Villiers, Alan John.   And Not to Yield.   London: Hodder &
       Stoughton, 1953.

2380   _____.   Cruise of the Conrad.   London: Hodder & Stoughton,
       1940.

2381   _____.   Whalers of the Midnight Sun.   New York: Scrib-
       ner's, 1934.

2382   _____, comp.   My Favorite Sea Stories.   London: Lutter-
       worth Press, 1972.

2383   Vincent, K. E. B.   Sea Change.   London: Jenkins, 1934.

2384   Volk, G.   Island Schooner.   London: Paul, 1950.

2385   Vorhies, John R.   Pre-Empt.   Chicago: Regnery, 1967.
              The captain of a U. S. nuclear sub offers the world an
       ultimatum: form an international council and surrender all
       atomic weapons to the wreckers or he will loose his 18
       Poseidon missiles.

- W -

2386 Waddel, Charles Carey. The Lady of the Green and Blue; Or, The Magic Figure Head. By Charles Carey "of the United States Navy, " pseud. Boston: George H. Williams, 1848.

2387 Walkey, S. Yo-Ho! For the Spanish Main. London: Cassell, 1910. y.
Pirates seek a treasure galleon in the 1700's.

2388 Wallace, John. Dope Runners. London: Popular Publications, 1940.
Smuggling at sea.

2389 Wallace, William M. East to Bagaduce. Chicago: Henry Regnery, 1963.
Conflict with the British off the Maine coast during the Revolution, featuring the disasterous patriot operation in Penobscot Bay in 1779.

2390 _____. Jonathan Dearborn. Boston: Little, Brown, 1967.
Privateering in the War of 1812.

2391 _____. The Raiders; A Novel of the Civil War at Sea. Boston: Little, 1970.
Based on the exploits of C. S. S. Alabama in the Civil War.

2392 Walsh, Jill P. The Dolphin Crossing. New York: Macmillan, 1967. y.
Two boys in the World War II Dunkirk evacuation.

2393 Walsh, Joseph P. King's Arrow. By Joseph Patrick, pseud. Philadelphia: Lippincott, 1951.
How Englishmen smuggled their goods to America, via the West Indies, to avoid the heavy taxes current in the days just before the American Revolution.

2394 Walton, Elizabeth C. Voices in the Fog. New York: Abelard-Schuman, 1968. y.
Twin girls encounter mystery in their father's 19th-century shipping business.

2395 Walz, Jay and Audrey. Undiscovered Country. New York: Duell, 1958. y.
Arctic exploration; scandalous love affair between explorer and spiritualist; early 19th-century setting. Based on the life of Elisha Kent Kane.

2396 The Wanderings of Tom Starboard; Or, The Life of a Sailor, His Voyage and Travels, Perils and Adventures, by Land and Sea. London: Harris, 1830.

2397 Ward, F. <u>Wolfingham</u>. Oxford: Parker, 1860.
      The introduction of convicts to Australia, 1795-1812.

2398 Warner, Oliver M. <u>Best Sea Stories</u>. London: Faber, 1965.
      An anthology.

2399 Watson, Helen H. <u>Andrew Goodfellow</u>. London: Macmillan,
      1906.
          A lieutenant of the Royal Navy who finds romance and
      action at the time of Trafalgar.

2400 Watson, Salley. <u>Jade</u>. New York: Holt, 1969. y.
          A captured girl decides to join in the exploits of female
      pirate Anne Boney.

2401 Watt, Lauchlan M. <u>The House of Sands</u>. London: Secker,
      1913.
          Another tale of the Barbary Pirates, this one having a
      Scotsman as its hero.

2402 Watt, W. M. <u>Home from Callao in a Hoodoo Ship</u>. London:
      Heath, 1933.

2403 Webb, Christopher. <u>The Ann and Hope Mutiny</u>. New York:
      Funk & Wagnalls, 1966. y.
          A New Bedford lad is involved in the mystery of a miss-
      ing sailing ship. Based on the <u>Mary Celeste</u> legend.

2404 _____. <u>Quest of the Otter</u>. New York: Funk & Wagnalls,
      1963. y.
          An 1840's whaling voyage forms the backdrop for a lad's
      search for his lost father.

2404a Webb, Forrest. <u>Caviar Cruise</u>. Garden City, N. Y. : Double-
      day, 1975.
          Two conspirators run great risks to loot the cruise ship
      <u>Niad</u> in the Mediterranean.

2405 Webster, Henry K. <u>Traitor or Loyalist</u>. New York: Mac-
      millan, 1904.
          Civil War blockade of southern cotton commerce. Em-
      phasis is on Yankee cruisers on station off the North Caro-
      lina coast.

2406 Weekley, William G. <u>The Ledger of Lying Dog</u>. Garden City,
      N. Y. : Doubleday, 1947. y.
          Lying Dog is an island where a shipwrecked boy lands
      and manages to outwit the rather evil local inhabitants.

2407 Welch, Ronald. <u>Ferdinand Magellan</u>. New York: Criterion,
      1956. y.
          A biographical novel.

2408 _____ . The Hawk. New York: Criterion, 1967. y.
       A young lieutenant aboard the Galleon Hawk pretends to
       join an assassination plot against Queen Elizabeth I in order
       to protect her.

2409 Wellman, Manly W. Carolina Pirate. New York: Washburn,
       1962. y.
       An 18th-century English lad is captured by pirates and
       forced to be their navigator.

2410 _____ . Jamestown Adventure. New York: Washburn, 1967.
       y.
       The settlement of the Virginia colony, including the role
       of Captain John Smith.

2411 _____ . Rebel Mail Runner. New York: Holiday House,
       1954. y.
       Civil War adventure afloat.

2412 _____ . The River Pirates. New York: Washburn, 1963.
       y.
       Pirates on the Mississippi in the 1820's and 1830's.

2413 Wellman, Paul I. Ride the Red Earth. Garden City, N. Y. :
       Doubleday, 1958.
       The French king sends Louis de St. Denis to Mobile in
       1715.

2414 Werstein, Irving. Civil War Sailor. Garden City, N. Y. :
       Doubleday, 1962. y.
       Adventures of a young Union bluejacket on the Atlantic
       blockade.

2415 _____ . The Cruise of the Essex. New York: Macrae
       Smith, 1969. y
       The American frigate's Pacific exploits in the War of
       1812.

2416 Westcott, Jan. Captain Barney. New York: Crown, 1951.
       A sea tale of Joshua Barney during the Revolution.

2417 _____ . Captain for Elizabeth. New York: Crown, 1948.
       The hero, Tom Cavendish, is modeled after Sir Francis
       Drake.

2418 Westerman, Percy F. Cadet Alan Carr. London: Blackie,
       1938. y.

2419 _____ . Call of the Sea. London: Blackie, 1938. y.

2420 _____ . His First Ship. London: Blackie, 1938. y.
       Alan Carr.

2421 _____. In Eastern Seas. London: Blackie, 1939. y.

2422 _____. A Lad of Grit. London: Blackie, 1908. y.
        Buccaneers, pirates, and gold on the Spanish Main at the
    time of the English Restoration.

2423 _____. Midshipman Webb's Treasure. London: Blackie,
    1938. y.

2424 _____. Ocean Bandits. London: Oxford University Press,
    1938. y.

2425 _____. The Quest of the Golden Hope. London: Blackie,
    1911. y.
        The search for a fugitive of Monmouth's Rebellion,
    whose pirate ship is named in the title.

2426 _____. The Red Pirate. London: Blackie, 1935. y.

2427 _____. War--and Alan Carr. London: Blackie, 1940. y.

2428 _____. When the Allies Swept the Seas. London: Blackie,
    1940. y.

2429 _____, et al. Tales of the Sea. London: Tuck, 1933. y.

2430 Wharton, Anne H. A Rose of Old Quebec. Philadelphia:
    Lippincott, 1913.
        The 1780-1790 romance between Mary Thompson and
    Captain Horatio Nelson set in Quebec and London.

2431 Wheeler, Keith. The Last Mayday. Garden City, N. Y.:
    Doubleday, 1969.
        When Kirov, the ex-First Secretary of the Communist
    Party, decides to defect, the Allies send a submarine to pick
    him up. All goes well until the Red is aboard and then the
    Soviet Navy moves in to sink them. A few survive the en-
    suing battle in a small boat and a cat-and-mouse game is
    on between the Russian and American navies to see who can
    "save" the men first.

2432 White, Leslie T. Look Away, Look Away. New York: Ran-
    dom House, 1943.
        A look at the Southern passengers aboard a single boat
    who were emigrating to Brazil in 1867. Between 1865 and
    1870, over 3,000 former residents of the Confederacy so
    embarked.

2433 White, Randall M. Salute to the Marines. New York: Gros-
    set and Dunlap, 1943.
        World War II in the Pacific.

[2434 no entry]

2435 White, Robb. <u>Flight Deck.</u> Garden City, N. Y. : Doubleday,
      1961. y.
          A yarn of pilots and crew aboard an American World
      War II carrier.
          White is one of America's most prolific authors of sea
      novels and stories concerning the U. S. Navy during World
      War II and after. Among his many titles are the following,
      all of about uniform consistency:

2436 _____. <u>The Frogmen.</u> Garden City, N. Y. : Doubleday,
      1973. y.
          Underwater demolitions teams.

2437 _____. <u>In Privateer's Bay.</u> New York: Harper, 1939. y.
          War of 1812.

2438 _____. <u>Midshipman Lee.</u> Boston: Little, Brown, 1938. y.

2439 _____. <u>Midshipman Lee of the Naval Academy.</u> New York:
      Random House, 1954. y.

2440 _____. <u>No Man's Land.</u> Garden City, N. Y. : Doubleday,
      1969. y.

2441 _____. <u>Sail Away.</u> Garden City, N. Y. : Doubleday, 1948.
      y.

2442 _____. <u>Sailor in the Sun.</u> New York: Harper, c. 1941.
      y.

2443 _____. <u>Secret Sea.</u> Garden City, N. Y. : Doubleday, 1947.
      y.

2444 _____. <u>Silent Ship, Silent Sea.</u> Garden City, N. Y. :
      Doubleday, 1967. y.
          A look at life aboard the U. S. destroyer <u>Caron,</u> dam-
      aged during the 1942 American invasion of the Solomon
      Islands.

2445 _____. <u>Smuggler's Sloop.</u> Boston: Little, Brown, 1937.
      y.

2446 _____. <u>Surrender.</u> Garden City, N. Y. : Doubleday, 1966.
      y.
          A tale of naval action in the Philippines in the five
      months following Pearl Harbor.

2447 _____. <u>The Survivor.</u> New York: Doubleday, 1964. y.

2448 _____. <u>Three Against the Sea.</u> New York: Harper, c.
      1940. y.

2449 _____. <u>Torpedo Run. Mutiny and Adventure Aboard a</u>

Navy PT Boat During World War II. New York: Doubleday, 1962. y.
        Pacific action.

2450 _____. Up Periscope. New York: Doubleday, 1956.
        Ken Braden, just out of underwater demolitions training,
        matures aboard a submarine during World War II.

2451 White, S. Tall Ship. London: Heinemann, 1958.

2452 Whitehorne, Earl. Supercargo. New York: Funk & Wagnalls,
        1939.
        A mysterious ship is found floating off Japan in the late
        1860's.

2453 Whitham, Grace I. Basil the Page. London: Wells Gardner,
        1908. y.
        A lad's adventures with Drake and at the court of Good
        Queen Bess.

2454 Whiting, J. D. The Trial of Fire. Indianapolis: Bobbs-
        Merrill, 1930.
        The Civil War duel between the Alabama and the Kear-
        sarge.

2455 Whitney, Phyllis A. Sea Jade. New York: Appleton, 1965.
        Post Civil War; sea captain plots a marriage to keep
        alive a company dealing with oriental trade.

2456 Wibberly, Leonard. Flint's Island. New York: Farrar, 1972.
        y.
        A sequel to R. L. Stevenson's Treasure Island (q. v.),
        complete with Long John Silver.

2457 _____. The Hands of Cormack Joyce. New York: Putnam,
        1960. y.
        Chronicles a great storm striking the islands off the
        County Galway coast

2458 _____. King's Beard. New York: Farrar, 1952. y.
        How Sir Francis Drake, his seamen, and two Devon boys
        managed to "singe the King of Spain's beard, " figuratively
        speaking, at Cadiz in 1587.

2459 _____. Leopard's Prey. New York: Farrar, 1971. y.
        The son of Revolutionary War Captain Manley is im-
        pressed aboard H. M. frigate Leopard a few years before the
        outbreak of the War of 1812.

2460 _____. The Lost Harpooner. London: Harrap, 1959. y.
        Whaling in the 1840's.

2461 _____. Sea Captain from Salem. New York: Farrar,

1961. y.
During the Revolution, Captain "Peace of God" Manley
is asked by Ambassador Franklin in Paris to raid English
shipping in the Channel.

2462 Wilder, Robert. Plough the Sea. New York: Putnam, 1961.

2463 _____. The Sea and the Stars. New York: Putnam, 1967.

2464 _____. Wind from the Carolinas. New York: Putnam,
       1964.
       Covers about 140 years of the period in which wealthy,
       aristocratic families from the Carolinas, Virginia and Geor-
       gia, who, after the American Revolution, remained loyal to
       Britain and moved to the Bahamas; epic of the islands.

2465 Wilkins, William V. The City of Frozen Fire. New York:
       Macmillan, 1950.
       A Welsh diamond mine owner is threatened by pirates
       in South America in 1826.

2466 Willans, Geoffrey. Admirals on Horseback. New York: Van-
       guard, 1955.
       First published in Britain as Admiral on Horseback,
       this tale is made up of three parts demonstrating the life of
       a British naval officer in 1941, 1952, and 1954.

2467 Williams, Ben Ames. All the Brothers Were Valiant. New
       York: Reynolds, 1919.
       Pirates in the Pacific.

2468 _____. Black Pawl. New York: Dutton, 1922.
       An evil English sea captain notices his son is growing
       up the same way.

2469 _____. Come Spring. Boston: Houghton, Mifflin, 1940.
       Maine during the Revolution, ashore and afloat.

2470 _____. Once Aboard the Whaler. London: Hale, 1933.

2471 _____. Strumpet Sea. London: Hale, 1940.

2472 _____. Thread of Scarlet. Boston: Houghton, Mifflin,
       1939.
       Privateering in the War of 1812; set around Nantucket.
       Williams wrote numerous stories and shorter works during
       this period as well.

2473 Williams, Charles. Dead Calm. New York: Viking, 1964.
       John Ingram and his wife Rae are bound for Tahiti in a
       small trim craft when an obsessive peril meets them in the
       plausible presence of a good-looking young man becalmed after
       a trio of deaths from botulism.

2474   Williams, R.   Memoirs of a Buccaneer.   London: Mills &
       Boon, 1909.
           Piratical adventure on the 17th-century Spanish Main and
       naval battles between the British and the Spanish.

2475   Williams, Wirt.   The Enemy.   Boston: Houghton, Mifflin,
       1951.
           World War II; life aboard a Pacific fleet warship is
       realistically portrayed as "bbb," boring between battles.

2476   Willingham, Calder.   Providence Island.   New York: Van-
       guard, 1969.
           A Madison Ave. tv executive is shipwrecked on a Car-
       ibbean island with two lovely dames for four months.

2477   Wilson, Erie.   Adams of the Bounty.   London: Criterion,
       1959. y.
           A look at the famous mutiny from the viewpoint of a
       long-suffering English seaman.

2478   Wilson, Hazel.   Tall Ships.   Boston: Little, Brown, 1958.   y.
           Naval action in the War of 1812.

2479   Wilson, Margaret.   The Valiant Wife.   Garden City, N. Y.:
       Doubleday, 1934.
           War of 1812; Dartmoor Prison.

2480   Wilson, Richard.   A Book of Ships and Seamen.   London: J.
       M. Dent, 1921.

2481   Wilson, Sloan.   Voyage to Somewhere.   New York: A. A.
       Wyn, 1946.
           World War II problems of human nature afloat.

2482   Winchell, Paul.   Fifty Fathoms Klondike.   New York: Funk
       and Wagnalls, 1959.   y.
           The Gold Rush to Alaska.

2483   Winn, Godfrey.   Home from the Sea.   London: Hutchinson,
       1944.

2484   _____ .   P. Q. 17.   London: Hutchinson, 1947.
           World War II on the Murmansk Run.

2485   _____ .   Scrapbook of the War.   London: Hutchinson, 1943.

2486   _____ .   Scrapbook of Victory: Further Extracts from a
       Wartime Scrapbook.   London: Hutchinson, 1947.

2487   Winterton, Paul.   Hero for Leanda.   By Andrew Garve, pseud.
       New York: Harper, 1960.
           An idealistic young woman and an Irish adventurer and
       amateur yachtsman attempt to rescue a Middle Eastern

revolutionary leader interned by the British on a remote island in the Indian Ocean.

2488 Winton, John. Down the Hatch. New York: St. Martin's Press, 1962.
      A study of Lt. Cmdr. Robert Bollinger Badger, alias "The Artful Bodger," and the strange goings-on aboard a submarine of the Royal Navy.

2489 _____. The Fighting Temeraire. New York: Coward-McCann, 1971.
      In the silent war between the U.S.S.R. and the West, a British nuclear submarine enters the Black Sea on a secre mission which becomes an international incident.

2490 _____. H.M.S. Leviathan. New York: Coward-McCann, 1967.
      A struggle between the old navy and the new aboard a huge warship of the modern Royal Navy.

2491 _____. Never Go to Sea. London: Joseph, 1963.

2492 _____. We Joined the Navy. New York: St. Martin's Press, 1960.
      A step-by-step look at the problems encountered by a few of the trainees in a class at the Royal Navy school at Dartmoor.

2493 _____. We Saw the Sea. New York: St. Martin's Press, 1961.
      In this sequel to We Joined the Navy, we follow two newly commissioned British naval lieutenants aboard their first ship, H.M.S. Carousel, which is stationed in the Far East.

2494 Wise, Henry A. Captain Brand of the Centipede. By Harry Gringo, pseud. New York: Scribner's, 1867.
      Wise created a number of highly praised sea tales similar to those written by Frederick Marryat (q.v.). An active American naval officer all of his adult life, this Southerner retired as a captain after the Civil War.

2495 _____. Los Gringos: Or, Inside View of Mexico and California, with Wanderings in Peru, Chile, and Polynesia. By Harry Gringo, pseud. New York: Charles Scribner and Baker, 1845.
      Interesting allusion to Melville and various characters from Omoo and Typee (q.v.).

2496 _____. Scampavias from Gebel Tarek to Stamboul. By Harry Gringo, pseud. New York: Charles Scribner's sons, 1857.
      Autobiographical travel fiction.

2497 _____. Tales for Marines. By Harry Gringo, pseud.
Boston: Phillips, Sampson, 1855.

2498 Wonderful Disclosure! The Mystery Solved; Or, Narrative of
Dr. M. Lorner, One of the Passengers of the Steamship
President, Which Vessel Left New York, Bound for Liver-
pool, March 11, 1841, Since Which Time, Until Recently,
Nothing Has Been Heard Respecting Her Fate. New York:
W. L. Knapp and E. E. Barclay, 1845.

2499 Wood, Eric. The Flaming Cross of Santa Maria. New York:
Appleton-Century, 1923.
A search for treasure on the Spanish Main coupled with
the adventures of Sir Francis Drake.

2500 Wood, James. The Sealer. New York: Vanguard, 1961.
Jim Fraser, a Scottish shepherd and fisherman, relates
his World War II mission to ferret out a secret German
raider in the waters of Tierra del Fuego. Other "Fraser"
tales published by Vanguard include: Fire Rock (1966);
Friday Run (1970); Lisa Bastian (1961); Northern Missions
(1954); Rain Islands (1957); and Three Blind Mice (1971).

2501 Wood, James P. The Queen's Most Honorable Pirate. New
York: Harper & Row, 1961. y.
Sir Francis Drake sails again.

2502 Woodrooffe, Thomas. Best Stories of the Navy. London:
Faber, 1947.

2503 _____. Best Stories of the Sea. London: Faber, 1945.

2504 _____. Naval Odyssey. London: Cape, 1936.

2505 _____. Yangtze Skipper. New York: Furman, 1937.
Published in England under the title River of Golden
Sand, this story tells of the experiences of a first lieutenant
aboard a British river gunboat on patrol duty in China during
the 1920's. Similar in vein, though more understanding of
the natives, to the American novel, The Sand Pebbles, by
Richard McKenna (q. v.).

2506 Woods, Edith Elmer. The Spirit of the Service. New York:
Macmillan, 1903.
Spanish-American War at sea; typical of the genre of
inspirational novels written for naval officers; features
Battle of Manilla.

2507 Woods, William H. Manuela. New York: Hill & Wang, 1957.
A beautiful half-English girl, Manuela, who has been
left alone in Brazil, strikes a bargain with the lecherous
chief engineer of the Conway Castle to smuggle her to Brit-
tain. But it is the freighter's captain with whom she falls

in love--until a shipwreck alters all plans.

2508 Worboys, Anne. The Way of the Tamarisk. New York:
      Delacorte, 1975.
            A yarn of murder and suspense aboard the good ship
      Tamarisk.

2509 Wouk, Herman. The Caine Mutiny, A Novel of World War II.
      Garden City, New York: Doubleday, 1951.
            The tyrannical Captain Queeg of a Pacific minesweeper
      brings his crew to rebellion; a psychological dilemma. As
      important to the sea literature of the war as Monsarratt's
      The Cruel Sea (q. v.).

2510 _____. The Winds of War, A Novel. Boston: Little,
      Brown, 1971.
            World War II epic, featuring an American naval family,
      among others.

2511 Wren, M. K. Curiosity Didn't Kill the Cat. Garden City,
      N. Y.: Doubleday, 1973.
            When a Navy captain is found dead in Oregon, the
      grieving wife requests a security investigation.

2512 Wright, Constance. Their Ships Were Broken. New York:
      E. P. Dutton, 1938.
            The English vs. the Chinese in the Opium Wars.

2513 Wyeth, Newell C. , ed. Great Stories of the Sea and Ships.
      New York: David McKay, 1940.
            An anthology, by the famous illustrator.

2514 Wylie, Ida A. R. Ho, The Fair Wind. New York: Random
      House, 1945.   y.
            Post Civil War Martha's Vineyard; whaling.

2515 Wynd, Oswald. Death the Red Flower. New York: Harcourt,
      1965.
            A tale of East-West tensions set aboard a Chinese ship
      and involving British agents attempting to prevent a surprise
      attack which would start World War III.

2516 _____. The Forty Days. New York: Harcourt, 1973.
            In September 1943, a freighter puts out from Singapore
      for Japan with 1200 Allied POWs aboard. The work focuses
      on the relationship between the senior British and Japanese
      officers aboard as well as their translator. Sort of a nautical
      Bridge on the River Kwai.

2517 _____. The Golden Cockatrice. New York: Harper, 1975.
            Paul Harris is caught in the middle of a Chinese-
      Russian shipping rivalry.

2518 _____. The Hawser Pirates. New York: Harcourt, 1971.
The captain of a British ocean tug and French and
Dutch tug crews race to reach disabled ships first.

2519 _____. A Time of Pirates. New York: Harper, 1971.
Harris is involved with a group of murderous modern-
day buccaneers operating off the coasts of Malaya.

- Y -

2520 Yerby, Frank. Captain Rebel. New York: Dial Press, 1956.
Story of the daring exploits of the blockade runners out
of New Orleans during the Civil War.

2521 _____. The Golden Hawk. New York: Pocket Books,
1959.
First published in 1948, this is a rousing good pirate
yarn.

2522 Young, Edward P. The Fifth Passenger. New York: Harper,
1963.
A London solicitor is on the spot when a defecting naval
officer who once saved his life calls on him for help.

2523 Young, Francis B. The Island. London: Heinemann, 1944.

2524 _____. Sea Horses. New York: Knopf, 1925.
Passengers aboard an old liner encounter difficulties in
reaching their East African destination.

2525 Young-O'Brien, Albert H. Windship Boy. By Brian O'Brien,
pseud. New York: Dutton, 1961. y.
A boy's two-year apprenticeship aboard an American
clipper ship.

INDEX OF PSEUDONYMS AND JOINT AUTHORS

A pseudonym is to an author what camouflage is to a war-ship: protective covering designed to hide a true identity. A number of sea story writers have chosen, for several different reasons, to make their contributions in disguise. Among these reasons are the fear among some active naval officers of being found out for undue "book learning" by their seniors; the fear by women or ministers that if their true names or pursuits were known their books could not compete with others of a genre conceived to be basically and robustly male-oriented; and the desire by some to segregate their stories by historic period.

The joint author in a literary adventure is sometimes overlooked; nevertheless his or her contribution to a work is often as important as the first-named person.

Aldon, Aldair, pseud. See Meigs, Cornelia L.

"Aurora," pseud. See Smith, Arthur G.

Baldwin, Bates, pseud. See Deck, Mrs. Lily M. A.

Barrington, E., pseud. See Deck, Mrs. Lily M. A.

"Bartimus," pseud. See Ritchie, Lewis A.

Bird, Horace V., jt. author. See Karig, Walter

Bowen, Marjorie, pseud. See Long, Gabrielle C.

Brace, Jack, pseud. See Kaler, James O.

Brentano, Lowell, jt. author. See Lancaster, Bruce

Buntline, Ned, pseud. See Judson, Edward Z. C.

Burgoyne, Alan H., jt. author. See Clowes, William L.

Cameron, Ian, pseud. See Payne, Donald G.

"Captain Barnacle," pseud. See Newell, Charles W.

"Captain Ringbolt," pseud. See Codman, John

Carvey, Charles, pseud. See Waddel, Charles C.

Castleman, Harry, pseud. See Fosdick, Charles A.

Cato, Conrad, pseud. See Cox, Cyril

Clark, Dorothy, jt. author. See McMeekin, Isabel

Coffin, Geoffrey, pseud. See Mason, F. van Wyck

Collingwood, Harry, pseud. See Lancaster, William J. C.

Connell, F. Norreys, pseud. See O'Rierdon, Conal C.

Copplestone, Bennet, pseud. See Kitchen, Frederick H.

Daviot, Gordon, pseud. See Mackintosh, Elizabeth

Divine, David, pseud. See Divine, Arthur D.

Doerflinger, William, jt. author. See Barker, Roland

Doherty, Edward J., jt. author. See Davidson, Louis B.

Ford, Ford Madox, jt. author. See Conrad, Joseph

Slaughter, Frank G.
Theeluker, Phyl, pseud. See
Champness, Francis Q.
Truck, Bill, pseud. See Howell,
John
Twain, Mark, pseud. See
Clements, Samuel L.
Vaughan, Carter, pseud. See
Gerson, Noel B.
Waters, Frank, jt. author. See
Branch, Houston
"Wave," pseud. See Batchelder,
Eugene
White, Tandal M., jt. author.
See Bruce, George
Williams, Joel, pseud. See
Jennings, John E.
"Windlass," pseud. See Hicks,
John B.